ONCE UPON A TIME
ON THE BANKS

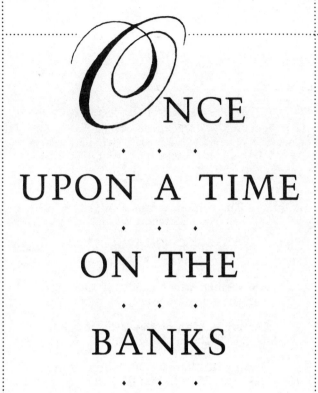

ONCE UPON A TIME ON THE BANKS

Cathie Pelletier

HUTCHINSON
London   Sydney   Auckland   Johannesburg

This edition published in 1990 by
Hutchinson

Century Hutchinson Ltd., 20 Vauxhall Bridge Road,
London SW1V 2SA

Century Hutchinson Australia, 20 Alfred Street,
Milsons Point, Sydney, NSW 2061

Century Hutchinson New Zealand Limited
PO Box 40-086, Glenfield, Auckland 10, New Zealand

Century Hutchinson South Africa (Pty) Ltd
PO Box 337, Bergvlei, 2012 South Africa

British Library Cataloguing in Publication Data
Pelletier. Cathie
Once upon a time on the banks.
I. Title
813'.54 [F]

ISBN 0-09-174283-8

Printed and bound in Great Britain by
Mackays of Chatham PLC, Chatham, Kent

DEDICATION

This novel is dedicated to all my French-Canadian ancestors, namely to Abraham Martin (1589–1664), my great-great-great-great-great-great-great-great-great grandfather, who came to New France as ship's pilot with Samuel de Champlain, and for whom the Plains of Abraham, overlooking the St. Lawrence River in Quebec City, are named. He is now a Trivial Pursuit question, one that I answered correctly.

To Hélène Langlois Des Portes, my great-great-great-great-great-great-great-great grandmother, who was the first white child born in Canada.

AND

To my father Louis Allen Pelletier, Sr., for the gift of childhood, and to my grandmother, Edith Thibodeau Pelletier, who learned to speak English from her grandchildren.

Civilization is a stream with banks. The stream is sometimes filled with blood from people killing, stealing, shouting, and doing things historians usually record, while on the banks, unnoticed, people build homes, make love, raise children, sing songs, write poetry. The story of civilization is the story of what happened on the banks . . .

—Will Durant,
The Story of Civilization

GENEALOGICAL SKELETONS IN SOME OF THE FINEST CLOSETS

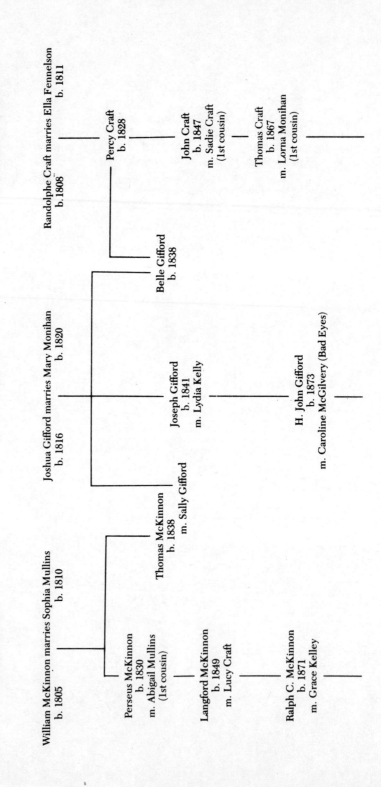

MCKINNON

GIFFORD

CRAFT-FENNELSON

William McKinnon marries Sophia Mullins
b. 1805   b. 1810

Joshua Gifford marries Mary Monihan
b. 1816   b. 1820

Randolphe Craft marries Ella Fennelson
b. 1808   b. 1811

Thomas McKinnon
b. 1838
m. Sally Gifford

Belle Gifford
b. 1838

Percy Craft
b. 1828

Perseus McKinnon
b. 1830
m. Abigail Mullins
(1st cousin)

Joseph Gifford
b. 1841
m. Lydia Kelly

John Craft
b. 1847
m. Sadie Craft
(1st cousin)

Langford McKinnon
b. 1849
m. Lucy Craft

H. John Gifford
b. 1873
m. Caroline McGilvery (Bad Eyes)

Thomas Craft
b. 1867
m. Lorna Monihan
(1st cousin)

Ralph C. McKinnon
b. 1871
m. Grace Kelley

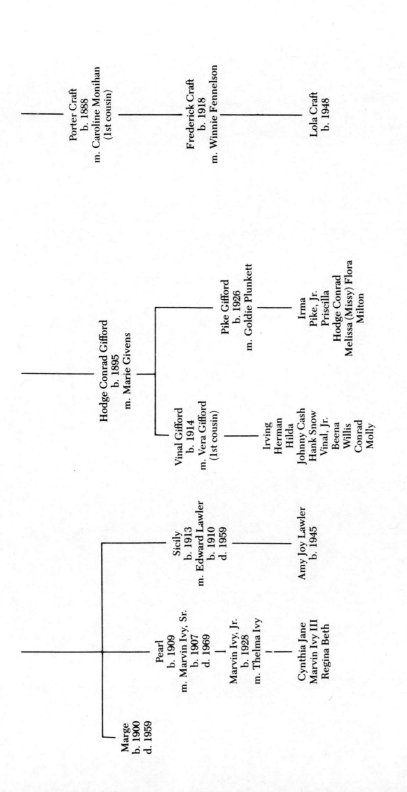

Porter Craft
b. 1888
m. Caroline Monihan
(1st cousin)

Frederick Craft
b. 1918
m. Winnie Fennelson

Lola Craft
b. 1948

Hodge Conrad Gifford
b. 1895
m. Marie Givens

Pike Gifford
b. 1926
m. Goldie Plunkett

Irma
Pike, Jr.
Priscilla
Hodge Conrad
Melissa (Missy) Flora
Milton

Vinal Gifford
b. 1914
m. Vera Gifford
(1st cousin)

Irving
Herman
Hilda
Johnny Cash
Hank Snow
Vinal, Jr.
Beena
Willis
Conrad
Molly

Sicily
b. 1913
m. Edward Lawler
b. 1910
d. 1959

Amy Joy Lawler
b. 1945

Pearl
b. 1909
m. Marvin Ivy, Sr.
b. 1907
d. 1969

Marvin Ivy, Jr.
b. 1928
m. Thelma Ivy

Cynthia Jane
Marvin Ivy III
Regina Beth

Marge
b. 1900
d. 1959

AUTHOR'S NOTE

The French surnames in this novel were chosen with great respect, and are the surnames of the following ancestral grandparents:

Zacharie Cloutier (born ca. 1590, Perche, France, son of Denis Cloutier and Renée Brière) married Xainte Du Pont (born 1596) on 13 July, 1616. A seigneur and master carpenter in New France, he arrived there in 1634 with Dr. Robert Giffard. Giffard (Gifford) is also a surname in this book, as well as in *The Funeral Makers*.

Julien Fortin (baptized 9 February, 1621, son of Julien Fortin, grandson of Simon Fortin), who left Normandy at the age of twenty-nine to battle head winds for three long months at sea before arriving at Quebec in late summer of 1650. He married Genevieve Gamache on 11 November, 1652. Cape Tourmente, "The Fortin Coast," where I go to watch snow geese gather by the thousands, is named for him.

Paul Vachon (born in France in 1630, son of Vincent Vachon and Sapience Vateau), Seigniorial Notary, who came to New France in 1650. He married Marguerite Langlois on 22 October, 1653. Paul Vachon helped to build the chapel of the Hôtel Dieu in Quebec City, as well as some of the sick wards. He and many of his children died in a terrible epidemic of 1703.

My apologies to them and to the French-speaking residents of the St. John Valley in northern Maine, where a skunk is called "bête puant." I chose "putois" from Cassell's French Dictionary for poetic reasons. I also apologize to any offended skunks.

ACKNOWLEDGMENTS

Again, to Jim Glaser, singer extraordinaire, scop, gleeman, birder, wine-maker, lover of astronomy, animals, books, good scotch, and with whom I have managed to fight in many other cities of the world since the dedication to him in *The Funeral Makers*. I would leave him, but then, why should *he* enjoy the rest of his life?

To my mother Ethel Tressa O'Leary Pelletier, who bravely recited Kipling's "If" at each family crisis (of which there were many) as well as lots of other poems.

To Rhoda Weyr. Among the listings in *Roget's Thesaurus* for *agent* one will find: *doer, actor, performer, worker, salesman, deputy, factor, broker, go-between, tool, procurator, institor,* and *gomashta* (I love that last one, from India: "I'm sorry, you'll have to talk to my gomashta . . ."). In Rhoda's case, Roget forgot to mention these: *friend, confidante,* and *magician.*

To my editor Amanda Vaill. I must borrow from Mark Twain, when he said that "Kipling knows all there is to know, and I know all the rest." Amanda is my Kipling, but behind her back I call her *Maxine Perkins.*

Louis Lee Pelletier, Jr., my big brother, who gave me info on everything from chain saws, to classic cars, to the dimensions of ice floes in the St. John River. My apologies to him, and to my father, for stating in *The Funeral Makers* that tamarack trees have *leaves* instead of *needles*. One day, in the university parking lot, I found a limb from a tamarack tree on the hood of my car, left there by elves as a visual fact. It *does* have needles. Everyone's a critic.

To my godchild Ashley Norris Gauvin, who was five months along in the womb for her *Funeral Makers* dedication. I witnessed her birth, her first steps, and listened as language exploded suddenly inside her precious little head. She's moving to Texas tomorrow and everything, even the moon, will remind me of her.

To Charles Baker, who pulled me from the St. John River when I was four and a half years old, unconscious, and in need of a saving. Nowadays, little kids don't swim in deep swift water, a half mile from their homes, as I did back then. Things have changed, Charlie, but I've never lost my respect for the river, a respect we both learned that day. I gave my feelings about it to Albert Pinkham in "The River Explained" chapter, but you were the one I thought of as I wrote.

Joe Taylor and Doug Leatherwood, who loaned me their *Rock Island Farm* for four days, allowing me to write the last eighty pages of this novel.

Those incredible Nashville songwriters, and their publishers, for letting me quote from their songs.

Dr. Roland Burns, who continues to say, "There, there now. It's not so bad, is it?"

My niece Diana Pelletier, who gave up typing (Praise Jesus) for marriage to Steve O'Neal and Veterinary school.

Joel Sonnier, whose record albums have never included one called *A Potpourri of Cajun Songs*, but who gave me permission to lie.

Dr. Joseph E. Sofranko, my ophthalmologist, who was kind enough to give the Giffords *retinitis pigmentosa*, their inherited eye disease.

Dr. Anthony E. Trabue, who took great pains to describe a heart attack to me. (The pun is intended.)

ONCE UPON A TIME
ON THE BANKS

APRIL IS A BITCH:

THE CRUELEST MONTH BRINGS

HYPOCHONDRIA AND FROST HEAVES

....

> We camped in the picturesque Mattagash River Valley in northern Maine, on the Canadian border, where the inhabitants are known to outsiders as Mattagashers. These are the Anglo-Saxon inheritors of ancient Indian soil once owned by the Mattagash Indian tribe. I was told by a townsman that the residents prefer being called Mattagashers to Maniacs, which is how the rest of Maine refer to themselves.
>
> —Horace Thud, author and canoe enthusiast,
> September 1927

WINTERS ARE LONG IN MATTAGASH, MAINE. THEY ARE LONG AND white and icy. They arrive when they please, bawdy landlords, and they depart when they are good and ready, well looted, leaving behind the soggy fields of molded hay, the houses peeling their summer paint, the potholes a foot deep in the one good road twisting its way to Watertown. When the winters finally leave, they leave of their own accord, and behind them lie the cabin fever dreams, those sentiments which have lain dormant as autumn seed, waiting for the right temperature, the right caress of sunlight, the proper texture of soil to sprout. And after five months of snow, what man is so hardened that he does not melt at the sight of buds on the wild cherry? What deer does not lift its ears to the first music of the old river running free again, shed of its blanket of ice? What woman does not scan the damp earth in the field near her house so closely that her eye can finally trace the ghostly outlines of cucumber beds, sweet peas, and all the fiery carrots she will grow there in a garden when the land is dry enough? When the last rooted cold leaves the earth, what child does not dust off the baseball bat, trim the string from last year's softball, and wait patiently for the muddy slush around home plate, and in the dip near second base, to go deep into the soil, to go down to ancient riverbeds and streams and leave the field alone long enough for a few solid games of ball before school recesses for the summer?

It is true in Mattagash, Maine, as it is true in all the cities and towns of the world, that spring is medicinal. Spring is a messenger. Spring is a politician wanting all votes. Spring does not discriminate between the socially established families of towns and the antisocially established, the lawfully inhabited and the unlawfully inhabited. Neither do potholes. Or frost heaves. And it is common knowledge in Mattagash that a barrage of frost heaves on the road to Watertown will bounce all the spongy pink curlers off a female McKinnon head as quickly as it will off a Gifford's. Potholes, born from seventy tons plus of logging trucks loaded down with logs, if hit at even a moderate speed will suspend the brain of any resident in its cranium for a split second or two. This will happen whether the brain is full of good deeds or bad deeds. A pothole will rattle a hippocampus enough that scenes from the driver's childhood flash quickly before the eyes. Then he or she jolts out of the pothole again, out of the bleary past, still happily on the way to Watertown, but experiencing a bit of difficulty in recalling the errand that had precipitated the journey. The sage who said that into every life a little rain must fall surely suffered at least one spring in Mattagash, Maine. It takes such a sage to know that with every fifty thousand cherry blossoms comes a pothole, with every promise of a bountiful garden comes the looming frost heave.

The spring of 1969 was not much different from any other spring, at least to the meteorologists down in faraway Bangor. But if you've wintered successfully in Mattagash, or in any other snow-bogged geography, each spring is handpicked. Each spring is best. Such was the spring of '69, when more rugs than in any other year seemed to float like large colored stamps from clotheslines, more storm windows were put sleepily away, more paint jobs brushed to perfection, more gardens planned and plotted, more mason jars bought and stored for the bounty.

It was in the heart of this rebirth, amid the first ragged strains of the old Mattagash River running free and pure, that Amy Joy Lawler broke the news to her mother, Sicily. There would be a wedding. There would be no long and polite waiting period. After twenty-three years of living, and with one foot flat into spinsterhood, Amy Joy knew perfectly well what she wanted to do with her life. She knew how she must set about doing it. And it all included Jean Claude Cloutier from Watertown, Maine, known as Frogtown to Mattagashers. At first Sicily was thunderstruck. At first she was only able to mouth the words.

"A Frenchman?" she asked of her only child, her voice raspy with grief. "You're going to marry a *Frog?*"

Amy Joy ran a brush through her hair, a brown forest with two silver streaks adorning the sides. The streaks were artificial, coming from a can of Clairol spray-on color rather than from any genetic coding, and were reapplied after each shampoo.

"No, he's a Russian," snapped Amy Joy, and then sucked some Pepsi up from its bottle. "He's from Watertown, for crying out loud. Of course he's French."

"Is that the creature who's been driving into our yard for a solid month, tooting the horn for you instead of coming to the door?"

"I guess," said Amy Joy. "That must be the creature. Besides, everyone in Mattagash toots the horn instead of knocking. Why is it suddenly so bad if Jean Claude does it?"

"Are you telling me that my future son-in-law, the only one I'll ever have I might add, assuming *please Jesus* this is your only marriage, are you telling me that a man I recognize only by his *toot* will be a part of the McKinnon family?" Sicily had been a McKinnon before her marriage to Ed Lawler, and after all those years of marriage, after all those signatures of "Sicily Lawler" on checks and letters, she still thought of herself as Sicily McKinnon.

"Affirmative," said Amy Joy. "That's what I'm telling you." She slapped a stick of spearmint gum onto her waiting tongue and then took a long drink of Pepsi.

"Oh Lord," said Sicily, and sank back into her chair. She had to think fast. How was she going to blockade this all on her own? She had managed to keep Amy Joy out of stewardess school in Missouri and a junior college for hotel-motel management in the Virgin Islands, not to mention having protected her from a Peace Corps job teaching English somewhere in Africa. That last thought was appalling to Sicily. She imagined her only child sand-logged in a sweltering school tent, surrounded by little black heathens, in a country she'd never seen, teaching English, a language she didn't know. It had, after all, been her worst subject all through high school.

But Sicily had managed to forestall all of Amy Joy's cabin fever dreams. And that's just what they were. Amy Joy had all winter to lie around the house and eat Fig Newtons and ponder the mysterious places of the world. She had plenty of time from October to March to fill out every application form in every single *True!* story that passed through her hands. And one, to Sicily's gravest displeasure, had even been for a diesel mechanic school in Nashville, Tennessee. Another had precipitated a visit from an air force recruiter who told Amy Joy that if she lost thirty pounds they'd send her to Lackland Air Force Base in Texas.

"She's as bad as the birds," Sicily had said to Winnie Fennelson Craft, on the Lawler front porch, just a month earlier. "When something inside her says *go*, she just wants to take off for anywhere."

"At least the birds know where they're going," thought Winnie Craft, who had never liked Sicily's only child. "Too boy-crazy," she told her own daughter, who was a constant crony of Amy Joy's.

"Texas. Imagine," Sicily had said to her best friend.

"Wasn't that where the girl who married Percy Mullins was from?" Winnie had mused. "You remember her. She was the one had the black blood in her."

"She hates to get up before noon," Sicily had said tartly, trying to jar Winnie into a sympathetic understanding of the situation. "What would Amy Joy do in the air force? They blow that bugle at dawn."

"They had a baby black as tar pitch," Winnie had replied, and fingered the fine hairs pushing out gently as little brushes from the tip of one nostril, a habit popular with all the Fennelson women.

But big wide Texas, full of the scorpions Sicily had seen on *Nova*, was not nearly as dangerous as Frogtown, not when it came to the possibilities of Amy Joy tying herself up for life to a Frenchman. Sicily remembered the last time they had clashed above and beyond the usual mother-daughter wrangling about dates. It had been a decade ago. It had been when Amy Joy was about to bust if she couldn't marry Chester Lee Gifford, a man almost old enough to be her father, not to mention his *Gifford-dom*. The Giffords had been the scourge of Mattagash since times immemorial. Yet if someone dug Chester Gifford up from among the dead, which he was, and stood him next to a Frenchman, so help her God, Sicily McKinnon Lawler would be hard-pressed to choose between them. So she used the same tactics to squelch the wedding plans that had proved themselves worthy against the air force scrape and the Peace Corps fiasco. She took to her bed, citing a flare-up of several organs that had been accommodating for years but had suddenly turned on her. Kidneys could rule a person's life if they got pissed off. This was, unbeknownst to Amy Joy, the same tactic Sicily had pulled on the hapless Marge McKinnon, her oldest sister, when Marge refused to let Sicily marry Ed Lawler. *Ed Lawler.*

"What would your father say?" Sicily asked weakly, from her bed, on the third day of her discomfiture.

"He'd be all for it," said Amy Joy. "He always said the French people around here were twice as smart as the Scotch-Irish. He said they speak two languages and the Scotch-Irish can't even speak one."

Amy Joy leaned in the doorway and stared at the paint-by-the-numbers Jesus hanging over Sicily's bed. He was holding a woolly lamb. It had confused her greatly as a child, this painting. The lamb looked as if it really wished to be put down, to be let loose, to be gamboling in some meadow. In the fourth grade it preyed upon Amy Joy's mind so that she had rewritten a nursery rhyme: "Baa Baa, Jesus, have you any wool?"

"Did he really say that?" Sicily asked, and stared vaguely at her toes beneath the blankets. Ed had committed suicide, ten years ago this September, during that rainy, rainy autumn. The autumn her sister Marge expired. The autumn Chester Lee Gifford ran a stolen car into a tree and died before he could crawl out.

"Did your father really say that?" Sicily asked again. Ten years later, ten years down the road of forgiving him for his abandonment of her and her daughter, she was still finding out secrets about him.

"Why don't you get rid of that old painting?" Amy Joy asked.

"That painting?" Sicily was horrified. "Aunt Marge would roll over in her grave. She loved that painting. She used to tell of the long afternoons Mama spent working on it, with only the sound of the clock to keep her company. It's very old, Amy Joy. It'll go to you when I die." Sicily coughed slightly to emphasize that this might be at any moment.

"And on to the dump," Amy Joy said, muffling her words.

"What, dear?" asked the stricken Sicily. The "dear" was an added mountain of guilt. It said *even after all you're putting me through, I still love you.*

"I have something to tell you." Amy Joy pushed one of the silver streaks of hair behind an ear and folded her arms. These pained Sicily, these two shimmering strips down her daughter's hair. But she would not begin on them now. She was saving her voice and her displeasure for the wedding issue. Sicily did notice, happily, that Amy Joy had lost weight since the weather had changed and she'd gotten out for more exercise.

"God only knows how she's getting it, though," Sicily thought. She winced as a picture of Jean Claude Cloutier, revving up his

Chevy super sport in her driveway, and beating on its horn, flashed through her mind. "Even that awful horn sounds French," she thought. "A real Frog mating call."

"I'm going to say this just one more time," said Amy Joy, and took her eyes away from Jesus and the lamb to focus them instead on her mother. "I will get married in three, count them, *three* weeks." She held up three fingers, each nail sporting a different colored nail polish. Sicily took note. After the wedding plans were safely squelched, she would work on the nails.

"And I will do so," continued Amy Joy, "whether you are there or not. Is that clear?"

Sicily groaned slightly and then rolled over on her side, her back pathetically to Amy Joy.

"Furthermore," Amy Joy continued, her eyes back on the painting of Jesus and the unwilling lamb now that they'd lost contact with Sicily's, "I don't care which of your body parts *explodes* because of this."

Sicily felt her kidneys kick at her insides, like little bean-shaped fetuses. They were warning her. Amy Joy could really make her physically ill by marrying Jean Claude. Serious stress had done that to many a formerly healthy Mattagash woman, and the McKinnon name had turned up, not infrequently, among their lot. June Kelley had nearly died from fatigue and shock when her daughter married that divorced man from New Jersey she'd met at Loring Air Force Base. And he spoke English!

"I don't care, I promise you, if your pancreas flies out the window," Amy Joy told her mother. "So there."

Sicily felt an embarrassing jab from her pancreas and was surprised she knew where it lay. How, then, could she be imagining this, as Amy Joy claimed she was, if at just the mention of its name her pancreas throbbed? This was an organ she might have guessed was in her *head*, for all she knew, a minute ago. Now here was a soft jabbing from behind her stomach, an elongated finger poking. Her pancreas discovered, thanks to a thankless daughter.

"I don't care if your bladder bursts at the church," Amy Joy railed on.

Suddenly, Sicily's bladder lurched forward, tipped, and threatened to spill its warm yellow contents in her very bed.

"Oh dear God," Sicily murmured. "Please."

"I have heard of every illness known to a heart, a lung, a kneecap. You've used them all, and you've used them out. They don't work no more."

Sicily rolled over in bed and stared pliantly at Amy Joy.

"There are four hundred and fifty-six people in this town and I will die a thousand deaths in front of each and every one of them," she said. "You'll kill me with this. You mark my words."

"I'll take my chances," said Amy Joy. "If I'm wrong, I'm wrong."

"Great odds for me," thought Sicily.

"I'm marrying Jean Claude Cloutier in three weeks," Amy Joy said. "Whether your organs like it or not."

A large symphony burst forth in Sicily's interior. The pancreas clanged. The bladder blared. The heart and lungs rang like bells. The large intestine, an entity that had heretofore left its landlady in peace, suddenly twisted itself and coiled, snakelike. The thought of a snake inside her was enough to bring on a wave of pure nausea. How could Amy Joy call her a hypochondriac with all this commotion and upheaval going on inside her, against her will? *Hilda Hypochondriac,* she had heard her daughter whisper into the telephone, to that short-legged little Jean Claude from Frogville.

"Three weeks," Amy Joy said dramatically, and left the room.

Sicily rolled onto her back to let the organs and glands and tissues all settle down properly. She stared at the tired oil painting of Jesus and the lamb. Funny, she had always hated it too. Its colors were the faded tones of another era. Jesus looked more angry than benign. The artistry belonged to a world of zealous missionaries, willing to go around the globe to convert savages. Sicily's father, the Reverend Ralph C. McKinnon, had died in China of kala-azar, which had been administered by the bite of a sand fly. He had died among the Chinese, who were even shorter than Frenchmen. Sometimes, when the mosquitoes and no-see-ums got real bad during the summer months in Mattagash, Sicily thought of sand flies and wondered how big they were, what color they were.

Wondered if the reverend had managed to smack the one that bit him. She was surprised, remembering the little of him she knew, that he had even stood still long enough to be bitten. Maybe there was some of his restlessness in Amy Joy's genes, this strange need to abandon a way of life, quickly and once and for all. The reverend's daughters, Marge, Pearl, and Sicily, never saw him again, or cared to really. By 1927 he was already safely dead, just another missionary statistic slid between the flimsy pages of the Good Book and left there until the fat rewards were passed out on Judgment Day. *Judgment Day.* Sicily winced. She hated the thought of the McKinnons lining up on that special occasion, in their best clothes, with a Frenchman in their ranks. The shortness alone could make the line unsightly. It could spoil family pictures for generations.

Sicily eyed the lamb in the painting. It was pained. Its face reminded her of a sad dog she'd seen the Watertown pound cart away one afternoon as she was having her hair clipped and curled at Chez Françoise's Hair Styles. It really was an unsettling picture. Yet throwing it out seemed almost a sacrilege. Sicily decided to pray to it instead, about the situation with Amy Joy.

"Dear Jesus," she implored, but before she could finish her petition a thought struck her that was world-shattering. It would mean social eviction from Mattagash for sure. It would mean all hell breaking loose on Judgment Day. Earlier, it had seemed bad enough that Jean Claude Cloutier, with his phone conversations of *Al-lo. Dis is Jean Claude. His Amee Zhoy dere?* was infiltrating a pedigree that had, like royalty, remained within its own kind for generations. This was worse! Of course! A Frog straight out of the heart of Watertown. Why hadn't it occurred to her before? Organs Sicily had not dared contemplate stomped and wambled and scuffed inside of her. She would die, she knew this, and the room grew suddenly hazy as the stark eyes of Jesus glowered above the piteous eyes of the lamb. When she realized that Jean Claude Cloutier, be he short or tall, was inevitably a *Catholic*, Sicily McKinnon Lawler and her bedraggled organs stayed in bed a full six days longer than they'd planned.

SPRING BRINGS NO JOY
TO MUDVILLE: THE GIFFORDS ARE
STILL PISSED-OFF ABOUT
CHRISTMAS

....

"If you want them boys to love school you got to switch things around on them. Put their school books out there in the outhouse, and take that old stack of *Playboys* to school. They'll be there in the mornings before the teacher even rings her bell."

—Vinal Gifford to his wife, Vera,
after the fifth truant officer visit of 1969

AT VINAL GIFFORD, SENIOR'S, HOUSE THERE WERE NO RUGS beaten to cleanliness. There were no tulip bulbs or gladioli pried into the earth near the front steps. No marigold plants were set out. The same pile of used tires that had sprouted there last fall, before the first snow, was still blooming in the front yard. Hubcaps glistened in the soft April sun. Pickup trucks and discarded cars, gutted and useless, rested on hardwood blocks at various angles and locations about the yard, their tires and parts long gone to newer vehicles. When the weather outlook indicated there would be no more snow until October or thereabouts, Vinal Gifford, Senior, (Big Vinal) ordered Vinal Gifford, Junior, (Little Vinal) to rip away all the plastic insulation from the windows and let a few straggling bars of sun in past the greasy streaks of seasons gone by.

All spring really meant to Vinal Gifford was that the snow-filled path he followed to the mailbox to pick up his disability checks was now more accessible. And he left no snowy tracks, no large heavy imprint of gum rubbers to and from the mailbox in case some snoop from Augusta, some welfare revenuer, came poking his nose about the Gifford house, asking impolite questions about that bad back which had laid Vinal up in front of the TV for years now. Big Vinal wasn't worried about the innocent track that he clomped to the outhouse and back. Surely it was forgivable. An act of God. But the beaten trail to the mailbox kept him nervous as a long-tailed cat. He spied the road both ways, long and hard, before trekking out to the box. He had even asked Bond McClure, the mailman, if he would simply toot the horn if the check was there, in its familiar brown envelope with the lovely Augusta postmark. It would have made those few days during the third week of each month easier ones for Vinal if Bond had simply agreed to toot a positive signal.

"Sorry," Bond had said. "That ain't company policy." And he had driven off in a short, quick burst of pebbles and gravel. Vinal stood in the wake and watched him go.

"I didn't ask you to French-kiss me, Bond," Vinal had said to the retreating bumper of Bond's new 1969 station wagon with the U.S. MAIL sign dangling from the side. Vinal knew damn well that if a McKinnon or a Craft had asked Bond to shit in their mailbox each time the new Sears Roebuck arrived, he would. Giffords, on the other hand, got no favors from the government, although they were highly paid by the organization.

•   •   •

At the top of the hill, across the road from Vinal Gifford, at his brother Pike's residence, spring arrived in much the same fashion. It thawed out the flies around the windows, shook the sluggishness from them that they might begin a new assault on the delectable outhouse. Used tires flowered about the front and back steps at Pike Gifford's house as well. Hubcaps gleamed like large silver quarters from along the sides of the makeshift garage. They spilled out of the mouth of the garage itself, a mountain of silver spilling from a cornucopia. And if they looked spendable that's because Pike Gifford would turn them into money as soon as he was able to function better on his stiff leg. He had asked the Henley Lumber Company to make good on their workman's compensation, and as he was collecting heavily for the mysterious blow to his kneecap that had occurred when a stick of pulp jarred against it, an action only Pike and God had witnessed, Pike decided he'd better not venture just yet into the used hubcap business, in spite of how lucrative it might be.

"I didn't want to hire you in the first place, Pike," Mr. Henley himself had said. "I told you I didn't like to hire Giffords because they claim fake injuries. And your nickname is Pike 'Comp' Gifford around Mattagash. My insurance bill is sky-high because of you folks."

Pike had been sitting in a chair at Watertown's emergency room, waiting to be examined. Old Henley himself had driven him there, too angry to speak on the bumpy forty-mile ride from the work site to the hospital. Waiting for the doctor, he had broken his silence in the hopes of luring Pike into a confession.

"I wouldn't want a man to miss out on medical attention if he needs it," said Henley. Pike thoughtfully watched a nurse shimmy by in her clean white uniform, the kind of sterilized white that hypnotizes Giffords. Pike watched her buttocks beneath all that white and had difficulty listening to his employer. But Henley had wagged on.

"You assured me you had no intention of faking an injury," he said. "You told me your family was up against it financially. I trusted you and now *this*." He pointed at Pike's knee where a soft little violet bruise had spread. "I think you probably did that at home last night, Pike. Tell the truth now. Did you and Vinal go on a little spree?"

"I can't hear a thing you're saying," Pike Gifford had answered, his eyes on the disappearing rear end of the nurse. "I can't hear a thing for pain."

Goldie Gifford, Pike's wife, had a better eye for the scenery around her yard than did Vera, Vinal's wife, at the bottom of the hill. Goldie had coaxed, then threatened her children to help pick up all the pop bottles and candy bar wrappers. She would try to manage it alone, if she ever found time, but she rarely did. Beseeching Pike to transport the flowering black hill of tires to a secluded spot out under the back field poplars had been for naught.

"They're an eyesore, Pike," she had nagged.

"Beauty's in the eye of the beholder," Pike had answered her. "That goes for tires, too." Of all of Hodge Conrad Gifford's many sons, Pike, the youngest, had turned out the most poetic.

"There ain't a sight from here to Bangor prettier than that right there," said Pike, studying the snaky mass of tires until his eyes grew misty with appreciation. "And there's no smell on earth like a fresh pile of rubber just thawing out from the winter," he assured Goldie. Then, forgetting to limp in case Henley had a spy out from the insurance company, Pike trotted briskly to the tilting garage and began counting his trove of hubcaps.

♦   ♦   ♦

The two plots of land that Vinal and Pike owned had been given to them by the old man, Hodge Conrad Gifford. His huge acreage had been passed down, through many generations, from Old Joshua, the first Gifford to settle the land in 1838. On his deathbed, Hodge Conrad Gifford divided the three-hundred-acre plot among his eight children. Four of the Gifford sons and two daughters still remained on their plots, scattered up and down the road in country-style proximity and forming what the rest of Mattagash called Giffordtown.

Vinal Gifford had received the flat hayfield plot and built his house there when he married Vera. When Pike Gifford built his house across the road from Vinal, he cleared away trees along the hill that bordered directly on the river. This would afford him the prettiest view of the water, at the spot where the river turned sharply and seemed to disappear. It would also give him an unobstructed view of the forever burgeoning homestead of his brother Vinal, only four hundred feet down the hill. Goings and comings could be monitored by both sides, which proved useful when a childhood spat between Goldie and Vera, involving who had jumped up and down on whose pencil box, grew in later years to monstrous proportions. By then, the sisters-in-law had become dread enemies. Their husbands didn't mind this tinderbox situation; they rather encouraged it. It wouldn't be to either man's benefit if Goldie and Vera joined forces. "You can fight the Japs, or you can fight the Injuns," Pike often philosophized to Vinal. "But you can't fight the Japs *and* the Injuns." But the tinderbox finally erupted into full flame on December 26, 1968, when the *Watertown Weekly* advertised the biggest sale of Christmas tree lights ever to befall the J. C. Penney Company in northern Maine. Never before had the manager seen such an overstock, and so he marked the lights down in his after-Christmas sale to mere pennies. To mere shadows of their former prices. Goldie's oldest daughter, Irma, who wore the thick eyeglasses, was a part-time clerk at J. C. Penney's, and so had inside info about the sale two days before the newspaper officially announced it. Irma had come home for supper on Christmas Eve, worn to a holiday frazzle, and told her mother.

"It'll be in the paper day after tomorrow," Irma had said, as she blew on one of her thick lenses to clean it. So, after a busy Christmas Day, Goldie had risen before anyone's alarm clock rang in Mattagash. She had pulled the pink sponge curlers from her hair and brushed the little blond humps into waves. She did not risk taking the time to fry a few slices of bacon and brown a couple of yesterday's biscuits for breakfast. She'd breakfast in Watertown, after the sale, when the rear end of her car would be dragging with Christmas tree lights. Only then would she pull into Una's Valley Cafe and have one of those big Farmer Breakfasts. So she had downed a quick cup of Taster's Choice and then skimmed over the snowy road to Watertown in time for the store to open.

On December 26, 1968, known as Boxing Day just across the border in Canada, Goldie stood outside the J. C. Penney store waiting for its doors to open at nine. She stood there in that blustery winter's wind that poured down off Marquis Hill, gushed past the drugstore, and slammed into J. C. Penney's at the street's end. She pulled it off, too. Irma unlocked the door at nine sharp, and Goldie stomped the snow from her boots and went inside to buy every color of Christmas tree light known to man. There were forty boxes of firefly lights, big lights, blinking lights, non-blinking lights. Red. Blue. Green. Orange. White. It was Christmas all over again. Goldie knew she'd pull it off. No one in Mattagash would get their newspaper until Bond McClure brought it to them in his mail car around one o'clock. And no one in Watertown got early papers, either. They got theirs in the mail as well, or waited until the paper boy got home from school to trudge up and down the streets flinging them to and fro.

But even in the slow-moving cold of late December word got out. A lot of women from Mattagash drove all the way over to Watertown in the afternoon. They barely took the time to dress properly once they read about the sale in the *Watertown Weekly*. They snapped the strings off their aprons and whipped them through the air. They abandoned smaller children to larger ones for tending. They tried to hide bobby pins and curlers beneath woolen kerchiefs. They sent boys outside in the cold to shovel out their cars. Some, who hadn't plugged in their block heaters the night before, found to their disappointment that the engines wouldn't turn over in December's cold. They were out of the running unless they could trust a friend, because no one really wanted to let anyone else know about the sale. It was survival of the fittest. It was evolution in full swing. And it would seem that Goldie was the fittest of them all. It would seem that the descendants of Goldie Plunkett Gifford would be the first in line at any sale for many generations to come, and would always have the finest holiday display of tinkling, twinkling, blinking lights that a small amount of money could buy. And that may have been true but for one thing. Charles Darwin had not met Vera Gifford.

Vera had been scraping that morning's oatmeal out of a supposed-to-be-a-no-stick pan when she heard her dog barking beyond its usual enthusiasm. She looked up from the sink in the direction of the barking dog, right up Goldie's hill, and saw her sister-in-law carrying a box into her house. No, it looked more like a big box piled full of little boxes.

"What do you suppose got her out of the house so early?" Vera had thought. Then, when the pan was shining again and ready to be rinsed, Vera heard a car door slam. She looked up quickly.

"Just out of instinct," she later told Vinal. "Just pure holiday instinct." But there Goldie was, half dragging *another* box, and it looked full of little boxes, too!

"She was all nerves," Vera told Vinal, "like she was trying to drag a dead body into the house. And she kept dropping her purse and trying to sling it back on her shoulder."

The drama had deepened when Goldie's little white crocheted hat with the three big diamond shapes on it flew off her head and went tumbleweeding in the wind. That's when Vera's dog, Popeye, had gotten involved in the action, had gone after the hat and caught it up in his teeth. This perked up Vera's suspicions more than anything.

"No matter how hard he pawed it, or shook it in his mouth like he does one of the kids' socks when he wants to play, Goldie never give him a second of her time," Vera told her uninterested husband. "She let him chew that crocheted hat to smithereens and yet, if you heard her talk, it took her weeks to make it, and it was past perfection. No sir! She just went on inside her house, dragging that box."

Vera had watched out her window until there was just one big maroon diamond and a few strings left between Popeye's paws, but still no Goldie to rescue her hat.

"What jackpot do you suppose she hit?" Vera had thought. But that was before the newspaper had come, all snowy and damp because Vinal still hadn't welded the mailbox door back on. Little Vinal had turned the mailbox into a play horse just a day before Christmas. He straddled the box, cowboy style, then tied a rope around the open door for reins. The billowing gust from the Mattagash snowplow had knocked him off, reins in hand, and with the reins came the mailbox door. But the newspaper wasn't so snowy that Vera couldn't read about the Christmas lights sale, and she put away her puzzlement at Goldie's behavior in order to whiz to Watertown for several boxes of lights.

"It ain't just the Catholics who light up their yards," Vera told Vinal as she was leaving. "I need to get there before them goddamn Protestants hear about the sale. They're just greedy is all. What do they need extra lights for? There ain't a single Nativity scene among them."

When Mattagash surmised through its complicated intelligence network of telephone calls, both the legal kind and the *rubbering in* kind, through the countless cups of strong Canadian-bought coffee downed while in pursuit of some new clue, through the close scrutiny of car tracks so as to tell who'd been out of their yard on December 26 and who hadn't—when Mattagash set its mind to solve the mystery, it was just a matter of time until the icy finger of guilt pointed right up Goldie's long driveway to her house on the hill. And it was Vera, the sister-in-law whom Goldie loved to hate, who had come back from Watertown lightless and downhearted, who did the most effective sleuthing. She called the manager at J. C. Penney's to give him a verbal trouncing for exaggerating his sale. Madam, he assured her, there were forty boxes of the most colorful Christmas lights ever trucked to northern Maine. He had placed no purchase limitations on his customers. One lone woman had been there when the store opened and had bought them all. She was from Mattagash, he was certain. He had recognized the distinguishable old-country brogue which still survived in the accents of modern-day Mattagashers.

Once Vera remembered Irma's highly esteemed position at J. C. Penney's as a kind of clerk with tenure, it didn't take long to surmise what had happened. She put the phone down from bawling out the bewildered manager and marched out the door and up the hill to Goldie's. On the icy trip up she pondered their relationship. She had tried time and time again to be friends with her sister-in-law, but it had been futile. It had been like spitting into the wind and getting it back in your face. The real clincher had come when Goldie announced she was *born again.* She had spent a week in Bangor looking for her *real* father, and had come back a Protestant. No one in Mattagash was happy about the conversion. The Giffords and a few other families in town were Catholic, and so hated to lose a sheep to the Protestants. The rest of Mattagash wanted no part of a Gifford in their fold, and they were certain God would feel the same way. Goldie's own husband, Pike, was most confused over the transformation.

"I don't know why anybody would want to stop being a Catholic," he had stood in Vera's kitchen to announce. "Why would anybody wanna do anything wrong if they can't go and confess it?"

December 26, like all other wintry days in northern Maine, was freezing cold. Vera knocked loudly three or four times before Goldie came to the door, smoking a Virginia Slim and holding it precariously in her fingertips. The way Vera never held her Lucky Strike no-filters. The way no woman in Mattagash smoked a cigarette. Even though she was a Gifford by marriage, Goldie had always thought she was a peg above the other Giffords. It was Goldie who first brought the Jackie Kennedy hairstyle to town. She had to dye her goldish-blond hair dark brown in order to create the full effect. She had even lowered her regular speaking voice to a Jackie Kennedy whisper, but when Jackie married that little Greek man, Goldie forgot about her and went back to the gold-blond curls. She still, however, held her cigarettes as if they were needles. Oh, but Vera *hated* Goldie!

"What are you doing out without a coat?" Goldie had asked, opening the door just a crack, then barring it with her foot.

"Never mind my coat," said Vera. "I'm too hot to wear one. I'm fuming right now, Goldie. If I had on a coat, I'd set it on fire."

"You ain't been here in years, Vera. You ain't even sent a Christmas card up this hill by one of my kids. So what are you doing up here spitting icicles?"

"I come to buy some Christmas tree lights," Vera had said. "And

I figure the only other person who owns more Christmas tree lights than you do is Nelson Rockerfuller. I don't know Nelson personally, but I do know you, Goldie."

"You're off your rocker as usual," said Goldie, and tried to shut the door. But Vera pushed until the crack came back again. Goldie had a shoulder and hip against the door, holding it, a single eye glaring out at Vera.

"Irma told you about that Christmas-lights sale, didn't she?" Vera shouted, and pushed harder against the door.

"You're a crazy woman!" Goldie screamed hysterically. Vera pushed harder still, but Goldie managed, because of her foot, to hold her grip.

"I drove all the way to Watertown, over ice and snowdrifts, to buy three or four measly boxes of lights and I come home empty-handed to find out you bought all forty boxes!"

"You come home empty-headed, too," Goldie had answered, almost in tears. She was losing her position in the doorway; she could feel her foot slipping, millifraction by millifraction. And she'd always been a little afraid of Vera, who was a large woman with broad shoulders and a violent temper. Goldie was even more afraid of her since she'd heard that Vera was in the midst of menopause.

"I want four goddamn boxes of Christmas tree lights!" Vera had shouted against the wind. "For my goddamn Christmas tree next year that I intend to stick next to my goddamn mailbox!"

Goldie was sure this was a sign of pure menopausal frenzy, although it seemed that Vera was always lit up like that. Even as a child she'd been a handful. Vera was a Gifford *before* her marriage to Vinal, who was a first cousin, and she seemed much more intent on being a true Gifford than did Goldie. Goldie would have been Jackie Kennedy in a flash, if she could have been.

"You can't even keep a *mailbox* standing because of Little Vinal," said Goldie. "How are you gonna keep an outdoor tree?" Goldie had asked this question sincerely. She was truly wondering how Vera could believe, after all these years of knowing him, that Little Vinal, aged twelve, would allow anything not made of concrete and steel, and welded to the earth, to retain its original form and location. "Besides," Goldie had continued. "I ain't got no Christmas lights. You're crazy. This is a hot flash, is what it is."

"I'll give *you* a hot flash, girlie. I saw you dragging them in today." Vera was angrier than Goldie could ever remember. "You was so damned scared someone might see you, you let Popeye chew up your precious, handmade, hoity-toity hat."

"*Someone* has to feed him," said Goldie. "You sure as hell don't. That poor dog looks like a washboard walking around on four legs."

"He gets plenty to eat," shouted Vera, who rarely knew where Popeye *was*, let alone if he was nutritionally satisfied.

"Hell he does," said Goldie. "He lays in the yard all day eating the catalog. Even the kids joke about it. They say he's too weak to order anything."

It was Pike, who had fallen asleep on the sofa during *The Edge of Night*, who came to Goldie's rescue. He ordered Vera to go back down the hill and forget about the incident.

"Lick some Green Stamps and paste 'em in a book," Pike suggested to his brother's wife. "Git your mind off this foolishness." So Vera had loosened her grip on the door and retreated.

"She's so mad she's melting all the snow off the hill," Goldie had observed to Pike, and then had gone back to packing away the boxes of Christmas lights, some to be used the very next holiday, others during the many holidays to come, when the very mountaintop of Giffordtown would radiate for miles around.

For two solid weeks following the sale, Vera had made everyone in her own household miserable—all except Popeye, who was forced daily to eat bowls of chopped welfare Spam, mixed with powdered welfare eggs. The dining took place outside, and the sole purpose was to assure Goldie that the nutritional intake and daily diet of Popeye was a well-balanced, family-monitored affair. Popeye was delighted and, not one to look a gift horse in the mouth, added stomach weight so quickly that the entire length of his body turned round and wobbly.

"Now he looks like a big ball of yarn walking around on four toothpicks," Goldie said, lifting a curtain panel with one finger ever so slightly and watching the activity at the bottom of the hill. "Now he looks just like Orson Welles."

Pike Gifford was flattened out on the sofa, waiting for *Guiding Light*. Like kings, the male Giffords never worked, and they engaged with the public at special functions only, the kings *at* court, the Giffords *in* court.

"She ought to be mixing up a little meat for her kids," Pike had yawned to Goldie. "It might stop that little one's nose from bleeding all the time. It looks like somebody stuck a pig in that house."

While the snows fell and the land settled more serenely under the tonnage of winter, the battle between the two women became most military. Encastled on the top of the hill with her small army, Goldie had in her coffers a treasure wanted by the angry army camped at the base of the hill. They waited. They spied. Since party lines still plagued Mattagash in 1969, McKinnon and Gifford alike, they listened in on each other's calls. Each and every time, after hearing the *one long, two short* rings, Goldie would carefully lift the receiver.

"The blond witch is on the line, Maggie," Vera would snort. "Be careful what you say." And many times Goldie had to bite her tongue in order not to ask, "Who're you calling a witch, you gray-haired hag?" Instead she would wait her turn, wait until someone phoned *her*, knowing Vera would hear the *two long, two short* rings and be unable to resist a listen.

"The biggest mistake Vinal Gifford ever made just picked up the phone, Lizzie," Goldie would chortle. "Don't breathe deep. You might catch stupidity."

Vera and Goldie also waged their ornamental battle through the children. "They're as bad as the Viet Cong," Vinal commented to Pike one day, as the brothers sat before the final minutes of *Days of Our Lives*. "The next thing you know, they'll be strapping grenades on them kids and sending 'em back and forth across the road." But, quick to vie for parental attention, even if it came in the form of a slap, the Gifford progeny were happy to oblige. At school, one of Goldie's tripped one of Vera's on the playground. One of Vera's pulled a hank of hair from the head of one of Goldie's on the school bus. One tore up another's homework. Mittens were stolen. Swear words filled the air like old medieval curses. But those first weeks of sheer holiday rage cooled a bit when 1969 brought in the coldest February to settle down on northern Maine in a hundred years. It's difficult to stand outside, the Gifford first cousins soon realized, and cuss someone out when your nose is frostbitten.

But not even a windchill factor of sixty below could assuage the painful need Vera had to wrap her fingers around her sister-in-law's neck. By the time spring curled, doglike, about the crooked door jambs, the peeling paint flecks, the weathered outhouses, the mud-filled driveways, Vera was still seething. Had Goldie found the time to plant a row of daffodils in front of the unsightly tires, Vera would've taken Vinal's old .44 rifle and blown the heads off every one of them.

Diplomats that they were, the two Gifford patriarchs managed to stay untouched and unruffled by what they considered pure female hysteria. A pile of nice new batteries might be a different story, but only women could get so emotional over glass bulbs that did little more than rocket electricity bills. So, when April came around with the ancient sound of water dripping from eaves, of car tires finally touching tarred roads, of rips rattling again in the Mattagash River, Pike Gifford lay on the porch sofa and listened to it all, smiling widely. God was in his heaven at times like this, when neither he nor Vinal was in jail. What more could a man crave than a comely spring, a little bit of freedom, and a daily diet of soap operas? And he could almost *smell* the disability check already in the mail, already on its sweet journey from Augusta to Mattagash. Pike lifted his head and gazed down to the bottom of the hill for a sign of his older brother Vinal. His eye caught the magnificent flash of hubcaps simmering in the warm sun, like a vein of silver dug up from all those early boomtowns he'd seen in westerns. He shifted himself onto his side and smiled again when he heard in his pocket the soft sweet rattle of quarters and dimes and nickels that had, just the day before, been in a container for "Jerry's Kids" at Craft's Filling Station. He had also gotten some gossip from Craft's, gossip that wedding bells would be ringing in the valley soon. Wedding bells, like sirens, meant excitement. From his hilltop view of Giffordtown, Pike knew that all was right with the world.

SPRING SLAPS PORTLAND IN THE FACE: THE IVYS CLING TO THE FUNERAL HOME

....

I've been so depressed lately that if it wasn't for my little packet of birth control pills I wouldn't even know what day it is.

—Thelma Ivy, to "Dear Abby," one of thirty-four letters written from January 1969 to April 1969

PORTLAND, MAINE, LIKE A FAVORED HEIR AND THROUGH SOME natural sort of special dispensation, had received its glorious spring a few weeks earlier. The ocean salt and sea breeze served to hasten winter into a quiet retreat, and already folks were tiring of the canary-yellow daffodils in their last death throes along the neat lawns and walks. Soon the rigors of summer mowings and prunings would replace all romantic notions of April, would push them back into the gray attics of people's minds until they were needed again, when the first daffodils birthed themselves once more out of a thawing earth.

At one particular yard, mowed and pruned to heavenly perfection, sprawled the brick Ivy Funeral Home, a structure more closely resembling an educational institution than a mortuary. Vines toe-holed their way across the gray bricks. Sagging, intelligent elms lolled on each side of the entrance, and shapely hedges squatted along the paved driveway and adjoining parking lot. A somber lull lay in the architecture of the building. A mystical aura. It could easily have been Cambridge University, that place of great thought and deep learning, so much did the design demand one's highest respect. Old Man Ivy, who designed the building himself, knew the architectural reasoning behind it all, knew it was no accident that the Ivy Funeral Home could pass as a university in its insistence on being paid an academic homage. He had researched buildings for six long months before he came up with the creative spark that had burst, finally, into full flame. When the smoke cleared less than a year later, the Ivy Funeral Home was welcoming clients at the cul-de-sac on the end of Maple Street. "There are two things on the planet that people are most afraid of," Old Man Ivy once said to his son Marvin. "The first is a scholar. The second is a corpse. Put them together and you can sell a coffin for twice the factory price. Please remember that, son."

And the notion worked. The institution threatened revenge on any weeping family member who might stop crying long enough to question the dollars and cents that were accumulating on the funeral bill. Old Man Ivy had seen, before his own demise, the long lines of serene, reverent mourners filing into his chapel as though Leonardo had sculpted the J. C. Penney plaster-of-Paris statues about the altar and the fernlike designs on the heavenly ceiling. He had seen the faces, pale and divine, like pilgrims at Lourdes, their nostrils fluttering at the smell of flower shop carnations and gladioli. He had seen the eyes sneaking peeks at the floral banners: BELOVED UNCLE, CHERISHED MOTHER, DEAREST FRIEND, SON, DAUGHTER, SISTER, BROTHER.

"Schmuck," the old man told Marvin one night, as they studied the newly arrived corpse of one of Portland's more prominent Jewish citizens. "They should print a banner that says BELOVED SCHMUCK."

But his son Marvin was as oblivious to the professional tricks of the trade as were the clients of the Ivy Funeral Home. He was caught up in the promotional thrust of the scheme. Driving to work each morning, to what he called "the office," Marvin Ivy felt like a professor about to enter the chalky halls of academia, where he might be prompted to deliver a lecture on Anglo-Saxon runes. Several years earlier he had begun wearing tweed suits and carrying a two-hundred-dollar calfskin briefcase to house his colored pamphlets on casket models and monument selections. He grew a small fuzzy mustache. The secretary began finding vestiges of Grecian Formula on the rest room towels. Then an 8 × 10 photo of Winston Churchill appeared in his office, among toothy school pictures of the Ivy grandchildren. "You have nothing to fear but fear itself," he began telling the secretaries and other "upstairs employees," who were skittish about the embalming room. Another innovative splash in funeral jargon which Marvin Ivy had coined himself was "houseguest." No corpse entering the Ivy Funeral Home was referred to as "the deceased," or even "the departed." Maybe behind Marvin's back his employees verbally roughhoused the bodies, calling them stiffs, or goners, or "Friday's paycheck." But to Marvin Ivy's face all incoming dead were to be referred to, politely, as houseguests. "We are not a *parlor*," he told his melancholy group of employees, "because we do not give massages. We take in *houseguests*. We are a *funeral home*. Think of yourselves as *hosts*. And don't slump in your suits," he warned, as they itched in their colorful tweeds and looked more like overgrown Scottish delinquents than workers at the Ivy Funeral Home.

It was in response to hearing this speech for the first time, the one about the employees being innkeepers of sorts, that Jimmy Driscoll was prompted to pipe up and ask Marvin Ivy why he didn't put out a welcome mat and stick a candle in the window. Marvin said nothing in front of the others, but the very next day Jimmy Driscoll was sucking on a milk shake in the Portland Mall and

talking about getting a job selling life insurance. So no one spoke
up again whenever the home-versus-a-massage-parlor lecture came
down. Marvin Ivy may have thought he loomed large and author-
itative as Winston Churchill before his employees, but in truth he
was barely in his car, on his way home from a busy day at the
office, before the barbs began to fly. "Has anyone seen the boss?"
they would ask one another. "He must still be here," someone
would say. "He left his calfskin briefcase." And then a soft moo
could be heard throughout the funeral home, until all the employees took up the chorus and a loud litany of moos filled the
establishment. Once, a secretary, who was biding her time until
an autumn marriage, told a prospective client who had phoned for
information, "Sorry. There's no more room at the inn." Everyone
in the casket showroom had cracked up when they heard about it.

One more time before he died, Old Man Ivy tried to get some
light to leak in through Marvin's tightly sealed lids.

"Don't let none of this fool you, boy," the old man said. "This
has been going on ever since the first caveman threw a few daisies
onto a grave. Think in terms of dollars only, son, and you'll be all
right."

The advice had fallen on ears as receptive as those belonging to
an Ivy Funeral Home houseguest. The old man's words had beat
against the hard walls of the embalming room, had circled like
doves around the chapel and then escaped into the wide sky over
Portland, Maine's, finest funeral home. They must have been in-
terred with the old man. They must have gone back to dust next
to the rattling bones in his coffin, because they simply disappeared.
Now, twenty-three months before his retirement, Marvin Ivy still
felt a literary jostle to his gut while driving in to the office each
morning. As he cut the sharp corner onto Maple Street, the first
thing that struck his corneas was the building, vine-covered, kingly,
aristocratic as hell. A building that had seen some things, this
building, like the Tower of London. It occurred to Marvin Ivy that
if his own son, Marvin Ivy, Junior, didn't get his cow patties collected soon, rather than pass the funeral home on to the foolish
boy he would turn it into one of those historic monuments and

charge tourists a buck apiece to tramp through it. That's just what those broke aristocrats did to their castles in England. That's how most of those English big wheels paid their light bills. Fifty cents here and there from Ohio and Missouri and Delaware. Yes sir. Junior Ivy had better get his horse manure into a meaningful pile soon or Marvin would change the very history of the building. Maybe he'd do it anyway. Even if Junior got his dog turds rounded up it would be only a matter of years before Junior's son, Randy, Marvin's only grandson, would inherit the family business. When Marvin Ivy thought about his vine-clad business being passed on to Randy Ivy, when he thought of his beleaguered houseguests being invited in for their brief stay by his grandson, it caused a sweat to form all over his body, a dangerous thing for tweed.

As Marvin Ivy left the office for the day, remnants of spring were lounging, still, around the squat hedges and along the prim drive. He hoisted his briefcase under his arm and sighed a heavy sigh as he surveyed his empire. It had been a busy week last week: eight from the local nursing homes, a heart attack at the new mall construction site, three automobile fatalities on Interstate 95, and a stillbirth. Thirteen houseguests made a nice tidy number that would add silver to the pockets of even the most undiscerning innkeeper. But that had been last week. So far this week every living soul in Portland seemed healthy enough to toss Marvin Ivy into bankruptcy. Last week thirteen. This week nothing. That number *thirteen* could grab hold of a man's superstitions, if a man let it.

In the midst of his monetary reverie Marvin Ivy, Senior, was bombarded by a hideous whine that had just cut the sharp corner onto Maple Street. The amplified sound of an outboard motor, he thought at first, or worse, a high-powered chain saw on wheels. It loomed suddenly out of the setting sun that had temporarily blinded him, and burst forth up the drive in a deafening squall, loud enough, perish the thought, to waken each of the slumbering houseguests at the Ivy Funeral Home, had any checked in.

"Sssshhhh!" Marvin said, a finger to his lips. He pointed to a sign near the door which said: QUIET PLEASE. THIS IS NOT AN

AMUSEMENT PARK. Marvin was proud of the sign. It was a minor example of the imaginative sparks that illuminated his lucrative career in funeral undertaking.

"We can't have one group bawling their heads off and disturbing another group of mourners," he had said to his wife, Pearl McKinnon Ivy, when she inquired as to the tastefulness of the wording.

"Sssshhhhh!" Marvin warned again, as the wall of sound pushed itself off the paved drive and burst across the newly sprouted grass of the funeral home lawn. It halted before him, with a rude abruptness, an inch or two from his shoes.

"SHUT IT OFF!" Marvin Ivy bellowed. "SHUT—IT—OFF!"

"What?" asked Randy Ivy, his hair dirty and dangling down his back in a limp ponytail.

"I SAID SHUT THAT GODDAMN THING OFF!" His grandfather was purple-faced by now. Randy turned the ignition key and the sound melted away.

"How do you like my new wheels, man?" Randy Ivy asked. The flare in the legs of his jeans had been wrapped around his skinny ankles and bound there with elastics to avoid any transportation hazards. Randy Ivy had learned this during the years he was confined to the noiseless, smokeless bicycle.

"And don't call me *man!*" Marvin shouted.

"Gramps," Randy corrected.

"God, that's worse," thought Marvin. "What if the mourners hear him?"

"What do you think of my new Kawasaki, Gramps?" Randy asked. His eyes glowed red as little campfires.

"Get it to hell off my lawn," Marvin warned, wondering what chemical Randy was experimenting with now. He knew a little bit about chemicals himself. They all did the same thing to the dead *and* the living. They were meant to embalm the body. In Randy's case, the brain.

"You seen my old man?" Randy asked.

"Your *father,*" Marvin snarled. "He's your father."

"Yeah," said Randy. "You seen him?"

"No," said Marvin. "I haven't seen him. I don't especially want to see him. And I don't especially care to see *you*. You're obviously higher than a Chinese kite. And you're tearing up my goddamn front lawn!"

"Hey. Cool it, man," Randy said. "Calm down. You'll end up a houseguest." Marvin Ivy, Senior, boiled. Blaspheme his institution, would he, this product of the ungodly sixties?

"Listen, you greasy-haired little squirt," he said, trying to sound menacing without disobeying his own sign behind his tweeded shoulder, the one outlawing amusement park activities. "You get your *wheels* to hell out of here. And your ass, too."

"How's business?" Randy asked his beet-faced ancestor. "Anybody's grandmother croak today?"

Marvin Ivy stood, slack-jawed, his tweed turning almost a full-colored navy in the sun setting over the Portland treetops. Marvin stood in front of his establishment, which looked, as the sun turned gold as wheat, more like Cambridge University than ever. He looked away from his grandson to the lot across the street which had been purchased for the sole purpose of housing the Ivy Funeral Home memorial stones. He counted to ten, his eyes moving from one sparkling, highly polished baby's monument to another. He kept his eyes on those newly arrived kiddie memorials adorned with angel wings. The monument addition to the family business was another one of Marvin's lucrative ventures, and it had proved a wise one. It was just last month that he had decided to try out an entire line of small sad children's markers, and now they lolled in the sun, the embossed lambs weary with waiting, the angel wings that embellished the tops too heavy to fly. One. Two. Three. His eyes counted until they marked off ten memorials. As he fought to keep his blood pressure from rising, he imagined what the tenth marker, with its granite wings fluttering, might say. MARVIN RANDALL IVY III. KNOWN AS RANDY. SADLY MISSED BY GRANDMOTHER ONLY.

"Do you see that sign?" Marvin was finally able to ask, evenly, of his grandson. "Right there?" He pointed to a mound that would soon be flowering with pansies, those somber yet summery flowers.

The sign in question said in heavy black letters: STAY OFF THE GRASS! Randy read it slowly, thought hard about it.

"I'm trying to, man," Randy Ivy said, reaching into his jacket pocket and taking out a Baggie full of what his grandfather estimated to be large chunks of parsley flakes. "But this shit," Randy said, wetting a ZigZag paper to his lips and beginning to expertly roll a joint, "this shit is pure Colombian."

◆ ◆ ◆

Marvin Ivy, Junior, turned away from Monique Tessier, in bed at the Portland Ocean Edge Motel, and checked his watch. He hoped to make it back to the Ivy Funeral Home in time to satisfy his father that he was just away on a short business call and would be back on the job until six-thirty, his usual departure time. Marvin Senior left the office by five o'clock every day, with a timed precision Junior had never been able to acquire.

"He'll probably die right on time, too," Junior had said to his wife, Thelma. "He'll probably kick off at five o'clock sharp someday to go to that casket showroom in the sky."

Junior squinted his eyes, gathering up enough afternoon light flitting past the thick motel curtains to read the digits. Five-thirty.

"Damn," he muttered.

"Mmmmmh?" Monique stirred beside him. It was most likely Marvin had already noticed that Monique was not at her desk in the reception area. The other female employee at the Ivy Funeral Home, the secretary-accountant, was supposed to cover for Monique if Marvin Ivy came around, smelling of sweaty tweed and calfskin and asking questions.

"Tell him I have a dental appointment," Monique had beseeched Milly Bishop. So when Marvin Ivy turned up at four-thirty to inquire as to Junior's whereabouts, Milly was ready for him.

"He had a business appointment," Milly lied, "and will be back any minute."

"Where's Miss Tessier?" Marvin had further asked, noticing the empty chair and paperless desk.

"Dental appointment," said Milly, too flustered with lying to look her boss in the face.

"Dental appointment?" Marvin bellowed. "That's the fourth one this month. How many teeth has the woman got?"

"Thirty-two," said Milly sheepishly, as if Monique had urged her to say this as well if asked. "I think humans have thirty-two," she repeated, and then went back to mailing coffin bills to the still-stricken relatives of houseguests.

"Damn!" Junior said again, and threw back the covers. Monique pushed brunette hair away from her eyes and then opened them.

"What?" she asked.

"The time," said Junior. "The old man is gonna raise the roof over this."

"Well, why don't we meet *after* work, sweetheart? Wouldn't that make it so much easier?" Monique walked her fingers among the forest of hairs on Junior's chest.

"You know why," Junior grunted and lurched forward to a sitting position. The acquisition of belly that he had worked for all his life, a nest egg of fat tissues and fat cells and skin dimples, jiggled as he hoisted his pants up over his hips.

"You know damn well Thelma would have the fire department out looking for me if I came home ten minutes late." Junior studied his face in the motel mirror. He hated the lighting in motel rooms. It had all the ambience of a police lineup. His image filled the tiny mirror, towered dark and heavy, like some Citizen Kane.

"Well just let her then." Monique snipped the words. "The trouble with Thelma is that she has nothing better to do with her time."

"Don't start," said Junior, and slipped his feet into his shoes.

"I swear when she comes into the funeral home she talks like she's been drugged. I know those Valiums her doctor gives her keep her on another planet."

"Don't start," said Junior.

"And Randy would be such a nice boy if he only had a little discipline." Monique said this as she pulled her cotton sweater over her head and then fluffed her hair. She took her skirt off the chair by the side of the bed and stepped carefully into it.

"I don't know why you don't just put your foot down," Monique said. She applied a fresh layer of lipstick to each lip, then rolled them together to smooth the effect. "The girls will be space cadets too, with Thelma as a role model."

"Don't start."

"And where does that leave us? Sneaking off like high school kids. Hiding from your wife *and* your father. Why can't we go to dinner? Spend a weekend in Boston? See a movie now and then? We never do anything but go to bed in the middle of the afternoon at the same damn motel. Day after day after day."

"Jesus Christ," said Junior, as he opened the door for the Ivy Funeral Home secretary. "You're gonna start."

◆ ◆ ◆

Pearl brought Marvin's after-dinner coffee in to where he lounged in the living room. He was reading the obituary page like a broker scouring the *Wall Street Journal*.

"Sicily called today in a panic," Pearl said. "It seems some boy is stupid enough to marry Amy Joy. Can you imagine?" But Marvin wasn't listening to matrimonial news.

"I don't understand it," he said to Pearl, who was milking his coffee just the way he liked it. "They seem to be dying just fine in Bangor, and Brunswick, and Lewiston. What the hell is Portland holding out for?"

"People are living longer nowadays," said Pearl. "People are healthier."

"Healthy is one thing," said Marvin, as he flung the newspaper aside. "Immortal is another."

"Oh, it can't be that bad, can it now?" asked Pearl. She settled back with a large thump onto the sofa. Her body had deteriorated more this very year than any other. She could feel it happening, the joints stiffening with rust, the skin loosening, the yellow growing in her eyes as though they were gardens of weeds. Every

morning since the twenty-fifth of January, when it had first occurred, she had awakened before daylight and lain beside Marvin
Ivy and whispered to herself over and over again, "I am sixty years
old now. I am sixty years old."

And so she was. The Reverend Ralph C. McKinnon, her father,
had seen her last when she was thirteen. Now she was sixty. Would
he recognize her when her turn came and she died and went to
heaven? Would he know that the graying woman, large and solid
like the McKinnons, with the arthritic hip and crow's-feet smile
was the same little girl who wore the brunette braids in 1922? That
was the day of goodbye, as the reverend set out for China, never
to be seen again. He had died there of a disease transmitted by
an insect of some kind. Pearl could no longer remember what. But
the reverend wasn't her problem in the gray morning hours as the
first light of dawn settled over Portland, over her house, over her
very bedroom. It was her mother's face that got her up long before
daylight and kept her awake long after Marvin's heavy snores were
cascading from his side of the bed. She was little more than four
years old when Grace McKinnon died giving birth to Pearl's
younger sister, Sicily. Yet Pearl could see her mother's face, pure,
calm, with the dream of life still unbroken. When she was not quite
awake, or not quite asleep, that's when it filtered in to her clearly.
A mother's face, awash in plainness, the skin pale and milky. The
thin hair that fell along the sides like silver willows was soft with
forgiveness. She was not a pioneer, Grace McKinnon, but delicate
and sickly. And she proved that by dying as Sicily was born.

Sometimes her mother's face turned into her sister Marge's, dead
a decade, who had raised Sicily and Pearl after the reverend em-
barked for a career and death in China. Poor Marge. What a sad,
lonely life for such a young girl. Pearl felt a twinge of guilt. She
and Marge had not always been on the same team. Sometimes
they hadn't even been in the same ballpark. But she missed her
dearly. Marge had died of beriberi—had refused to eat anything
but polished rice and Chinese tea as a tribute to the great missionaries of the world. Marge had died unmarried, unhappy, un-
fulfilled, and now Pearl wanted to tell her that—although she

herself had a husband, a son, three grandchildren—she was feeling that life had dealt them the same round of cards, but in different games.

"This dry spell keeps up and I'll have to fire Barney," said Marvin, and sucked up some more coffee. "It's getting to the point nowadays where nursing homes are teaching exercise and fitness. What do people want, for Chrissakes? To live to be a hundred?"

"Fire Barney?" asked Pearl. Barney Killam had been with the Ivy Funeral Home for thirty-eight years. Old Man Ivy himself had hired him. "Isn't he about to retire?"

"We've been saying that for almost ten years," said Marvin, and retrieved the paper to glance at the sports page. Perhaps it was business as usual in that category at least. "He'll never retire. We'll just embalm him one day and stand him in the corner. Retire? Ha!"

"Good heavens, Marvin. It seems to me that firing Barney after thirty-eight years of service would be a tad unfair."

"Well, I can't let any of my new blood go just to keep Barney working," Marvin said abruptly. Pearl pondered the situation.

"Well, don't tell Barney *why* you're firing him," she offered. "He may be tempted to bump somebody off."

"You can't blame a man for loving his job." Marvin sighed and put his shoeless feet up onto the ottoman. Pearl thought about this. She had come to accept almost every tenet and ism of funeralology over the forty years they'd been married. Had even grown used to Sicily and Marge's inability to deal with death and its earthly ministers, the undertakers. "Funeral directors," Pearl was still correcting Sicily after forty years. "Please, Sicily, not undertakers." But some notions were blacker and harder to swallow. This was one. That white-headed Barney might slink in dark alleys in hopes of slaying potential houseguests in order to keep his job was too much. Pearl tried not to imagine him in court, bent as an old willow tree, weeping about missing the embalming room. And he *had* been the best embalmer. A real artist. But now the trembling in his hands limited him to shaking hands with mourners and offering his quivering condolences. Pearl realized that Barney's hands were probably incapable of murder these days. She imagined the raised silver knife glancing off the victim and skittering like a fish along the pavement. She saw the bullet refusing to go into the gun as brittle old fingers pushed at it. The match unable to ignite with such a slight scratch of itself down an alley wall. Old Barney couldn't hurt a fly even if he were a spider and wanted to. He was too fragile with age, Pearl decided, and let the issue drop.

"Speaking of firing," Marvin said, his voice tight with tension. Pearl's jaw grew taut as she felt her molars clamp together, quietly but firmly. She waited. Nothing.

"Yes?" she asked, finally. "What about it?" The tension floated like a balloon between them, ready to burst at the first sharp word.

"If I ever run into Junior at work, I may just fire him." Marvin said this quickly, hoping to make it sound as matter-of-fact as the possible firing of Barney Killam. But this was different. This was treading upon ground higher and taller than any sacred mound an Indian even conceived of building, for this Junior, this large, pinkish philandering heap, was, at thirty-eight years old, Pearl's one and only baby. *Juniorkins,* she had called him in his baby years, and on occasion she still slipped and called him this. Juniorkins. And it seemed, she was sure, to please him. She had done all a mother could to protect Junior for years. His classmates had been cruel, she knew, singling him out on the basis of his father's profession. So she had cradled him from those awful creatures all she could, had plied him with cakes and candies and high-caloric meals, insisting his bouts with unhappiness were a sure sign of low sugar. When Junior jilted her to marry batty little Thelma Parsons, Pearl had felt, family business metaphors aside, that a great grave had opened up wide and swallowed any chances for future happiness for her only child. Now Thelma Parsons Ivy had proved true to Pearl's expectations of her. She was battier than ever. She was driving poor Junior to his wits' end. Pearl knew this. A mother senses inner turmoil, regardless of how many layers of fatty tissue she must go through to reach it.

"And Monique, the secretary with the big tits, was gone again.

Another dental appointment." Marvin offered more evidence, but to Pearl it was even further proof of poor Junior's marital unhappiness. Thelma could have had breast implants. Pearl had seen her bras in the laundry room. Thirty-two-A's. "Walnuts," Pearl had thought, "could fit in these cups." How then could Junior *not* be tempted when veritable melons were flaunted before him, day after day? Pearl did pale at the thought of Monique, a fortune hunter, a gold digger if she ever saw one, trying to finagle her way in through the showroom doors of the Ivy Funeral Home as Junior's second wife. And that was what Monique was after, to be sure. What woman wouldn't want to be first lady of Portland's largest, most academic funeral parlor? *Parlor*. Pearl grimaced. Thank heavens Marvin Ivy was unable to weasel his way into her thoughts. The last thing she needed that evening was the "we do not give massages" lecture. Pearl shot an innocent little look of inquiry at Marvin, but he was staring straight ahead, still consumed with the anger he had brought home over Junior's habitual disappearances.

"All he thinks of is sex and food," Marvin said grumpily. "In that order."

Pearl wished suddenly that Junior would come to *her* for the food, and for some motherly consolation. She might not be able to compete with Monique Tessier in some departments, but she could hold her own with quick, drive-through restaurants and the seedy sort of menus one might find in sleazy motels. She would make her son a fat three-tiered sandwich of homemade bread, cut him a monstrous slice of cake, fill a glass of Shulman's Dairy milk up to a frosty brim. She would rub his shoulders and call him Juniorkins.

"Maybe it was just a coincidence," Pearl offered vaguely, of Junior and Monique's magical co-disappearance.

"Any more coincidences like that and the woman won't have a tooth left in her head," said Marvin. He finished off the last sip of coffee.

"This is Thelma's fault," Pearl muttered, her eyes welded to Junior's bronzed baby shoes, which glittered on the top shelf of the bookcase. Pearl could, if she listened hard enough, long enough, still hear the lovely patter of those plump little footfalls. "My God, where does the time go?" she wondered.

"No. He's a grown man," said Marvin. "It's no one's fault but his own. He has a business thrown into his lap, for Chrissakes, and he's still too lazy to do a single day's work."

So here it was, the continuing argument between Marvin and Pearl for years, between husband and wife, between father and mother.

"The funeral business makes him nervous," Pearl said.

"Yeah, well let him shovel shit somewhere and see if *that* makes him feel any better. Any other boss would fire him anyway. He's lazy, Pearl. You might as well admit that."

Pearl sat softly and watched the bluish light from the turned-down television set as it bounced off the bronze laces of Junior's first pair of shoes. She had bought them at The Blessed Stork, a children's store now long swallowed up by a swath of shiny new office buildings.

"If he hadn't married Thelma," she said resolutely.

"Thelma Shmelma," Marvin said, as he always did. "You'd put the blame on anyone he would have married. If he had married *Elizabeth Taylor* you'd have blamed her." Marvin had Liz Taylor on the brain, since all the funeral home employees had commented many times on Monique Tessier's resemblance to the star.

Pearl tried to imagine Junior driving up to the front door of the Ivy Funeral Home with Elizabeth Taylor happily ensconced in the front seat, the three Ivy grandkids bobbing noisily in the back. "Large breasts," Pearl thought, visualizing Elizabeth—no, she would call her Betty—opening the car door and waving a warm, diamondy hello to her in-laws. Pearl could even see the angle of Portland sunlight as it bounced along Betty's ample cleavage. She was reminded of the tiny path that wound between Thelma's walnuts, with not even the slightest trace of curve or hint of a hill. This was back road stuff, a dirt trail, when compared to the six-lane freeway on Betty's chest. "Yes," thought Pearl. "Betty Taylor Ivy. It might have worked."

"Ever since he was a kid," Marvin barged on, "you blamed other kids for his wrongdoings. You're not helping him any, Pearl. Believe me. I know. I work with him, when he's there." And with that Marvin had gone up the stairs to take a long leisurely soak and ponder the new no-corpse situation befalling Portland, Maine.

"Something in the water, maybe?" he wondered as he turned the tap and warm water gushed out to fill the tub.

Pearl sat alone on the sofa, staring at her wedding band, wondering how all that young skin around it had grown so miserably wrinkled and dry. When she married Marvin he had been studying to become a lawyer, and thus she felt she was marrying a lawyer. But she had married an undertaker instead. Sicily was right. Funeral director. Undertaker. It made no difference. The end result was the same. Somebody died. Somebody *undertook* to bury them. It had been going on since time immemorial, this dying-burying business. Someday, and someday soon, no matter how she looked at it, someone at the Ivy Funeral Home would take Pearl McKinnon Ivy in as a houseguest and drain and stitch and powder her to a lasting perfection. This would happen to Marvin Ivy, Senior. It would happen to Marvin Junior. It would happen to his wife, Thelma. To the Ivy grandchildren. Someday.

"I am sixty years old," Pearl said softly, and the television flickered a blue response. Junior's baby shoes sat gathering the dust of the years. Petrified. Embalmed. "I am sixty years old now," Pearl said again. And she tried to call her mother's face to her mind's eye, to picture a visage that was soft and loving and peaceful. But instead of her mother she saw Thelma Parsons Ivy. Pale and breastless. Thief of sons. Purloiner of only children.

"Damn her," Pearl muttered. She was suddenly struck with a film image of Junior, spread across the Portland drive-in theater. Junior in *Butterfield Eight*. Junior on horseback in *National Velvet*. She could see him eating peeled grapes as Antony, while Cleopatra lounged at his feet.

"Damn her," Pearl said again, and decided that one day soon, she would take a hammer and chisel and pound away at those bronzed baby shoes, just to see how the soft leather inside, like the aging meat of an old nut, had been holding up all these years. She struggled up from the sofa and turned off the TV set. It was an older set, a model with tubes, but Pearl still hadn't the heart to chuck it out for a newer one. Junior had watched his favorite cartoons on this set. And Ed Sullivan playing straight man to Topo Gigio. Arthur Godfrey, the redhead, dug up the best talent in America. And Milton Berle dressed up as a woman on Tuesday nights with Texaco sponsoring. Pearl had read that the streets of America emptied on this night, so folks could gather around televisions and radios to see and hear Uncle Miltie. "My God, where does the time go?" Pearl asked again. On the television screen, the white line of the picture tube drew slowly inward, until it became a white, flickering dot. It hung there like a tiny soul, like the ghost of every one of the old television performers who had come and gone in the lives of curious, forgetful Americans. *I Married Joan. You Bet Your Life.* Edward R. Murrow chain-smoking on *Person to Person.* The picture screen fell to a grayish haze and grew darker. Suddenly the little white dot was gone and the screen turned black as death. "I am sixty years old now," Pearl said again, as though it were the latest answer to the sixty-four-thousand-dollar question.

◆　　◆　　◆

One of the *adult* shoes belonging to Junior Ivy pressed down on the accelerator as he flew down Beacon Street and swung into his wide driveway. He saw the curtain flutter gently in the window. Birdlike. *Thelma.* Junior walked around the back end of the car after he parked it. It was the longest route to the house, but even a few extra feet would give him added time to think. His eye spied a sticker on the rear bumper that one of the kids had pasted there during the family's spring vacation. I WISH I WERE IN FLORIDA, it stated.

"God, ain't that the truth," Junior thought, as he saw the curtain go limp in the window.

Inside, Thelma popped a Valium into her small bird's mouth,

and it disappeared down her throat in a wash of ginger ale. She flew across the room and flopped onto the sofa in front of the evening news. She straightened her dress and waited. Junior stopped to pet the family's miniature collie on the front steps. More time to think. Thelma glanced out nervously and saw her husband's head bobbing up and down outside the window.

"There, boy," she heard him say. "Good dog."

"That's me," Thelma thought. "A good dog."

Junior came in and closed the door softly.

"Whew. What a day!" he said. He threw his suit jacket on the sofa and leaned over to lightly kiss the top of Thelma's head. "And how was your day?"

"The same," said Thelma. "Nothing new." He heard the thin layer of ice forming among the words, molding them into a cold sentence. *What now?* He moved nervously to the bar and poured himself a gin and tonic.

"Where's the kids?" he asked. This would be okay. There was no trap in this sentence waiting to snap shut. Something had riled her, to be sure, so he must step the way soldiers do to avoid live mines. He was good at this. Very good. He'd had plenty of qualified training. He dabbed a napkin at the bottom of his glass. Christ, but he *was* good. If it hadn't been for the funeral home, he might have tried his hand at drama. His confidence pushed the words out again. "I said, where's the kids?"

"Where's Monique Tessier?" Thelma asked suddenly and Junior's glass slid a full inch down, out of his hand. He caught the bottom of it with his other hand, but Thelma had already seen the damage caused by her explosive remark.

"Who?" Junior croaked. The Muse had abandoned him, the bitch. Suddenly his feet hurt, as if he were wearing shoes that were too small. *Mama*, his subconscious mind all but shouted. His clothes began to shrink, to hurt him badly, an embalmed suit of skin.

"Monique Tessier," Thelma said again, and turned to look at him. He had grown even more portly, this man she had married.

He had grown chins, and unusual habits, and away from her. She took a Polaroid picture from beneath the sofa cushion and handed it to him.

"Look familiar?" she asked, sultry almost. Calm. Beneficent. This surprised her. Wasn't she usually flighty, illogical, overly emotional? This must be, then, the new her. She must have grown already from the news of this nasty business. In truth, she had forgotten the day's handful of Valiums, and the obvious character-building they supplied her.

Junior took the picture with a trembling hand and gazed at it. Polaroids. How he hated them. What ever happened to the old-fashioned way of processing film? How nice it would have been if Thelma had had to drop her film off at the mall for three days. Or send it to Boston. Or Hong Kong. It would have given him *days* to think. Yes, there they were, him leaning on the door of Monique's old Buick, just about to give her a last little goodbye peck. His lips were moving with words. What had they been? Oh, yes. *You'll see. Things will get better, honey.* That's what he had been foolishly saying just as the blasted Polaroid had snapped and frozen his guilt forever. Bronzed it. *Things will get better.* Sure, but for whom, that's what he hadn't asked himself. Christ, there were land mines everywhere.

"Is that," Thelma fairly sang with calmness, "or is that not Monique Tessier?"

Junior struggled for an answer. He pondered heavily, as if to be of help to Thelma in her identification of the culprit, to ingratiate himself, to fling himself into her side of the ring. His eyebrows knitted with disgust. He wanted to say, "Good Lord. What's she doing away from her desk? She's supposed to be working! Me and the old man will need to look into this tomorrow."

"Ah" was all he said. He was struck with the fullness of Monique's breasts in her cotton sweater, with their pendulous appeal. And right there, even upon the burning coals of this fiery inquisition, he wanted to bury his head between them. "God, but she does look like Elizabeth Taylor," he thought.

"What are you looking at?" It was Cynthia, his oldest daughter, engaged to a young dental student.

"Nothing," said Junior, and stuffed the photo into his hip pocket.

"A picture," said Thelma, gleefully, smugly. She had no idea she was capable of such magnanimous composure.

"Where's Regina Beth?" Junior asked quickly, hoping to lead Cynthia to the sidelines and away from the heat of the action. If Thelma kept it up, the goddamn picture would be in the *Portland Telegram* in the morning.

"In her room reading. Where else, but with her nose in an old book?" scoffed Cynthia, and turned up her own nose, which looked as if it had never even *smelled* a book, much less been in one. She tugged at the legs of her jeans, pulled them down, away from her crotch. She had been born, Cynthia Jane Ivy had, long-waisted. At least that's how Thelma described the malady. Shorts and pants tended to ride up into the crotch area. Cynthia was chafed constantly as a young child, and Thelma had kept a steady supply of talcum as a powdery buffer. But as she got older, Cynthia found the best remedy was a constant relocation of clothing and she perpetually tugged her garments down into more comfortable locations. As a result she fidgeted constantly, and was even sent to the principal's office in the fifth grade by an insensitive teacher who incorrectly diagnosed a kind of civil disobedience as the cause. Thelma had gone, red-faced, to the principal's office to explain. "A birth defect," she had told the man, her eyes lowered to the floor by the weight of what she thought was a family secret. "She lives with pain," she had added. The nervous affliction had even kept the poor child off the cheerleading team. At tryouts, while the other five girls flew like balloons into the air with shouts of "Give me a *P*, give me an *O*, give me an *R*, give me a *T*," Cynthia had remained with her feet flat on the gymnasium floor, trying desperately to come to amicable terms with the stiff red cheerleading panties.

"She'll probably die someday with her nose in an old book," said Cynthia, tugging at her jeans.

"A lovely, lovely picture," said Thelma, and smiled broadly. Junior flinched.

"Listen," he said to Cynthia. "Why don't you go get your sister and we'll all go out to a nice little dinner? That way your mother won't have to cook. What do you say?" Junior was grasping— surrounded by the children he would be temporarily safe. How far had Thelma gone in uncovering his deceit? Had she hired a detective? A lawyer? God, he hated lawyers. Smug sons of bitches. They almost never smelled of formaldehyde. But no, there was her Polaroid camera sitting on the table in the entryway where she'd obviously left it, hastily, on her way in with the spoils. Her purse sprawled in a nearby chair. She'd done the act herself, no doubt. Yes, her car had been in the garage when he'd come home for lunch, and now it was parked haphazardly near the curb in front of the house, threatening to tip over. She must have nearly broken her neck driving there and back. It saddened him, suddenly, that she seemed in such a great rush to catch him red-handed. What had happened to honor, and trust, and emotions like that? Couldn't she at least have given him the benefit of the doubt? He was suddenly angry at her lack of faith in him. He glared out at the little yellow Corvair, Thelma's accomplice. Her right-hand man. Her sidekick deputy.

"I never should have bought her that car," Junior thought. "She keeps this shit up and she's losing it." But how the hell had she pursued him in that canary-yellow thing without his seeing her? He imagined her following him, her mind somewhere in the ozone as she sneaked from stoplight to lilac bush to stoplight, all the way from the funeral home to the Ocean Edge Motel. How downright disgusting of her! No! Of course. Now he had it. She had followed Monique. Men were too damn smart to be followed in bright yellow cars by their wives. Especially if they were on their way to a rendezvous. But one woman following another, well, that was a different story. Thelma could have followed Monique in the *Queen Mary*, in the Goodyear blimp, and gotten away with it. Monique rarely thought to look up, or even ahead sometimes. She was too busy with inspecting herself in the car mirror, fluffing her hair, smoothing her lipstick, checking for food particles in her teeth. He'd seen her do this a thousand times, had followed her to the Ocean Edge Motel so often he knew every detail of her method of operation. Thelma could have maneuvered the Hindenburg up behind Monique's old Buick and no one would have been the wiser for it. There now. The intrigue was over. The next part would be planning the defense. He hadn't lost the battle yet, by Jesus. Not by a long shot. Thelma would have to start getting up a whole lot earlier in the morning if she was gonna play detective with Junior Ivy, Vice President of the Ivy Funeral Home.

"Well, what do you say, girls?" Junior asked cheerily. "Is it a night to eat out, or what? Where's Randy?" The more children he had around him, the better.

"Oh, that's another thing!" Thelma bleated loudly. Her joy was akin to hysterics. Her glazed eyes filled with tears of laughter. "Randy's in jail!" she hooted.

OLD LEAVES AT
MATTAGASH'S FINEST MOTEL:
THE PROPRIETOR SEES PINK

....

"If Albert Pinkham had owned the only inn in Bethlehem, he would have charged Jesus for a hot plate."

—Kevin Craft, after making
a down payment on his honeymoon motel bill, 1964

ALBERT PINKHAM FINISHED SWEEPING THE CRINKLY LEAVES OF autumn off the cement sidewalk that encircled the Albert Pinkham Motel. He would need to repaint the doors to rooms 1 and 2, which faced the road. Rooms 3 and 4, hidden from view, could wait another year. By the time guests saw the peeling paint of the back rooms, they had already checked in, they were usually exhausted from the bumpy ride, and besides, Albert had no competition. His was the only place a weary traveler could sleep from Mattagash to Watertown, short of sleeping on the old-settler ground itself.

Albert had built the motel so that its end was pressed firmly against the side of his two-story house. There was no entryway between the two buildings, but Albert wanted what was his to remain nearby, close. He wanted to keep a proprietor's eye on his belongings. He had explained himself years ago to Ed Lawler, who once commented on the logic of the architecture.

"If I hadn't nailed the motel to the house," Albert Pinkham had told Ed, "the Giffords would have carried it off by now." But Ed Lawler had gone on, a year later, to commit suicide. So what did *he* know about motel architecture?

Hoping to keep up with progress, Albert added tubs and running water to his rooms in 1965.

"You have to be careful," Albert said to a group of men at Blanche's Grocery, when asked why he still hadn't furnished his rooms with hot water. "City slickers are spoiled all year long. They appreciate a little inconvenience when they go on vacation. It makes them feel like they're really in the country. Makes them pretty damn sure they must be roughing it."

But after a slew of complaints, Albert had taken it upon himself in 1967 to add hot running water to the rooms. Tourists complained so heartily about having to rent a hot plate to heat their own water that Albert conceded. And, of course, those who had paid for a large galvanized tub of bathwater had to come to Albert's house to retrieve it from the stove. On occasion, Albert's dog, Bruce, had bitten potential bathers as they knocked on the kitchen door. The most unfortunate bite occurred when Bruce sank his teeth into a white-water enthusiast from Baltimore, who then threatened to sue the Albert Pinkham Motel. But nothing came of it. The white-water enthusiast had gone back to Baltimore to bathe, a little less enthusiastic about H_2O. Bruce had lost the tip of a good tooth and a little enthusiasm himself. Destined to miss out on many a juicy groundhog due to miscalculation of bite, he moped around the house for several days until the miniature poodle tied to a stake in Winnie Craft's backyard was besieged with estrus. Albert had learned a lesson from the near lawsuit. He decided to pipe the luscious hot water into the rooms, sparing both Bruce and the customers an unnecessary embarrassment. But if hunters and fishermen wished to dangle a tea bag in a cup of *very* hot water before they began their day, then, by God, they would fork over a buck fifty for a hot plate. Albert also rented radios, his ancient pair of binoculars, kitchen utensils, electric fans on those two or three fairly hot days in the summer, and tire pumps.

"You're a *maniac!*" one Rhode Islander had gasped at Albert when the latter charged him fifty cents for the quick use of a pop opener.

"Yes sir, I am," Albert had answered with pride. "Born and raised right here in Maine. In God's country."

It may indeed have been God's country, but it gave many a tourist pause as to why God would want to fill his country with so many mosquitoes and blackflies and no-see-ums. Bugs aside, Albert made a killing. Complaints from customers fell on deaf ears and rattled like coins inside the drums. It was all money to him, this motel business, and he had it wrapped up. For years. A mogul. A hostelry tyrant. Until the spring of 1969 came around and Albert cleared up the wintry aftermath as best he could to set his motel in order. He expected the sight-seeing tourists first. The real nature enthusiasts who never hunted or fished but *walked*, for Chrissakes, in the woods and took short, meaningless canoe trips.

"The stuff city folks think up during the year," Albert had said, many times, of these bird-tree-flower cultists.

But nobody came. Albert also expected to be getting phone calls from Macabee's Sporting Store in Watertown. It was at Macabee's that he had tacked a large sign firmly to the bulletin board.

GREETINGS FISHERMEN, SPORTSMEN, AND NEWLYWEDS!
The Albert Pinkham Motel
Welcomes You Greatly.

Beneath this sign was a black-and-white photo of Albert stroking the massive head of his aging German shepherd, Bruce, on the very steps of the motel. Beside the photo was a plethora of paper strips, Albert's business cards, waving in the sweet breeze of Macabee's electric fan, like small white flags. Albert had taken a sheet of typing paper and had torn twelve strips, two inches long, on each side of the sheet. Then he had carefully scrawled his phone number on each strip—an idea he had gotten from baby-sitters who advertised their services at the IGA. It had worked wonderfully in the past. By March of each year more than enough reservations had come in, roaring like lions. But the 1969 season was coming in like a lamb and goddamn dying in his front yard. He had not received a single nibble from the transient buyers of equipment and such at Macabee's. He was perplexed. Surely at this point in the game, ten successful years into the motel business, he would not be expected to, heaven forbid, pay for an advertisement in some dastardly newspaper or magazine?

"What next?" Albert muttered, as he flopped into his outdoor rocker and reached a long arm down to pet the tangled fur of his German shepherd. Bruce yawned heavily in the mild sun that had splattered itself across the porch steps. Tourists could be fussy, if you let them. One woman from New Jersey had even gone so far as to ask for a matchbook with "Albert Pinkham Motel" printed on it. For a souvenir, for Chrissakes!

"Get yourself a Bic, lady," Albert had told her, and slammed the door of his house in her pale, whining face. There she was, covered with a hundred large mosquito bites, a few moose fly welts, the catlike scratches of raspberry bushes on her calves, a huge grapelike bruise where she had fallen out of a canoe, and now she was wanting a *souvenir* of her vacation to take back to New Jersey with her. Jesus H. Christ. Let her take herself back. Let her take her wounds with her. Albert could envision her at the next meeting of her bridge club, bandaged like a mummy, saying, "And the mosquitoes there are large as butterflies." Women. It amazed Albert that the government had ever agreed to give these creatures the right to vote. And nowadays, during deer season, some of them were even turning up in the woods with guns, shooting the branches off trees.

"Trying to impress the men," Albert said, scratching now behind the dog's ears. Bruce yawned again, exposing his broken canine.

But one woman in Albert's past had been most memorable, a

Miss Violet LaForge, a customer who neither fished nor hunted. A customer who did not care a fig for white-water rapids or walks amont the thickly rooted pines. She had been a dancer, performing nightly at the Watertown Hotel, shedding her clothing as easily as reptiles shed skin. There had been no customer come to the Albert Pinkham Motel as exotic as this stripper who danced the light fantastic, the vision in black leotards, with eyes like real violets. He had barely opened his business when Violet drove up in her little Volkswagen and rented a room, number 3, beneath Albert's own bedroom window. And she had altered the outcome of Albert's little time upon the planet. How could he have known, on that red and orange and yellow autumn day, when he handed her the key to number 3, that he was handing fate the key to that door? His wife, Sarah, wanted Violet off the premises. Even when Violet had painted the bed and the walls pink, Albert held out. He cited money as the reason and, knowing him, Sarah believed it. But, oh, it was so much more delicate than money, this hold Violet had on him. It was pink as her room. Soft as the blanket on her bed. Pink as a flower bud. He had wanted to sink down into that softness, that pinkness, to nibble at it, collect it in one place like a pile of coins. He had wanted to own it. But Albert had been a sexual pawn, Violet's instrument to strike back at Sarah Pinkham and the Mattagash Eviction Committee that had formed to oust her. When Sarah caught Albert inside number 3, with his pants literally down, she had taken their daughter, Belle, and left him. That's when Albert changed the name from the Albert Pinkham Family Motel to, simply, the Albert Pinkham Motel. He had to, expensive as it was. He had no family left. The family had left Mattagash. At the time, Albert felt as though his life had shattered, an icicle falling. But he and Bruce had adjusted well to bachelorhood. Belle visited in the summers. And Albert certainly didn't miss that nagging, wagging tongue of Sarah's. Oh, it was grand, after years of servitude, to be able to toss his work shirts into a pile near the foot of his bed. To tromp all over the house in muddy boots. To allow the dirty dishes to pile up in the sink like a crusty little pyramid. To let Bruce paw the sofa at will. Albert was even known to put on a

Sunday shirt while it was still Saturday night and sit out a few beers on a barstool at the Watertown Hotel, leaving Bruce to wait outside in the truck. Yet a little companionship would be nice now and then. Sometimes, and no one in Mattagash knew this, when Albert Pinkham had a beer too many, he found himself back at room number 3, sitting on the edge of the bed, remembering the wonderful pink moments in Violet's bed before Sarah had knocked. He had even let the room remain pink. Hunters didn't mind. It was just a lighter shade, a different shade, of blood. And on those nights, Albert often wondered what he might say to Violet LaForge if he ever had the opportunity to run into her again, face-to-face. He might say thank you, even before he said hello. But no one at the Watertown Hotel ever knew what happened to Violet. Rumor was she got on the Greyhound bus for downstate, from whence she had come, and never bothered to look back. She was swallowed up by the new interstate which was slowly inching north to meet her. She was swallowed up by the passage of time. It had been ten years now.

"Skipped the light fantastic," Albert told Bruce, as the dog rolled over on his side and placed a huge head on Albert's old brown boot. A breeze rushed quickly through the budded lilac bushes, rattled the leaves, stirred them up like old memories. Yes sirree, Albert Pinkham had fallen into bachelorhood just fine. Now if he could only figure out why his business was in the seasonal pits. He had just heard through the grapevine, which in Mattagash was the telephone wire, that Amy Joy Lawler was getting married. June Kelley had rubbered in when Sicily, distraught as hell, called her sister Pearl down in Portland and told her. May first. That could mean a motelful. The money would be nice, but Albert wouldn't count on any wedding guests as juicy as Violet LaForge turning up.

"Number 3," Albert said musically, as he tugged a burr from last year's crop out of Bruce's coat. Bruce was perplexed. He raised his head and tilted it at Albert, questioning.

"The stripper with the big tits," Albert reminded him, and Bruce yawned again, a long and lazy yawn, and remembered.

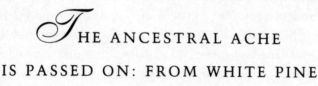THE ANCESTRAL ACHE
IS PASSED ON: FROM WHITE PINE
TO OLD SPICE

....

> In the pines, in the pines
> Where the sun never shines
> We shiver as the cold wind blows.
>
> —B. Williams,
> S. Bryant, J. Doris,
> "In The Pines"

AMY JOY FLIPPED THROUGH *BRIDE* MAGAZINE HURRIEDLY. SHE would have liked to browse but none of the magazine's contents applied to her, really. How could she possibly plan on ordering anything when her wedding was only two weeks away? This saddened her. She had always imagined herself in a swirl of delicate lace, the train falling like a path of pure Maine snow behind her. She had, many times, envisioned her name in silver letters, along with the name of her betrothed, on cocktail napkins. A day the whole town of Mattagash would be hard-pressed to forget. The

Reverend Ralph C. McKinnon's only granddaughter, padding down the sweet aisle of matrimony. But none of it was turning out the way Amy Joy had planned it, all those late nights she lay in bed unable to fall asleep and listened to the Mattagash River beating itself to pieces against the river rocks, like a downpour of thick, heavy rain. Her ancestors' river. The one that had brought the first McKinnon settlers, in hand-hewn pirogues, up from New Brunswick in search of white pine. That had been almost a hundred and fifty years ago. And now here she was, a product of that long-ago journey, of those faraway people. Here she was, about to marry. It was something, wasn't it?

Amy Joy had even thought about starting a notebook of memories about her aunt Marge, dead ten years now. She had known Marge well, better than most knew her. She had lived with her those last months, before Aunt Marge died of beriberi. Her job was to pay close, sharp attention to her aunt's every whim. The truth was, and this pained Amy Joy now that she was an adult herself, she had kept a closer eye on Chester Lee Gifford, the infatuation of her teen years, than ever she did on Aunt Marge. And there was some guilt, now, that it had happened that way. But love and life had taken hold of Amy Joy at fourteen and shaken her so badly her brain was just now settling into place. At least Amy Joy assumed it was. According to Sicily it was looser than ever.

"A *Catholic*," was all Sicily could mumble nowadays, from her bed. "Dear sweet lovely Jesus, have mercy on us all. A full-blooded *Catholic*."

Amy Joy opened a can of cream of mushroom soup and stirred it into a pan along with a can of water. She stared out the kitchen window as the occasional Mattagash car drove by, and identified the owners. Cars were as recognizable as faces. In Mattagash there were few secrets. In Mattagash your greatest fears were memorized like license plates.

Amy Joy's main problem had been getting the invitations sent off in the mail, but she had done that and they were gone. A future bride had to invite three fourths of Mattagash, except the Giffords, whether she wanted to or not. There were usually that many relatives on the list. But the remaining one fourth would show up anyway if they felt like it. It was as if the whole town believed that they owned the Mattagash gymnasium, newly acquired in 1963, and that an eternal invitation was issued to Mattagashers concerning functions given there. The gymnasium had become like a large family living room, where all were welcome. And the Giffords presented a problem, as they did at any special function in Mattagash, from chicken stew dinners to fudge sales and town meetings. Amy Joy knew that the Giffords couldn't be bothered with the notion of a church wedding but they would turn up at the reception to lurk in doorways and around the gift table, to push food into their mouths and, when the punch bowl had been sufficiently drained a thousand times, the big Giffords would eventually end up in a brawl. This could be among themselves, with strangers, or with one or two local boys still testing their hormones. And the littlest Giffords had to be watched every second or the gifts would slowly disappear, one by one, from the gift table until just the decorations were left. Little Vinal Gifford had carried off Patsy McPherson's toaster, waffle iron, electric can opener, and popcorn popper before the best man tracked him down and retrieved the merchandise.

Amy Joy stirred the soup. Should she marry Jean Claude Cloutier? Should she marry anyone? Amy Joy liked Jean Claude. He was a very nice boy. She knew this, despite what Sicily said about his leg length, his accent, or his religion. A person's real worth went deeper than all of that, she knew, although few people in Mattagash realized it. But she had heard her father say such things long before she understood the meaning of it all. And now she was trying desperately hard to remember what he had said. He had left lessons behind him, Amy Joy sensed, if she only knew how to retrieve them. His suicide hadn't been easy on his survivors. There had been jokes when no one knew Amy Joy was listening, in the girls' bathroom, on the school bus, at the swimming hole. There had been whispers and embarrassed glances for months after that bullet tore into her father's brain. And lately she'd been dreaming of the bullet, of the loathsome gun. She'd been hearing the *Bang!* in all her best nightmares.

Amy Joy fingered one of the two silver strips of hair that lined her face, curled it around her finger. *Should* she marry? She left the mushroom soup popping in small bubbles to answer the ringing phone. It was Jean Claude, who must have divined by some sort of Catholic telepathy still unknown to the Protestants that Amy Joy was having second thoughts.

"Is dis Pu-tois?" he asked. This was his pet name for Amy Joy, one he had chosen after careful deliberation of the two silvery Clairol streaks burning up the sides of her hair. Putois. Skunk. And Amy Joy rather liked it.

"Affirmative," she said, and giggled. It still made her laugh to hear the nickname verbalized. Thank God Sicily was unable to understand French.

"Dis is Jean," he said. Of course it was. Who else called her Putois? Sometimes, it seemed that Jean Claude was capable of living up to Sicily's low expectations of him.

"If she *had* to pick a Frenchman," Amy Joy had heard Sicily telling Winnie Craft only yesterday on the phone, "couldn't she have picked one of the smart ones? There are, you know, Winnie, smart ones."

"I know who this is," said Amy Joy. "Why are you calling so early, cupcake? Is something wrong?"

"No," said Jean. "I jus have some bad tots go in my head, me."

"What kind of bad thoughts?"

"Da bad kine," he replied.

"Oh well. That explains it, don't it?" Maybe she *should* marry one of the smart ones.

"I tink, may-bee, you and me, we break hup, hus."

"Oh cupcake," said Amy Joy, and twirled the skunkish curl. "Don't be silly."

"Caw-liss," said Jean Claude. This was a French Catholic swearword, and it always made Amy Joy laugh to hear it. Caw-liss. Chalice, actually. This was the chalice used during the Catholic mass and apparently even a reference to it was a blasphemy. So was "ta-barn-nack," the tabernacle of the church. Strange things to her Scotch-Irish Protestant upbringing where a swearword was, by Jesus, a *swear*word. But Amy Joy didn't mind, not the way Sicily and Mattagash might. She rather liked the change.

"Maybe I'm becoming my father's daughter," she thought, and smiled at the notion.

"Ta-barn-nack," Jean Claude swore softly.

"What is it?" asked Amy Joy, and let the silver curl unroll from her finger.

"Hit's jus, well, my mudder, she doan want for hus to tie da knot, her."

"Your mother don't want *what?*"

"For hus to get marry."

"Well, to hell with her *and* the horse she rode in on," said Amy Joy, and opened a Pepsi to accompany her mushroom soup. "What does she think I'm stealing from her?" Amy Joy thought. "The Hope Goddamn Diamond?"

"Caw-liss," Jean Claude swore again. "Vee-aje!" This last one was a Catholic verbal assault on the Virgin Mary. Vierge. Virgin.

"We're both plenty old enough to do what we want, Jean Claude." Amy Joy was a bit hurt. She thought Mrs. Cloutier liked her. But this religion thing ran deep, deeper than she ever imagined. "I already sent the invitations. Your mother can sit next to mine at the church. It'll do her good."

"Caw-liss de ta-barn-nack," said Jean Claude, and let a long tired sigh pass over the telephone wires. "De Vierge." He had just gotten off work from Thibodeau's Auto Repair, an occupation much desired over the woods-working jobs of his father and brothers. "She's habout to send me crazy, her," he told Amy Joy.

"Do you want to drive up, then, and talk some?" asked Amy Joy, knowing the bumpy, twisting ride was a long one. Jean lived and worked in Watertown, thirty long miles away. On weekends the trip didn't seem so terrible, but during the week that awful distance of thirty miles, *one way*, of narrow, time-consuming turns and dips and frost heaves and potholes, worked on Amy Joy's guilt. How it would tire him after a hard day's work. What if he missed one of the jagged turns and ended up drowned in the river? She still hadn't shaken the memory of how Chester Lee Gifford died, twisted and gnarled as an old oak, inside her cousin Junior's new Packard. But if he did drive up, they could sit in the car after Jean Claude had tooted her out of the house. Dates rarely came to the door in Mattagash, preferring to sit with a beer can between their legs, behind the wheel, and simply toot their arrival, a modern mating call. He could drive the car below the house, and they would sit together where the bright yard light on the telephone pole would not reach them, and they could kiss each other and feel each other's body heat, and listen to the occasional fade-in of songs from WPTR, nearly five hundred miles away in Boston.

There had been many of these moments in the three months they'd dated. They had met at a dance in Clair, New Brunswick, just across the river border from Watertown. What set Jean Claude apart from the other regulars at Perrault's Dance Hall was his extreme good looks. And he was tall and muscular, not short-legged as Sicily had described. A real Quebecer, Sicily had called him. But Jean Claude was by far if not the brightest then the best-looking boy in St. Leonard or Watertown, or on the Canadian side of the border. Or in Mattagash, for that matter. He had thick, rich hair, as Chester Lee had had. And eyes black and large as all of his old French ancestors combined. A handsome boy, at twenty-one, and it was most unusual that he was still unmarried. Such young men were usually snapped up quickly, unless they had plans to go to Connecticut to work in a factory, or in construction. Northern Maine was losing more of its young blood every day to industrial Connecticut.

"We're making the toilet paper down there at Kimberly-Clark that you're wiping your asses on all the way up here in Mattagash," Ronnie Monihan had bragged to a group of gaping listeners at the Watertown Hotel, on his first Fourth of July vacation back home. Mainers always came home for the Fourth.

"Ain't that something?" Ronnie had asked them, and his listeners had nodded in awestruck agreement.

"Drive up and we'll talk about it," said Amy Joy softly. Brains aside, she could smell, mixed in with a little Old Spice, a smell that caused an ache within her, a deep wish to marry and then propagate. As her ancestors had done. Maybe it was all linked to smell alone.

"I doan give a shit, me, what she say. May-bee we should halope, hus." Jean Claude coughed loudly into the receiver.

"Come on up, then," Amy Joy said, and knew that by nine o'clock she would be sitting next to him in the front seat of the Chevy super sport, watching the orange glow of his Marlboro bob up and down in the black night. By 9:10 she would have talked him out of eloping and into a glamorous wedding on May first. And beyond the rolled-down windows of the car she would hear the perpetual sound of the river that had carried her ancestors to Mattagash where they would settle, and bear children, and die. That's what it was all about, wasn't it? A pirogue one day. A red super sport Chevy the next. But the script was the same. If it wasn't Old Spice back in those days, then it was something else. Maybe it was the sweet smell of fresh water combined with white pine. The dried papery bark of the yellow birches, soft animal hides drying, the sticky line of resin oozing from the spruce tree. And dried sweat on a hard-working man, well, that hadn't changed a bit, had it? Even the antlike men whose bodies broke beneath the weight of the pyramid stones smelled sweet to some woman. And so did kings. The pirates. Old West cowboys. It had been going on a long time, this smell-and-touch-and-ache business. Amy Joy *ached* to see Jean Claude, to feel the water from his comb still beaded among his deep curls, holding them in place. She wanted to run a finger around the thick muscle of each arm, to trace the French jaw, to fill her nostrils full of enough Old Spice to drown them.

"Look out for the frost heaves," said Amy Joy, and smacked a kiss into the receiver. Thirty crooked miles each way of potholes and frost heaves. There must be true pioneer blood still coursing within their veins. Sixty dangerous bumpy miles because of an *ache*.

"Chalice de Tabernacle," Jean Claude said, and put the greasy receiver back in its cradle.

THE GIFFORDS RETHINK
THE AMBULANCE BUSINESS:
THE MAILBOX
AS A DIVINE RECEPTACLE

....

"He didn't do it, Sheriff. He's as pure as the driven snow."

—Goldie Gifford, of her son Little Pike,
in reference to the broken windows at the grammar school

"Of course he is. Have you ever seen snow once it's been driven on?"

—Vera Gifford, Little Pike's aunt, when she quit laughing

VERA GIFFORD HAD NEARLY GIVEN UP HOPES OF KEEPING A MAIL-box standing erect and in good condition by the side of the road in front of her house. In the twelve years that Little Vinal had been on the planet Vera had lost eight shiny aluminum mailboxes to bicycle accidents alone. Two other boxes had been mown down by a late-night, drunken Big Vinal and his tanklike old Plymouth, when neither he nor the Plymouth had enough good sober sense to execute the sharp turn into the driveway. This infuriated Vera. The sickly taste of S&H Green Stamps had barely worn off her tongue when another six books needed to be filled, page by page, to replace the last box. A mailbox was more essential to the Giffords than running water, electricity, or a telephone. Without a functional mailbox, one that fit governmental standards, Bond McClure refused to deliver the daily handful of mail. Vera and Vinal were not very interested in the pamphlets from stores in Watertown, or the occasional personal letter from downstate relatives, or the light bill, or the *Reader's Digest* Sweepstakes giveaway of the dream house. But they were obsessed with that narrow brown envelope that arrived every month with its familiar Augusta postmark: the treasured disability check.

It was just two weeks after Vera had received another new mailbox with her S&H Green Stamps that Little Vinal dragged his fenderless rusting bicycle out from beneath the mound of tires in the lopsided garage and took his first quick ride of 1969. The road was still a bit muddy in places but the air was April's finest and the long winter months of bicycle-dreaming were finally over. Little Vinal was beset, as usual, with a flood of adrenaline to his loins when he came barreling down the main road in Mattagash, over the one-way bridge and then onto the short stretch of road that would take him home. He saw the sun on the mailbox first, a silver bounce of light that glowed, clean and pure as money. His breath caught up in his throat. There was the red flag, waving at him, taunting him, daring him on, the way a matador teases the bull. Little Vinal gulped in the April air, a big mouthful of it, and bore down on the mailbox. His aim, as he often told spectators, was only to see how close he could come to the box without hitting it. But April got to him, the budsy trees lining the roads, the birds mate-singing back and forth along the telephone wires, the black swath of beautiful tar he had not seen since last October. Added to this, he spied the younger Gifford children, those waiting to inherit the bicycle the way they did hand-me-down clothes and shoes, gathered as audience on the warping front porch. Little Vinal put his hands on his hips, a large smile on his smudged face, and shouted to his siblings, "Look! No hands!" It was at this moment that the opened mailbox door caught his left side and hauled him violently off the speeding bicycle. The door clattered onto the road behind him. But this time the damage done to the perpetrator was much more noticeable than the missing mailbox door, and the little boy and girl Giffords on the front porch danced up and down and clapped their dirty hands in appreciation of some fine and unexpected entertainment.

Little Vinal lay sprawled, the April air knocked out of him, on the warm tar in front of the Gifford house, his ancient bicycle several yards away. His shirt was torn open to reveal a deep gash that had blossomed on his arm. His eye, which had struck against a handle bar during the fracas, had already begun to swell into a bluish hill, on its way to turning into a hideous black mound. When the air came again to Little Vinal's lungs, he sat up and inspected the tear on his arm. It was very deep and bleeding heavily. In his pain he tried to weigh the two dangers he faced: bleeding to death quietly, or informing his mother of the injury, thereby incurring her wrath over the mailbox. But the dilemma was settled for him by one of the smaller Giffords, who kicked the screen door loudly and shouted, "Mama! Little Vinal done it again!"

Vera was about to pulverize Little Vinal as she stood over him at the scene of the accident. But he quickly turned his injured arm up to her, a broken bird's wing, so that she could see that he was already badly wounded. Vera gasped. The cut would require stitches. The closest doctor was in Watertown, thirty miles of frost heaves and potholes down the road. Vera wished Grammie Gifford were still alive. Grammie G. could have stopped the blood with her blood charm and then stitched the gash herself with regular thread. She had had an eye like a hawk when it came to stitching, whether it was fancy-material sewing, or skin sewing. But old Grammie was peacefully reposing in the Catholic graveyard, her days with the needle finally over.

The accident threw Vera into a dilemma of her own. How would she get Little Vinal to Watertown? Big Vinal had left in the rattling Plymouth, the battered fenders shaking off mud until he had disappeared over the hill. God only knows where he had ended up. Calling the ambulance in Watertown would be a useless endeavor—Vera might just as well call the moon. The Watertown Ambulance Service had no intention of hightailing it to Mattagash to pick up an injured Gifford. They didn't give a damn what the first name was, but if the last name was Gifford, you might just as well stand by the side of the road and whistle when it came to calling *them*. You might just as well hold your breath and bleed to death. The Watertown Ambulance Service had had it up to their neck with the Giffords.

It was all Big Pike and Big Vinal's fault. Where the idea came from in the first place no one remembers. Perhaps their ancient cars had broken down either with misuse or with sheer disgust over the owners, but Vinal and Pike concocted the brainstorm of phoning the Watertown Ambulance Service whenever they desperately needed a ride to Watertown, feigning once a ruptured appendix and once a severe heart attack. Vinal always played the victim, as he was in his mid-fifties, in horrid physical shape, and thus made a more believable potential corpse than did the younger Pike. Once Vinal was lifted into the ambulance Pike, beset with worry, climbed in as consoling relative for the breakneck ride to Watertown. It was always at the city limits that Vinal recovered, rubbing his side or his chest, mumbling that it wasn't as bad as he thought. Maybe it was the heat. Or something he ate. But the pains were, yes, by Jesus, gone. He and Pike would get out right there in front of the Newberry store. Friends were in town who would drive them back to Mattagash. The tired ambulance drivers, sick of the narrow, twisting, hairpin road, were only too happy to be free from the drive. It was not until the gunshot wound that the Watertown Ambulance Service got wise to Vinal and Pike Gifford.

At the city limits of Watertown Vinal had sat up with his usual mien and asked plaintively where in the hell he was.

"You're in the am-boo-lance," Pike told him gently.

"Why?" asked an incredulous Vinal.

"You've been accidentally shot," Pike reassured him.

"Hell no, that wasn't me," Vinal said. "That was Alphonse. I'm sleeping off a drunk."

"Shit! You're right," Pike Gifford said, and slapped the side of his own head. "Sorry, boys," he told the irate drivers, as though the joke were on them. "In all the excitement we grabbed the wrong man."

"You just let us out here at the Newberry store," Vinal was offering as the ambulance promptly drove them to the Watertown police station.

"Looks like it backfired," Pike whispered to Vinal, while they waited for the drivers to finish the story they were telling the chief of police. "I guess they must of recognized us," Pike said.

"That's a small town for you," Vinal had whispered back. "If this was the big city, we could start our own cab company this way."

With Little Vinal spread-eagled in the road and bleeding profusely, Vera was at her wits' end. She retrieved the wobbly bicycle, held it upright as one of the littler Gifford boys, his head a mass of dark curls, climbed up onto the seat. He positioned his feet on the pedals and clasped the handlebar tightly.

"Are you the one who just learned to ride this goddamn thing?" Vera asked the child. When he nodded a positive response, she pushed him off in the direction of the steep hill that would take him down the slope to Alphonse Gifford's house.

"Go see if Daddy's at Uncle Alphonse's," Vera shouted to the retreating back of the small Pony Express agent. "If he ain't, get Uncle Alphonse or Aunt Lucy to come quick with their car."

The child nodded again, frozen on the seat of the bike, his feet barely able to keep pace with the frenzy of spinning pedals. He disappeared over the line of hill, like a bird falling. Vera knelt next to Little Vinal, who was now over the burst of pure adrenaline and in the midst of some very real pain. Vera pushed a handful of her bunched-up dress onto the gash to discourage further bleeding.

"You'd think," she said to Little Vinal as her other children gathered quietly around her like sturdy weeds, "that of all the stuff Alphonse Gifford has stole in his lifetime, he could at least steal a telephone."

Luck, knowing no prejudice, was with the Giffords. Vinal was indeed at his brother Alphonse's. The two men were in the backyard dividing up a cache of used car batteries when news of the catastrophe swooped down off the dangerous hill to reach them. Vinal rattled home, leaving the helpless bicyler to huff and puff the cumbersome bike up the long, steep hill that had been his launching pad.

In the emergency room at the Watertown Hospital, Little Vinal was pale as snow.

"You're not too big for a lollipop, are you?" a nurse asked as she slid a strawberry sucker into his trembling hand. Little Vinal clutched it to his side. No matter what degree of pain might be filtering through his body, he would eat the lollipop on the bumpy ride home, somewhere on the thirty-mile span back to Mattagash. One lollipop, Little Vinal knew from experience, had a pauper's chance if tossed into the living mass of little Giffords waiting back at the house.

"I was playing 'Look, no hands,' " Little Vinal told the doctor, when asked the particulars of the accident. The lollipop had already disappeared, thanks to his one good arm, into the pocket of his trousers.

It had taken Vera a great deal of mental concentration to summon forth motherly concern instead of anger. She could still taste the Green Stamps from the last mailbox. But she was in Watertown, and in the company of a doctor and a nurse. The last thing she needed was social workers sticking their noses in her front door and inquiring as to how she was treating her kids, instead of staying home and looking after their own.

"It was almost 'Look, no arms,' " Vera said, and tampered as lovingly as she could with Little Vinal's prominent cowlick. Big Vinal was not so magnanimous. He didn't give an old boot about what social workers had to say, and besides, he had been in the midst of a very important business transaction when the urgent plea for assistance had biked down to interrupt him.

"He rips the door off one more mailbox," said Vinal, "and it'll be 'Look, no teeth.' "

"Sounds more like 'Look, no brains,' " the doctor told his nurse, after the Giffords had taken their son and begun the trying exodus back to Mattagash.

Little Vinal recovered much sooner than the doctor would have anticipated. Tired of seeing him with his legs drawn up and his face pouting, Vera urged him to experience once more the new spring days that April had so lovingly brought them.

"Get your ass off my couch and out into the yard," she told him. "And you better be standing by the road with your hand stuck out when the mailman comes."

Little Vinal sat in the warm sun for a few minutes, kicking one foot against the other and babying his sore left arm. Then he threw several large rocks at Tinkerbell, the cat. Still bored, and with two hours to pass before Bond McClure would inch slowly around the turn in his mail car, Little Vinal went off to the garage to find his BB gun. It was right where he had hidden it from the younger children, behind the case of powdered welfare eggs and the large air compressor which said HENLEY LUMBER COMPANY in red letters. Standing in the garage door with a wounded left arm and sighting along the barrel at Tinkerbell, Little Vinal let a BB whiz across the yard. The cat yowled before it disappeared into the black open spaces beneath the garage. With no other wild game in sight and still an hour to pass before mail time, Little Vinal was at his wits' end until it occurred to him that a good capable scout such as himself would trek out across enemy country, just to see what the scoundrels were up to.

It was a beautifully soft day, with a small spring breeze wafting up from the river, and Goldie had taken her canary outside in its little wicker cage so that it could enjoy a panorama of Mattagash, Maine, and all the places it would never fly.

"Oo needs to shake-um off that old cage fever," Goldie said, and tied the cage to the front porch clothesline. Feathers was the only pet she had ever owned, the only one she didn't have to share with others. Goldie's mother had never allowed pets: "If there's any extra food in this house, it ain't going into the mouth of a dog or cat." Goldie used to stare at pictures in storybooks of little girls holding furry kittens on their laps or tugging well-groomed puppies about on fancy leashes. And she promised herself that one day, when she was in her own home, she would have one of these delightful creatures. But it seemed the human babies came so quickly, pink and wrinkly and crying, that Goldie, still seventeen when she had her first one, forgot about the luxury of owning things just for pleasure. It was true that Pike Senior had dragged home a stray dog after the first kids were toddling along, but that was the *family's* pet. Then, the day her youngest baby started kindergarten, Goldie put down her usual cup of morning coffee, slung her purse over her shoulder, and drove Pike's old clunker all the way to the Newberry's in Watertown. She had no idea what she might buy as she stood there in the back of the store where they kept birds, white mice, hamsters, and big bowls of tropical fish. But when she saw Feathers, his tiny head canted, his perky eyes focused on her, she knew the answer.

"This is the first pet I ever owned all by myself," Goldie told the clerk behind the Newberry cash register.

"We got a big sale on them white mice," the clerk had answered. But Goldie had the pet she wanted. On the way home Feathers had flitted happily about his cage, singing sweetly. It didn't seem to matter a hoot that he was on his way home to Giffordtown. He didn't even wish for a McKinnon or a Craft to come to his rescue, Goldie could tell. She would share the family dog with the kids, but Feathers was all hers.

"Now oo stay wight here," Goldie cooed to Feathers, and blew a soft kiss into the cage. Then she went back to the drudgery of her housework.

As she did so, Little Vinal was crawling up the long hill on his stomach, dragging the BB gun behind him. Occasionally a stab of pain echoed through the bruised arm if he applied too much weight to it. But war was all blood and guts. He had seen Patton in a television movie saying so just that week. The canary suspected something, and cocked its head every now and then before it returned to its preening. It felt relatively safe where it was. After all, it was in a cage, protected from freedom, and dangling high enough in the air to outwit any cats.

"You ain't built the fort that'll keep me out," Little Vinal sneered to the enemy, and let fly a dozen BB's.

Goldie herself saw the sharpshooter bounding away, guilt in every leap. But which of Vera's kids it was, she was at a loss to say. They all looked alike to her. And for some strange reason she could never understand, they all seemed to be the same size, all eight of them. She suspected it was the steady diet of surplus food given out begrudgingly by the town. Goldie watched until the boy running down the hill disappeared into Vinal's teetering garage. An hour later, when she went out to see what Bond McClure had left for her, she found Feathers already stiffening in his cage. He was obviously not out there enjoying the spring day, as she had thought. He was absolutely oblivious to the sunshine and the sweet breeze.

"Dead as a doornail," muttered Little Pee, who stood by his mother's side and stared down at Feathers.

"Oh, Feathers," Goldie said softly. She took the stiffening bird up into her hands. A whispery breeze rippled over its body, the soft, sad caress of spring.

"Don't cry, Mama," Priscilla, Goldie's thirteen year-old, pleaded. "You can get you another one."

"I don't want another canary," Goldie whispered.

"Let's get one of them white rats," Little Pee excitedly offered. "They been at the Newberry's forever."

Little Pee and Priscilla were able to find several of the little gold beads about the porch and ground. They were obvious misses or—and Goldie grimaced to think of it—ricochets. Now her grief billowed into a pure, fine anger. How dare they kill her bird! She was certain now of the culprit's identity. Little Vinal had already built a wide reputation around Mattagash for escapades with his BB gun. All of the Giffords at the top of the hill had heard how Little Vinal had picked the candy beads off his teacher's birthday cake and replaced them with BB's. Several of his classmates ate plenty until the teacher bit firmly onto one and destroyed her new dental bridge. Questioned by an irate principal as to why he'd done it, Little Vinal said, "Because she's always shooting off her mouth." It brought in quite a large guffaw back home, at the bottom of the hill.

"By God, they won't laugh about this," Goldie threatened, and stomped in to wake Big Pike. She promptly snapped off *As the World Turns,* his favorite program, and insisted that he pay heed. The world wasn't turning very well in Mattagash, Goldie let him know, and she demanded that he take Feathers down the hill and collect the five dollars she had paid for him.

"Who?" asked a sluggish Pike. He wondered for a second if they had named one of their own kids Feathers and if so, who would want to shoot BB's at the creature. Flora, he suddenly remembered. They had one named Missy Flora. That's what had tripped him up. The naming process had always bothered Pike, as it would any thinking man. When two people get married and set about having a herd of children, why not just alphabetize them according to birth? It would make things a whole lot easier when talking to the welfare people.

"But there's no amount of dollars they can pay for my broken heart," Goldie wept. "And you can tell them that!"

Pike watched as the little white dot, the same tiny ghost that appears in the old-fashioned televisions of rich and poor alike, in Mattagash or faraway Portland, flickered like a Sominex tablet on the black screen. Inside that little dot was Penny Prescott, who had just found out that husband Linton was cheating on her with her sister Ingrid, who had just adopted Korean twins—all this at a time when Penny had made arrangements at the hospital for her hysterectomy. All those problems were inside that small white dot. Then the dot vanished and the screen was blank. Pike wished his problems were like that, too. Switch-off-able.

"Linton Prescott don't know the half of it," thought Pike, and pulled on his boots. He grabbed Feathers from Goldie and pushed open the screen door. Goldie, Little Pee, and a mob of smaller mourners followed on his heels, the screen door slamming behind them.

At Vinal's house the door was opened slowly by a small girl's hand. Then a tiny head covered with the dark Giffordish curls poked around the door and demanded, "What?!" Big Vinal appeared behind her.

"That's Molly, my baby," he said to Pike. "Can you believe how big she's getting? She's already wanting to drive the car."

"There's no stopping them once they take it in their heads to grow," Pike said, and gave the child a token pat on the head.

"Tell him about Feathers," whispered Goldie, poking Pike's back and hushing the smaller children behind her.

"Well, we got us a little problem," said Pike. "Goldie here says she saw Little Vinal shoot her canary with his BB gun, and the whole family's up in the air about it."

Vera appeared behind Vinal with her swarm of children situated on both sides. They pressed forward eagerly, all the same height and width. Goldie tried not to look at them. They reminded her of a bed of pansies.

"Little Vinal!" his father shouted, and a gangly boy with freckles came forward, looking like a Norman Rockwell creation until he squirted a frothy plug of spit off the porch and exhibited a skull and crossbones inked on his upper right arm. The left arm was wrapped in what had been a pristine bandage the day before at the Watertown hospital, but was now a murky brown rag.

"You shoot this canary?" Vinal thrust the remains of Feathers under Little Vinal's nose. Before the boy could shake his head no in a plaintive denial, his father gave him a sharp slap across the face. Little Vinal slumped back, and then disappeared into the mass of children around Vera. His footsteps sounded inside, heavily, angrily, on the steps leading upstairs.

"I'm sorry about this, Vinal," said Pike, to Goldie's dismay. "I guess boys'll be boys."

"Yeah," Vinal agreed. "But he knows he's supposed to shoot birds that ain't store bought." He sucked on his toothpick, which was a piece of yellow straw from Vera's broom. Food stamps didn't include fancy toothpicks.

The two brothers had talked in depth about how to keep their women happy. It was far better to go along with them as best they could, as long as they themselves didn't get riled up with them. All women were silly, but Gifford women would come to blows. And both Pike and Vinal were certain Goldie wouldn't stand a chance against the burly Vera.

"It'd be just like that Cassius Clay–Sonny Liston fight," Pike once said to Vinal as they sat in the battered Plymouth, beer bottles foaming between their legs. "We're talking six, maybe seven seconds," Pike had said as he took a dangerously large gulp.

"We want the five dollars we paid for him," said Goldie, over Pike's shoulder.

"What for?" asked Vera, over Vinal's. "It can't be to say a mass. Not over at the Holy Roller church you been going to."

"You ain't been to a church in so long, Vera, you couldn't tell a mass from Merv Griffin's theme song," said Goldie. "And besides," she went on, from the safety behind Pike's shoulders, "I read in *Reader's Digest* that juvenile delinquents pee the bed, then they're cruel to little animals, then they set fire to something. You know damn well the only thing that child ain't done is burn us out of house and home. And that's next. He's gonna end up in jail, in the same cell as Irving."

"Don't talk about my boys like that," Vera shouted, and lurched forward, but Vinal caught her arms.

"Send Goldie up the hill, Pike, so you and I can talk," said Vinal. He shoved Vera back into the faces of her children, into a scattering of bony arms and flying ponytails.

Outside on the front steps Vinal pushed his hands deep into his pockets and listened as Pike scolded Goldie back up the long hill. She went, with the children's blond heads bobbing around her, all of them looking back at intervals to see what the men were doing. From her kitchen window Vera watched them go.

"Them kids remind me of dandelions," she said to Molly, who was retrieving lint from her navel.

Vinal lit a cigarette and tossed the match out into April's soggy grass. He stared down at the patch Vera had glued to one of his rubber boots to keep the slush out. It could get damp on the way to the mailbox, or kneeling by the hubcaps of some stranger's car.

"How about this?" Vinal asked, and squinted at his brother. "You tell Goldie I give you the five dollars. I'll tell Vera I never give you a cent."

"Let's hope they don't git on good terms someday," said Pike, and winked. "If they ever start talking, look out."

Vinal spit a large plug of snuff from under his lip. The juice of it sprayed the tomato fledglings that Vera had placed on the front steps. They grew out of milk cartons the kids had brought home from school. GRANT'S DAIRY MILK, they advertised. Vinal kicked one and it flew like a small red and white football into the air until it landed with a loosening thump of dirt and seedling.

"Them two women," said Vinal, and reached down to pick up a set of shiny hubcaps he had selected earlier from out of the pile near the back steps. The rightful owners were probably driving around Watertown without them at that very minute, their drab wheels turning sadly. Vinal enjoyed this thought, and smiled at it.

"Them two women will be the death of us yet," he said to Pike, who nodded.

"They're a couple of mean ones," Pike agreed.

"Well, Vera takes after her old man," Vinal said. "I'll admit that. Uncle Frankie was Hitler without that little mustache." He picked at his back teeth and freed a piece of relief meat that had been bothering him since noon.

"Hell, you know Goldie," said Pike, and scratched his crotch, then his chin—the Giffords did most things backward. "She gits uppity and that sets Vera off. It'll pass. By the way, how *is* Irving making out?"

"He oughtta be out in five months," said Vinal, of his eldest son. "I don't know what in hell he was gonna do with that snowmobile in April. He should've waited until December. Not only would it have been easier to sell, but it's hard to send a man to jail right before the holidays."

"Well," said Pike sympathetically, "his timing was just a little off. Looks like a storm coming over from Hayfey Mountain."

"I got to get me a new mailbox," Vinal said, and motioned with his head to the road. "Little Vinal tore the door off that new one."

"You must be expecting a wedding invitation from Amy Joy Lawler, too," said Pike. "Special delivery, with Sicily licking the envelope herself."

Hearing with satisfaction that his brother found the joke worthy of a belly laugh, Pike started off across the road, scuffing his heavy boots. He lifted one finger high in the air to test for raindrops.

"A good rain won't hurt us none," Pike said with authority.

"It'll eat up the last of that snow," Vinal shouted after him. Then he went back inside his house, where Vera was waiting to hear that no way in hell did he give one penny to pay for some foolish dead bird.

Vera listened with satisfaction as she shoved another pair of grayed long johns through the wringer of her washer, and then sent the littlest children to close all the windows from the rain.

"What high-class stunt will she pull next?" Vera asked gruffly. "Can you imagine buying a bird in a store when your garden is so full of starlings nothing will come up?"

THE HOUSEGUESTS WELCOME
RANDY: HOLLYHOCKS, VALIUMS, AND
A CRANBERRY SWEATER

....

"Well, what do you expect her to do? It isn't like she can *take them off* 'til after the party."

—Marvin Ivy, to his wife, Pearl,
with respect to Monique Tessier's bosoms,
Ivy Funeral Home Christmas party

RANDY IVY TAPPED HIS FINGERS NERVOUSLY ON THE DESK AND waited for his grandfather to acknowledge his presence. Junior Ivy, his father, sprawled in a chair next to him, his belly threatening to pop all the buttons on his shirt. The elder Ivy was on the phone, engaged in a frustrating conversation with an irate customer.

"But we can't guarantee a monument against *vandalism*," Marvin was saying. "I'm sorry to hear that hoodlums would go into a sacred place and do such things but . . ."

Randy's fingers tapped more slowly. It was a Steppenwolf tune he was drumming out on his grandfather's desk. *Don't Bogart that joint, my friend*, the fingers sang. Junior Ivy sweated in his tight shirt and tried to ignore the gestures of Monique Tessier, whom he could see through the open door of his father's office. She was at her desk, in a splendid cranberry-red sweater with an unabashedly low neckline. She held up a sheet of typing paper, quickly, for Junior to read. CALL ME TONIGHT! the message demanded. Junior nodded a nearly imperceptible agreement, then glanced nervously at Randy to see if he had witnessed the communiqué between his father and the Ivy Funeral Home secretary. But Randy was tapping a fast-paced rendition of "Born to Be Wild." Marvin put his hand over the mouthpiece of the phone and said, "You want to lose those fingers, keep on doing what you're doing." Randy's fingers stopped. Marvin nodded.

"No, we certainly did not guarantee that the angel wings wouldn't break off, not if someone went at them with a sledgehammer, for crying out loud." Marvin grimaced. People could be so irrational during a reign of grief. "Well, have your lawyer do that, then," he said finally, and hung up.

"Hoodlums in the graveyard with sledgehammers," Marvin said to Junior. "What will the world do next? They were probably all high on drugs," he added, and cast a remonstrative eye on his grandson. Randy Ivy didn't catch the slur. He had become awestruck with the fluid movement beneath Monique Tessier's cranberry-red sweater. Junior felt a surge of jealousy sweep over him when he followed his son's gaze. Ignoring Monique's eyes, he got up abruptly and closed the door.

"Was that Dale Porter's wife?" Junior asked.

"Yeah," said Marvin. "Crib death, remember? I don't know why she just doesn't have another baby and leave us to hell alone."

"Hoodlums in the graveyard," Junior mused. He was hoping to ingratiate himself by repeating Marvin's contempt. "What next?" he scoffed.

"Speaking of hoodlums," Marvin said, and turned his attention to his only grandson. "If it hadn't been for your grandmother, I want you to know, I'd never have agreed to this."

"Swell," said Randy. "Like you're really doing me a big favor letting me work in the boneyard."

Marvin's face tightened, and his hairline receded slightly.

"That'll be enough," said Junior. The old man was already on the warpath about him and Monique. Randy needn't add to it. "You tell your grandfather thank you."

"Thanks, man," said Randy, and his fingers went back to "Born to Be Wild" on his grandfather's desk top.

Randy's offense was a first one so his father had managed to get him released on probation. Speeding on the Kawasaki had alerted a policeman, who pulled him over and discovered the Baggie. It was not, as Marvin first suspected, parsley flakes but some of the best Colombian gold to hit Portland in months.

His driver's license, a hefty fine, an apology, and a promise is what the judge wanted from Marvin Randall Ivy III. The judge took the license. Junior paid the fine. Randy apologized. And Marvin, at Pearl's prodding, promised to give Randy gainful employment at the Ivy Funeral Home. The probation would last a year, and would be over when spring bounced back again with daffodils and sharp blades of grass. The kind that doesn't get smoked.

Marvin was explicit about what tasks Randy would *not* be expected to perform as part of his official duties.

"Stay to hell away from the mourners," he warned his grandson. "Don't touch a thing in the embalming room. And don't even *think* of going into the chapel."

Marvin was in a grandfather-employer quandary. Maybe the boy would be capable, later on, of learning the line of caskets. He could be a salesman of sorts in the showroom. Junior could teach him. It might keep them both out of trouble.

"Balls," said Randy. "So like, what am I supposed to do then?" He ran his musical fingers through his closely cropped hair. He felt bald. He longed for his ponytail, but a barber had heartlessly disposed of it on Saturday. It had been one of Marvin's strictest demands. Almost a year of growth, gone down the drain at some stranger's barbershop. "Like, what is my *job?*"

"I'll tell you what your *job* is," Marvin said, and pulled out a file before him. "It says here your take-home pay will be sixty-eight dollars and ninety cents every week."

"So whadda I do?" asked Randy, wishing he could see through the wooden door to the reception room where the secretary was lounging.

"Let's see," said Marvin, as he pondered with business details in his head. "Sixty-eight ninety a week. Looks to me like you sit in the coffee room, stuff your face with doughnuts, and keep your mouth shut."

"It's a deal, man," said Randy, suddenly enlightened by the world of big-time employment.

◆　◆　◆

Ever since the wedding invitation had arrived from her niece Amy Joy, Pearl had been in the doldrums. Maybe it was because she hadn't seen Amy Joy in ten years, and this wedding suddenly reminded her of the cruel passage of time, as everything did these days. Time had become Pearl's mortal enemy. Time was gobbling up everyone and everything she ever loved. Time would be coming for her, soon.

Pearl McKinnon Ivy turned the thick pages of the old McKinnon scrapbook as she sat on the edge of her bed, still in housecoat and slippers at ten-thirty in the morning.

"What would Marge have thought of that?" Pearl wondered, as she stared down at a picture of her older sister. Marge was brown-haired, with a wash of freckles across the straight bridge of her nose. Hollyhocks swam in the frame around her. The picture was taken, then, just outside the old McKinnon homestead, famed for its display of the flower.

"What would Marge say about me sitting here on my bed, still in my nightclothes, in the middle of the day?" Pearl wondered again. "Marge was always up with the birds." The hollyhocks began to swim a bit around Marge's head as Pearl's eyes filled with warm tears. The memory of the old homestead, with its charming summer kitchen, drenched in all those colored flowers of China, had unlocked another kind of memory inside her. Suddenly her bedroom in Portland, Maine, was overpowered with the smell of hollyhocks. Their fragrance burst out of the closet, killing the formaldehyde aroma of Marvin's suits. It fairly flew from the drapes, seeped out of the rugs, was so strong it stirred up a small breeze and moved the loose strands of hair still clinging, uncombed, around Pearl's face. Or was that just a regular breeze, billowing up from the disenchanting streets of Portland? Who could tell anymore? Hollyhocks. Marge. The Reverend Ralph. The old homestead.

"Why are you bothering me now?" Pearl asked Marge's faded picture. "Why now, after all these blasted years?" she asked the fragile hollyhocks, and suddenly the fragrance of them was so thick that Pearl closed the scrapbook and lay back on her bed. The flowery perfume moved in on her, the way a heat wave presses down, blanketed, solid as a wall. She could even hear bumblebees, which unnerved her at first. The last time she heard bees was when she had her nervous breakdown. That was the balmy spring of 1928, when Marvin came into their small apartment and announced that he was dropping out of law school to become an integral part of the family funeral business. Pearl heard bees buzzing in her head, loud enough to be a swarm of little airplanes. *Undertaking,* instead of *law.* How does one adjust to that? But it had been forty-two years now. She had recovered. The bees had eventually flown away. Today was different. These were different bumblebees. These were the bumblebees of 1922, the year her father left. There had been hollyhocks that day, hadn't there? And Marge had put one hand on Pearl's shoulder, one on Sicily's, and they had watched the reverend bounce away in a horse and buggy. To catch the train in Houlton. To go to China. To die of kala-azar. When he had disappeared, Marge said—oh, what *had* she said? It was something straight out of the Bible, word for word, but Pearl couldn't remember. What she did remember was that she had gone immediately and stuffed her nose into a hollyhock, a lavender one.

"My God, yes," she thought, as she lay on the bed. "It *was* lavender, wasn't it?" And lavender had always been her favorite color. Did it begin there? Or did she choose that flower because she had always loved the color? Things of the mind were so complicated. The fat smell of hollyhocks was fingering its way around her on the bed. She undid the top buttons of her nightdress and loosened the garment away from her throat. Her hand brushed the skin of her neck and she pulled it back quickly, outraged at the work nature had done there, the loosening, the harrowing, the furrows. The way one readies earth in order to plant a garden. Useless work. What seeds could come up after sixty years? What plants could prosper?

"Weeds," Pearl whispered. She heard the mailman flop her mail into the box and the cast-iron thud as the cover fell. Then she heard the neighbor's dog barking as mail was delivered in the next yard. The phone rang many times, but she did not even consider answering.

"Some people are more patient than others," Pearl thought, depending on how long they allowed the phone to ring before giving up. Perhaps this was a secret of life, of why some succeed where others don't. It all has to do with how long a person will sit with a phone to his or her ear and listen to it ring.

A housefly landed on her nose, and she squinted her eyes to stare at it. But she hadn't been able to read anything up close for so many years now, what did she expect to see right on the very end of her nose? Her eyes were growing toward cataracts, had been for years. That's what the eye doctor told her. *It happens to all of us*, he had said. She wrinkled her nose and the fly, with its head of magnificent compound eyes, launched off for new territory.

Pearl heard her next-door neighbor, Mrs. Tinley, hosing down her car.

"Washing off the mud," Pearl thought, and even this seemed significant in life, another clue perhaps as to how some folks manage where others don't.

"A little matter of washing the mud off," Pearl thought. She had lived in Mattagash long enough, eighteen years of her life, to know that this could be an effective maneuver. The McKinnons, Pearl had come to realize, were famous for such. She and Sicily were the only McKinnons left in Mattagash. The name, at least there, had died out. But she thought of the old aunts and uncles. The second cousins. If one had a drinking problem it was shoved into a closet. None of the McKinnons drank in public. They preached "Love thy neighbor" a good part of the day, then spent the rest gossiping about that neighbor.

"Real good Christians," muttered Pearl. She wondered if Amy Joy was in the family way. Why else would anyone shiver and shake to get married on May first? Well, if she was, so be it. She was always boy-crazy. Yet Pearl knew that if someone else's daughter found herself "up the stump," to use Marvin's expression, and still unmarried, she would be nothing short of scandalous. But if a McKinnon ended up in the same predicament, or a Craft, or a Fennelson—and many of them did—it was another matter.

"The Lord will take care of her," Pearl remembered her great-aunt Caroline saying of her pregnant daughter Lydia. Pearl was very young then. And she believed her great-aunt. She felt there *was* a difference between a Gifford getting pregnant out of wedlock and a McKinnon doing so. Now she was too many miles down the road from Mattagash, too many years, to believe any of that non-sense. *The Lord will take care of her.* Great-aunt Caroline was dead. So was Lydia. And that child was God-only-knows where. Lydia had never come back to Mattagash after she'd had that baby. Baby. Pearl still thought of it as a small woolly bundle kicking its feet, yet in real years it would be almost as old as she was now. *The Lord will take care of her.* Just a matter of washing off the mud.

"The Lord didn't knock her up," Pearl thought. She listened as the lunchtime traffic in front of her house increased. Folks putting food into their bodies just to keep going. Time was moving on, with or without her. She felt around on the bed for the scrapbook, and walked her fingers over the cover. Marge's old book, passed on to Pearl because she was next in line. And, of course, that meant she was next in line for a lot of things. Marge was dead, and she, Pearl McKinnon Ivy, was *next in line*. Thanks a lot. Thanks a hell of a lot.

When she heard Mr. Tinley turn into his driveway, his car door slam, his dog bark, his house door shut behind him, Pearl smiled.

"My God," she thought. "It's so routine, I don't even have to look to know what's going on. Or what's gonna happen next. Marvin will be home in a half hour. Him and Mr. Tinley are as regular as good old clocks." Pearl closed her eyes. "They're real good soldiers, them two," she said.

There was a scurrying, micelike, in the attic. She opened her eyes and stared up at the ceiling. It must be the wind rustling about. It would actually be nice to have mice living up there. How Marge had fought the mice, back at the old homestead. Yet it was as if they were part of the family. Nowadays, especially in Portland, you got to be pretty damn hard up before you get a few self-respecting mice to settle down in your house. Yes, it would be nice to believe there were mice living in her attic, in her nice house on Hillsboro Street, a little secret from the neighbors. She imagined Mrs. Tinley standing on a chair screaming at just the thought of *those mice next door*. It would be nice to have something living up there besides dusty trunks of old clothes and letters. Some of Marge's personals. Some of the Reverend Ralph's. Some of her mother's delicate china. Letters and papers, mostly. Articles it seemed only the spiders were interested in these days. Junior's kids certainly didn't give a damn. They must believe she had always been from Portland, Maine, their grandmother Pearl. They had never bothered to ask her one single bit of family history. She even brought it up one day, when Cynthia Jane, the oldest, was a senior in high school.

"Did you know that you're descended from the first settlers of Mattagash, Maine?" Pearl had proudly told her first grandchild. She had waited years for that day.

"Where?" Cynthia Jane had asked, and turned up that little nose that looked so much like Thelma's.

"Did you know that your great-grandfather Ralph was a missionary who went all the way over to China and died there?" Pearl had gone on, determined to leave behind her this special oral history. To give it to her grandchildren as something to be protected for years to come. The way you might give a high school graduation gift. The way you might give them luggage, or money, or bicycles.

"Who?" Cynthia Jane had asked. So Pearl gave up within seconds of her first try. And she was tired of watching Cynthia Jane tug at the crotch of her pants, rather than listen to her heritage being unfolded for her.

Pearl closed her eyes. She did not want to look up at the wide open ceiling anymore. It reminded her too much of the clear night sky over Mattagash, of the late night sessions with Marge when the three sisters had sat with legs dangling off the back porch and spied on the sky for falling stars.

"There's one!" She could hear her own voice at twelve years old. Yes, she could still hear it. Now how many people who don't have such things preserved on a tape recorder can say that?

"There's one, Margie!" And Sicily would be asleep beside them on the porch. Old Chad, the dog. My God, how had she ever let Old Chad slip out of her memory? The day he died she and Sicily had simply *known* they would never be happy again. And here she was, in Portland, Maine, with a family who didn't even know she existed, and with not even a sliver of memory about Chad.

"Old Chad," Pearl whispered, and tried to swallow the lump in her throat. "There's another one! Wake up, Sicily! Wake up and look!" My God. It had been so much better than she had ever remembered it. Why didn't she know that, when she was way back there right in the heart of the action?

"We were washing off so much mud all the time, the way we were taught," Pearl thought, "that we never realized how good we really had it."

So it had come to this, then? Sixty years of living and learning and raising a family had brought her to stretching out on her bed, in her nightclothes, and letting a whole day inch by. She hadn't even had an urge to go to the bathroom. If she had made her morning coffee, perhaps it would have been different. But she hadn't. The only energy she'd put into the day had been to sit up, swing her legs over the edge of the bed, and pick up the old scrapbook where she'd left it the evening before. The rest was history. Yet she'd worked out a lot of things, more things than if she'd gotten up and puttered about her kitchen in another useless day of routine. She would call Sicily as soon as possible. Yes, she would be coming to the wedding, even if she was the only one in the Ivy family to do so. She would even set her mind to picking out a perfect gift for boy-smitten Amy Joy. But no, she would not be staying at Sicily's.

"Please have someone clean up Marge's old house," she would tell Sicily. "Please have someone sweep all the cobwebs off the old homestead. And tell the mice I'm coming home."

◆　　◆　　◆

When Marvin walked in the front door half an hour later, sharp as a clock, Pearl was in a lavender dress, with her hair swept up and sprayed in a nice coiffure. The electric teakettle was singing, and the radio was tuned in to a local talk show. The newspaper had been brought in off the front porch and all the houseplants had been given a drink of water. Who would know that there had never even been any breakfast dishes, or lunch dishes, to wash and put away? For forty years now, Marvin had preferred to eat one or two doughnuts in the Ivy Funeral Home coffee room for his breakfast. How would he have known any different if, over the years, Pearl had been starving herself during the day? If she had been lying crazily on her bed for hours, every damn day? He never noticed if she waxed a floor, or bleached a sheet, or dusted a lamp. Would forty years of dust have piled up to his nose and eventually choked him? A *houseguest* in his own living room?

Marvin smiled as he plunked his calfskin briefcase down and took off his tweed jacket. He made a quick assessment of the kitchen. How nice it would be to have nothing more to worry about all day long than washing a few dishes and cooking a bit of food. Maybe dust a vase every couple of days. Bring in the paper. Open the damn mail. Search for a purse. He almost envied a woman's life. They were as content as flealess dogs on a sunny porch. Marvin sniffed the air. Usually he could identify the fare of the evening by keen smell alone. He knew pot roast immediately. Steaks and pork chops were more elusive. So was meat loaf. But there was no mistaking the spicy air of stuffed cabbages, or a boiled dinner. Marvin sniffed harder. Ham. Yes, it was definitely ham. Boiled ham dinner. Good. It had been at least a month since he had tasted the sweet broth, the carrots, the small whole potatoes, the tender ham. Boiled ham dinner, that old New England fare that had put muscle on all the frail bones of their ancestors. Helped them cope in a harsh new land. Good for her. Good for Pearly.

"And how was *your* day?" Marvin asked, as Pearl put a bowl of canned pea soup and a hastily built ham sandwich in front of her starving husband.

◆　　◆　　◆

"Come on down!" Thelma Ivy screamed, along with the *Price Is Right* audience on television. The trick was for the three contestants to pinpoint the price of a new 1969 Maytag washer. Thelma searched her memory bank of female knowledge. Her very first washer had been a Maytag. She purchased it in 1948, the year she and Junior were married. What had they paid for it? Yet that was over twenty years ago. What had been the rate of inflation over that period? And how much would that amount to in dollars and cents right now? Right at this minute? My God, they only gave contestants *seconds* to figure this all out. Even game shows demanded so much of a person's intellectual and emotional responses that three or four a day was enough to leave Thelma supine on the floor in front of the TV, literally drained.

"I'll be a basket case if I watch *Let's Make a Deal,*" Thelma decided, and she reached out a trembling hand and shut the demanding monster off. Thelma shuddered at the sudden disappearance of Bob Barker. It was as if she had murdered him. Had murdered the whole audience. Had ripped the very guts out of the shiny new Maytag. But it had been the most positive movement, she was quite sure, her hand had taken upon itself in ages. Thelma had been cheating on Junior for three months now, and he didn't even suspect it. Maybe he thought he was the only one to have affairs, but he was dead wrong. Thelma had loved Bob

Barker ever since she found out about Junior and Monique Tessier. Ever since she'd heard Milly, the secretary-accountant, laughing about it in the rest room at the Ivy Funeral Home, during the employee Christmas party. She was telling one of the ambulance drivers' wives about it. They had come into the rest room to arrange their hair, fix their lipsticks, and smoke a quick cigarette since Marvin didn't allow it in the funeral home.

"I'm surprised he allows *dying*," Milly had said to Buddy Simlac's wife, about the no-smoking situation. Then she had gone on to spill the marital beans.

"Oh yes, it's been going on for months," Milly had giggled. "I think Monique is bored. Good God, what other reason could there be?"

Thelma had pulled her skinny feet and ankles up off the floor to avoid detection. By the time the women had doused their cigarettes beneath the water faucet and disappeared back into the dullness of the party, Thelma had heard all. And hard as she tried she could not pee a drop.

"I'm all shriveled up," she thought, but she meant her heart.

After that, Thelma fell so deeply in love with Bob Barker that every time she looked at her husband, she saw Bob's narrow face plastered at the top of Junior's fat body. At night she had lain beside Junior in their bed, and she had *known* it was not really her husband lying there, lost in his snores. It was Bob. Bobby. And several times in the past few weeks, she had lain *beneath* Junior Ivy, and while he grunted himself to satisfaction and whispered things like "Oh, Thel. Yes," she had heard Bob whispering instead, gently, encouragingly, "Come on down, Thel. Come on down, baby." And she had moved rhythmically beneath Junior and shouted "Yes! Yes!" as she heard the crowd behind her catch its breath and wait to see if she was lucky enough, this time, to win. "Yes! Yes!" God, she wanted that refrigerator so badly that she could taste all the food that might go in it! And Bob wanted her to win. She could see it in his eyes. He wanted all his women to win. It was she and Bob *against* the sponsors. "Oh, yes. Come on. Come on down."

Yet, rather than be jealous, Junior had become, she noticed, more energetic about lovemaking. He was less tired at night and more demanding of her. They were barely in their bed lately before he started. The night-light bulb was still hot to the touch when she felt his heavy hand stirring the blankets, searching for her in the darkness.

"How about it, Thel?" he would ask, as he patted her barely perceptible buttocks. "Do I get to hear my little cheerleader tonight, or don't I?"

So *that* was it. He thought the new Thelma was nothing more than a revival of the old high school cheerleading days, when they'd first met, rather than the work of a mature woman with an experienced lover in tow. A lover who also happened to be the king of the game shows. What else, then, could she do? Would it take a ménage à trois with Monty Hall to get her husband to sit up, despite his cumbersome belly size, and take notice?

It was Christmas Day that Thelma had taken her first *extra* Valium, a week after hearing Milly's seasonal conversation in the rest room. And on Christmas Day she didn't bother to give Junior his biggest, best present. It was a belly toner called Belly Beautiful, complete with an exercise program to help him shed his burgeoning gut. Thelma had wrapped it three weeks earlier, but she left it right where it was, behind the summer dresses in her walk-in closet. Instead she let him poke sadly among the balled-up wrappings and flattened bows that covered the floor of the family room. And when his sad eyes met hers they almost cried out to her, "Didn't I hint a thousand times that I wanted a Belly Beautiful?" But she had ignored them. Even when he rounded up his ties and socks and Fruit of the Looms into a somber heap and sat looking at it vacantly, she said nothing. Two days later she took Belly Beautiful back to Sears.

"It wasn't something my husband needed," she had told the holiday returns clerk. On the drive home, she had barely noticed the fat flakes of snow as they pelted against the warm windshield and were eaten up by the wipers.

"Let Monique Tessier fight for breath beneath him, the way I did for years," Thelma thought as she drove. "I won't help him get rid of his belly just so he'll have an easier time crawling into bed with *her*." She had driven around for an hour, past other people's happy holiday homes, up and down the streets of Portland, like a delivery woman of some sort, until she remembered she had a house of her own, with a family, with a Christmas tree in a den full of scrunched-up paper. Until she remembered she had a fat-bellied husband. Thelma had parked her little yellow Corvair in the driveway, and then gone straight upstairs and found the ring Junior had given to her as her big gift. It was an opal. Her birthstone. She didn't want it. It would be like a birth certificate around her finger, reminding her.

"I'm sorry I was ever born," Thelma had said, as she stood staring out into the streets, into the heavily falling snow that could cover up mistakes so easily if you let it. She took another Valium, another sort of snowfall, a warmer kind of covering.

Now Thelma looked out her spring window at the balmy April day, at the same scene that had been freezing and snow-filled, and so like a New England Christmas card, just a short time ago. The day she had flushed her birthstone ring down the upstairs toilet. Where the mounds of snow had been, there now were flowers. There were no longer white things everywhere, but green things. Green as money. Greener than envy.

Thelma went to Junior's tiny bar and washed another Valium down with a splash of club soda. She had never dreamed the day would come when she would abuse her prescription. She felt about the prescription the same way she had felt about her first credit card. A mark of maturity. Dr. Phillips would never believe that his little Thelma would take more pills than he told her to. It was like disobeying her father to disobey Dr. Phillips. He had been the doctor who was there when she was born. *Born. Birth. Birthstone. Christmas. Junior. Junior and Monique. Ocean Edge Motel.* Oh, wasn't the mind a terrible thing sometimes? Sometimes it seemed that even if you started out with nice thoughts, it could lead you right back to painful ones. She thought of Hansel and Gretel following the bread crumbs, and she smiled widely. That's a good story for children. It's all about bread crumbs in the woods and how to follow them. It's a good lesson for when you get older, and become an adult, and have to follow secretaries to motel rooms. Only you don't know it at the time. At the time, you think it's only a children's story! Good Lord, but Valium really helped her to sort her thoughts, to philosophize wonderfully about life's sudden twists. And this was not to mention the smooth, calm equanimity that seemed to engulf her. She was ready *Yes! Oh yes! Come on, baby! Come on down!* for any sweet little bump that might pop up, just to throw her off her guard. But she wouldn't let it. She would relax. She would play her favorite music. She would be damn fine. *Come on down!*

Thelma was still sitting in the den when Junior arrived home on time for a change. Randy, his son, and now Junior realized, his *chaperon*, was with him. Junior looked at Randy's hair, cut so short you could see the sickeningly white scalp. He looked at the tweed suit, which had once belonged to Jimmy Driscoll before Marvin fired him for insubordination. The tweed hurt his eyes. The sight as a whole reminded Junior of his own first days in the family business, sans tweed.

"I have seen and heard all of you today that I care to," Junior said to Randy, and the boy went promptly up the stairs to his room, where he had cleverly hidden a fat joint for a rainy day. "Thank you, though," Junior said as Randy slammed his door, "for sharing yourself with me."

In the den Junior stopped at the bar to pour a quick drink. He also wanted a few seconds to size up Thelma, determine her mood, before he interfered with it. He found the opened wedding invitation from his cousin Amy Joy where Thelma had left it, leaning against a bottle of club soda. He hoped the notion of a wedding, of sacred vows, of words like "honor" and "obey" hadn't thrown her into a emotional dump. He never knew what might set her off. One time it was a radio advertisement for Chicken Delite. The description of juicy thighs had reminded Thelma that Monique Tessier had such attributes.

Junior eyed his wife steadily. She seemed fine. She was sitting on the sofa, her legs crossed, holding a record album and thinking heavily, brows knitted.

"Trying to remember some old song," thought Junior. He prided himself on being as good as any damn disc jockey when it came to the whos and whens of music trivia. He would help Thelma out. Things were better between them, weren't they? A few months ago she'd come alive in bed. Even after she caught him with Monique it hadn't put a damper on things. Just last night he'd tried again, and sure enough. It was so good he thought she might accidentally wake the kids. Stir up the neighbors. He even imagined a fire truck pulling up and turning a spray of water loose through the bedroom window. Maybe that's what women needed sometimes. A little push now and then. A little jealousy to stir up the old home fires.

Junior stared at Thelma's thoughtful brow curiously. He would help her out, the way she'd been helping him through the nights lately.

"She keeps that up," Junior thought, "and I might start coming home on time, with or without Randy." Besides, he didn't want to be like his father. A million times in his childhood he had heard Marvin ask Pearl, "And how was *your* day?" and then never bother to listen to her answer.

"What are you trying to think of?" asked Junior. He noticed Thelma had *The Hits of Bobby Vinton* in her hands. What could be puzzling her? The year "Roses Are Red" was a hit? 1962. "Blue Velvet"? 1963. Come on, it was Thelma here he was dealing with. How tough could it be? Vinton's nationality? Polack.

"What's the problem, hon?" Junior prodded. "Are you trying to think of a year?"

At the sound of the question, Thelma burst into loud sobs. She shook her head angrily. She stomped her feet.

"It was 1948, you asshole!" Thelma screamed. She made a motion with her hand, quickly, the way one throws a Frisbee, and Junior ducked as Bobby Vinton sailed through the air and struck the wall behind the bar. "Just tell me what we paid for that damn Maytag!"

$\mathcal{S}$ICILY GRAPPLES WITH HER CONSCIENCE: ARSENIC, OLD LACE, AND YOUNG FRENCHMEN

....

"Ed Lawler run around on that woman every chance he got. He pillowed and plundered and bedded, I tell you, all he could. But Sicily's a saint. She stuck with him every inch of the way."

—Winnie Craft, as though this were wise of Sicily, at the 1962 Avon party

SICILY MCKINNON LAWLER TOOK HER WEDDING DRESS, STILL IN its original box, down from a shelf in her bedroom closet. She wiped away a cobweb that had attached itself to one corner. There had been no spring cleaning done that year, thanks to the wedding revelation by Amy Joy. Sicily no longer cared if cobwebs festooned the entire house. The spiders could have it, for all she cared, and the few acres of land too.

The dress was still softly beautiful. The lace design had always reminded Sicily of frost creeping across icy windowpanes during

Mattagash's wintry months. What is it about spring that old memories seem to thaw out too, along with the flies, the fields, the river, the buildings? Sicily remembered Ed Lawler, so nervous on his wedding day that he had vomited heartily, leaning out of John McRyder's new Pontiac. Sicily had always suspected nerves had little to do with it. John McRyder, Ed's old college classmate and best man, was famous for the bottles of alcohol that poked out from the springs of the Pontiac's seats. A rainy August day in 1931, the skies so dark and foreboding that someone not so much in love as Sicily might have taken it as a bad sign. A kind of matrimonial omen. Funny that John McRyder came to mind. She had looked at Ed's old college class book just a few days ago and had found them both, John and Ed, arms around each other's shoulders, cocky in their football uniforms, faces so young they were almost unrecognizable. "John 'The Flying Scott' McRyder, Captain," is what the caption said, "Gets a Pat on the Back from Ed 'The Lawless' Lawler. Championship Game, 1929." It was in the late forties that John McRyder had gone up in a little yellow airplane at the Houlton state fair for a five-dollar joyride and the entire shebang had come plummeting down to earth in a potato field. For years afterwards, during the harvest, kids found pieces of yellow like chunks of sun turned up by the digger and tossed among the rows and rows of russet potatoes. Sicily had always liked John, despite his philandering ways which she worried would rub off on Ed. But John had even managed to get himself married to a nice girl, and he had settled down before he died. And didn't Mrs. John McRyder cry at the funeral! Ed and Sicily had driven all the way to Houlton to attend.

"Can you imagine?" Emily McRyder had cried out to Ed in her grief. "Can you imagine going up in an airplane *just to look down?*" The McRyders had enough little kids by then to fill that old Pontiac. It pained Sicily dearly to see Emily McRyder so.

"They might just as well have buried that woman along with him," Sicily had told the women who gathered around her, back in Mattagash, anxious for news of the wake. Little yellow airplanes never took enough interest in Mattagash to crash there. They were always flying *over*, toting hunters and fisherman from the city into the virgin lakes which had once been safe from such creatures. But now Mattagash's geography was being plundered, thanks to yellow Piper Cubs and red Stinsons, which never landed for a chat but chose instead to stay above it all, tipping their wings mockingly.

John McRyder. He had been so dashing in his day. Sicily realized years after his death, when it was perfectly safe to admit such things, that she had had a passionate crush on John McRyder. She held the wedding dress beneath her chin and studied herself in the mirror. She had never been thin—none of the McKinnon women had ever been accused of that. But it was all tied in to the reason their ancestors had been strong enough and sturdy enough to withstand the raw country that faced them, to be the first in that country. Yes, the McKinnon women, like the men, were all big-boned and solid, a compliment for young girls of that place and time. But Sicily had become a little more big-boned and solid over the years than she cared to be. And besides, it was all over now, this pioneering notion, this striking out to hinterlands unknown. Why did she need the childbearing, water-carrying frame of a woman you see nowadays only in *National Geographic* pictures of Russia? It all seemed a bit unfair in 1969. Oh, maybe a great-grandchild of hers would end up on the moon one day. It was possible. They were getting ready to send a man there, a Mr. Neil Armstrong.

"Imagine that, Ed," Sicily thought. "A man on the moon. You always said we were close." And then Sicily smiled to remember how Ed used to tease old Mr. Fennelson about going to the moon.

"There's gonna be trouble," the old man would sputter. "You mark my words. God don't want mankind on the moon. God wants to keep as far away from mankind as he kin." Now they were both dead, moon-walking or not. And soon man *would* go off to the moon, seeking rivers maybe and warm places sheltered from the snows and winds, just as Sicily's ancestors had done.

"Look out, God," Sicily thought. "Here we come." And then

she was suddenly very unhappy that she had been caught between pioneering ages, the way some young men complain of being lost between wars.

Sicily folded the dress carefully and tucked it back inside the shell of its box, like a sad white seed waiting to sprout. The dress, her very own wedding dress, did not fit her anymore, it was true, but with a few adjustments it would fit Amy Joy just fine. Tears filled Sicily's eyes. All the times she had dreamed of seeing little Amy Joy gussied up in her mother's wedding lace! What had she expected, all those years? Perhaps that Amy Joy would meet a nice young boy at Loring Air Force Base, a boy from Delaware or New Jersey or one of those civilized states. Or perhaps Amy Joy would go off to college somewhere, since a high school degree didn't create the brouhaha it used to. In Mattagash the hot new item was a year or two of college. So perhaps Amy Joy *would* go off to college and at that college, all hidden mysteriously in those intelligent green vines, Amy Joy would sip a Pepsi in the cafeteria next to some young boy whose family was influential in some way or another, like the Rockefellers or the Kennedys, and they would fall in love and marry. And the whole influential family would come to Mattagash to meet Sicily, and their entourage would stay at the Albert Pinkham Motel, and Sicily would fix a pot of Tetley's so that they could all come by her house for a cup of tea, and they would sit on the back porch and listen to the Mattagash River and be thankful that their son had the foresight to chase down one of the descendants of Mattagash's founding family.

"Damn that Jean Claude Cloutier!" Sicily said. "Or however you pronounce that god-awful French name." She could actually *poison* him, if she thought she would get away with it. She could actually give him a plug of arsenic hidden in the creamy center of a home-made Whoopie Pie. But a Frog probably wouldn't eat a Whoopie Pie.

She took the fragile dress back out of its box and held it to her body again, for one final look before it went off to belong to someone else, to become a part of someone else's future. She turned before the mirror, for a side view. If someone had told her years ago, when she first started dreaming her wedding dreams for Amy Joy, that this dress would flounce its way down the aisle to weld Amy Joy to a French Catholic for eternity, she would have burned it, veil and all. Or better yet, she would have marched right down to the banks of the Mattagash River and heaved it far out into the rips. Let it float all the way down to the ocean at St. John, New Brunswick, if it wanted to. Let it go back down that old river in the *opposite direction* to the one that the first McKinnons had taken. That's just what it was like for Amy Joy to be marrying in the territory of Catholics. It was the opposite direction from any McKinnon before her. If you so much as glanced at the McKinnon family tree you would be able to pronounce in a second any name that your eye spied. Just how did they say "Cloutier" in Frogtown? "Clue-tier"? Or, worse yet, "Clue-tee-yay"? My God, you'd sound like a cheerleader. Her poor little grandchildren. Yes sir, the way Sicily felt about weddings and trousseaus and bridal showers now, she might just as well toss the dress into the Mattagash River and let the young girls down around St. John, New Brunswick, pull it out of the water and wear it. They were Canadians, true, a short-coming. Yet they could still speak the King's English down there, by God. But she kept forgetting. Jean Claude wasn't a Canadian. He was American, like the rest of them on that side of the border, on that side of the Mattagash River. And his family had most likely been American for a hundred and fifty years. Maybe more. Yet, and Amy Joy had told her this, Jean Claude's parents could barely speak a sensible word of English. *Americans,* unable to speak English. Imagine that.

"You can't depend on a river to separate folks in a proper manner," Sicily thought. She had once said to Ed that she wished the French-speaking people in Watertown and St. Leonard would go back where they came from. And Ed had reminded her that a century and a half ago, her very own ancestors had come from New Brunswick, Canada. The loyalists. And that there were names in her family tree from Ireland who had been *Catholic* back in the old country, before the famine, before the passage, and they came here as orphans to be adopted by Protestants.

"Well, God meant for that to happen," Sicily had answered him. "Maybe God caused the famine to disperse the Catholics so that they could find good Protestant homes in America." Ed had only laughed, his "I know more than you" laugh. A snort, really. But it was true. And besides, why bring it all up now? Why bring it all back?

"Folks got no business remembering stuff that far back," Sicily had argued. "If God wanted us to remember things that happened so long ago, he'd have let us live longer." Ed had been a thorn in her side many times when it came to her religious beliefs. It seemed sometimes as if he felt it was his job to prove her wrong. Like he was some kind of devil's advocate or something.

Amy Joy knocked on the bedroom door and Sicily quickly put the dress away and slid the box under the bed. She kicked her slippers off and lay back. As a final touch she flicked some bangs down into her eyes and then pulled the spare woolen blanket, meant for cold winter nights and not balmy spring days, up around her neck.

"Come in, dear," she said meekly. The eyes that looked from beneath the heavy blanket were dull with remorse. Pain had erased all memory of a former, happy life.

"Oh, I didn't know you were taking a nap," said Amy Joy, and started to close the door.

"No!" said Sicily, showing much too much vigor. "No, sweet," she said, more calmly, remembering her condition. "What do you want?"

"Well," said Amy Joy, "I guess it's high time I got the wedding dress taken in. Rose Henderson said she'd do the seamstress work as a present, and the wedding is only a week away. Have you decided to give it to me yet, or not? It doesn't matter, you know. I can get something at J. C. Penney's at the last minute."

Sicily heard the awful words as they entered the external part of her ear. Once there, in the foyer, they were escorted on into the middle ear. Here the ruckus started. The awful words beat fiercely upon the tiny bones in the middle ear and caused something fluid to move around in the internal ear. It was in there, in the internal ear, that the awful words caused you-know-what to hit the fan. That's when those ugly little hair cells started blabbing their mouths off, and then her nerves took the whole kit and caboodle straight up to her brain. *The wedding is only a week away.* Her poor, poor brain. What it had been through, these past days. Amy Joy, her own daughter, her only daughter, was going to cause deafness in her, one way or another. How did Sicily even remember all this nonsense about the ear? Why had this disgusting information about *hair cells* filtered back from her school days if she weren't on her last hearing legs? Hairs belonged inside the nose, not the ear.

"What?" asked Sicily sadly. "What?"

"I said do I, or do I not, wear your wedding dress? If it's going to bend you out of shape, I'll pick up something in Watertown. It doesn't matter to me what I wear." Amy Joy sucked down some Pepsi.

Bend you out of shape. What in the name of God did *that* mean? What was happening to Mattagash's youth? Once, they were content to skate all night around a fire on the bogan, or slide on pieces of linoleum down Russell Hill, or swim all day long in the patch of good swimming water by the bridge and then drink pops while the sun dried them again. And the next thing you know, they want cars to drive to Watertown *for no reason at all.* Not for shopping, or to go to the doctor's office, or even to trade in a few books of Green Stamps at the redemption center. For no reason at all. Amy Joy had given that answer herself a thousand times. Now they wanted television sets instead of old-fashioned story-telling. They turned their noses up at handmade clothing, hand-knit mittens, home-given haircuts. The outside world had reached its hand into Mattagash, dirty fingernails and all, and had grabbed up the fancy of the youngsters. There was something missing now. A sense of heritage, maybe. What young girl would not beg to wear her mother's precious wedding dress? *I'll pick something up in J. C. Penney's at the last minute. If it's going to bend you out of shape*. Whatever that meant, it was happening. Sicily *was* being bent out of shape. Her ears were bending out of shape. Her heart was twisting out of shape.

"Speak up please, dear," said Sicily, and held a shaking hand to her right ear. "I can't hear a thing," she said loudly. "Not even the river."

Not hearing the river, that downpour of water that rushed past all the houses in Mattagash clinging to its bank, was unimaginable. If you'd lived there all your life, it's true that you wouldn't notice it. Like the soft ticking of a clock, it went away with time. Only the tourists remained wide-eyed about the river, as they did with most foolish things. But if you listened for it, by God, the river was there. It was your family scrapbook strung out, page after page. It was the watery line of your heritage which pointed straight toward the ocean, then across the ocean, to the old country. It gurgled and rippled and snarled. In Mattagash, say you don't hear the wind, and no one will pay you much mind. Say you don't hear the heaving pulp truck, or the whining skidder, or the grating chain saw that has replaced the old-timer's broadax. Say you don't hear the throaty loon in the swamp of the black bogan. Say you don't hear your own heart washing its beat against your rib cage. But, for Christ's sake, *say you hear the river*.

"No," said Sicily, straining toward the river window. "I'm quite sure. I can't hear a single drop."

It was the first unauthenticated case of traumatic deafness ever to trek that far north.

THE PINKHAM MOTEL
SUFFERS FROM MALNUTRITION:
EXTRATERRESTRIALS PARTY
WITH THE GIFFORDS

....

"Well, let's see. He started two years ago, the same fall that
Kennedy got himself shot, and he hasn't stopped since. I can't
sleep nights for him. Even the cat is going crazy."

—Albert Pinkham, long-distance to the receptionist
at *Guinness Book of World Records* office,
about his German shepherd's hiccuping bout, 1963–65

ALBERT PINKHAM LEFT BRUCE, THE GERMAN SHEPHERD, WITH
his head lolling from the side window of the pickup truck and went
inside Macabee's Sporting Store to inspect his business cards.
There they were, all twenty-four, still flapping happily in the breeze
of uninterested passersby, without a single care for the financial
burden their unpicked presence thrust upon a motelier. Albert
rubbed his chin and pondered the situation. Where the hell were
the naturalists who usually flocked to Maine before the hunters
and fishermen could swarm in? Where were the *snobs of nature*,

for Chrissakes? Had they discovered some other little niche where the air was pure and the scenery picturesque? He wished he knew. He wished someone would goddamn tell him because he and Bruce had lain awake all night, watching their fates race across the ceiling with the casual spray of lights from cars passing by the Albert Pinkham Motel. *Passing by.* He might just as well have a motel in the Yukon, as in Mattagash, Maine. He might just as well stick his motel in Siberia and throw out the welcome mat to Russian prisoners. At least that's how he felt when he looked at all the blank pages in his Big Chief tablet, which he used as a registration book. Surely this didn't mean that he was doomed to leave behind him the wide open spaces of the country and move to the smog-filled, clogged places of the big city. He could see his tiny four-room motel swallowed up by high rises and big fancy city buildings. Surely this didn't mean he would have to move to *Caribou!*

Albert followed the writhing Mattagash River home, over thirty frost-heaved, potholed miles from Watertown, and contemplated his fate. Bruce bounced sadly on the seat beside him but kept a sharp eye out for female canines trotting along beside the road or lounging seductively on front lawns. Bruce even spied a black jockey on one lawn, wearing a red jacket and holding a riding crop. This greatly confused him. He sniffed the air heavily for an odorous clue. What was it? One of those fancy little Chinese dogs that actresses like Zsa Zsa Gabor dragged onto *The Merv Griffin Show*? But the truck rolled on and the jockey was soon gone from his sight and mind. Albert had noticed the black jockey when it first appeared, a couple years back. At first he thought that the French family who lived in the house must have adopted a small black child to put to work during the potato harvest. On his return trip that same day, he was forced to ask himself why any child would want to stand erect in the same place for so long? Was he being punished? That was when Albert had slowed for a better look. It almost surprised him at first. But then he was pleased to realize that no matter how far Mattagash was from civilization, at least according to city folks, here was a sign that anything was possible. Here was proof that fine art from the faraway South could drift casually north. At Christmastime, Albert noticed, the family placed a Santa's cap on the jockey's head and strung him with firefly lights. Albert worried that the jockey might not be accustomed to such extremely cold weather, but, after all, it wasn't a *real* coon. There had been real ones come north to Maine, back in the heart of the logging era, past the turn of the century. They were lumbermen, or tried to be. Albert's father told him how they nearly froze to death in the thin clothes they wore and how the women and children ran from them in fear. There's even a brook in Mattagash called Nigger Brook, and some say it's because one of those darky lumbermen drowned in that brook during a log drive. And it was also true that a KKK organization sprang up in the Mattagash River valley in the 1940s, but there weren't any niggers around, not even wooden ones, so the group had gone out of business due to apathy.

Albert reached a heavy hand over and rubbed Bruce's neck fur.

"What do you think, pal?" Albert asked his traveling companion. "Could you put up with the big-city life in Caribou? They can come in a truck, you know, and take you to the pound if you don't have a collar, and put you to sleep." Bruce whined sadly, and canted his head.

"No, of course you wouldn't," Albert interpreted soothingly. "But if this keeps up you might see the Albert Pinkham Motel go by one day on a flatbed. This keeps up and we might both end up in the pound." Bruce *rahoooooo*ed loudly from deep in his throat.

"There," Albert soothed. "There, there. We won't go to the pound."

Albert stopped in St. Leonard to gas up at Henri Nadeau's Quick Lunch and Gas.

"Tank you," Henri said, replacing the gas cap and waving Albert on. "Tanks ha lot!" Henri shouted.

"Tank yourself," muttered Albert, back on the road now. Bruce growled back at Henri until the gas pumps, and the large sign displaying a lovely giant hot dog in its fat roll, disappeared around a turn in the road. Henri charged too much for his gas. And his quick snacks were gourmet meals after they were added up on the cash register. But, like Albert's motel, his gas pumps were the only ones from Watertown to Mattagash, and Mattagash had only recently acquired theirs. Peter Craft had finally saved enough money by working at Pratt & Whitney aircraft plant in Connecticut for ten years to come home and launch into the filling station business. Albert disliked Peter Craft. Peter Craft had a habit, every time a jet flew over Mattagash on its way to Europe, of pointing and saying, "Look, that might be one of them planes I stuck the little metal piece on at Pratt and Whitney." What a show-off. At times like that, Albert always hoped the passengers on board had plenty of them little aspirin bottles of booze. They'd probably end up needing it somewhere in the middle of the ocean if Peter Craft had been allowed to stick things on their plane. And Albert didn't like the one other businessman in Mattagash, either. That was Charles Mullins, who slung sandwiches and doughnuts, damn near off the Mattagash bridge, to starving canoeists just coming to shore from two weeks of roughing it on the Mattagash River. Albert didn't mind Blanche, whose grocery had been around long before the motel opened, and who was a woman anyway. That didn't count. But he had enjoyed being the only big fish in a small pond, and did not encourage other Mattagash men to leave the woods-working business of their heritage. This wasn't New York City. There wasn't room in Mattagash for that many entrepreneurs. He should have recognized the business philosophy of Henri Nadeau: It was his own "I got something and you want it" style. But he didn't.

"He's as bad as the A-rabs," Albert told Bruce, of Henri's high gas prices. "One of these days he'll come out to pump gas with a checkered tablecloth tacked to his head." Bruce's lip curled up involuntarily at the displeasure in his master's voice, exposing the broken tip of his left fang.

Albert waved at nearly every car he met, especially after he left the Watertown line and entered St. Leonard. He knew all the drivers from St. Leonard to Mattagash. If teenagers were driving, well, he still recognized the cars as belonging to their fathers. Little towns grew up next to each other, regardless of religion and nationality, and since they were *little* towns, everybody knew everybody for miles, whether they liked it or not.

Among the cars Albert met was Vinal Gifford's old sharklike 1960 Plymouth, black as a killer fish, with dangerous fins sprouting from its back. The Plymouth looked to be hunting, *preying*, its headlights beady and attentive, its fins hurling it forward to Watertown. Pike, as Albert could plainly see before he was compelled to leave the tarred road for the gravelly ditch in order to let the sharky creature pass, was clutching the door on the passenger side. Even if Vinal was in the habit of braking, which he was not, the Plymouth had probably seen its last abrupt halt around 1966. Its brake shoes were worn to a frazzle.

Albert came to a complete stop in the ditch. The Plymouth rocked over the frost heaves and then bobbed out of sight. Everyone in Mattagash marveled that Vinal could keep such a bouncing vehicle on the road, especially since it had no shocks whatsoever and only a whisper of brakes. Why, everyone wondered, doesn't the first frost heave it hits send it to Mars? Or even Boston?

"That's why Pike and me drink a bit," Vinal had answered Henri Nadeau, when asked about the mechanical miracle that seemed to chart right up there with how bumblebees can fly. "We're both afraid of heights," Vinal said, just as Henri finished pumping two dollars' worth of gas into the shark. And then it was off again, looking for smaller, weaker fish.

"There won't be a battery, a hubcap, or a virgin safe from here to Watertown," Albert Pinkham said to Bruce, as he steered the sensible gray pickup back onto the road, back onto the trail of thought. He had had his own run-in with the Giffords just two years before, and he had, by God, taken the whole nest of them to court. Folks in Mattagash had warned him to leave things be.

"You'll end up like them big crime bosses," Tom Henderson told Albert. "You'll end up in the trunk of some Plymouth, I ain't saying whose."

But Albert took the Giffords to court, and he garnered a pile of respect near and far by doing so. The whole trouble began when he discovered that the Giffords had converted an empty, two-story house into a motel by adding several rickety bunks. A good strong wind could have leveled the establishment in a second, not to mention what a heavy snowfall would do. Albert couldn't possibly see how Gifford & Gifford Sportsman's Lodge & Sons had a prayer, and he wasn't too worried about it until he found out, after a quick visit to Macabee's Sporting Store, that all his business cards had been picked and pocketed by small children with dirty hands and faces, who all appeared to be the same size, and who had heads of massive curls.

"They all looked like bottle brushes," Macabee told Albert.

But cute misdemeanors turned into grim felonies when the *Bangor Daily News* ran a sensational story about Gifford & Gifford Sportsman's Lodge & Sons. Vinal Gifford had phoned a reporter, collect, at the *Bangor Daily News*, and told him that a UFO had landed several times in front of the lodge. The reporter didn't believe one word of the story, but he foresaw the humorous impact of printing it.

Vinal also claimed that two of his sons had been taken aboard the spacecraft and whisked about Mattagash before being plunked back down on the front steps. The two boys, only eight and nine years old, had managed nonetheless to give several interviews themselves, one stretching as far away as the *Boston Globe*. Albert stopped by the sheriff's office in Watertown and filed a massive complaint of deceptive advertising. He couldn't have a Boston paper doing this to the Albert Pinkham Motel. He depended too heavily on out-of-staters. So the Giffords had come grudgingly to court, thanks to one brave lone man and his loyal dog. Let other, lesser men say that the lone man was prompted by avarice.

The Giffords were a lot less willing to be interviewed by the judge than they had been by the *Boston Globe*. In court they snapped shut, tight as oysters. Oysters a little too far north in Maine to be near the safety of an ocean. That's how Giffords were, once you got them away from the thickly sprouted pines of Mattagash, where they could disappear like wild men in a split second. But, oh, and Albert seethed to think of it, hadn't their lips flapped to reporters! Their Christian names alone had garnered much limelight. Vera Gifford had been a country music fan from birth, and she had named a parcel of her kids accordingly. The two sons who had been taken on a carnival ride through the clear skies over Mattagash in a souped-up spaceship were Hank Snow Gifford and Johnny Cash Gifford. The newspapers had a field day.

But, by Jesus, Albert and Bruce put a foot and paw, respectively, down. Asked by the judge what the inside of the spaceship looked like, Hank Snow and Johnny Cash went white as pillows. They hung their heads, a Gifford genetic coding, and shrugged.

"Well?" the judge demanded.

"Considering all them lights," Johnny Cash Gifford finally answered, "it looked just like Bangor."

"At Christmastime," added Hank Snow.

Rehashing the Pinkham Versus Gifford Act, Albert and Bruce swept by the very spot where the shady lodge had boasted visitations. A good swift northeasterly, like a needed kick in the ass, had leveled it all before the first snow of 1967. Albert had mourned that it was not chock-full of Giffords at the time. But there the old building was, a pile of weathered lumber, birds circling in search of nest-building sites, last summer's hay bent about the doorway. It couldn't be the Giffords causing his latest lack of business. All of Albert's business cards were still flapping tearfully back at Macabee's, tacked up high enough that little delinquent hands could not reach them.

"I hope you don't have any Quebecers for clients," Macabee had mentioned to Albert. "They won't be able to reach up that high either."

Albert rolled his window down and let April hit him fair in the face. A golden splash of afternoon sun was lying on the river, rippling there. The river was high and dangerous, having been free of its ice for only two weeks. It was an act of nature that could make you believe in God, if you didn't, when the Mattagash River ran. Sheets of ice thirty feet wide and five feet thick could stand straight up in the water and look down on you. And trees a chain saw could barely cut through would uproot and find themselves fifty miles down the river before they came to. And the sound of it! The noise! Well, it wasn't until them supersonic jets from Loring Air Force Base, seventy miles away, started flying low over Mattagash, shattering sound barriers, and windows, and ear drums, that Albert Pinkham finally had something to compare to the natural noise of a river breaking up in the spring. It was nothing to toy with, the river. At any time of the year. Yet you can't tell a tourist that. They're used to city ways. Tourists think it's okay if they accidentally drown in the Mattagash River. They think they can just go back to the city when it's all over and sue somebody. But Albert and Bruce knew the truth of it. They knew what a tourist looks like who's been vacationing at the *bottom* of the river for two weeks. They'd seen cute little firm-thighed college girls so black and bloated even the flies wouldn't go near them.

Could he have been too harsh on the naturalists last year, Albert wondered, as he tooted hello in answer to Winnie Craft's wave from her front porch.

"Winnie's too afraid to go inside and shut her door," Albert said to Bruce. "Too afraid she'll miss something."

As Albert turned the truck into his own wide drive, Bruce wagged his tail furiously. The Albert Pinkham Motel sign always set the dog to twitching in the front seat, and by the time Albert opened the front door to release him, Bruce was often drooling.

"You love this place as much as I do, don't you, boy?" Albert asked. Bruce's tongue flapped from the side of his mouth in anticipation of the bound he would make from the front seat once the open door had given him clearance. But something stopped them both. A car was waiting for them, pulled in snugly below the house. Sicily's car. Amy Joy lolling behind the wheel. McKinnons in blood. Lord, how Albert and Bruce loathed uppity-ups. The rumor that Albert had heard about Amy Joy getting hitched was true, for a change. He had read in the *Watertown Weekly* just yesterday that she was betrothed to the French grease monkey at Thibodeau's. Maybe Albert should say grease *Frog*. There was a picture of the two of them, their engagement picture, taken as they leaned against someone's refrigerator in someone's kitchen. It was a French kitchen, Albert knew that much. He had spotted two crucifixes over the refrigerator. Mattagash women might have the snazziest items Avon can offer plastered all through their houses, but there wasn't a single crucifix among them. The Giffords maybe had one or two, if they hadn't pawned them. Albert thought of the picture. Didn't the McKinnons think they were meringue on the pie, though? Bruce growled throatily, as if reading Albert's thoughts. But engagement pictures meant weddings and weddings meant honeymoons. And honeymoons meant cozy nights of squeaking bedsprings at the all-new Albert Pinkham Motel, replete with hot running water in all the rooms.

"You people need *cold* showers, not hot ones," Albert told two shivering newlyweds who complained heavily upon checking out. That was before he had broken down and added hot water. Had pampered the sex-crazed imbeciles who graced the doors of numbers 1, 2, 3, or 4.

"They'll be wanting one of them Gee-coo-sees next," he told Bruce. But in fact Albert planned, if business would only pick up, to buy a plastic swimming pool from Sears, one of the big fancy jobs, twelve feet wide with a little diving board, and with a most colorful design. He would plant it where Sarah Pinkham's old flower garden had been and charge the bastards $1.00 to dip in it. For the local kids he would even go so far, being a philanthropist of sorts, to offer a $25.00 seasonal pass, a virtual giveaway at that price. Quite frankly, it wouldn't be a great variation from the price he charged tourists. If his motel was in Florida, maybe, he'd have to charge $365.25 for a seasonal pass, so as not to lose money. But in northern Maine, with a summer that comes and goes on mosquito wings, Albert could make a killing on seasonal passes. Bruce agreed.

Amy Joy got out of her mother's car and slammed the door.

"Goddamn McKinnons," Albert thought. "Just because a door is there, they gotta slam it." Bruce's teeth scraped, top against bottom. His tail went slack. Albert calmed him with a quick stroke of the neck fur, right where Bruce dearly loved stroking, and opened the door. *Weddings meant honeymoons.*

"Well, if it ain't little Amy Joy," Albert said, most pleasantly. "What's this I hear about you getting married and breaking all them bachelor hearts? Good gravy, I remember when you was no higher than this," said Albert, and held out a hand, knee-high, to demonstrate the awful passage of time. He smiled widely, displaying his motelier smile while Bruce, recognizing the salesmanship involved, rushed forward to insert a cold nose into Amy Joy's hand.

CYCLES, RECYCLES, AND
BICYCLES: VINAL AND PIKE AWAIT
THE TIRE CONVENTION

....

"I'll say one thing for the Giffords. If you're in trouble they'll
take the shirt right off your back."

—James Henderson

GOLDIE GIFFORD SAW AMY JOY'S ENGAGEMENT PICTURE IN THE
Watertown Weekly and showed it to Pike.

"What a shame we ain't been saving our money for the past ten
years," Pike said. "We could buy her something real nice." They
laughed together, Goldie and Pike, and so did a portion of small
Giffords who happened to be doing homework within hearing distance. But a somber thought crept into Pike's mind as he lay on
the sofa in front of yet another episode of *The Edge of Night*. A
wedding like that was bound to be the social event for years to

come. And the McKinnons had rich relatives from Portland. They had a bushel of friends and acquaintances from out of state. Ed Lawler himself was born down south somewhere, near Massachusetts. Only God would know who might be capable of coming to that wedding. *Massachusetts.* Lord, that had a magical ring. Pike was smitten with out-of-state places the way the young girls in Mattagash were. Marriageable maidens, tired of the few old family names that never seemed to change, swooned over the strange names of men from the cities. They loved going off to marry, and then dragging back to Mattagash some Polish or German name so long you couldn't fit it onto the back of a pulp truck. For Pike, however, this flirtation with other states was purely artistic. He imagined those were the places that first received all the latest hubcap designs straight from Paris, France, or wheresoever they designed them. And tires! Lord, four to a car. Pike could almost sniff the whitewalls. He tried to imagine what an entire school yard full of fancy cars might smell like. There was no doubt in Pike's mind that the high school gymnasium would be used for the reception. Everyone had their receptions there, no attention paid to the last name. And Missy had already come home from school in a tizzy to tell Goldie that the entire fifth-grade class spent their activity period making carnations out of pink Kleenex to decorate the Mattagash gym.

"For Amy Joy Lawler's wedding reception," Pike had heard her say, and warmth had spread throughout his groin at the thought. He stretched out longer on the couch, but inside he was curling up. In spirit, he was all bent over, rolling a tire quietly away into a soft April night.

◆   ◆   ◆

Vera Gifford Gifford read of the wedding plans, too. She wondered how Sicily McKinnon Lawler was handling the affiliation with a Catholic, not to mention one that was French. Being a Catholic herself, Vera understood the religious persecution that went hand in hand with such a thing in Mattagash. But she was never really sure where Catholic began and Gifford left off. She knew one thing, though, having lived all her life on the outskirts of the social wake the McKinnons and Crafts had always caused in Mattagash. Sicily McKinnon Lawler, and Vera knew this, would no more welcome a Frenchman into the fold than she would a Gifford. Look at all the fuss, years ago, when little boy-crazy Amy Joy got herself tangled up with Chester Gifford. Vera's first cousin. You'd have thought someone was selling Amy Joy up the river to slavery, to hear the backlash. Well, good enough for Sicily. Let her get what she deserved. You spit up into the air, and it's bound to come back down. At least Chester Gifford spoke English, even if it was mostly lies.

But the wedding wasn't nearly as interesting to Vera as were her troublesome relatives at the top of the hill. Retribution over the assassinated canary had finally arrived, two days earlier, when Little Pee stole Little Vinal's cumbersome bicycle. He had stripped away the paint, sawed off the bar that designated the sex of the bike, painted it a bright blue, added a jaunty little horn. Then he presented it to his sister Priscilla, who had ridden the bike proudly up and down the road that ran between the two Gifford houses. Little Pee told Goldie that he and Priscilla had pooled their pop bottle money and bought the bike for five dollars from Old Sambo, who owned the little junk shop at the St. Leonard–Mattagash town line.

"I can't imagine him selling such a nice bike for so little," Goldie had said to her son. She even left a huge pot of macaroni boiling on the stove to come outside and admire the glistening bicycle.

"His granddaughter who lives in Caribou left it," Little Pee lied smoothly. "She's too big for it now."

"I didn't know Old Sambo had any kin in Caribou," Goldie had said vaguely as she shook the outdoor rug, made of plastic Sunbeam bread wrappers. Then she had gone back inside to add some hamburg and two cans of stewed tomatoes to the macaroni.

At the bottom of the hill, Vera and her children had watched Priscilla riding up and down, up and down, in front of their house for two days before they recognized the bicycle as Little Vinal's.

"She looks like she's selling apples," said Vera, the first day she spotted Priscilla. "Look at her. Wearing out her legs to give her ass a ride." But the bicycle did look spectacular. Little Pee was handy at welding, painting, and sanding. In fact, the only course he was passing at school was shop. And the skills he had picked up that aided in disguising the bicycle would someday be applied to automobiles that mysteriously disappeared outside the Watertown movie theater, and other establishments, to emerge again as mere ghosts of their former selves. No, it wasn't that the quality of the job on the bicycle was shoddy that tipped off the bottom-of-the-hill Giffords. It was because the very bicycle that Little Vinal had bought, a few autumns ago, with what he claimed was his potato-picking money had suddenly vanished. It was as if the old settler soil had opened up and swallowed it. And the new bicycle upon which Priscilla was traipsing the roads looked alarmingly like Little Vinal's. *If* you looked closely. *If* you imagined it black, instead of a dazzling blue. *If* you stuck a bar back on and made the bicycle male. For a usually unmathematical family, Vera and her offspring had put two and two together to come up with the whereabouts of Little Vinal's bike.

"Little Pee could make the *Titanic* look like a canoe if you left him alone with it for an hour," Vera had said, and waited with her fists opening and closing like petals for Big Vinal to get home. She forgot about supper. She let her big washing machine sit with dirty loads of clothing all about it on the floor. Where the hell had Pike and Goldie gotten the money to pay for a new bike, that's all Vera wanted to know. She even forgot about the new mailbox that Vinal was thoughtful enough to get her. She had planned to touch it up with a quick paint job until she spied Priscilla's meanderings. Now the mailbox was leaning sadly on the back porch, its red flag lowered, the lettered announcement MR. & MRS. WALTER HEBERT, RR #2, WATERTOWN, MAINE 04774, awash in April sunlight.

The kids were eating sandwiches from sticky jars of already mixed peanut butter and jelly when Vinal Gifford finally sauntered in and slammed the kitchen door.

"Is it too much work to mix your own?" he asked his wife, the jar of premixed peanut butter and jelly in his hand. He was already tired from a day of imagining how the parking area of Amy Joy's reception would fill up. He expected some peace, Vera could tell, so she put her rantings in limbo. Instead of starting with the bad news, she broke ice with the good.

"Look here at Amy Joy Lawler's engagement picture," Vera said, and thrust the newspaper into Vinal's face. "Ain't she the picture of old Marge McKinnon? Look how that little nose turns right up into the air."

"Maybe we should wrap up a battery and give it to her," Vinal joked. "Do you think she'd like a pair of hubcaps? Some booster cables?" He chuckled again, imagining Amy Joy Lawler's face as she tore open the heavy box. But then Vera broke in upon his pleasant reverie with sordid details of the bicycle.

"I want it back," she warned her husband.

"If you and Goldie would keep your traps shut," Vinal complained, "them kids would play together, like they should. God didn't put us on the earth to fight. He put us here to relax."

"He did?" Vera countered. "Well, if he'd knowed how much you and Pike was planning to relax, he'd have put you both on the moon. Where it's quieter."

So Vinal was obliged to trudge up the hill for a short conference with his brother Pike. When he came back, he brought the pristine blue bicycle down the hill, leading it like a tame deer, and gave it to Little Vinal.

"Don't say a word," Vinal told his son. "You know damn well he turned that old clunker into what looks like a brand-new bike. And he's gonna weld the bar back on so no one'll call you a sissy. Take it and shut up. It didn't cost you a penny."

"She had her heart set on tramping the roads on that bike," Vera said, as she lay in bed that night next to Vinal. "She's as boy-crazy as they come."

Vinal reached over and clasped a limp breast in his hand. Vera tried to avoid the hand by rolling on her side, her back to Vinal, but he followed the sagging breast.

"Lord, I did five tubs of wash today," Vera hinted, and yawned heartily. Vinal slipped off his long johns and rested a hairy leg on Vera's thighs.

"This'll keep her mind off fighting with Goldie," Vinal thought, and smiled. "As long as she's fighting *someone*, she'll be okay."

PEARL PACKS ESSENTIALS, THELMA PACKS PORTLAND, MARVIN PACKS OFF THE RESIDENT MISTRESS: RANDY THINKS THEY'RE A PACK OF FOOLS

....

"I already smoked Genesis, Exodus, and a good part of Leviticus."

—Randy Ivy, on where to find the best substitute for reefer papers, April 1969

PEARL PACKED EVERYTHING SHE MIGHT TRY TO GRAB IN CASE OF a fire. Her concentration was no longer on dresses or purses, or which pair of shoes. She wanted the important things now. The things you couldn't replace if flames raged through your home. And there *was* a fire curling around the old memories in Pearl's brain. Eating them up. Pearl put *the little things* in her suitcase, the kind of items that people look at once you're dead and marvel at what you ever saw in them. She remembered how she and Sicily had jokingly belittled the contents of Marge's moldy trunk, the leftovers of her life.

"Why would she keep these old clippings from World War One?" Pearl had laughed. "And look, here's a tattered old handkerchief from France. It says 'Argonne Forest' on it. Now who do you suppose ever sent her that?" Well, Pearl saw things differently now. Lives were like wars. You could only study them years after they were over.

"Margie was only fourteen when that war broke out," Pearl thought, and packed the battered locket Marge had given her for her ninth birthday, January 25, 1918. The locket opened out into two very young faces of Pearl and Sicily. "The war was almost over when she gave me this," said Pearl. "Who might she have known in that war that worried her? Where did she ever find the money to buy this little locket? Where did she buy it?" She wished with all her heart she still had Marge's old trunk so that she could look at the items anew, with a fresh interest. All they had saved from it were things that had been passed down from the reverend, and the papers of Grace McKinnon. The other things had seemed of no consequence. Personal letters from Marcus Doyle, the missionary Margie had loved so dearly, who had abandoned her for some reason or other. Pearl remembered seeing the two of them walking among thick fields of goldenrod, Margie's brown hair tossing in the wind, her skirts picking up burrs and dead dandelion spores. She loved that missionary, and Sicily and Pearl had thrown away his letters. Had thrown away all the secrets of her life. Because there must have been important clues there, Pearl knew. If they had only known it at the time. Had known where to look. Pearl had read how archaeologists could dig up cities thousands of years old and tell all sorts of things about the people just from what they ate, what they wore, how they set about housekeeping. And she and Sicily had opened their own sister's trunk, only a few years old, and had seen *nothing*. Now here she was herself, on the threshold of being the owner of a trunk of items that held more interest to moths, and spiders, and the inching dampness of rot, than to her grandchildren.

Pearl packed the McKinnon family scrapbook, its back broken from bending, its pages loosening like wings. Family members, *flown into death*. She took Junior's bronzed baby shoes. Maybe he hadn't turned into the most perfect son. She would admit that. But why should she forfeit those early years of waking in the night, of standing over his bed, sometimes for hours, watching his tiny red upper lip blowing outward with the small pop of his sleeping breath. What a beautiful child he had been, and what a precious thing to own this creature. How had the reverend gone off and left three of these soft, darling things behind?

"He loves the flock," Marge had said once, of the reverend, after he was gone. "He loves the damn flock, but he has no need for the lamb."

Pearl packed the engagement ring she had not worn in years. Her finger had grown too large for it. The wedding band was let out to accommodate the growth of her finger. A jeweler had enlarged it for her. But the engagement ring, like the virgin it truly represented, was left untouched. Its little stone sang out as Pearl held it up to the light so that the facets could catch fire.

"How tiny it is," she thought. Had it shrunken with age? Had it shriveled up the way old people do, until one day there's just a dusty outline left? Or if she had stayed in Mattagash, where things were kept safe from their tininess, would the ring loom larger than ever? This was true of small towns. Things are big there. And you are sheltered from the oddities of foreign cities and phrases, from menus you can't read, from wines you can't pronounce. You're protected from fancy tables where there are no paper napkins, but linen ones you're reluctant to soil in case someone's mother has to wash them. You're saved from silverware around your plate, enough for a whole family, but it's all for you, and you struggle with which fork to use first. Which wine with fish? How much tip? Oh, the questions involved in just trying to get something to eat when you leave a small town and move up in the world! *When? Where? To what extent? How often?* The horrible adverbs of the city. Yes, a small town is safe enough for some things, but if you make a mistake there, a mistake that might otherwise be lost in the casual rush hour of the city, it will follow you around a small town all your life, like an unrepentant dog.

Pearl packed the grandchildren's most recent pictures. They might not be perfect either, these children, but they had not asked to be born. And for that, surely, they could be forgiven some things. She stared a minute at the wedding picture of her only son and his bride, Thelma Parsons. Pearl left it on her dresser where it had been since the day Thelma excitedly gave it to her. Pearl left the picture where it had stood all those years. She was still in the city, after all, and while in the city she *could* put some unrepentant dogs to sleep. This was one mistake she didn't want following her back to Mattagash, nipping at her heels.

She did pack clothing, but they weren't special clothes. There were no "Look at me, I've gone off to the city" clothes. No silk blouses, no fancy dresses. No things that would tear easily if you were planting in the spring earth. She packed none of the impractical clothes that Mattagashers wouldn't even wear on a Sunday. Mattagash saw those clothes differently than the wearer did. Mattagash saw them as "Look at her come home from the city and who the hell does she think she is?" clothes. Pearl had been a victim of that kind of dressing. Sometimes you can't help wanting a pat on the back from your heritage, and when one doesn't come, well then, some ex-Mattagashers dress themselves up a bit too fancy, and they vacation in Mattagash with accents they've borrowed from the city. Pearl knew. She'd done it herself. But after a while you're gone from the small town longer than you've ever lived there. Gone a lifetime. And then you realize one morning that there's no more pretense. Your accent *has* changed. Your style of dressing *has* changed. Your taste in food *has* changed. You find out, quite suddenly, that you're the genuine article. The real McCoy. And there's no backtracking. You're gone for good. You're caught between two worlds now because Mattagash will never accept you as the genuine article. They remember you from the day you were first born. They remember you without silk clothing. They've seen you in the buff.

"Well, I'm going home anyway," Pearl answered her own train

of thought. And she believed she'd have the good fortune to go home alone. The way she'd left years ago. On a Greyhound bus with its cold nose pointed toward adventure. Maybe she could *retrace* her path, if she tried.

"I'd go back to when it was just me and Margie and Sicily, finding Orion in the sky, and making snowhouses for fairies. The year Daddy left for China. The best year of my life. I'd go straight back to a soft September day in 1922. I'd go back to the first leaves of autumn falling."

But very modern footfalls stepped upon the crinkly leaves of 1922 and mashed them well when Marvin announced that he would drive his wife back to her birthplace. To the old McKinnon breeding grounds.

"You're as bad as them salmon I've read about," Marvin said.

"But you hate Mattagash," Pearl protested. "You know you do. And what about business?"

"I'm worried about you, Pearly," Marvin had said as he left for the office, the calfskin briefcase obediently in tow. "And business is so slow Randy could handle it, for Chrissakes. Just kidding," he added, when he saw Pearl's utter consternation. "I wouldn't leave Randy alone with a house*plant*, much less a *guest*."

Good Lord. Did Marvin actually notice when things had risen up inside Pearl's emotions and refused to settle back down? Was there an understanding there all those years that she had overlooked? Or was it something else? Was it something akin to how the crows start up before a storm? Or how rabbits sense the earthquake in their feet? Did Marvin look at her the way you look at a good gold watch, one that's not been keeping accurate time lately, one that's been squandering seconds and minutes? Yet if you took it apart for a look inside, all you would see would be whirling, complicated mechanisms that meant nothing to you, and you would be very, very sorry you pried in the first place.

"Bless him," thought Pearl. "He tries."

Once in Mattagash, Pearl would announce her need to stay on at the old McKinnon homestead for a time. "At least for a while," she would tell Marvin. "I want to walk in that blue vetch, that cow's vetch that fills the back field. I want to lie awake to the noisy river. I want to find holes drilled in the birches and catch the sapsucker at it. It might be a pile of bones to you, Marvin, and to Junior and the kids, that old house might be. But even elephants have got a place to go. Even dogs can find the right field to die in." She would tell him all that. Sort of. She'd probably leave out the part about the cow's vetch and the birches and sapsuckers. Men weren't much for poetry. Not even men from Portland, Maine. And it wasn't dying she was going home to achieve. At least not in the flesh. But the spirit was ready, like some beaten, misunderstood snake straight out of the reverend's Genesis, to shed sixty years of old skin.

"Absolutely *not*," Pearl told Marvin, when he went on to say that Junior, Thelma, and Randy would be going, too. "Not one inch will I drive with Thelma," Pearl threatened. And she meant it. "You remember the last trip north we took with her. We ended up in a clover field."

"That was better than the river," said Marvin.

"Yes," said Pearl. "You're right about that. But the only reason we *didn't* end up in the river is that Thelma is not real good at wrecking cars. She's not real good at anything."

"Well," said Marvin. "I'll tell you one thing, Pearly. I'm real worried about this family. Whether you want to admit it or not, the truth is that we've got to get Junior away from that secretary."

"What secretary?" asked Junior's mom.

"Come on, Pearly," said Marvin, and smiled. Pearl was almost girlish when she coyly took Junior's side. "First of all, I'm gonna fire Monique Tessier. I was hoping this little infatuation would run its course but it doesn't look like it will. I don't want that woman to step one step back inside my funeral home, unless it's as a houseguest. Houseguests are always welcome." Pearl grimaced. Must he always consider business?·

"I know that Thelma, and this is putting aside what you think of her, Pearly," Marvin continued, "needs a good rest away from here."

"How about Bangor?" Pearl asked. "How about a week at the nuthouse?"

"I see a lot more than you do, Pearl. I work with Junior and, God help me, Randy too. I overhear the employee gossip. Thelma's been taking a lot of some prescription drug. She's wired up most of the time."

"She was wired up when he married her," Pearl muttered. She remembered how silly Thelma had been on her wedding day. She had giggled aloud when it was time for her to say "I do," and later, at the reception, she had dropped wedding cake all over the floor and thrown a bridesmaid's bouquet instead of her own.

"A real little hamster," Pearl remembered thinking of her newly acquired daughter-in-law.

"And Randy can't be left alone. You know that. We'll have to take him along. Maybe it's time we started pulling together as a family, Pearly," Marvin offered gently. "It doesn't matter what the occasion is, really. I don't care if Amy Joy is getting married or divorced. I don't care if she just got out of jail and they're throwing a big welcome-home party for her. What matters is us. The Ivys." He squeezed Pearl's hand. "Come on, Pearly," he said again, with great verve. This wasn't like him at all. Something had jarred him out of his complacency. So he recognized, did he, that his good old watch, his forty-years-of-marriage gold watch, was losing some costly seconds. Was ticking like a live bomb.

"Junior says the girls don't want to go," Marvin added. "He says they both hate Amy Joy." Well. At least Pearl wouldn't have to watch Cynthia Jane tug at her crotch for eight hours, one way, to Mattagash.

"Not in the same car," Pearl said finally, and meant it. "I *will not* ride in the same car with her."

"All right," said Marvin. He had anticipated this reply. "We'll separate, then. Junior can take his own car, and we'll take the company car. I'll deduct it as a business trip. You know I've been wanting to check out that funeral home in Watertown. The one that's for sale."

"The one you were going to buy and set Junior up in?" Pearl asked meekly. What a strange reversal of feelings! When Marvin had first suggested this business expansion idea, just last Christmas, Pearl was all against it. She hadn't liked the notion of Junior being so far away from Portland. From her. Now that these homecoming notions had sprouted inside her and she secretly planned to stay on in Mattagash, she didn't want Junior and his family in Watertown because they would be too close.

"Junior needs to get his rabbit raisins counted, if he expects me to buy him his own damn business," Marvin snapped, forgetting his recently uttered words, now deceased, about families pulling together.

Pearl thought it all over quickly. Two cars. Thelma in one. She in another.

"Okay," she said.

"That's my Pearly!" said Marvin. "That's my girl."

"To hear Sicily talk about the wedding," Pearl said, changing the subject, "maybe it would be better if Amy Joy *was* just getting out of jail."

♦   ♦   ♦

Thelma, on the other hand, packed everything, including her fox stole.

"Good Christ," said Junior when he saw the fox's head hanging languidly from the suitcase. "You can't wear that in Mattagash! People will be shooting at you!"

"Let them, then," said Thelma sharply, and packed a stapler.

Randy refused to go. He had grown to love his job of sitting in the coffee room, eating doughnuts, and keeping his mouth shut. All for sixty-eight fifty a week. His grandfather had even noticed, much to his own pleasure, that Randy had been taking a Bible to work every day. What Marvin did not notice was that the Bible was slimming down daily. The Bible was imploding, as though some biblical censor were at work, scratching out the ancient sex scenes and all that unnecessary violence.

"I don't want to go, and I'm afraid *that's it!*" Randy told Junior.

"Them people are real hicks. It's like driving to the Lost Continent. Forget it, man."

"No," said Junior, maneuvering his belly straight in front of him in case they came to blows. That way the belly could serve as inflatable protection, the kind they were talking about putting into cars soon. "No, you've got it all wrong," Junior said. "It's not a case of 'Forget it, man.' It's a case of 'Forget it, Randy.' Now you go upstairs and pack, and I mean only things that are legal."

"Balls," said Randy. He stared threateningly into Junior's eyes. He was almost as tall now, though nowhere near as hefty. Yet it was a most frightening thought for Junior. "This is my little boy," he thought, and his eyes misted. "This is the kid on the rocking horse." He was relieved when Randy relented, for he had no idea what he'd have done otherwise.

"Lord love a duck," said Thelma, as Randy stomped every step down the hallway to his room. "Are you packing *those?*"

"What?" asked Junior, and stared down at his hands. They held only the most essential items of underwear, neatly folded, fruits of the proverbial loom. He was notorious for packing only what he needed. An army packer, his own mother called him. He glanced quickly, a small peek so as not to rile her, at Thelma's burgeoning suitcase. A large sewing basket teetered on top of Thelma's Wooly Bully Bear from childhood. Junior would let the teddy bear pass, chalking it up to Thelma's lifelong insecurity. But did she think there were no needles or thread to be found in all of Mattagash? Well, maybe there weren't. But that still didn't explain the stapler. Or the flashlight. He looked again at the innocent accoutrements in his hand.

"Why?" he asked cautiously.

"Oh, nothing," Thelma chirped. "Lord love the helpless, is all."

◆　　◆　　◆

Monique Tessier didn't take the firing lying down. At least, she and Junior were not in bed when he told her. They were sitting in her old Buick in the parking lot at the new IGA where they would be lost in a sea of cars. Monique's cleavage, legendary back at Wally's Service Station, where she usually tanked up and then checked her own oil, was now relaxing inside a buttoned-to-the-throat blouse. Junior was relieved. It would make the job less difficult.

"I'm sorry, babe," Junior said, and watched a shopper load her groceries into the trunk of a car in front of them, then send her shopping cart reeling in the direction of the little station where the other carts were corralled. So *that* was how carts wound up wandering aimlessly about the parking lot, annoying customers and looking generally homeless as dogs. Junior resented this. He had always taken the time to waltz his own cart back to its station. How dare this woman! He was about to comment to Monique about the rudeness of some shoppers but she stopped him.

"That motherless son of a bitch," Monique said, and slapped the steering wheel.

"Aw, Neeky, come on now," said Junior, and tossed an arm around her shoulder.

"Don't you Neeky me," she said.

"All right," said Junior. "Monique."

"Why didn't he have the balls to tell me himself?" she asked.

"Look, all I know is that he called me in, told me he knew what was going on, and said it was time I put an end to it."

"What did he say?" asked Monique. "How did he say it?"

"How?" asked Junior. Monique nodded.

"Word for word," she said. "And don't lie to me."

"He said, 'It's time for you to fire the bitch.' " Junior spoke quickly, then grimaced.

"That spineless little *corpse lover*," Monique snarled.

"Now, now. Come on, Neeky. Remember that it's my job you're talking about, too," Junior whined.

"That no-good *grave robber*," Neeky went on.

"Look, this doesn't mean we can't still meet occasionally, sweetheart. We'll have even more freedom now." Junior spied another shopper about to hurl her shopping cart out into the swirl of things. What the hell is it about these women shoppers, he wondered. Are they so pissed about conditions at home that they willfully

abuse the IGA's property? Male shoppers would be different. Junior knew damn well that if someone took a poll they would discover
that at least 95 percent of all men parked their shopping carts in
the rightful spot, and with the same care they took in parking their
own cars in garages.

"That *bone sucker*," said Monique, tearfully.

"I think that's enough," said Junior.

"It's just," Monique sobbed, "what am I going to do? I got
payments, Junie. I got an overdose of bills."

"He's giving you two weeks' severance pay," said Junie.

"That's not the point. Where do I go about getting another job?
After me and Tony got divorced this is the only job I've had. My
only experience. How is that going to look on a résumé? Two years
at Corpse City." Monique began to sob a bit.

"I really wish you'd watch what you say," said Junior, and focused
his concentration on a group of pigeons pecking away at some
littered food.

Monique blew her nose and inspected her face in the mirror.
Lipstick came out of the purse and went to work immediately. A
comb was employed. She looked like her old self, but she was still
seething. She really had hoped Junior would divorce squirrelly
little Thelma and marry her. Everyone knew the Ivys were swimming in money, and the funeral parlor business wasn't like Hula
Hoop, Inc. It would be around as long as there were people around.
Once married, Monique would never have to darken a single door
at that god-awful place. She would have long leisurely lunches with
her friends, both male and female. She would have her nails done
weekly at Très Nails!, and she would open accounts with the very
best Portland stores. K-mart would not see her face again. Junior
would see it rarely. Now look what had happened. The old fart.
She had underestimated him.

But then, he had underestimated her, too. She was not done
with the funeral parlor, yes, goddamn it, *PARLOR*, by a long shot.

"Junie?" she cooed. "June Junes?"

Junior had, in the few seconds' silence between them, watched
three more women careen their carts out across the parking lot

rather than park them! They were throwing carts about the place like the aluminum in old gum wrappers. Sweet Jesus Christ! Were they *all* on Valium? Was it a goddamn big conspiracy that men had no idea was going on unless they sat for an hour in the parking lot? What did those lanky bitches think they had there? Bumper cars, for Chrissakes?

"Junie, take me to Mattagash with you."

Junior forgot all about the brainstorm he had just had for Valet Cart Parking, an idea he pondered on selling to the IGA, when he heard Monique's latest utterance.

"You can't be serious!" he all but shouted. "To my cousin's wedding?"

"Of course I'm serious," Monique snapped. "Why should *I* have to stay home when *she* can go?"

"Because. That's why. What would you do in Mattagash? What would people say?"

"They wouldn't have to know."

"Monique, you've never *been* to Mattagash. Believe me. *Everyone* would know."

"But how? I promise I'll lay low," Monique said, as she playfully tugged at Junior's tie.

"Lay low? In Mattagash? Do you even realize what you're saying? There's no place to lay low in! D-Day would have flopped in Mattagash. It's a regular hotbed of communications. Forget it."

Monique pouted heavily, her red lips pursing out to twice their normal size. She would not let go this easily. Not on the old fart's life, she wouldn't. She had invested too many months to bow out gracefully. Big fat tears rolled easily out of their ducts and splattered her cheeks. Junior was aghast when he saw them.

"Oh, babe," he said. "Cutie pie. Don't. Now come on. Be realistic. I'll take you to Boston when I get back. Maybe we can even spend the night there. In Boston a person can lay low."

Monique howled. All the facial repair work she'd done earlier was washed away in the April freshet that cascaded down her face.

"No, I'm sorry," said Junior, and patted her. "Cry if you want to, but when it comes to this, the answer is no. *N. O.*"

Monique halted her tears. What was this? A *man* denying her something? Holy shit! Was that what she could expect from her forties, only two years away? A goddamn no-good *undertaker* telling her no, and then spelling it for her? Well, we'd see. We'd just see.

THE FIRST TIME

FOR SECOND THOUGHTS: AMY JOY

INHERITS SOME ART

....

"I can't help but get sentimental about weddings. After all, a man only gets married three or four times in his life."

—Irving V. Gifford, to his cellmate,
after reading a letter from home

AMY JOY LAID HER HEAD BACK ON JEAN CLOUTIER'S SHOULDER and listened to the music that was winging on invisible waves all the way up from WPTR in Boston. It was an unusual thing, this notion of unseen forces penetrating one's mind. Maybe ancestors could do that, too. Could send out messages to you, down the years, over centuries and lifestyles. But if that were so, Amy Joy's ancestors would be telling her *not* to marry this young French-speaking Catholic. At least according to Sicily, the ancestors would be highly peeved to be dug up and informed of the wedding.

"They're not rolling over in their graves," she told Amy Joy plaintively. "They're *spinning*."

The bright red Chevy super sport was parked in the darkness below Sicily's house, its nose pointed over the hill at the Mattagash River. The April night engulfed them, a lingering chill still in the air. But Amy Joy wanted the windows rolled down, and they were. The Mattagash, high with its April load of water, thundered along in front of them. Old Man River was what Amy Joy called it. Old Man Mattagash River.

"Woman, oooooooh Woman," Gary Puckett asked all the way from WPTR. " 'Have you got cheating on your mind?' "

"Putois?" asked Jean Claude, pensively.

"What?" Amy Joy leaned toward him and bit the lobe of his ear gently.

"Chalice!" said Jean Claude, and jumped. "Cut dat out! It gives me tickle, me."

"It gives you what, *you*?" Amy Joy teased him. The French teacher at Mattagash High School, who lasted just a half year since Amy Joy and one other boy were the only Mattagashers interested in learning French, had told her that French-speaking people talk this way because that's how they actually speak in their own language. "They repeat the pronoun," he had said, and from then on Amy Joy didn't laugh to hear this done.

"Putois?"

"What?" No biting this time.

"Do you tink dat your mudder she'll be hokay, her?"

"She'll be fine," Amy Joy said. She was still angry at Sicily for her behavior earlier in the evening.

"Is it true that Catholics burn their dead?" Sicily had asked Jean Claude.

"How can you be so *stupid*?" Amy Joy snapped.

"Well, I'd hate to see my future grandchildren go up in smoke one day," Sicily had defended herself. "That's the only reason I ask."

"I hope she begin to like me some, her," Jean said, and let his fingers intertwine with Amy Joy's.

"You're marrying *me,* Jean Claude," said Amy Joy. "You're not marrying *her.*"

"Holy Shit de Tabernacle!" said Jean Claude. Just the thought of marrying his future mother-in-law caused such a rush of adrenaline that his English quickly co-mingled with his French, a habit among his generation.

"Ta-barn-nack is right," said Amy Joy, and flung her head back on the seat for Jean Claude to kiss her. He pushed his tongue deep into her mouth, in search of hers.

"Talk about *French*-kissing," thought Amy Joy, and let the blessed smell of Old Spice send her reeling.

A curtain panel moved gently in the kitchen window, overlooking the scene in the super sport. It moved gently enough that human breath could have propelled it. However, it was not Sicily's breath but the pinkish nail of her index finger that separated the curtain panels and gave her a ringside seat. What were they doing out there in the cool night?

"She's worse than an old tomcat," Sicily said, and her own tomcat, Buster, left off his tedious licking to listen to her words. Sicily let the curtain flap back in place and plugged in the teakettle. It quickly began to hiss. A nice cup of tea would help greatly to settle her nerves. Ed used to be irked when Sicily called it a *nice* cup of tea.

"What the hell is a *nice* cup of tea?" he would demand. "How would it be different from all other cups of tea? Do you realize that in over twenty-five years of marriage I've never known you to drink a cup of tea that wasn't a goddamn *nice* cup of tea?" Oh, he could be upset at the silliest things. Sicily hoped that it wasn't hearing her state one time too many that she was having a nice cup of tea that sent him down to the grammar school to plant a bullet in his brain. She shuddered. She missed Ed greatly, but she had come to realize that what she missed most was the common ground they shared. She had long gone past any romantic elements and prevailed instead upon the companionship in their relationship. That happens sometimes. Most times, in fact. Sicily was no fool. She'd seen enough marriages in her day to take note. There comes a time when the honeymoon is over and the preacher's words ring true as bells. *Until death do you part.*

"Death from boredom," Winnie Craft said one time to Sicily, about her own marriage to Fred Craft, and the two had laughed heartily. It was probably true of city folk as well. Men and women have a tendency to settle in with one another like old oaks, too well rooted, too stubborn to transplant.

"Instead, they keep a close eye on the acorn," Sicily said, and lifted the curtain panel one more time. She let it flop back quickly. The interior light had burst on suddenly in the super sport and Sicily could see Amy Joy gathering up her sweater and her purse and giving that Frog a good-night kiss. She had been bringing him in, right into their house, every chance she had since she announced her plans. And she expected Sicily to talk to him!

"But I can't understand a single thing he says," Sicily had protested just that morning, when Amy Joy had shamed her for her manners. "I'd talk to him if I *could*. Of course I would." Well now she was talking, all right. Now she was asking him important theological questions about Catholic cremation rituals. See how Amy Joy liked them apples.

When Sicily heard the front door slam she pretended to be busy with her teacup, and saucer, and spoon. Amy Joy came into the kitchen and draped her sweater about a chair.

"Hi," she said.

"Oh, hi there," Sicily answered, and her cup rattled dramatically on its saucer.

"Making tea?" Amy Joy asked. Sicily heard that little ring of sarcasm known so well to mothers.

"Of course I'm making tea," she said tartly. "Why else would I be out here in the kitchen?" Amy Joy smiled that little smile, also well known to mothers, and then went to browse in the cupboard. Sicily dunked her tea bag slowly as she took a quick inventory of her daughter. Amy Joy was looking slimmer by the day. Gone was the plumpness of childhood upon which Chester Lee Gifford had so cleverly hitched his wagon. If Sicily could just snuff out the marriage plans, maybe one day she could even convince Amy Joy to have that Pepsi bottle surgically removed from her right hand.

Amy Joy took a can of whole-kernel corn from the pantry and opened it. She put it in a pan to heat.

"She'll eat that with one slice of bread and butter," Sicily told herself. "She's done that since childhood. She's had her one slice of bread and butter before bed. Except *I* used to butter it for her, and then cut it into four squares, and she used to munch the squares slowly, one at a time, counterclockwise. But she used to drink milk back then, not Pepsi."

"Where's Puppy?" Amy Joy asked, of the family's large dog.

"I don't know," said Sicily. "If he's not on the sofa, I don't think he come in yet. Why?"

"Oh, nothing," said Amy Joy. "It's just that I thought I saw him peeking out of the kitchen window just a few minutes ago."

Sicily bristled. The little ingrate. She ought to take her right now, across her knee, and let her have a good old-fashioned Scotch-Irish licking. A Protestant one at that. Sicily hadn't had the opportunity to know her own mother. Grace McKinnon had died a few days after giving Sicily birth. *She died of birth*, is how the old-timers described the malady. Sicily had always hated to hear this fact conveyed, as it had been over the years. *Died giving Sicily birth.* It was not an easy fact to live with. It was the word *giving* that bothered her most of all. As if the *giving* of birth meant a *taking* as well. As if, by being *given* life, Sicily had *taken* life. Her mother's as well as her own. But if Sicily had known her mother, she would have obeyed her and respected her, that was for sure.

"I wish I'd had a mother myself," Sicily said to Amy Joy. "I would to this day give my eyeteeth for the opportunity to have a mother of my own." Then she spun on her heels, her nice cup of tea in hand, and went off up the stairs to bed.

"Only dogs have eyeteeth," Amy Joy muttered, and dished her warm corn into a bowl. She buttered one slice of bread and cut it into four squares. Sicily used to do that for her. It was her midnight snack when she was a child. And she'd kicked her legs happily beneath the kitchen table, long after Sicily had crawled back into bed beside Ed. She'd dangled her legs and pretended that each square was a field of yellow hay, like the ones around the house.

"I've eaten a lot of hay in my lifetime," Amy Joy thought, as she ate the first two squares, counterclockwise. She was suddenly remorseful for tricking Sicily into the joke about spying out the window. The truth was, Amy Joy was lonely for her mother's company. Sometimes, at least before the betrothal, they had been more like friends, playing dominoes until after midnight, doing crossword puzzles from the *Bangor Daily*. Sometimes Sicily surprised Amy Joy with what she remembered from school. Puzzle words like *tine* and *supple*. Old-fashioned words that Amy Joy had never heard before. There were many good things about Sicily that Amy Joy would miss. A quickening of heartbeats pounded in her chest.

"I'll be leaving here soon," she told herself. "I'll be leaving my childhood home forever." Breathing was difficult, and Amy Joy reminded herself to breathe slowly to avoid hyperventilation. It was a horrible thing to want to leave, to desire to go off and test the new places of the world, even if they were in Watertown. And it was another thing to want to stay. It was an emotional tugging, this going-out-on-one's-own business.

Amy Joy heard Sicily stomping heavily upstairs. The bathroom door slammed and, minutes later, Sicily's own bedroom door.

"She's pretty keyed up for a woman who's only got a few weeks left to live," Amy Joy said to Buster the cat, who was begging for crumbs. She left a square of field uneaten, for the first time since she could remember. Only a serious illness had caused such things before. The truth was, and Amy Joy had to admit it, she was having second thoughts. Or *tots*. Whatever they were, in whatever language. She would even like to tell Sicily of them, to ask her advice, but she knew she couldn't.

Amy Joy knocked quietly on Sicily's door. It was ajar, so she pushed it open at the sound of her mother's voice.

"I just came in to say good night," said Amy Joy, and flung herself onto the bed next to Sicily. Her mother was reading, and quickly slid the book under a pillow. Amy Joy waited for the right second and then whisked her hand in after it. As Sicily fought to wrench the book from her, Amy Joy held it high and read aloud, *"Troublesome Teenagers: The Key to Discipline."* She hooted wildly as Sicily fought harder for the book. " 'By Dr. Rosalind K. Wooster. Child Analyst and Mother of Five'! Oh God, I'm not a teenager."

Sicily fetched the book back to safety under her pillow.

"Nevertheless," said Sicily, and smoothed the blankets over her. Amy Joy laid her head on Sicily's shoulder.

"What's different in here?" she asked.

"Different how?"

"I don't know," said Amy Joy. "But there's something different."

"Well, you tell me," said Sicily, and tried not to notice the silver streaks in her daughter's hair. They lay side by side in silence.

"I miss you," said Amy Joy.

"I miss you, too," said Sicily.

"And I miss Daddy."

"Me, too."

"Can we be friends?"

"Will you cancel the wedding?"

"Okay. Let's stay enemies."

"Amy Joy, your trouble is that you've always been too head-strong. I just wish you'd take things slow is all," said Sicily, and discovered to her horror that she'd been lovingly twirling one of Amy Joy's awful silver strips around her own finger. She let it loose.

"What is different about this room?" Amy Joy asked again.

"Honey, you must be imagining things," Sicily said, and smiled. "Remember when you thought the troll from the Billy Goats Gruff story lived in the flush? You peed standing up for weeks. Your father said people at school were gonna think you were a boy."

"What's that?" asked Amy Joy, and pointed at a beautifully wrapped box sitting on the floor under Sicily's bedroom window. The occasion paper was definitely wedding. Small bride-and-groom couples smiled happily from all over the box. The bow was magnificent. Sicily was an artist when it came to gift wrapping. Amy Joy was aghast. Her mother was coming around.

"Is that for me?" she asked Sicily, and Sicily nodded. Amy Joy hugged her. She had always known that if she was firm with Sicily things would work out. What had she bought them? The box was fairly large. How sweet. How very, very precious. She cuddled up to Sicily and planted a small kiss on her mother's hand.

"You can be the sweetest thing when you want to," she said.

"So can you," said Sicily, and hugged back.

"But why did you black the teeth out on the groom?" Amy Joy asked.

"I was just doodling, dear," Sicily lied. "Are you cold?"

"Affirmative," said Amy Joy.

Sicily had lifted her window two inches to let in a bit of April's balminess. She had covered the bed with an extra blanket. April's nights were most welcome after the winter, but they were terribly chilly. There was still snow in the deep woods and along the edges of the trees. Sicily liked to sleep cold. The heavy pressing of an extra blanket soothed her. She pulled it up over Amy Joy as well and thought how nice it would be if her little girl, the one who ate a slice of bread and butter every night, would fall asleep there in the bed beside her. The big bed had seemed large as a boat lately, what with Amy Joy's insane wedding plans. Sicily was about to suggest that Amy Joy hoist off her boots and jeans, and slip into bed with her. Spend a loving mother-daughter night, the way they used to all those times Amy Joy was afraid of the dark.

Amy Joy opened one eye slowly and focused on the wall near her mother's bed. The other eye opened. They stared hard at the bare space that virtually hung there, as though someone had tacked it up.

"Damn her," thought Amy Joy.

"What is it, dear?" Sicily asked her daughter. Amy Joy sat up and threw off the extra blanket.

"I've just realized what is missing in this room," she said.

"Oh?" asked Sicily, and seemed to drift farther back, into the downiness of her pillow.

"Thank you for giving me Aunt Marge's old painting of Jesus and that awful lamb, which I dearly hate, for my wedding gift," Amy Joy told her mother.

"You're welcome, sweetheart," Sicily said, and pulled the extra blanket back up about her. "Don't mention it."

"Oh, I won't," said Amy Joy, disappearing from Sicily's bedroom. "Nor will I forget it."

WOMANHOOD SLAPS PRISSY IN THE FACE: LITTLE VINAL GOES FISHING TWICE

....

"We'll flip a coin. If I win, *you'll* drink of the pint of hooch. Then I'll take the hatchet and, *snip*, before you know it, it'll be gone. Come on, Vinal. You don't use that little finger for anything but picking your nose."

—Pike Gifford, on whether he and his brother should take out some accident insurance

PIKE GIFFORD'S BROOD OF CHILDREN GATHERED NOISILY AROUND the large Formica breakfast table with the wobbly aluminum legs and grabbed toast off the plate faster than Goldie could pop it from the four-slice toaster. "A four-seater" is how Pike Gifford referred to the appliance. When the last Cheerios bowl was empty, the last toast lying soggy and unwanted on the plate, Goldie sat back with a cup of Taster's Choice to relax. The morning breakfast was over well ahead of time. Usually the school bus was out in the dooryard honking itself silly while the kids were still stuffing doughnuts into their mouths, digging under the sofa for papers and books, searching for a mitten or shoe. Spring must have had a hand in getting everyone up on time. There must have been something in the April air that blew in under the blankets when the alarm clock rattled the sleepers awake.

"I even got time to finish my homework," said Missy, aged nine, the smartest of Goldie's six children. The oldest girl, Irma, had already quit school to begin her job in Watertown, at the well-respected cash register of J. C. Penney's. The baby, Miltie, aged seven, was now in the first grade. Hodge, the shy one among the children, had just turned ten. With Little Pee past eleven, and Priscilla now thirteen, Goldie could envision a future without children. She could possibly land a job at one of the sewing machines at Stitches Incorporated in Watertown. Maybe she would even take an adult education course. Let Vera say she was uppity. Goldie would do just what she wanted when the children were gone.

Goldie sipped her coffee at the kitchen table where Missy was busy ciphering math problems. The coffee was a well-earned treat, but the price of it was getting higher and higher. Goldie feared the day might come when she would have to give it up entirely. Lord God in heaven, what would school mornings be like if there was no coffee waiting for her after it was over?

"I heard a coffee analyst talking on the news yesterday," Goldie said loudly to Pike. He was still sprawled on the living room sofa where he had fallen asleep the night before. "He said that from a political point of view it's good for the U.S.A. to support higher prices because it helps out countries like Brazil and the Ivory Coast." Goldie took a long breath. Pike closed his eyes tightly and wished Goldie would choke on her coffee, regardless of how much it cost. What in hell was a coffee analyst, anyway? If someone who simply pondered the consequences of coffee could be called an analyst, well then, Pike Gifford was a lot better off than he imagined. Once, when a welfare worker had asked Pike Gifford his occupation, he rolled over on his side on the sofa and said "television viewer." Well, he had moved up in the world, by Jesus. Now he was *hubcap analyst*.

Quite frankly, Goldie embarrassed him, especially when she made such highfalutin speeches in front of Vinal and others. "She says that she's trying to expand her mind," Pike had red-facedly told Vinal once, minutes after Goldie had gone on and on about how great Lyndon Johnson had been for the highways in the country, those busy roads she would most likely never see in her lifetime.

"That's perfectly all right," Vinal had told his little brother, and then patted him on the back sympathetically. "You're still better off than I am. The only thing Vera's expanding is her ass."

"It seems that Brazil and the Ivory Coast are having foreign debt problems," Goldie now explained to Pike.

"Oh, I see," said Pike. "What a shame. What a goddamn pity. And here I've been, up here in northern Maine, enjoying myself in spite of it all." God, that woman wore him out. He hadn't even swung his legs off the sofa to begin the day and he was already completely exhausted. And the herd of cattle that came down the stairs every morning for breakfast was not exactly a lullaby to his ears. He usually had one beer or a slug of cheap vodka too many to climb the long stairs up to his and Goldie's bedroom. Once in a blue moon he stayed sober enough to make love to his wife. Or he caught her early in the day, before the kids got home, and let her remember what it was she saw in him in the first place. When warmer weather arrived he would just sleep on the soft seat of the old Ford pickup, hiked up on wooden blocks below the garage. The whole family could tear the house down and be damned. He would never hear them. He wouldn't even be dreaming of them.

"And why should we give a damn about countries in Europe?" Pike asked. He sat up on the sofa and rubbed the residue from the corners of his eyes—his morning bath. "Let them pay their own goddamn bills and keep to hell away from our coffee," he added.

Missy folded her paper and stuffed it inside her math book.

"Stupid," she said. "Brazil and the Ivory Coast ain't in Europe. That's all *you* know."

Pike stared at his daughter with hard, early morning eyes. She was getting more and more like her mother every day. Goldie was even encouraging this one to finish high school.

"You read too damn much," Pike said, and pointed a finger directly at Missy. "You just remember, one day when it's too late, that I told you so."

"Did you go to school, Daddy?" Missy asked haughtily. "I bet you didn't even get past kindergarten."

"You're wrong there," Pike said, and wished suddenly for a cup of that Brazilian coffee. "I went all the way to where the two men was fighting in the book." Missy and Goldie both laughed at this, but it was true. Sometimes Pike Gifford dreamed of those burly men in that old fifth-grade primer. Sometimes he was even tempted to go back to school, just to see who won.

But education was not to be the major issue on this glorious spring day, not if Little Vinal Gifford had his way. With the birds chirping noisily and the buds almost popping on the trees, Little Vinal decided it was the perfect time to avenge himself for the manhandling of his bicycle.

Priscilla came home from school early, in tears and a torn dress. One of the teachers drove her up the long hill and then helped her climb the rickety front steps to where she folded herself in Goldie's warm arms.

"Little Vinal threw me on the ground behind the schoolhouse," she sobbed as Goldie cradled her, "and said he was going to give me a baby."

"Oh my God!" screamed Goldie. "Did he do anything to her?" she asked the teacher, who shook her head.

"What did he say to you?" Goldie asked her daughter.

"He said," Priscilla sobbed as she primped her ponytail back into place, "that he was gonna make a real woman out of me."

Goldie hit the ceiling. Since Pike had driven to Watertown to sell a spare chain saw that had suddenly come into his possession, she took the matter into her own hands. Besides, she was good and tired of the manner in which Pike settled family matters. First, she phoned the sheriff in St. Leonard, and then the principal of the Mattagash Grammar School. Before Pike came home in the evening with seventy-five dollars snug in his pocket, Little Vinal had been expelled from school for two weeks, thanks to a principal who agreed with Goldie that thirteen was too young to become a real woman. The issue was out of Pike's hands. It was a school matter. But Pike told the sheriff from St. Leonard to let snarling dogs go back to sleep.

Vera accused Goldie the next day, over the phone, of ruining Little Vinal's academic future. She was talking to her sister and Goldie was rubbering in. Priscilla, who had stayed home from school, was behind Goldie's shoulder, pressing an ear in close to the receiver. She was, after all, the subject of the present skirmish.

"He's refusing to step another step inside a school building," Vera told her sister.

When Goldie dialed her own sister, just a half hour later, she said, "We needn't worry about Little Vinal. When a twelve-year-old has hair on his lip and is still in the sixth grade, you ain't exactly losing a Shakespeare. When a kid has to sit on a special chair because the desks are all too small, there ain't no Albert Einstein going down the drain." When Goldie heard Vera's angry intake of breath on the line, she was pleased.

"It's poor little Priscilla that I feel sorry for," Goldie went on. "She sat up in the middle of the night last night and screamed her head off. And she'd only watched a rerun of *My Three Sons* before she went to bed. But even Fred McMurray scares her now. I tell you, she's a changed child."

Vera hung up with a loud click. If Priscilla was a changed child, it could only be for the better. She turned to Little Vinal, who was eating a ketchup sandwich and drinking an orange pop.

"Who does she think Priscilla is? The Flying Nun?" Vera asked of no one in particular. There was only Little Vinal, who was sitting at the kitchen table, eating his sandwich, happy with his sabbatical. And the gray cat, Tinkerbell, slinking about the boy's feet, waiting for a crumb to fall, if even from a ketchup sandwich.

"Molly tells me that Priscilla goes into the girls' bathroom and stuffs bobby socks into her bra," Vera said.

As if in answer to his mother's statement, Little Vinal kicked

Tinkerbell, suddenly and with such violence that the cat slid on its side several feet across the kitchen floor. When it was able to breathe again, it staggered to its feet and beat a path to the back door, where Vera let it out.

"I *will* agree with Goldie on one thing, Little Vinal," she said as the screen door banged shut. "Billy Graham, Jr., you ain't."

It was two days later that Priscilla was over the trauma of premature womanhood enough to conspire with Little Pee in an attempt to regain her feminine honor. The plan was to lure Little Vinal into the thick woods near Haze's Brook. Priscilla sent a note down the hill by Miltie when she saw Little Vinal out and about on his bike. The note said that she was sorry she fought him off. She'd changed her mind. That becoming a real woman months before her fourteenth birthday wasn't such a bad idea after all. Could he meet her, then, at Haze's Brook, after making absolutely sure no one would see or follow him?

Little Vinal even bathed for the event, and then splashed about his pimply neck some of the unused Raleigh aftershave Vera had given her husband for Christmas. He then pulled on Big Vinal's stiff Sunday shoes. They were shit-brown in color, and two sizes too big for him, but Little Vinal knew Priscilla deserved a certain amount of worldliness for the sacrifice of herself, and he intended to supply her with it.

Little Vinal approached the expanse of budding poplars around Haze's Brook and stood waiting patiently for Priscilla. He rocked back and forth in the giant-sized shoes as though they were brown boats. He recounted the hairs on his upper lip. He studied the silvery zipper on his pants. For the hundredth time that week, Little Vinal wished he knew more about the workings of the penis. Wished he'd been born with an owner's manual, supplying him with a storehouse of bodily information. But there had been enough gossip buzzing around the schoolhouse about Priscilla that Little Vinal rested assured he would have a well-educated instructress. And it would help greatly for him, the educatee, to learn the sexual ropes from his first cousin. That way, when he met women outside the family he would be aptly schooled in what to grab first, what to shove where. He was pondering what would be a good way to pay Priscilla back for this needed initiation when he saw the hazelnut bushes rustle dramatically along the footpath leading back up to the highway. His heart froze. He felt a small throb in his genitals. *Fool*, they said to him. *This is just the beginning. We'll be getting you into messes like this all your life.* He sensed a truth in this throbbing admission, but before his mind could process it he saw faces emerge like flowers from the bushes. Miltie and Hodge, his little cousins. He saw Priscilla—that visage which had launched at least a dozen ships from landlocked Mattagash, if one believed gossip—smiling mockingly from up on the footpath, taunting him with her secret female knowledge. When he heard Little Pee's voice rise up from behind him, Vinal Gifford, Junior, knew what it meant. *Sexual ambush.* The mounds of toilet paper he had shoved into the toes of the shoes had enabled him to walk functionally, but running was another matter. The shoes turned on him.

The Gifford cousins surrounded Little Vinal the way those tiny people did poor Gulliver. Heads of curly hair, like roving tumbleweeds, were everywhere. Instead of seducing the plump, ravenous Prissy, he found himself tied to a medium-sized birch tree and stripped down to his shorts. His clothing was gleefully tossed into Haze's Brook by the revelers. So were Big Vinal's shit-brown Sunday shoes. Little Vinal sucked in his breath. He would, even after all the humiliation, probably have let it pass, blaming himself for the blunder. He would simply have counted it as a game lost, although well fought. It would've been Little Vinal *zero*, his genitals *one*. And he certainly didn't dare tell Vera the real reason he'd gone down there in the first place. Yes, he would have turned the other cheek had it not been for Little Pee, in a spontaneous gesture even Prissy was against, urinating upon his helpless cousin. Hands tied, Little Vinal could not even wipe away the warm strings of pee that lashed against his face. He listened to the disappearing laughter of his cousins as they raced home along the narrow footpath, and considered firsthand the irony in Pike Gifford, Junior's, nickname.

When Little Vinal finally worked himself free, after an hour of twisting and turning within his nylon stocking bonds, he'd devised a good reason for being where he was. He had been innocently fishing. He'd cut himself a nice pole. He'd tied a line, hook, and sinker to it. He'd dug a few worms. Yes, he'd gone fishing, just to test his luck. They had attacked him from behind. Had thrown his clothes into the brook. And then Little Pee had peed on him, the ultimate disgrace. And, Little Vinal told his group of avid, livid listeners back in the warm kitchen, they'd made off with a thirteen-inch trout that he'd just pulled, all shiny and wiggling, from the brook.

No one in his family questioned Little Vinal about the logic of fishing in April, much less catching a fish. It was still possible for a sudden shift in the weather to bring the snow back. And the brook, like the Mattagash River, was bursting at its seams from the spring freshets. It would take a brick, not a foolish sinker, to sink a fish line in those burgeoning waters. But Little Vinal could have told Vera that he'd caught an alligator in Haze's Brook and she'd have believed him. That's how much she hated Goldie. And no way in hell had she forgotten the Christmas lights incident.

"They're probably sucking its bones dry this very minute," Vera said, of the trout, and slammed a fist into the palm of her hand.

Goldie didn't believe a word of it when she heard. Perhaps because Little Vinal, in his emotional state, in his urge to bestow himself with a hunter's prowess since he'd bombed as a lover, had made the story too dramatic.

"If he'd throw that trout back," Goldie told her sister over the phone, "I might believe him. But if Little Vinal caught a trout in April, he must have been fishing in Vera's Frigidaire."

But even this distasteful skirmish was kept in hand by the two senior Giffords. Pike dragged Little Pee down the long hill and deposited him on the front porch where he apologized, however angrily, to Little Vinal.

"And say you're sorry you peed on me," Little Vinal demanded, with all the intensity that comes with repressed sexual energy.

"I'm sorry I peed on you," Little Pee said, between clenched teeth.

On the ignominious climb back up the hill, with all the bottom-of-the-hill Giffords burning their eyes into his back, Little Pee was seething.

"I should've shit on him, too," he said to Priscilla, who had come halfway down the hill for a report on what was said.

Certain panels moved in the front windows of both Gifford households for nearly an hour. Vera looked up and Goldie looked down. The battle over the Christmas lights might still be waged through their children, but neither woman was getting any relief. They were hot as firebombs.

"And they threw your good Sunday shoes into the creek," Vera added, hoping *that* would spark anger in Vinal. She failed to consider that he might take that anger out on Little Vinal for wearing the shoes in the first place.

"Now that's a goddamn shame," said Vinal, as he headed for the outhouse with a copy of *National Geographic* that had come home as part of a child's schoolwork. Vinal had developed a sudden interest in the Auca Indians of Ecuador, especially the women. "Now what am I gonna wear to Amy Joy's wedding?" he asked, and disappeared on the well-trodden path.

THE IVYS GET OUT OF DODGE: UNWELCOME VISITORS FROM PORTLAND AND A PAIR OF THIRTY-EIGHTS

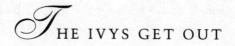

> Oh, every year hath its winter,
> And every year hath its rain—
> But a day is always coming
> When the birds go north again.
>
> Oh, every heart hath its sorrow,
> And every heart hath its pain—
> But a day is always coming
> When the birds go north again.
>
> —Ella Higginson,
> "When the Birds go North Again"

THE IVY WEDDING ENTOURAGE PULLED OUT OF PORTLAND, Maine, in the thin gray morning as the herring gulls oversaw the departure north. The lead car scurried up front with Pearl lounging comfortably in the front seat, happy to be free of Thelma for the trip. It was a chance to redo old mistakes, shape up old automobile accidents.

Behind, in his 1969 cream Cadillac, Junior anxiously followed his father's taillights, the only advice he had taken from Marvin in years. But it was a relief to get out of town for a while. Monique had begun calling him at home the day before. Junior himself had answered the phone three different times to hear her say, "It's me. Monique. Call me." The last time he answered she'd been curt. "I'm not fooling around, Junior. Now get out of that goddamn house and call me." Each time Junior could not race Thelma, or one of the kids, to the phone, Monique had simply hung up. But how long could he count on her doing that? Thelma knew about the affair. Granted. She had caught them at the Ocean Edge. But why in hell let his kids know? It was a constant battle to garner even a modicum of respect from them as it was. This would squelch any father-child relationship. And he had been planning to look so parental yet dashing in the tuxedo he was to wear next month at Regina's Father-Daughter Dance at school. Goddamn it, but he wished he knew what Monique was up to.

Junior had found out one valuable piece of information from the whole miserable experience: A mistress was worse than a wife. When a mistress wants to *be* a wife, look out. And that's what Marvin had told his son when he decided to fire the temptation. "She's after our money, son," Marvin had said. "There ain't a woman in Portland who wouldn't want to be in Thelma's shoes. They want to rise up in the world, women like Miss Tessier. You got to realize that we're sort of like the Kennedys of Portland, Maine. We got a responsibility. We got to look out for Camelot, son. Tell the bitch to walk."

Junior glanced in the rearview mirror and caught his son Randy's face glowering there. In the backseat, Randy bit at pieces of thumb cuticle and thought about his unpleasant circumstances. There was a hot shipment coming in from Mexico over the weekend. Buddy had promised to buy a couple ounces for him with some of the money Randy earned by eating pastries and acting like a house-guest. But that wouldn't do him much good right now. He was going to Mattagash, *Mattagash* for shitsakes, with half an ounce. That was like throwing them poor, straight Christians to the lions. And Randy was leaving behind Leslie Boudreau, the waitress at Cantina's. Leslie Boudoir, the guys called her. Sweet, womanly, leggy Leslie. She was the reason he crawled out on his father's veranda every single night and shimmied down the massive elm to the ground, which he hit running. Leslie had been teaching him things that sex manuals were yet to print. She smoked too much of his dope, it was true, but she was his first, his very first, his usherette on that magical journey into the land of the libido. A burning erupted suddenly in his groin area. It had been there for days now, even when he wasn't thinking of Leslie. It was different from burning, really, this adult passion to which he had been so recently introduced. *Itching* might be a better word for it. Whatever it was, Randy itched and sulked for the entire eight-hour, uneventful drive to Mattagash, Maine. The tiny visitors he unknowingly brought with him snuggled down beneath his pubic hairs, as though they were the thick massive pines of Maine, and waited patiently as burrs for their next excursion.

In the front seat, on the passenger side, Thelma Parsons Ivy stared out the window with eyes that needed sleep. When the car rolled past Tusculum Street, Thelma's eyes misted heavily. She used to wait for the school bus right there, right where the stop sign still was. She used to be a little girl on her way to school one day, waiting for a bus, with loving parents waiting back at home for her. She should have stayed there, beneath that stop sign. Better yet, she should have stayed at home, in her bedroom, with the diamond-pattern curtains in the window. She should have told her mother, "Never let me out of bed. Never let me out of this room. Out of this house. Keep us here. All together. Don't you know what's about to happen to us all?" But she hadn't said any of that. Life had pulled the covers off her and shoved her out into the street with an armful of books. And at Portland High School she had finally met and fallen in love with pudgy Junior Ivy. Was it love, or pity? Now she wondered. But she knew one thing, as Tusculum Street fell far away behind the Cadillac, like an old movie reel being rewound.

"I wasn't waiting for no school bus all them mornings," Thelma thought, and fingered the hidden bottle of Valiums in her purse. "I was waiting for a hearse."

A few hours later, in Millinocket, the two cars stopped to gas up and to order a hasty sandwich at The 95'er restaurant. Pearl barely glanced at Thelma, but this time the insult fluttered by unnoticed. Thelma had rushed into the ladies' room as soon as Junior brought the big car to a lurching stop and now, if Indira Gandhi were across the table from her giving her dirty looks, Thelma would simply smile at India's leader.

"Did you see her eyes?" Pearl asked Marvin, when the entourage, like a miniature version of a funeral procession, progressed on. "Talk about piss holes in a snowbank. She's beginning to look like an owl."

"That's what I've been trying to tell you," Marvin said, and signaled to his son that he would be pulling out in the left lane to pass a dawdling pickup truck ahead of him. Junior immediately complied and Marvin saw the creamy Cadillac follow his move. It made a warm glow in his stomach, the way a good scotch or two can simmer down there. This was the relationship he'd always wanted with his only son. Junior didn't have what it takes to sweep up moose cookies, for Chrissakes. But if Marvin had a steady hand on the broom, well, that was a different matter. Marvin passed the pickup, signaled right again, and saw the reflected Cadillac follow suit.

"Like father, like son," thought Marvin, and smiled broadly.

"It'll be good to see the old house again," said Pearl. "But it's going to be strange with Margie not there."

"All things must pass away," said Marvin. This would have been soothing to Pearl, in its poetical, philosophical way, except that it was also on a sign Marvin had tacked up in the coffee lounge at the funeral home. Knowing this made it sound to Pearl's ear more like a work slogan, an advertisement, than inspirational advice. He could very well have said "Sooner or later, you'll own General." As though Marge had driven off on four new tires, rather than into death.

"Sicily said she'd have someone go in and do a bit of cleaning," Pearl said. "Get the old place in order for us."

"The last time I slept in that house," said Marvin, "we'd only been married a few years. It always seemed haunted to me."

"It *is* haunted," said Pearl. "I'll be the first to say that. But I'd rather fall asleep with ghosts in the house than Thelma." Thank God that Junior and his family would be staying at Albert Pinkham's motel. They had been thrown out ten years ago, but Albert Pinkham was most forgiving and hospitable on the phone. Junior and his family could have as many rooms as they wanted, he assured them, and for as long as they wished.

"Now, Pearly," said Marvin. "Remember what I've been telling you. We need to get this family straightened out. Get it running smoothly again." He felt suddenly like old Joe Kennedy, and sat a bit more upright behind the wheel.

"Why me?" asked Pearl. "I didn't give her that prescription. Why do *I* have to listen to her loony tunes?"

"You're both women," Marvin said. "She probably could use a mother's advice. How long has her own mother been dead, anyway?"

A mother's advice! Pearl felt suddenly nauseated. It could have been the hot dog, a half hour ago, but more likely it was the notion of mothering Thelma Parsons Ivy, Pill Addict.

"Well," said Pearl, turning her face to the window and gazing out at the rain that had begun to fall lightly. "We'll see what happens," she added, remembering that soon she'd be back in the safety of her childhood home, and free from all of them.

In the car behind, Thelma turned her own face to the window, to the passing pines. They were going deeper and deeper into the heart of the forests. They were going up, up, up the road just to surface nowhere. You could get the bends going to Mattagash. At one time in her life, Thelma had not been able to envision anything north of Bangor. No houses. No hospitals. No schools. No people. Now, thanks to her marriage, the world had expanded for her. But now she wished greatly that the world had indeed dead-ended at Bangor, and that if you ventured any farther you would fall off the edge. She wished that Maine had been flat, the way the world was once believed to be. Knowing that something and someone lay north of Bangor had not enriched Thelma's life, had not expanded it. Stretched it, maybe. She had had a terrible vacation there ten years earlier, when the kids were still small, when she could still halfway cope. Now here she was on the road back, the road north, the road into the heart of the wilderness. Thank God for pills.

"And just think," Junior was saying, "if we'd had more time we could've taken Route One. That road starts out in Fort Kent, Maine, and runs all the way to Key West." The Cadillac passed a small blue car by the side of the interstate, its hood up, its owner thumbing.

"Yes sir," said Junior, as the car whisked by the stranded driver without a thought. "Good ole Route One. Two thousand one hundred and nine miles long. Ain't that something?" He heard Thelma mumble. Good. He was finally getting a response. It was all a matter of patience. His father had been right about that. In just a few hours of driving, Junior had managed to interest his wife and son in some interesting highway facts about the state of Maine.

"What?" asked Junior. "What did you say, hon?"

"I said 'God love the traveler,' " Thelma replied loudly, as the distraught driver and his little blue car disappeared in her side view mirror. In the backseat, a large snore cascaded from Randy's nose and mouth as Leslie Boudreau undid her blouse in his dreams.

The procession continued north, each in his or her own reverie. What it did not know was what everyone back at The 95'er restaurant already knew: that behind the Ivys, only minutes away, as the gray Portland morning turned into the overcast midday of Millinocket, a lone Buick was in pursuit, its driver scorned and bosomy and furious as hell.

"She looks just like Elizabeth Taylor," Petey Simpson, back at The 95'er, had said to the waitress, as Monique Tessier ordered a ham sandwich to go.

"And make it damn quick," she had said.

THE RIVER EXPLAINED: ALBERT CONTEMPLATES BARNS, TINTYPES, AND THE OCEAN, AS HE WAITS FOR THE CITY SLICKERS

....

The river glideth at his own sweet will;
Dear God! the very houses seem asleep;
And all that mighty heart is lying still!

—William Wordsworth,
"Composed Upon Westminster Bridge"

AS A PROPER WELCOME FOR HIS PORTLAND GUESTS, SOON TO arrive, Albert Pinkham swept the leaves from last autumn, crinkly and broken, into a respectable windrow on the cement walkway. He felt like a successful businessman again. It was true that he had thrown the Ivys out of the Albert Pinkham Family Motel ten years earlier for disruptive behavior. But forgiveness is the mark of a good Christian man, especially if that Christian man is going broke. And ten years was enough time for that awful little Ivy boy to grow up. He'd be a young man by now. Albert Pinkham had never liked

Pearl McKinnon, it was true, with all her city airs and bloated sense of self-importance. Somebody must have told Pearl, early in life, that her shit didn't stink, and she had believed them. But Pearl wouldn't be staying at Albert's establishment. It would be only that wimpy son of hers, Junior, and his simpleminded little wife, and the child that such a union might expect. He would put the two adults in number 1, in the front, and the kid around back, in number 4. It would be a show of sudden prosperity to have a big fancy car from downstate idling on the gravel driveway of the Albert Pinkham Motel. And, by jiminy, it was about time the Pinkham coffers began to hear coins clinking about in them again instead of mothballs. Almost overnight, Albert Pinkham had gone from being barely able to keep his head above water to walking on the stuff.

The Ivys weren't the only boost to his good fortune. Another room had been reserved by a woman who was also from Portland, coincidence of all coincidences. Albert didn't give a damn if she was from Mars, as long as she paid with good ole American moolah. A nature enthusiast, he assumed by the gravelly quality in her voice. He had learned to read his clients over the phone, just from the cadence of their speech. This was a nature enthusiast all right, longing to hoof about in the slushy woods and tramp her feet off along the Mattagash River. Blisters for nature. He had intended to put her in number 2, but there was something in the way the smooth April breeze was rearranging the noisy leaves of another year, another time, creating something like a sad music, an old song, that prompted Albert to change his mind. He would put her in number 3. Violet LaForge's old room. For old time's sake. She had sounded quite young, younger than Violet, and yes, damn it, she had sounded sexy. He would put her, nature enthusiast that she was, in the pink room, with its pink wooden bed, and its pink walls that could loom over her in the morning like a reddish dawn.

Albert opened the doors to the three rooms and raised their single windows. April rushed in and pushed out the mustiness of non-use. He noticed cobwebs in each corner of each room, those finely knit doilies that spoke of Sarah Pinkham's disappearance from the premises. She had kept things spick-and-span, it was true, but Albert didn't mind that in her stead was the gauzy embroidery of insects.

"I get along better with spiders than I ever did with that woman," Albert told Bruce, who had jumped onto the bed of number 1 and stretched out for a little spring nap. Albert left him there, and the door ajar for his escape when nap time ended. He decided to leave the cobwebs clinging. Some city slickers liked such things. They don't have cobwebs in New York City, Albert knew. Cobwebs don't stick good to concrete and steel. You need some nice old-fashioned wood to make spiders feel at home. Albert had redone the walls of rooms, 1, 2, and 4 when he discovered that barn boards were a hot new item with tourists. He simply went out to the flat field behind his house, behind the thicket of jack pines, and he tore boards from the old barn of his youth. His grandfather, John Pinkham, the best goddamn barn builder of his day, had built it. The passage of years and the heavy snows of so many winters no one could count them anymore had tilted the barn. It had already begun its aging plans by the time Albert was born. But he remembered it still strong enough, solid enough, that he could climb up into its loft and lie back on the molded hay of another time, hay meant for workhorses whose bones lay beneath the gravel pit and whose names no one could remember. Even the sunlight that splayed in rickety streams through the spaces in the boards was sunlight of a different era. You could lie on your back in that old hay, with all the sweetness leaked out of it, and you just knew that the ball of sun outside the timeless barn was not a real sun. It was round and yellow as a summer apple and only *painted* in the sky. It was like the sun that comes up on picture puzzles, the pieces of it easily found because of the blazing yellow.

Nowadays even Albert's grandfather was no longer real to him. Nowadays his grandfather peered out from a daguerreotype with the eyes of a terrified man lost to time, lost between the pages of the years. His grandfather didn't exist anymore. Now he was just a face full of whiskers, with hands folded in his lap like a carpenter's tools, with a fat ridge of snuff protruding his lower lip. And even this sparse remainder of his grandfather was disappearing into bits and pieces because Albert didn't take good care of the old tintype. It was slowly eroding, flecks of the silver nitrate peeling away like paint. The damage had begun at the base of the photo, but as Albert tossed pens and knives and coins into the drawer where he left it lying unprotected, the face was beginning to peel away, as it must in death, exposing only sockets until even those are gone. Albert hoped one day to give the picture to his daughter, Belle, so she could at least catch a glimpse of the old man, the old barn builder himself, before he disappeared for good.

Albert Pinkham leaned against the front wall of the Albert Pinkham Motel and closed his eyes. On the far ridge, where the wild cherry and ash still grew thickly, he could hear the metallic *tok tok tok* of a solitary northern raven and he knew, if he opened his eyes, he would see it gliding on its flat wings, a shadowy black plane skirting the horizon above the old river. Albert felt like that sometimes, that he was skirting, skimming through life. Things had changed, it was true, from the days of the old barn builder, so what then was the grandson to do? Was it wrong for him to leave his barely used Jonsered chain saw on a flat stump one day and just turn his back on it and walk out of the woods forever?

"Things ain't the same anymore," he had come home in the middle of the day and said to Sarah Pinkham, who was terrified to see him. Men never left the woods during good daylight working hours unless a falling tree had crushed someone, a pulp hook had embedded itself in a fleshy foot, a chain saw had bounced off a tree and into the muscles of a meaty leg. A woman could usually see blood coming from somewhere if a man left the woods early.

"Times ain't what they used to be," Albert muttered to Sarah, and he lay in broad daylight on the sofa, like a crazed man, like a Gifford, until nightfall came with his solution. The Albert Pinkham Family Motel. Why should the innkeepers in Watertown make all the money from tourists who tramp Mattagash into the ground? Why shouldn't a native son prosper as well? Everyone in Mattagash had laughed behind his back at the new venture. Albert could see it in their eyes. But folks had sneered at Fulton. At the Wright brothers. At Henri Nadeau's mini golf course behind his filling station. Yet the steamship had puffed away. The Wrights had taken wing. And Henri Nadeau could be seen every Sunday behind the wheel of the only goddamn Lincoln Continental this side of Caribou.

Times had been hard, very hard, at first. Damn hard. Sarah could tell you, but she would be too proud. Bruce could tell you, if he could talk. His daughter, Belle, couldn't see well enough to know what was going on, and instead stayed cloistered behind her thick eyeglasses. But after he borrowed five thousand dollars from the Great Northern Bank of Watertown to open his business, Albert Pinkham had to go to the town for support. There just wasn't enough money coming in to put food on the table for his family and clothing on their backs. It was rough sitting there with a list in his hand upon which Sarah had written the necessities—groceries, medicines, and so on—and waiting for the town's first selectman, like some kind of god, to sign it so Albert could go shopping. Albert remembered that Frederick Craft, Winnie's husband, had been the town's first selectman that year. He went over each item thoughtfully, Winnie peering over his shoulder like she was *second* selectman, or treasurer, or something, instead of just a nosy wife, which she was. And Frederick Craft had, almost gleefully, crossed out the occasional "3 lbs. hamburg" to make it "2 lbs. hamburg." Once, he deleted altogether "1 tube toothpaste," as if a grown man and woman didn't know for themselves what was required to make a household run efficiently. As if it took some foolish first selectman to tell them. As if Albert and Sarah Pinkham were trying to cheat the entire town of Mattagash, Maine, out of a goddamn tube of Crest.

Albert opened his eyes and saw the raven this time. He could still hear its grating *prruk, prruk* after it disappeared from his line of vision. He knew where it was. Most likely everyone in Mattagash, including little kids, could tell an outsider that the bird had landed in Old Mrs. Mullins's backyard birch, where it would survey the odd scraps of bread and doughnuts and the skin-colored chunks of suet before it swooped down to carry off its supper.

Two herring gulls, now becoming a common sight to such an inland part of Maine, appeared from behind a twist in the river. Upon spotting the raven they sounded their anxiety notes, *gah, gah, gah*. Albert heard, and anxiety sounded in his chest as his heart drummed rapidly. Now only the gulls and the ravens, ospreys and the occasional bald eagle used the river as a highway. Albert's generation had come, and now it was going. He was a member of a group who still had a foot in nature's door. He was among a rare cabal of storytellers who now had no one to listen to them. They were replaced by radios with speakers the size of car batteries, by fancy television sets, and driver's licenses for all, and movies every weekend in Watertown. My God, but Albert Pinkham could remember the day when a strange man and woman came from somewhere downriver, and they invited the whole town to pay a nickel to watch as they made shapes with their hands in front of a lantern. As the shadows fell on the wall behind them, it came to life with birds and deer and horses. Oh, no television ever emitted such lovely visions! And that woman's voice was almost as deep as any man's as she told stories for these shadowy animals. Even the grown-up men, immovable at the sight of bodies busted beneath pine trees, of wounded horses spurting blood from their chests, even these tough, wizened woodsmen who thought they'd seen everything, sat with mouths fallen down like trapdoors and knew their minds had been pried open and tampered with, and that they could never be certain of anything again.

Albert Pinkham looked long and hard out across the winding Mattagash road. He let his eyes settle down on the river. It used to be a *road*, that old girl did. The Indians had broken it in years before the white man knew it was there. But Albert easily remembered when it was still functioning. He remembered the cold mornings of being bundled, still frozen, in the bow of the canoe as he and his father whipped over the fast rapids to Watertown. With their sugar, and their flour, and their molasses neatly packed, they would begin the long tedious poling upriver, until finally they saw smoke from the Pinkham chimney curling like a white man's signal up into the evening sky. Nowadays, no one used the river for anything. No one, that is, but the tourists. There were still the local fishermen, but they searched for out-of-the-way lakes and ponds to avoid the onslaught of city slickers. Youngsters barely swam in it anymore, preferring the public pool in Watertown. Was Albert wrong, then, to offer them a plastic pool himself?

For Albert and his forebears the river was a directional device, a compass, even after the canoe was replaced by the automobile and it became a dusty back road no longer trodden.

"Guess I'll go downriver today," Albert Pinkham would tell Sarah, "and find me a used snowplow." It meant direction, and no matter how crooked it twisted, in the end it always pointed right to the spot you meant. The river had social connotations, too.

"He married a girl from downriver somewhere," Sarah would say, and Albert knew that it meant someone from outside Matta-gash, past St. Leonard and Watertown. Albert knew what else it meant. Everyone knew.

"He married a stranger," Sarah could have said. "He married a girl no one here in town even knows. He went and married himself a stranger and, because of that, God only knows what will become of him." And whoever heard it would sip their tea with the loud sucking noise that Albert's generation liked—it meant good strong hot tea, by Jesus. They would sip their tea and feel real sorry for anybody who had to go all the way downriver looking for a mate. Nowadays, the young regarded it as a blessing to "marry away." And more and more of them were growing discontented with bo-redom, which their ancestors had considered a good rest. Matta-gash was losing its young blood to factories downriver, to the makers of toilet paper and jet planes, and in their place more and more sea gulls were coming to Mattagash with the news that there was an ocean out there somewhere. And you could almost hear the jackhammers and the graders down around Portland and Ban-gor, building, building, coming north, inching upriver, until one day maybe the ocean itself would sweep in to wash them all away.

The river meant safety, too. Sometimes the river was your mother, or your father, or the best friend you've ever had. Some-times Albert Pinkham would be all the way down to Madawaska, below Watertown, tacking his business cards to only the busiest bulletin boards, when he would spy a shift in the weather. He would see a grayness creeping up into the sky over the treetops. He would see the birds panicking. He would feel the very air around him tense in anticipation.

"We'd better head *upriver*," he'd say to Bruce, and the two would disappear into the soupy grayness, only their red taillights telling the rest of the world that they were pointed toward safety, they were headed upriver, they were running back into Mattagash's arms before any storm, any stranger, any handmade bird flying crazily in the lantern light on some wall, could catch them.

◆　◆　◆

Dusk had come and was turning into evening when Junior's creamy Cadillac rolled into Albert's yard and tooted rudely. What the hell did he toot for? Did Junior Ivy expect Albert to run out to the trunk like one of them tip-hungry city doormen and carry in all their shit? Let that son of Pearl's, that big undertaking turd, carry in his own junk. And that littler turd, that grandson, let *him* understand a few seconds of work. Albert Pinkham hadn't sacrificed his back to the woods, to over thirty years of spine-snapping work, to tote the fancy suitcases of the idle rich. What did the Ivys have to do to earn their money but stand around and wait for folks to shuffle off their mortal coils, for Chrissakes. Nonetheless, Albert was a man who had nearly gone under as a motel proprietor.

"Be on your best behavior," Albert instructed Bruce, who bounded out into the yard to greet the human nitpickers from Portland.

Albert did as he intended. He checked the burly Junior and his scrawny little wife, who seemed to be under a spell of some kind, a real zombie, into room number 1. He put the kid, another story altogether, in number 4.

"Well, at least you've got hot running water this time," Junior said, staring down his snobbish nose at Albert. The latter was aghast. Didn't this pork-bellied son of a bitch remember being thrown out of here? Evicted, for Chrissakes? Tossed to the winds?

Now here he was, like he was doing Albert some kind of favor by breathing the same air.

"You got color TV, man?" Randy asked.

"What about room service?" asked Thelma.

"Phones in the rooms?" Junior queried, as he looked sternly at his watch, a harried businessman.

Albert felt weak in the knees. They were as bad as the sea gulls, these rude, loud ocean people. But the truth was that Junior Ivy and his companions *were* doing Albert a favor, so what else could he do but stand there and show his teeth in a smile that made him look like a happy, well-fed old dog? Bruce showed his own teeth, well tartared up to the gums, but Albert soothed him with a quick dig behind the ears.

"We aim to please," Albert said to Pearl McKinnon Ivy's three chips off the old block, and he and Bruce smiled widely in unison.

It was only an hour later that the dirty beige Buick turned with a slow uncertainty into the Albert Pinkham Motel. Albert had been anxiously awaiting this arrival, and he bounded quickly out of his house to greet this new guest and to gallantly offer to hoist every last bit of her luggage, be it plaid, or fur-lined, or leather, into the sanctity of number 3. There had been something in her voice that sang of spring, of April, that bespoke a kind of schooled poetry that men like Albert Pinkham never dared read, let alone dream they could write. There was a soft curl of womanhood in each letter of her name as she had spelled it out for him, her sensuality warm enough to push itself north, through the marrow of the cold telephone wires, all the way to Albert Pinkham's own telephone pole. Let others say this was Freudian. All Albert knew was that the voice was that of an angel. He had even pulled a white Sunday shirt from a hanger, patted some after-shave about his face, and brushed Bruce to such perfection that Lassie would yowl in jealousy to see it. Yet he left Bruce inside to watch the arrival from the living room window. There were some things a man could not share, not even with his dog.

The driver's window of the dirty Buick, splattered with April's muddy leftovers, wound cautiously down. Albert felt his breath catch. He could almost feel the pulse in his throat thumping about like a wild little drum. *Gah, gah, gah,* his Adam's apple cried out as the pulse jumped erratically around it. Albert Pinkham was fifty-seven years old, and one day last week it had occurred to him that he might never again know the pleasure of undoing his belt buckle and letting his trousers drop because some woman was waiting, wanting him to. Albert glanced nervously at Bruce, who had his nose pressed like a pig's against the pane in a frenzied inspection of the guest, his tail beating furiously.

"Go for it, boss," his eyes encouraged Albert.

A delicate head popped out of the window and the movement startled Albert. He had meant to rattle off his pitch about how the Albert Pinkham Motel welcomes you greatly, and all, but then he saw the face, the shapely nose, the aristocratic chin, and those brunette wisps of hair tumbling about like little feathers.

"My God," thought Albert Pinkham. *Gah, gah, gah!* Could it really be who he thought it was? Could it be *her,* tired of minks and Hollywood and Richard Burton? He was the sea gull now, spotting for the first time the glistening, violet-backed raven. *Gah, gah.*

"How in Christ can you people up here drive on these roads?" Monique Tessier asked the proprietor, in a voice unbecoming to any self-respecting angel. "I nearly bounced my goddamn tits off," she said.

*M*ÉNAGE À TROIS AT THE MAISON LAWLER: SIGHTS, SOUNDS, AND SMELLS OF MATRIMONY

....

Catholics, Catholics, ring the bell,
Protestants, Protestants, go to hell.

—Robert Gibbs,
lines to a childhood singsong

AMY JOY SAT IN FRONT OF HER VANITY MIRROR, ON HER DAINTY vanity chair, the set Sicily had gotten with Green Stamps as an eighth-grade graduation present for her daughter. Amy Joy sat in her bedroom, in front of her cans of Clairol spray-on silver hair color, deodorants, perfumes, and a half bottle of Pepsi. She sat with her chin on her hands and stared at her face in the mirror. She was fresh from a hot bath, which had opened her pores and soothed her muscles but troubled her mind with prewedding jitters. Now her face was waiting to be covered again with a layer of creamy makeup. Her eyes were waiting for the two blue swaths of shadow to render them alluring. The brows were in need of a penciled arching, the cheekbones an accentuating with rouge. The black eyeliner waited, on the table before her, to add an Oriental mystery to her bottom lids. And then the silver spray, as liquid as poetry, which would turn strands of hair around her face into tinsel icicles, shimmering, fluid, effervescent. Putois. Jean's little skunk. Amy Joy stared at her childhood face, unspoiled, pristine as an old school photo. She looked like Sicily a bit, it was true, with her McKinnon eyes that wanted to see inside people. But Amy Joy's thick frizzy hair, a drab brown, had none of the red highlights that had raged in her mother's hair. Now Sicily's hair was rusty, scattered with a wash of gray.

"Spraying gray into your hair!" Sicily had criticized the streaks about her daughter's face. "My God, child. Mother Nature is gonna spray that onto your head permanently. Just wait a few years. You'll get it for free."

"It's not gray," Amy Joy had quit protesting months ago. "It's silver." What was wrong, then, with trying to brighten up something as drab as medium-brown hair? Why not spray a patch of silver into a bleak world, like pure money. Like art, even. What was wrong with bringing a little tinsel to Mattagash, Maine?

"You're making yourself grow old too fast, Amy Joy," Sicily had warned, as if a pulse on aging was a talent her daughter had. *You're going to grow old too fast.* This always reminded Amy Joy of those poor little children with that awful aging disease. She had seen them on television, the little old men in baseball caps, toothless, rickety. Tiny Grandma Moses look-alikes in dresses sewn for ten-year-olds. Little girls with hair thin as spiderwebs, breastless and dying. Only their eyes spoke the secret. Only the absence of worldliness gave these wizened little dolls away. The pupils were void of romance, of marriage, of parenthood. There was no future lurking in them. The future had twisted itself like a snake, had coiled back around and caught itself at the beginning. Life and death cohabited. Only the eyes and the hearts were young and round and innocent, looking out of bodies belonging to their grandparents.

"You're just making yourself age," Sicily had said. That showed how much *she* knew.

Amy Joy sprayed one side of her hair. The color clung like wet beads to the strands until it grasped on and hardened. She was reminded of the wet drops of snow that splatter against a windowpane. She had seen twenty-three Mattagash winters. She knew snow. It was pliant at first, and soft, and on a warm window she had seen it glisten in drops, had seen those drops catch the outdoor light. And then, in the morning, when Jack Frost had ravaged his way across the pane, the drops were frozen solid, embedded, married to the glass. Fossilized snow. When Amy Joy and Jean Claude signed their marriage certificate they would be crystallizing themselves. The letters of their names would be like ancient little fish that have died in some old rock and are now sealed forever.

Amy Joy watched as the spray attached itself like silver flakes to each strand. But before she could finish the paint job on her hair, she was overwhelmed with sadness. There was something tragic in how her face, without the makeup, reminded her of crawling out of the Mattagash River, fresh from swimming, in need of a good toweling, in search of whatever food Sicily had cooking on the stove. What a simple time it had all been—and look at her now.

"I feel like dying," Amy Joy said, and she laid her head upon the circle of her arms and cried.

When she heard Jean Claude's super sport shift downward for the turn into the Lawler yard, Amy Joy went into the bathroom and splattered her eyes with cold water. They were still puffy but makeup would disguise the problem. She applied her second silver streak. Putois. Jeans and a sweater were suitable for the quiet occasion. She wished, however, that she'd had the opportunity to imbibe one of those stiff drinks Jean Claude promised to swallow down before he left his job in Watertown. It could only help. It was three days to the wedding. The Ivys were descending upon Mattagash at any minute, no matter how Amy Joy wished she could have avoided inviting them. The truth was, she never thought for a second they'd accept. And then there was the problem of the future in-laws. Jean Claude's mother was praying to saints that the Vatican had yet to canonize.

"She even make some up, her," Jean Claude had explained. And now Amy Joy's betrothed was downstairs, about to partake in what was to be a kind of get-acquainted-with-the-mother-in-law party. Sicily had promised this would happen. In fact, she had initiated the event. And then she had placed her whispery wedding dress into Amy Joy's arms. It was, strangely enough, this sudden change in Sicily that had precipitated the sadness in her daughter. Amy Joy almost hated to see Sicily relent, let go, give up. After all, it was Amy Joy as a child Sicily was finally relinquishing. And it was that same child Amy Joy was desperately holding on to.

"We nearly pulled the arms off her," Amy Joy said to the mirror as she touched her lips with gloss. Now *there* was the Amy Joy who was ready to take on the bilingual world. The eyes were blue almonds above the black liner. The sides of her face glittered in silver. The lips shone like ice. The cheekbones blossomed red. All right. It was time to go down and make an appearance. All soon-to-be brides got the jitters. Amy Joy had been forced to read *Our Town* in high school. She knew all about that prewedding shit. It was pure jitters that created such a bridal glow when the big day finally arrived. If you avoided throwing up, tension could be downright rosy. Now Amy Joy was ready to go downstairs and see just what the hell Sicily was really up to.

Sicily welcomed Jean Claude into the living room and watched as he sat uncomfortably on the sofa. The future mother-in-law sat in the chair across from him. She had smelled a quick flash of whiskey as he passed her. It may have been merely beer or wine. No matter. To Sicily it was all whiskey.

"A nice cup of tea?" she asked him.

"No tank you."

"Coffee?"

"No tanks," Jean Claude said. He bit carefully at one, then another of his fingernails. They smiled greasy black smiles up at him.

"A Coke?"

"No."

"One of Amy Joy's Pepsis?"

"No."

"Orange juice?" Chalice de Tabernacle. Would he have to tell her in French? Jean Claude shook his head negatively. Merde. Merde. Merde. Shit. Why had he agreed to this?

They sat in silence and listened to the clock in the kitchen reminding them that in just three days they would be legally bound. They sat like indifferent travelers on a train until Amy Joy bounded down the stairs and allowed the pent-up sighs to escape from both their throats.

"Water then?" asked Sicily. "From the spring?" Christ de Calvaire! (This anathema was taking a potshot at Christ's unfortunate visit to Calvary.) Ever since he was a little boy, Jean Claude knew that he would grow up one day to acquire a mother-in-law, and when he did he must call her la belle-mère. The pretty mother. How then, even with years of practice, could he accomplish this successfully? La femme avec une grande bouche, Jean Claude whispered to himself. This would be a much more appropriate title. The woman with a big mouth.

"She hask too much question, her," he had complained to Amy Joy, when he was told of the tête-à-tête that would take place.

"So?" Amy Joy had been indifferent, used to a lifetime of Sicily's interrogations. "*Hanswer* them."

Jean Claude stood up when he saw Amy Joy and smiled transparently. She saw right away that he was quite drunk. She might have smiled with him had they been at the Acadia Tavern in Watertown. Jean Claude could be clownish in the most sensitive way when he was nipping, his smile crooked, his curls tumbling about on his forehead. But this was not the place for crooked smiles and loose curls. This was a crew cut occasion, if ever she saw one.

"Hello, sweetie," Amy Joy said, and saw her mother cringe as she leaned over to quickly kiss her future groom.

"Al-lo, Putois," said Jean, and Sicily cringed noticeably to all.

"How was the drive, darling?" Amy Joy intended to throw out as many endearments as she could. It was plain to her already, by

the look on Sicily's face, that this was not some warm family function. Sicily had shit up her sleeves.

"Holy Tabarnacle," said Jean. "Hall I can see, me, for tree or
four mile, is dem pothole and fross heave. Chalice!"

Sicily canted her head at the unusual sound of the words, like
a curious dog, but semantics didn't arouse her tonight. Tonight she
wanted Amy Joy to see this Frog for what he was. She wanted
Amy Joy to realize what the social aspects of her life would be like
from then on, if this marriage occurred.

Amy Joy was at first relieved that her mother didn't recognize
the swearwords. Then it occurred to her that Sicily would probably
endorse any condemnation of the Catholic Church and its accoutrements, having done so herself, often, and in English.

"And how is your mother?" Sicily asked. She had even tried,
unbeknownst to her daughter, to phone the Cloutier home and
rouse up Mrs. Cloutier as an ally. She had heard Amy Joy telling
Lola Craft that Jean's mother was against this wedding, too. *Why*
Sicily couldn't imagine. It was obvious to her that marrying Amy
Joy Lawler amounted to several rungs up the social ladder for
anyone from Frogtown. But Catholics were strange folks, Sicily
knew. They lit candles for the dead and then played bingo by the
light of them. She'd heard it all when it came to the Catholics. But
Sicily couldn't find the right Cloutier in the phone book. There
were so many listed that she might as well be looking for a Smith
or an Adams in New York City. And the two she did ring up
answered their phones in French. They merely hung up when
Sicily asked, meekly, "Parley vouse some English?" Of course they
could all speak some English. They were just too proud to, was
all. And there they were, in the good ole United States of America,
living right off the fat of the land all these years, and still speaking
French!

"My mudder?" asked Jean Claude, and Sicily nodded. "She hokay, her."

"Well, that's good news," Sicily muttered. "Whatever you said."

"Mama, *please*," said Amy Joy, and rolled her eyes at Sicily.

"Where's da bat room?" Jean asked, suddenly. He had had a

few too many red beers, a favorite at the Acadia Tavern, a combination of beer and tomato juice. Alcohol for the soul, tomato juice for the hangover. Now the beer was pressing upon his bladder heavily.

"Go up the stairs and turn left," Amy Joy directed, motioning with her hands the proper directions.

"Just look at her," thought Sicily. "She's only been with that Frog for a few months and she's already talking with her hands." All of Mattagash knew that Frenchmen wouldn't be able to utter a word in either language if someone held their hands.

"As for you," Amy Joy spun around and accosted Sicily once she heard Jean Claude close the door to the bathroom. "What kind of stunt are you trying to pull? I thought this was going to be your chance to get to know him. All you've done for the past five minutes is make crude remarks and roll those McKinnon eyeballs."

"Oh, you're wrong," said Sicily. "I *am* getting to know him."

"You're making fun of him."

"He looks just like Chester Lee Gifford," said Sicily, and stood to smooth the fabric of the couch where Jean Claude had been sitting, as though the very action could make him disappear, could send him back to the old country, to France, where he truly belonged. "And you know it, Amy Joy."

"I've never heard anything so ridiculous in my life. As usual, you're grabbing for straws."

"Well, this straw has dark curly hair, a mustache, and real brown eyes. Except for the accent, you got another Chester Gifford."

Upstairs in Sicily's bathroom, Jean Claude Cloutier lifted a pint of Yukon Jack whiskey from his hip pocket and, as he had done all the way from Watertown, let it pour slowly down his throat. This was his second pint of the evening and it took hold of his stomach immediately, an assurance he needed. His gut had begun to tighten under the scrutiny of his future belle-mère. Anxiety was rampant in his entrails. He broke wind rather loudly and then smiled at the soft explosion. Une petite brise pour la belle-mère. A nice little breeze for the pretty mother. Something in which she could hang her English bloomers. As soon as the marriage was over, he would,

Jean Claude Cloutier, put his boot down. Already his childhood friends were warning him that this girl, this shimmering Putois, was a handful.

"She make a good woods boss, her," Philippe LaGrange had just finished telling him at the Acadia Tavern. "She pick up a stick of pulp, her, and hall da boys run for dere lifes." Jean Claude bristled to learn that his best friends, his fellow altar boys, his fellow drinkers, lovers, fighters, could even think that he'd let a mere woman dominate him like that. Vierge! Something had to be done before the merde hit the fan. But what? He was in love with Amy Joy. At least it felt like love, and Jean Claude reminded himself daily that all his big brothers had two or three children when they were his age. He was in a bit of a biological rush to catch up, so if Amy Joy was a little bossy, who was the worse for it? But he must make her understand that she shouldn't be so pushy in public. At home, push away, especially in bed. But in front of those old altar boys, well, that was another matter.

Jean Claude killed the pint of Yukon Jack, and then urinated quickly into Sicily's commode, trying desperately not to wet the fuzzy pink cover. He shook himself thoroughly, spraying the pink fluff with occasional drops of pee. What a stupid place to decorate, to put something fancy. The English, and to Jean Claude the English were anyone who spoke the language, were like that. They were always embarrassed of bodily functions, always trying to disguise the less than pleasant facts around them. At Jean Claude's house there had been so many boys in the typically large Catholic family that the commode seat stayed wet all the time. The girls, forgetting to look before they sat, complained heavily about the freezing drops of pee they were forever setting their warm bottoms down upon. Jean Claude's father, Théophile, had argued the point for all his sons when the females had sheepishly asked the males to lift the seat before spraying.

"Men have work to do. We have no time for this fool's stuff," he had lectured his wife and daughters, in French. "Be thankful that now you piss *in* the house, not out, in a snowbank."

Jean Claude shook a few final drops on the fuzzy pink cover, a final tribute to his father, before he tucked himself away. He was reminded of how, as boys, he and Philippe LaGrange and the others would write their names in the snow as they peed. Boys who had to dot *i*'s or cross *t*'s usually lost. Jean Claude's problem had always been the sheer length of his name, and the separation. No matter how he practiced his technique, his calligraphy always ran together in the snow as a sunken, yellow *JeanClaude*. On some days, he lost terribly, creating only *Jeanc* or *JeanClau* before his steaming pen ran out. Later, when he grew to manhood, and he and Philippe LaGrange stood out behind the Acadia Tavern, competing under the cold, blazing stars of the Big Dipper, bellies full of fifteen red beers, he had astonished even the old altar boys of his youth as they gathered around him, disbelievers. *JeanClaudeCloutier-Box274WatertownMaine*. Sometimes he even went so far as to add, as a final coup de theatre, a flourishing *USA*. When he stepped back to admire his handiwork, it always caused a shiver to run through him. He knew who he was at times like that. He was *JeanClaudeCloutier*. He knew where he lived, *Box274*. He felt as if he were hanging from the frosty handle of the Big Dipper, looking down on *WatertownUSA*, looking down on the tiny speck of the Acadia Tavern, where the altar boys of his past had gathered around some yellow writing in the snow.

"Mon dieu," he would mutter to himself, on those wintry, boozy, starry nights. And he wished he were a man who could take a pen to a sheet of paper and say clever things on it, so that it would last, instead of disappearing like this watery writing in the snow.

The stairs moved beneath him on his descent. He stopped dead in his tracks and shut one eye to survey the situation. There they were, eight, maybe nine steps, lying in perfect unison in front of him, and not one of them was moving. He lifted his right foot carefully and every step wriggled before him. He tried the left foot. The steps danced. Chalice de Vierge! He tried squinting. Then he opened both eyes wide. The steps were now bouncing themselves silly as they revolved before him like a belt. He was reminded of the cold mornings of the potato harvest, when he was hung over and sleepy on the harvester, trying to concentrate on

potatoes leaping before his eyes. Now here were stair steps coming
at him like giant brown russets. He shut both eyes, and things
quieted in his stomach. With a hand steadied against the wall, he
lowered himself to a sitting position. On the top step he comtem-
plated his fate. Putois would live up to her name for sure. There
would be a big stink over this. But Christ de Calvaire! These were
the last few days of his bachelorhood. Did anyone anywhere on
earth, including in the Papal City, expect him to stay sober just
days before the guillotine would fall? La belle-mère. *She* would.
Jean Claude slid his rear off the top step and bounced safely to
the next. He was a man. *Le diable avec la belle-mère.* She could
take her fancy pink cover and go straight to hell. She could put it
on the devil's toilet, for all Jean Claude cared. There would be
only Protestants in hell anyway, so she wouldn't have to worry
about any Catholics setting their toasty asses down. Smiling at this,
he bounced down to the next step, his eyes still shut tightly to
avoid the nausea of spinning stairs. He bounced again and smiled
broadly. By God, he could drink an oil drum full of whiskey and
still manage his affairs. It was a good mark to his ancestors, the
Québecois and the Acadians, that he could drink whiskey like a
workhorse. He farted loudly and the grating music of it caused a
tingling in his feet. He wanted badly to dance. He longed for his
father's fiddle and bow. He would play "Jolie Blonde" all night
long on la belle-mère's pretty pink cover, and he would dance her
around until she died, straight out, of a heart attack. More intestinal
wind escaped, and more loudly than before. He'd had too many
hot dogs at Henri Nadeau's Quick Lunch and Gas. The sign meant
what it said.

On the sixth step he sensed, as a blind mountain climber might,
that he was approaching the base of the stairway. He celebrated
by lifting his left hip and extracting more of Henri Nadeau's heaven-
reaching vapors. He *needed* to dance. There were Acadian fiddles
playing "Alouette" in both of his feet. It was true he rarely drank,
like most hardworking men of the valley, unless it was Saturday
night and then, Tabernacle! Look out! Jean Claude would stomp
his good dress shoes rhythmically upon the hardwood floor of the

Acadia Tavern, which had been, in its prime, the J. J. Newberry store. He would toss down shots of Yukon Jack and then dance, holding Amy Joy's buttocks fast in the palms of his hands during the waltzes. He must find Putois and take her to the Acadia Tavern and twirl her around the old J. J. Newberry store floor until they both dropped. He swung his left leg out dramatically, in a half pirouette, and felt it make contact with some object before he heard a soft *thunk!* on the floor. But he didn't care. He was celebrating. He wished he were lying on top of Putois at that very moment. He could almost smell her, the spray she used in her hair mixed with her perfume. But the smell nauseated him again. It did not mix well with Henri's hot dogs and Yukon Jack. He kept his eyes closed to avoid the topsy-turviness of the stairs, but it did no good. He felt the mixture of his afternoon's indulgences surfacing in his mouth, some leaking through his nostrils, and soon he had vomited heartily upon the bottom step of la belle-mère's stairs.

Jean Claude had not imagined the fragrance of Amy Joy's hair spray and perfume. Nor did he vaguely imagine hearing voices in some grayish, faraway reality, in some outer dream with which he could not connect. In fact, Amy Joy and Sicily had stood at the bottom of the stairs, mouths agape in sheer astonishment, and had watched and listened and involuntarily smelled the incredible descent of Jean Claude Cloutier. Sicily reached down weakly and picked up the pot of Irish shamrocks that had scattered on the floor. She had covered her ears and closed her eyes when the vomiting took place, but she was nevertheless fighting back her own nausea, brought on by the sickening event.

"These belonged to your grandma Grace," said Sicily, still faint. "They come straight from Ireland and they've been passed around the family for almost sixty years, and now look at them."

"They'll grow back," said Amy Joy. "Depend on it." She grabbed Jean Claude by his booted feet. He kicked to fight her off, but she pulled until he left the last step and lay spread out on the living room floor. Amy Joy's face was afire with embarrassment. She hoped Sicily was satisfied now. It was true that Jean Claude had lost that certain je ne se quoi in her eyes.

"Do you know what you did?" Amy Joy shouted at Jean Claude. She pointed to the vomit on the step. Jean Claude's head slowly followed her arm, down to the hand and out the pointing finger. His eyes rested on the mixture of food and booze.

"Non," he said, and shook his head. "It was le chien."

"Chien!" screamed Amy Joy.

"Please," said Sicily, who had sunk down into the sofa, still battling nausea from the sights, smells, and sounds of getting to know her future son-in-law. "Please don't swear in my house." She held a fistful of the pathetic shamrocks, which Jean Claude Cloutier had seemingly chosen for his symbolic attack upon the virtuous Irish ancestry of his future bride.

"You're blaming this on my *dog!*" Amy Joy shouted. "Chien my ass!"

"It's too bad your aunt Pearl couldn't have had the pleasure to sit through this," Sicily suddenly wailed. "How would I ever live that down?"

"Would you stop thinking about yourself, as usual?" asked Amy Joy. She had gotten Jean Claude to his feet and was leading him heavily to the door. "Come help me get him out to the car," she said, and Sicily begrudgingly tried to assist. But she could not bring herself to touch this French person.

"Allons danser!" Jean Claude shouted and began to stomp his feet. He could almost feel the old J. J. Newberry store floor sagging under his weight. "Dansons!" He clapped his hands and motioned to Sicily.

"Oh sweet Jesus," said Sicily, and mashed the shamrocks against her bosom. "He's gonna do one of them French dances right here in our living room!" she screamed. "Stop him, Amy Joy, before he breaks all my good Avon pieces!"

"Stop it, Jean!" Amy Joy yelled.

"Oh, it's no use," Sicily wept. "Once them people get it into their heads to dance, there's no stopping them. Their feet have minds of their own."

Jean Claude escaped Amy Joy's grip and jumped onto the sofa. So la belle-mère thought he wasn't such a good dancer, did she?

Well, he would show la belle-cochonne, the pretty pig, what dancing was all about. There wasn't a single soul in Mattagash, Maine,
with any rhythm. Everyone knew that. All the rhythm on the
American side of the border had been invested among the French
descendants of the old Canadian settlers. Yes, by Christ, the Catholics had all the rhythm in the state of Maine, even to the musical
kind. Jean Claude jumped off the sofa and into Sicily's face.

"Allons danser, belle-mère!" Jean Claude shouted to Sicily, who
recognized that she was being referred to as a *mare* before she was
swept off her feet and caught up in a frenzied dance. She screamed
lustily as Jean Claude reeled her around and around, occasionally
bouncing her off the wall. The smell of booze on his breath was
sufficient to put Sicily under its influence.

"Help me, Amy Joy!" she shouted at each pirouette.

"Are you satisfied now?" Amy Joy screamed back at her. "This
is what you wanted, isn't it? I hope he dances you to a frazzle!"
Amy Joy grabbed the new spring-summer issue of the Sears Roebuck catalog and began to wallop Jean on the backs of his knees.
The pounding knocked the dancers against the wall in a fast embrace. Sicily caught her breath, and then pointed to the catalog.

"Please don't tear that," she whispered to Amy Joy, in huffs and
puffs. "I've yet to order a single thing from it."

"You let that poor woman go this minute," Amy Joy ordered
Jean Claude.

"She dance good, her," Jean Claude said, heavily winded, and
even in the midst of such utter humiliation Sicily had to suppress
a blush. Amy Joy clouted him again, this time on the elbows. The
catalog ripped loudly.

"Please, dear," said Sicily. "Be careful with the outdoor furniture
section." The balmy arrival of April had reminded her to order a
new lawn chair. She and Jean Claude were still leaning with their
backs against the wall, harmonious at last in that they were both
fighting for breath.

"Well, this is one big happy family, if I ever saw one," Pearl
McKinnon Ivy said from the doorway. "Don't you people ever
answer a knock?"

"Good God, it's Pearl!" said Sicily, and broke away from Jean Claude's arms.

"You want to dance, you?" Jean Claude asked the burly, bosomy woman now standing before him. Chalice de Vierge! They were lining up to dance with him. This one would be like dancing with a plow horse, but no matter. He reached his hand out to Pearl and then proceeded to slide slowly across the wall until he hit the hardwood floor with a thump, taking an end lamp and two Avon candlesticks with him in a crescendo of breaking glass.

"Jean Claude Cloutier," Amy Joy introduced him to Pearl.

"The groom," said Sicily.

Pearl stared in disbelief. Suddenly Thelma Parsons didn't seem like such an awful addition to her family.

"We were practicing for the wedding," Sicily said quickly. Her hair was lopping in all directions on her head. Her face and neck were flushed red and her apron was twisted around to her side. "French people dance an awful lot at weddings," she explained.

"On sofas?" asked Pearl. So she had been watching from the doorway all along. The *snoop*.

"Sometimes," said Sicily.

"If there's one around," Amy Joy added.

"What's wrong with him?" Pearl asked, ever the detective, and still able to intimidate Sicily at a second's notice.

"He's exhausted," said Amy Joy. "He's been rehearsing for the wedding all week."

"Looks more like he's been rehearsing for the honeymoon," said Pearl. "Anyway, I just stopped by for the key to the old house. What's that awful smell?" She sniffed the odors heavily.

"It smells like someone's been grilling out," she said at last, proud of her nasal powers. "Have you?"

"Affirmative," said Amy Joy quickly. "We grilled all evening."

"Spring finally here and all," added Sicily.

Pearl walked over to the smashed pot of shamrocks. The trios of little leaves, which had already closed for the night, were clinging desperately to the pot.

"Is that a batch of Mama's old shamrocks?" she asked, and Sicily nodded mechanically.

"Is it a French custom to throw them on the floor before a wedding?" inquired Pearl.

"Oh no," said Sicily, as she bent to scoop dirt back into the pot. "I was right in the midst of repotting them."

"And you just dropped them there to go dance?" Pearl drilled on. "I see."

"Well, here's the key," said Sicily brightly. She fished it out of her apron pocket, which was now on her rear hip. She knew Pearl would be stopping for it, but she hadn't expected to give it to her under such circumstances. She had imagined herself driving over with Pearl and unlocking the big front door, and their going into the old homestead as *sisters*. The way women do in movies. And they would say warm things to each other, like "Remember this" and "Remember that," and the old house would come to life around them. But this is what happened when French Catholics infiltrated good Protestant, English-speaking families. They crumbled like cookies. Like that unleavened bread those Catholics were always chewing on during mass.

"The telephone man came yesterday and hooked you up a telephone, like you wanted," Sicily said meekly.

Pearl said nothing more. It was obvious to her that what was going on was nothing more than washing off the dirt. She wasn't sure what kind of dirt, or just how much, but it was typical of Mattagashers, especially of McKinnons, to hide every wart and mole they could, even from other family members. Sometimes *especially* from family members.

"I'll be running along, then," said Pearl. She was thankful that Sicily looked too distraught to follow her over to the old house. She wanted, for some reason, to walk inside alone. She had even asked Marvin if he would wait a few minutes in the car. "Marvin's out in the car. We're pretty tired."

"You get some rest, then," said Sicily, and attempted to swing the massive Pearl around, point her to the door. "It's good to see you," she said, shoving.

"What's that?" asked Pearl.

"Where?" asked Sicily.

"Where?" asked Amy Joy.

"Right there," said Pearl, and pointed to the moist, hot dog–pink pile on the bottom step of Sicily's stairs.

"Dog puke," said Amy Joy, and twirled one of her silver streaks.

 McKINNON IS A McKINNON IS A McKINNON: MARGIE'S GHOST IS BACK, BACK, BACK

....

"Our revels now are ended. These, our actors,
As I foretold you, were all spirits and
Are melted into air, into thin air . . . We are such stuff
As dreams are made on, and our little life
Is rounded with a sleep."

—William Shakespeare, *The Tempest*

THE VERY FIRST NIGHT IN THE OLD MCKINNON HOMESTEAD welcomed Pearl McKinnon Ivy with terrifying dreams. Maybe the coconut cream pie from which she and Marvin had eaten two extra-large slices before bedtime added a luster to the nightmare. Or maybe the old-settler ghosts were unhappy over being stirred up, fidgety with the intrusion from the outer world they never visited in their time, when their bones held flesh. Or maybe they had questions about that world to ask the prodigal daughter. One thing Pearl could be sure of was that they'd welcome her back, or at least wanted her there. It wasn't good, she knew, to stray off, far from home, *downriver*, across the ocean, away from the rituals.

"If you're a missionary, it's okay," Pearl had remembered hearing the day she bumped south on a Greyhound bus to Portland. The day she had abandoned (that's how Margie had put it) her family, her town, a way of life, and set off for Portland with the dream to become a hairstylist.

"If you're a missionary, it's all right," Margie had told her. "Then you got a purpose. Then God will watch out for you."

"Well, maybe that's why there's so many missionaries," Pearl had answered. "Maybe all that religious zeal is just nature's way of covering up for ants in the pants." Then Pearl had snapped the tiny padlocks shut on her aging suitcase. End of argument. But for years she sensed that Marge took pleasure in Pearl's having ended up married into an undertaking family. God wasn't watching out for her, as he surely would a missionary. God wouldn't let one of his sheep marry a gravedigger.

Pearl opened her eyes and adjusted them to the architecture of her old bedroom. She felt the row of beaded perspiration on her forehead turn suddenly cold, and reached up with her pajama sleeve to wipe it away. She lay next to Marvin and stared at the ceiling. Outside, she could hear the Mattagash River bursting at its old seams. When the water was lower and the boulders along the shore emerged out of the deep, the river would be even noisier. Pearl knew this. She *remembered*. She remembered a lot of things suddenly, like how to spy a good fishing hole after a heavy rain caused the water to rise just so. How to discover where the king-fisher's tunnel-nest was hiding by finding the telltale scratches around a hole in the riverbank. And Pearl remembered all kinds of wonderful things about the old-timers she'd grown up with. She recalled how Old Man Gardner could harvest a bucketful of earth-worms just by pounding a pointed piece of wood, what he called a stob, into the ground and then rubbing a piece of steel across the stob. The vibrations in the earth drove all those worms right out of their little minds, and Pearl remembered seeing them rush right up to the surface and give themselves up, like convicts of some kind. A kid could walk along and pick up enough fish bait for a week, just like picking wild strawberries. Old Man Gardner used to boast that on good days he could harvest over two thousand of the squiggly, wiggly things. Fishermen from out of state bought them up as if they were something good to eat. And old Mrs. Sophia Mullins was a case to remember, too. There was no one in Mattagash in that day and age who would even attempt to dig a well until old Sophia hobbled around with her willow switch jumping in her hands like something alive. Divining water. Pearl supposed backhoes and fancy hole diggers had replaced Old Sophia, who had been divining water in her coffin for at least thirty, forty years. And Samuel Gifford, the old half-Indian, would make a stick from a cherry tree and beat ash out so fine it looked like yarn.

"They never *built* an ash pounder that good," Pearl said aloud. "Yet I can barely remember Samuel Gifford." She felt Marvin stir sleepily beside her and, rather than wake him, she let the ghosts of Old Man Gardner, Sophia Mullins, and Samuel Gifford take their worms, and willow switches, and ash-woven baskets and go back to peddle their wares among the dead.

In the hallway Pearl followed the tiny night-light she'd left on in the kitchen. A glass of warm milk would help her to sleep. Margie used to do that. Often Pearl would wake up in the middle of the night and hear a soft clattering in the kitchen below. Margie. Unable to sleep again.

"She must have been damn lonely," Pearl muttered, and quickly settled a pan on the stove. She took milk from the refrigerator, Marge's same old Kenmore, and poured a generous amount into the pan. She turned the gas burner on and watched the flame engulf it with a blue hiss. The Mullins girls had done a good job of getting the house in order. It was almost as good as new. Almost. Pearl could detect a most noticeable sagging, with her older sister gone a decade. Marge had kept a discerning eye on every nook and cranny. But winters are cruel in northern Maine, and no matter how lovingly spring comes back to caress the bruises, to lick the wounds, there is a stiffness that never leaves. The joints of the old

McKinnon homestead, like the joints of its last human occupants, were stiffening with age.

"It's tired is all," Pearl whispered, as the floor beneath her feet creaked with her weight. "But it's still nice. It's still home." She stopped short a second, sure that she heard a scuffling in the basement, or outside, *somewhere*. When silence came back at her, she smiled.

"The mice must be as big as I remember them," she thought, and opened a box of graham crackers from which she selected three. She and Marvin had picked up a few things to get them through the night, but tomorrow it would be necessary to stock the fridge. She would also have to explain the phone to Marvin tomorrow, with some kind of lie.

"Why a phone when we'll only be here a week?" he was bound to ask her when he discovered it in the den.

"Oh, just to keep in touch," Pearl would say. "Anything can happen." Soon, though, she would be compelled to tell her husband that she was staying on in Mattagash.

Pearl stood in front of Marge's old china cabinet and bit into a graham cracker. The baby roses were still on all the dishes, a pattern Pearl dearly loved. How many Sunday dinners had the three sisters and the reverend spent hovering above those roses like a family of bees? Pearl even remembered how many roses had been on each plate.

"Twelve," she said, and pressed a finger against the glass door. And she used to count them as she ate, knowing that when a dozen flowers surfaced, sprouted, the meal would be over, her plate empty, dessert waiting. It was wise of Sicily to leave the dishes in the cabinet. To leave most of Marge's stuff right where it was, in the old house.

"There's no room in my house either," Sicily had agreed with Pearl. "I suppose I could rent it all furnished to one of the school-teachers who has to travel all the way from Watertown, but somehow it don't seem right. Some things shouldn't be moved. And they shouldn't be trifled with by strangers. But one day, Pearl, we need to sort through it all and divide it between Amy Joy and your granddaughters."

"Make sure the Giffords don't find out it's got all its furnishings," Pearl had warned, after Marge's funeral. "Put the word around town that you've boxed everything up and stored it in your attic. Let them think we picked the place bone-dry."

Pearl sipped her milk loudly. She was no longer in Portland, Maine. She could guzzle as she pleased.

"I can see Cynthia Jane with this china right now," Pearl said to her reflection in the cabinet glass. "She'd break a rose plate every time she pulled her pants out of her crotch."

Pearl went into the reverend's old study. Next to the cherry desk a small bookcase bulged with books. Pearl checked the spines. All old, mostly autobiographies of missionaries who had giant ants in their pants and who had inscribed their books to the reverend. Pearl had heard Marge tell of the days when Reverend Ralph had a stream of visiting missionaries come to entertain Mattagash with stories about the heathen world. That was before Pearl's eyes and ears started picking up information for themselves about her environment. That was another place, another time, when Grace McKinnon, still very much alive, floated about as a gracious hostess and the house itself was newly minted.

Pearl left the old books alone. Someone should check their value someday, it was true. In Portland, there was a rare-book store on every block. Yet it was funny how most folks in Mattagash regarded anything old as valueless. They wanted new things, store-bought things. The treasures of the past embarrassed them now. Mattagash was going modern.

Pearl closed the door to the study behind her. It caused her mouth and her stomach to tighten, just walking into the room. There were no good memories of the reverend. There were no bad ones, either, when she thought about it. He was like a Mattagash winter, Pearl realized. When it's all over, and you're standing in the midst of summer again, you only *remember* that there was something harsh and unforgiving that happened to you.

"The old devil," Pearl said, and laughed as she closed the door.

She remembered the look on Sicily's face the first time she heard Pearl call him that. A man of God as the old devil himself.

Pearl went back into the kitchen to rinse her glass. When she was a girl there used to be two silver pails of water sitting on the counter at all times. She and Sicily shared the chore of lugging it up from the spring. Marge had running water installed years later. The pails, Pearl realized now, were galvanized, but when you were a child a winter's morning sun could transform zinc-plated tin into pure silver.

Pearl opened the back door cautiously and the full sound of what spring could do to a river hit her citified ears. The old summer kitchen sulked in the shadows outside, like the dinosaur it was. In its day it was used heavily in the summer months for cooking and canning, to keep the heat out of the main house. In the winter it was closed up, ice on the linoleum and windows, a foot of snow on the roof. Marge had kept it shipshape, however, no matter that its functional qualities had been swept away with the dust of the years. Now Pearl understood all too well Marge's need to hang on to the past. Folks knew you by name there, and you were always welcome.

Pearl was about to abandon the bones of the old kitchen and the millions of gallons of Mattagash River water to the glittery April night when a flashy movement bounced into the corner of her eye. Above the cloudy puffs of her warm breath, cascading into frosty air, Pearl saw a light moving cautiously inside the summer kitchen. She felt her nostrils narrow with her frightened intake of breath, and threaten to freeze there. Was it a light? Oh, it was all so much like one of Junior's old Trixie Beldon books: *The Mystery of the Light Somewhere or Other*. Then Pearl remembered other things about lights. She remembered hearing the old-timers speak of them in graveyards, and hadn't she and Sicily seen a few themselves as children on Halloween nights? Yes, big balls of fire rolling about in the Catholic graveyard. It was always the Catholic graveyard. Protestant ghosts weren't so outspoken. The chilliness left Pearl, and she flushed warm to recall the terrifying answers to these things.

"It's the soul going off," Marge had said. "Round and blue and fragile."

Pearl stared hard at the light. It *was* a light, that was certain, bouncing in the darkness, in among where Marge's old mason jars must still be shelved.

"Sweet Jesus," Pearl whispered. She remembered that Flora Gumble, the grammar school teacher who taught so many generations of Mattagash children that she began calling the new arrivals by the names of their grandparents, had been much more scientific.

"It doesn't happen when folks are embalmed," she had said, still in her sixties then, to some of the kids who waited around after school to inquire about the tales. "It's human gas rising out of the body, is all. It'll glow like a little lantern." And Pearl remembered how Vinal Gifford, a little first-grader then, had asked solemnly, "Do you mean them balls of fire is ghost farts?"

But Pearl knew better. She'd seen a real one hundred percent genuine-article ghost when she was twelve. A young ghost. A pretty ghost. A woman ghost. Pearl had not only *seen* her, there had been words between the living and the spectral. Oh, sweet Jesus, when she remembered, all the wispy neck hairs on Pearl's nape stretched out to their limits. The only person Pearl told had been Sicily. She had no intention of being shackled and then packed off to Bangor and locked in a padded cell, due to unearthly visions.

"I'm looking for my children," the ghost had said softly. "Are you my child?"

Terror seized Pearl again, as it had that day out behind the lilac bushes, where rumor held that three little children had been buried after a bad spread of influenza. This was before the Reverend Ralph built the McKinnon house and started his own family. But even after all those years Mattagashers still told of how the mother of those three little kids had gone stark raving mad and had to be taken away. But she had managed, after death, to come back and ask a twelve-year-old the whereabouts of her children. Pearl believed in ghosts, and that's why she had run from the inquiring woman without answering.

"Why didn't you tell her to dig beneath the lilac bush?" eight-year-old Sicily had asked later.

Yes, Pearl believed in ghosts, but what ghost would be interested in ransacking the old summer kitchen, for the love of God? What ghost would be content to rattle dust off the mason jars and search through Marge's moldy trunk, read her mildewed letters? Fear drove a knife, suddenly, into Pearl's heart. *Marge!*

"Marge?" The word trembled out of Pearl's mouth, and her hand quickly flicked the switch. A fan of porch light fell out into the blackness, turned the lurking black beast into harmless gray shingles. Pearl looked again. The light was gone. She flicked the porch light off once more and tried again to find the eerie light. Sheer blackness confronted her, except for the worn stars which had patterned themselves over Mattagash before even the Indians found the place. This was way back when God first put stars in the sky there, so that one day the McKinnons could follow them upriver to found a town. And later the Giffords could utilize that same starlight to shine a path for them to the nearest hubcap or tire iron. There were only stars out there, behind Marge's old house, and the pounding swell of the spring river.

"Margie?" Pearl tried once more, before she closed the door and locked it.

It must have been only minutes after she had fallen asleep that the voice woke Pearl. She had lain snuggled up to Marvin for nearly an hour while she pondered the unearthly circumstances out in the musty summer kitchen, that haven for ghosts. And although she was sure it couldn't happen, she'd fallen asleep. At first it had filtered in to her as part of her dream, but then it grew louder and tugged her toward it until she opened her eyes and realized that it was coming from outside the house, from the back of the house, from the site of the summer kitchen.

"Marvin?" Pearl whispered. "Wake up." He answered by chopping off a snore in midflight and turning over on his side. Pearl was suddenly glad he hadn't wakened, considering the circumstances. If she let him see her like that, frightened in the night by ghosts, how could she convince him of the validity in her staying on alone? The voice again, a male's. Sweet Christ, had the old reverend himself come home from China? Could ghosts navigate such great distances? In real life he couldn't even drive a car.

Pearl struggled out of bed and tiptoed over to the window. Holding her breath, she leaned forward to the cold glass and peered down. Suddenly a male form moved out of the shadows of the house, into a pond of starlight. It stood stiffly, looking toward the river, toward the old highway. All Pearl could discern, from her crow's nest view, was the figure of a sturdy man with a full head of thick curls. She gasped. She remembered just such a dark curly head from her childhood, one connected to the summer kitchen.

"Marcus Doyle," thought Pearl. "Marcus Doyle." Who else but Marge's missionary lover, who had slept in the very summer kitchen during the autumn of 1923, who else would come back to cavort with Marge among the mason jars and old love letters of another time?

"He wrote those letters to her," Pearl whispered, and shivered involuntarily as she peered down on the phantom. Then it was gone, lost on the black trail that led around the house. Maybe he had followed the trail all the way to the river, past the lilac grave-yard where Pearl had seen the woman-ghost. Maybe he was inside the summer kitchen right now, had gone straight through the shin-gled wall, rather than follow any old river path. Maybe he was, at this very minute, huddled with Margie over her trunk of letters, reading them again, almost fifty years after they were written. Another thought occurred to Pearl, as she stood barefoot on the cold floorboards of her old bedroom and looked down on the sum-mer kitchen. And it frightened her more than the pale woman-ghost seeking her dead children. It frightened her much, much more than the Catholic fireballs that used to roll at little Protestant trick-or-treaters, fireballs from hell. This was scarier. Much scarier.

"Sicily and I threw them old love letters away!" Pearl thought, and leaned listlessly against the wall. Hell hath no fury like a letter writer scorned. Heavenly Savior, but Marge would be furious when she found out! Marge would be what Randy called really pissed off. Had she been waiting, then, these ten long years by the lilac bush, that favorite hangout of ghosts, for Pearl to innocently, unsuspectingly come home?

"Her ghost'll probably go into a tailspin," Pearl thought. "Her ghost'll probably hemorrhage right on the floor of the summer kitchen."

Pearl McKinnon Ivy developed such a genuine case of the jimjams that she was unable to sleep anymore on the first night of her long-awaited homecoming.

BABY JESUS RETURNS

TO MATTAGASH: LET THE GAMES BEGIN

....

"It's beginning to look a lot like Christmas,
Everywhere you go . . ."
—Sung by Bing Crosby. Never sung in Mattagash

THE LAST WEEK OF APRIL TURNED INTO A COLD ONE, WITH THE
ground reluctant to shake loose the embedded icy veins. Then, to
no one's surprise, a heavy wind decided to get involved. The last
week of April was not heralding wedding weather, by any means,
and the fact that Amy Joy Lawler was having hers on May first
suggested a *hurriedness* to the entire town that left it purring with
gossip. Both clans of Giffords had passed the notion that something
was afoul around the supper table several times since they first
heard of the quick wedding. It did not occur to anyone in town

that Amy Joy's *head* was in a rush for the wedding, not her *belly*.

It was not wedding weather that followed the Gifford kids out to the school bus on the last Friday of April. Cold still clung to the mammoth cakes of ice that lay like white Roman walls along the Mattagash River bank. Snow still peeked out from beneath the trees at the edge of the woods, and during the nights the dead grass in the fields crusted with frost so that the morning sun careened off it in glittering bounces. From the looks of it, it could have been sheer snow.

The last Friday of April found a school bus full of rambunctious children, with MATTAGASH CONSOLIDATED SCHOOL DISTRICT #12 on its side, winding its way along the main road, dropping off all the modern descendants of the old loyalist settlers. That daily bus ride home from school had been a ride of terror for everyone on board until Fred, the driver, grabbed Little Pee and Little Vinal and knocked their heads together. He then assured them that if they so much as breathed loudly on his bus again they would become acquainted with the two-by-four he had stashed beneath the driver's seat.

"If you two don't want the Watertown mortician visiting your mothers," Fred had said, "you'd better sew up them lips."

Although Little Pee and Little Vinal had quieted during rides, Fridays always contained an excitement that stirred up the whole busload. Freedom from school, and the elusive joy that creeps in as the weekend is about to roll around, precipitated a kind of People's Revolution on board. When the lumbering school bus pulled to a screechy halt in the heart of Giffordtown that Friday, all the school-age Giffords except for Little Vinal, who was enjoying the final days of his suspension, raced down the steps and out into the chilly air wafting up from the river. Vera's kids went left, across the road to their house, and Goldie's climbed the hill as the bus pulled away in a cloud of exhaust. Among the mountaineers was Miltie, Goldie's baby, who had been so congested during the notorious cough season that Goldie insisted he wear his mittens even before April turned cold on them. Preferring to tough the nippiness, as the big kids did, Miltie perpetually lost his mittens.

Sometimes they stayed sizzling on the warm register at school. They were often left behind in his seat on the bus. They were forgotten in the boys' bathroom or, worse, they were actually *lost*. On the last Friday of April, Miltie managed to come home with his mittens.

Slower than the older, long-legged children, Milton was the last off the bus. Despite Goldie's constant plea for Priscilla and the others to lag behind with him as protection, Miltie's siblings usually raced each other up the long hill, seeing who could tap their hand on the front door first. Miltie had long gotten over the insult of being left behind in such a fashion. He no longer even looked up in envy at the retreating soles of boots and sneakers. He consoled himself with the knowledge that one day he would be taller and faster than all of them. One day he would run up, tap the door, then run back to meet the losers halfway up the hill.

Running this imaginary race in his mind, Miltie decided he'd best put on his mittens, since they'd both come home with him anyway, and satisfy Goldie. The right one went on smoothly enough but, as Miltie's hands were also encumbered by a week-long accumulation of school papers, the other green mitten dropped like a heavy leaf to the roadside. Holding his papers in his teeth, Miltie squatted to retrieve the woolly nuisance. A gust of wind came roaring up like a truck and swept the mitten across the road and into Vera's yard. Miltie bit into his papers and chased it. He spotted the mitten, but so did Popeye, Vera's dog, who had long ceased to receive the hearty dishes that Vera insisted he eat last January. Popeye went for the mitten as if it was meat. Miltie was no match for the huge animal but he dived in anyway. Popeye was less frightening than his mother angry over another lost mitten.

Popeye had never taken sides in the Gifford family feud and instead wagged his tail diplomatically at all the children. But whether he meant to do it, or whether it was a freak accident, was not important. What was important was that Miltie's leg came out of the shuffle with severe tooth marks and some bleeding. Aunt Vera came running out and demanded to know what Milton Gifford was doing in her yard, on private property. Miltie was crying too hard to tell her. Instead he grabbed the mitten from Popeye, who was shaking it in an attempt to play, and raced up the hill, falling twice.

Goldie could not speak as she washed the wound and doused it with iodine. She covered it with a Band-Aid, planted Miltie on the couch, tucked a blanket about him, and snapped on *Bozo the Clown*. Then she bundled up in a scarf and coat and marched down the hill. But, like the January fight, nothing came of it except some extraordinarily loud shouting. Big Vinal came running from the garage, where he had been busy with some clandestine cuttings and skinnings that involved an illegally shot deer.

"She sicced Popeye on Miltie!" shouted Goldie.

"I did no such thing," said Vera, who was barefoot, and stepping on one foot, then the other, on her chilly front porch.

"That dog ain't all there," said Goldie. "He walks around all day with a rock in his mouth."

"I wish you'd do the same," said Vera, all ashiver. "It'd keep your tongue from wagging."

Back at the Gifford house on the hill Goldie told Pike Senior what had taken place. Still not wanting the roof to blow off, considering the weather, Pike inspected Miltie's leg wound and said, "That ain't too bad a bite, is it, Miltie?"

Miltie felt differently. It was indeed a monstrous bite, a trauma he might never get over, but then Pike said, "You're Daddy's little man, ain't you? You ain't gonna act like no old girl now, are you?" No. Of course Miltie wasn't.

"You can't blame Popeye," said Goldie. "That's the first time that poor dog's been near a bone with meat around it." She was briskly folding towels from her laundry basket. "Vera never feeds him. Half the time he walks around looking for low crotches to sniff. He's too weak to jump for the high ones."

The more Vera sat at the bottom of the hill and thought about it, the madder she became. Why hadn't she brought up the Christmas tree lights to Goldie? She had been waiting since December, in a kind of emotional hibernation, to remind Goldie of her greed. To reacquaint Goldie with the fact that all of Mattagash knew that the basement or the attic at the top of the hill must be bulging with boxes of lights. She wanted to rub it in Goldie's face like it was snow, or maybe even snot. Either one would be distasteful in April. Instead she had only shouted, and chilled her bunion-cursed toes to the bone. What a waste of a wonderful opportunity. And Goldie had been on Vera's land, in case the sheriff from St. Leonard had taken an interest in the family reunion. Well, suffering Jesus, she would let Goldie know one way or another that she remembered the lights. She would remind Goldie Plunkett Gifford in a big way.

Toward evening Goldie looked down the hill and saw Vera outside in the icy wind, trying to install what looked like *Christmas decorations!* A five-foot-long cardboard poster of Santa Claus, with a mittened hand on Mrs. Claus's shoulder, proved especially difficult. The wind caught the bottom of the poster several times and yanked the tacks out of the top where Vera was trying in vain to secure it. When the wind died down for a minute, Vera managed to get several tacks up and down the poster, and suddenly her door was no longer a dull brown but brightly emblazoned with the holiday husband-and-wife duo.

"It's one hundred percent pure menopause," Goldie said to Pike, who had been summoned off the sofa for a peek. "The Bible might call it a crown of glory, but let's face it. What you see down there is a crazy woman."

"Is Uncle Vinal gonna take Aunt Vera to Bangor?" Missy asked. "Is he gonna put her in the crazy bin?"

"He should," Goldie answered. "Lord knows she belongs in it."

Next, Vera lined the porch with Christmas lights, saving a meager string for the scrawny outdoor tree she'd told Goldie about last December. This was why she needed some of those extra lights that her sister-in-law had stockpiled. She instructed Little Vinal, who had to disrupt his sabbatical in order to do so, to pry a thin fir into the hard mud around the newly erected mailbox. Goldie watched with interest from behind the kitchen curtain as Vera ran an extension cord out to the tree and lit it up. It was still too early in the evening to catch the full lighting effects, but once Vera was assured it was working, she unplugged it and went about tacking sprays of pine branches at random about the porch.

Goldie stared down at the piteous tree driven into the mire near the mailbox. It was for the adoration of *this* that Vera had climbed the big icy hill four months ago and cried bloody murder?

"It looks like budworms lived off it all last summer," Goldie said to Missy, and let the curtain fall back into place. "I don't give a damn what the Bible says, you're looking at a genuine hot flash."

It was only ten minutes later that Goldie reappeared at her window, unable to resist, and peered down to see that Vera was arranging the plastic figurines of her Nativity scene in their usual place on the front lawn. By nightfall, all the plastic participants stood around the baby Jesus, who lay illuminated by means of an extension cord rather than a halo. The lighted faces of the group were in dire contrast to the low temperature that the black April night had swept over Mattagash. Goldie looked down at the tranquil, grinning visages. There was the perpetual Mother, smiling sweetly at her naked son. Naked, and the temperature was still dropping! Goldie looked down into Mary's peaceful face, where a layer of frost had begun to form.

"With the windchill factor what it is," Goldie said to Missy, who was eating relief peanut butter with a spoon, "you almost want to see Mary get up and take that poor baby inside."

"She could at least put a Pamper on it," said Missy, plopping her empty spoon in the sink.

It was only five minutes later when the telephone rang. Goldie was shocked to hear Vera's breathy voice on the other end of the line. The decorating had winded her, but her anger was in full sail.

"You can buy all the goddamn Christmas lights in Watertown!" Vera screamed. "But you don't own 'em all. Just take a peek down your hill."

"You should be taking pills or something," Goldie said. "You're under the influence of your hormones, Vera." Goldie was about to hang up, but Vera got in her last words.

"Your problem, Goldie, is that you was a bastard baby," Vera yelled. "Ed Plunkett marrying your mother ain't gonna make any difference with the Pope. You're gonna end up on the same cloud as them unbaptized babies."

Goldie put the phone back in its cradle. Then she went upstairs, away from the kids, and Pike, and the noisy television set. She went up to her bedroom, closed the door, and lay back on her bed, eyes closed.

When Claire Fennelson, Dorrie's mother, had told Goldie one day on the playground that Ed Plunkett wasn't her real father, she went into the bathroom and cried hot, salty tears. Then she came out with her head held high in the air. What else could she have done? And the other children had laughed—Giffords and not-Giffords alike—and said she was stuck-up. They said that knowing her real father was from downstate had gone to her head. But Goldie knew that it was best they think this. And when they weren't looking, she found out all she could about her real father. She coaxed it word by word out of her mother, her precious mother, when she was sober enough to talk. Goldie's last memories of this person were of the fine yellow skin and the yellowish of her eyeballs. Her swollen ankles and the huge round bloodspots on her shins. Her bloated stomach and her hardened liver. Goldie remembered how desperately those organs were fighting to get out of her mother's body. And so were the secrets, because she told Goldie the truth before cirrhosis took her off. Her father was in a nursing home in Bangor.

So Goldie had waited, and the day came when Pike went as far as that city to visit Clement, his second cousin. Clement had found Pike a good deal on a used Ford Fairlane and Goldie demanded to ride down with him. Once there, she got Clement's wife, Peg, to drive her over to the home. And then she went in with her heart full of forgiveness. He was too young to be in a nursing home, but he needed medical attention. The nurse whispered to Goldie short references to excessive drinking, ruined health, dying organs. She needn't have bothered. She could have saved her breath. Goldie had seen jaundice up so close it reminded her of how autumn came to the old vegetables in her garden, turning them to a sheeny yellow and then to mush. So Goldie had pushed quietly past the nurse and gone off down the hall in search of his room. Yes, he said, he used to live in Mattagash. Yes, he knew her mother, Mildred, but then, so did a lot of men. And no, he wasn't, he was quite sure, her father.

"Do I look like anyone in your family?" Goldie had asked. Everyone in Mattagash knew that Goldie looked like no one in Ed Plunkett's family, or in Mildred Gifford's. Surely she looked like someone in his family. A mother? A sister? Other daughters? A cousin?

"You got to understand," Goldie whispered to him. "All these years, I been lost out there. All these years, I been floating."

"No!" he told her. "Now shoo! Git!" He looked at her as if she were a fly and he wanted badly to swat her.

"I've waited my whole life for someone to belong to," Goldie said. "I don't look a bit like Mama, or the man she married. But I got your eyes, and your cheekbones. And I got your nose, don't I? And I bet your hair was blond once. That's why you can't even look at me."

Mildred's old boyfriend rose up out of his chair when Goldie said this, and tried to hit her. He swung something dark and rattling at her. As Goldie pulled back to avoid the impact, she saw that the weapon in his hands was a rosary.

"You've cursed yourself, old man," Goldie whispered. "I'd have taken you out of here. After all these years of *nothing* from you, I'd have taken you home. But now you've cursed yourself. That rosary ain't long enough to keep you out of hell."

Goldie ignored the receptionist at the front desk who asked if she'd be coming for the Father's Day get-together, and if so could she bring a covered dish. On the trip back to Mattagash, Pike had driven into a station to get some gas. There were only the first three kids back then, Irma, Priscilla, and Little Pee, and they were asleep in the backseat. They'd tired on the long drive down and were fussy and unhappy in the heat. Goldie was relieved when they finally drifted off, their little heads all golden and curly. This was like no Gifford hair she'd ever seen. The curls, yes, but that fine yellow flaxen was not at all like the dark chestnut hair of all their Gifford ancestors. And no one in Ed Plunkett's family had such hair. It was Goldie's own hair she was seeing on the heads of the children. As she shooed a fly away from Irma's sleeping face, she noticed the little arts and crafts shop next to the gas station. While Pike was pumping gas and checking the oil, Goldie got out and went into the little shop to browse. An old woman with a stiff leg came clumping out of a back room, wiping her hands on her sweater. She was just browsing, Goldie told her, while her husband gassed up the car.

"We got us a six-hour drive over a bumpy road," said Goldie.

"I make all this stuff myself," the old woman said. "It's how I get by. That little check the government sends me ain't enough to feed the cats. That little government check wasn't worth getting old for."

So Goldie shopped among the potholders and tea cozies, the dish towels and doilies and throw rugs. She walked past terry-cloth curtains and facecloths with "Maine, Vacationland" embroidered on them with bright red stitching. And in the back there were dried-apple dolls and pine cones tied with red ribbons. There were little crocheted Santa Clauses with cotton batting beards.

"Them's left over from Christmas," the old woman said. Goldie picked up a dusty set of salt and pepper shakers with a pine cone and tassel poorly painted on each. The old woman squinted at them.

"Them's the state flower," she said, and spit on a finger to wipe away the dust so that Goldie could better see the little tassels. "Just between you and me," she added, "that's a sorry flower for a state to have."

The little front room was full of the old woman's treasures, some dusty and yellowing, some fairly new. Handkerchiefs and kerchiefs. Little throw pillows. Violets stitched on place mats. Crocheted slippers. Mittens. Knitted wool scarves. On one wall Goldie saw a handsaw with a varnished handle. On the blade was painted a scene of a brook surrounded by trees in autumn. There were birds far off, doing something in the sky, and a small doe, almost too brown in color to be real, was drinking at the brook's mouth, its velvet lips pressed like petals to the water.

"I never would've thought of that," said Goldie, running a finger along the edge of the saw. "What a pretty thing to do to a handsaw."

"There's pictures in everything," said the old woman. And as Goldie looked past the white dinner plates, which had more scenes on them, which had rabbits, and a moose, and a pulp truck, she thought of the old woman's house as a special kind of museum. She thought of it as a gingerbread house in the forest where a good witch lived.

"Them can be used for ashtrays," she said, when Goldie lifted a plate and admired it. "Or candy dishes. Or to hold little cakes of soap." The old woman looked at them lovingly, imagining all their uses. On one plate was painted a picture of a little house sitting alone, a gray house with a single light in the window, with a Christmas wreath on the door, and all around it were globs of white-paint snowflakes swirling and whirling in a frenzy to come down. There was an expectancy about the little house, and the lone candle, and the deep green pines billowing in around it. There was a sudden sadness.

"That's my favorite, too," said the old woman, rolling a pair of socks into a ball and tossing them into a basket where something stirred and stretched, and Goldie saw that it was a huge yellow-striped cat. And she realized that in the dark corners of the room, even among the pot holders and little rocks painted to look like Easter eggs, among things Goldie didn't recognize—like colored strips of cotton a foot long and hemmed neatly, maybe bows for a little girl's braids—among the sachets and hanging chimes made of painted wood chips, were countless cats curled into round balls: tigers, calicoes, blacks, whites, grays, tortoiseshells. Cats dozing among the subtle shapes and colors. Goldie thought of the old woman's house now as a gold mine, and of all the cats as sleeping booby traps. If someone should try to take anything, there would be a quick snarl, a fast claw to the hand.

"That little check don't even feed the cats," the old woman said again, and she turned her old face up to Goldie, and Goldie saw that it looked like the dried-apple dolls on the shelf, all brown and wrinkled, the juice drained out.

When Goldie saw the Christmas angels, she knew she would have to buy one. To help feed the cats. To help keep the wheels turning. The factory rolling. To keep alive the stitching, tatting, crocheting, knitting, embroidering, gluing, painting, hemming, cutting, pasting. And so she bought one. There were several of them, nearly identical except for one. Its hair was blonder. Its face sadder.

"Their bodies is cardboard," said the old woman, whispering. "And their dresses is from an old lace dress I had years ago." She was telling Goldie precious secrets. And she was excited about the sale.

"Them wings is angel's hair left from some Christmas when my kids was small," she said quickly, just in case Goldie might change her mind and put the angel back. She counted out the change, wetting each bill with a finger spitty from her mouth, so as to be sure, counting each smooth coin tenderly.

"Once," she said, trying to raise herself up to Goldie's ear. "Once," she said, dry-throated, tearful, "they all caught on fire. All my things. I lost plenty, I tell you. Lost all the angels but them you see. And when I come to rescue them, they had raised their arms up to heaven." She smiled at Goldie. "They were like tiny children letting their mothers undress them."

When Goldie took her angel and went back out into the sun, the door tinkled behind her as she closed it. Back in the car she couldn't be sure if it had really happened, if the old woman really was in that shabby house, sitting there in the sun like an old mushroom. A house full of sleeping cats, and angels, and dark secret corners. A storybook house. A tale of the old woman's life. Her only statement. So Goldie *imagined* her inside, an old troll shuffling through the tiny rooms, arranging her trove. And every Christmas Goldie had remembered the tiny old woman. Every year she had wondered if she was now dead. If someone was feeding her cats and watering the plants. Dusting off the other Christmas angels. And every year the secret of her father sank deeper within her. She told no one, not even Lizzie, who *was* Ed Plunkett's daughter, that she had found her real father. It was her secret. And the angel's. And, in part, it was the old woman's secret.

Alone in her bedroom, with Vera's lights blinking happily at the bottom of the hill, Goldie thought about fathers. She had always wanted to possess one, hadn't she, the same way she had longed for her own pet. Ed Plunkett had paid for her food and her clothes, but he offered her little else. And Goldie had wanted to give her children a father, too. Vera's cruel words hadn't hurt, not in the way they were intended. Goldie knew she wasn't headed for some eerie kind of limbo, as Vera had prophesied. What did hurt was the whole notion of fathers. Of family. Of her never having had one as a child.

"Even dogs do," Goldie thought. Her own children were basically fatherless, but they weren't motherless. Goldie looked at their school pictures, scattered about on her dresser. Their heads of blond hair glistened in the reflections of Vera's Christmas lights like little yellow clouds. Halos. Even Little Pee had one. Goldie smiled. They reminded her of the Christmas angels she had seen in the old woman's house. They were Goldie's angels, bad as they were. And someday she would share her secret with them. One day, when they were ready, she would say, "You got that blond hair because you got Swedish blood in you. You can trace it back to New Sweden, Maine. From there, you got to go across the ocean to the old country. But that's the secret of the yellow. That's your hair, explained."

When Miltie came up an hour later to snuggle in for the night next to his mother's warm body, he found Goldie already sleeping peacefully.

JUNIOR CAN'T TEACH THELMA
NEW TRICKS: MONIQUE TESSIER
AS A BUSINESSWOMAN

....

> "If I had to drive over these potholes and frost heaves for the rest of my life, I'd be forced to start wearing a bra. As it is, I have to steer with one hand."
>
> —Monique Tessier, to the startled clerk at Blanche's Grocery

JUNIOR AWAKENED TO HIS FIRST MATTAGASH MORNING IN ALMOST a decade. He checked his watch through squinted eyes and discovered it was only nine-thirty. Saturday. There was plenty of time to lounge in bed now that Marvin Senior wasn't peering out of the funeral home like some kind of watchman, waiting to see if his son would get to the office on time. Junior had even thought of launching into his own business, but he never had the chutzpah, or the moolah, to do so. Now things were looking brighter. The evening before the Ivys set out for Mattagash, Marvin had beckoned Junior inside his leathery office and there had looked his son square in the eye.

"I'll put it to you this way," Marvin told his son. "You see to it that our old secretary stays gone, and you've got your own business in Watertown, Maine."

"Watertown?" asked Junior, at first disappointed to be offered a goody that lay so far north it would be frozen six months out of the year. Watertown was just thirty miles away from being another Mattagash. But then he began to ponder the future consequences. There was only one funeral home in Watertown. Surely, with Junior's years of citified expertise, he could easily swallow up all business until he had complete funerary control of northern Maine. Even Mattagash had stepped, albeit gingerly, into the twentieth century. Except for a few diehards, if Junior could use the pun, who were still holding wakes in their living rooms, most of Mattagash and St. Leonard were now availing themselves of professional undertaking. Junior would become a mogul. He'd be rolling in his own dough within a couple of years, and then goodbye northern Maine. He'd be off for Bangor, maybe, or Lewiston. It might even be time for a big city like Boston.

"You just see that Miss Tessier keeps walking, son, and it's as good as yours," Marvin promised.

"Yes sir," Junior promptly agreed. "You bet she'll keep walking. If *I* have anything to say about it."

"Good for you, son," Marvin said, and patted his shoulder. "The wedding's on Sunday. We'll go first thing Monday and take a good look at Cushman's Funeral Home, Watertown, Maine."

"Thanks, Dad," said Junior.

"You know, son." Marvin was feeling more magnanimous than he could ever recall. "I almost give up on you a thousand times."

"I know, sir," Junior squirmed.

"But I didn't."

"No sir, you sure didn't."

"Not many forty-year-old men have a business tossed into their laps."

"Not many at all," said Junior.

"We'll get Thelma straightened out next," promised Marvin. He was feeling more and more like old Joe Kennedy as the days went by.

"Good idea," agreed Junior.

"But keep an eye on her up in Mattagash," Marvin warned. "Gossip travels fast in Aroostook County. It ain't good for business to have potential clients talking about your family matters."

"I'll keep *two* eyes on her," Junior offered generously.

"Okay," said Marvin. "But you gotta promise me one thing."

"What, sir?"

"About Miss Tessier."

"Yes sir?"

"I wanna see dust coming from that whore's heels at all times."

"I'll keep her walking," Junior had promised.

Junior reached out a hand to touch Thelma but no one was in the bed with him. He sat up and looked about the small room.

"Thelma?"

He found his pants and slipped into them. He pulled on a bulky sweater and slid his feet into slippers. Goddamn cheap-ass Pinkham could at least install a telephone in the room. What if there were an emergency and Junior needed a phone desperately, only to discover Albert not at home? And even if Albert were home, Junior mistrusted that German shepherd. He looked as if he might have been Hitler's own personal guard dog. And he seemed just as two-faced as Albert Pinkham.

Outside on the cement walkway Junior easily found Thelma. She was lounging behind the wheel of the big Cadillac, sunglasses on, staring straight ahead at the Albert Pinkham Motel. When Junior opened the door the smell of gin hit him squarely in the nostrils. Oh Jesus. It was barely morning and she was already plastered.

"Thel?"

"Wha'?" asked Thelma.

"Come on back inside, sweetheart," Junior urged gently. "It's nippy out here and you'll catch a cold. Come on now." Thelma squinted her eyes. *Come on now. Come on down, Thelma Parsons Ivy of Portland, Maine.*

"Come on, Thel, feel your arms. Aren't you cold?"

"Cold?" Thelma asked quizzically. They were supposed to ask her how much a can of pinto beans cost compared to a bottle of Windex. They were supposed to ask her how much cars, and skillets, and vacuum cleaners cost. What was this "cold" business?

"Come on," Junior urged, and tugged on her thin arm. *Come on down!* Then she remembered. This wasn't Bob Barker, the genial host. This was Junior Ivy, the fat cheat.

"No!" Thelma shouted. "Can't you see that I'm very, very busy?"

"Let's go in, hon," Junior tried again.

"No!" screamed Thelma. "I said no! No! No!"

"Goddamn her," Junior thought. If it wasn't his mistress, it was his goddamn wife.

"Thelma, get to hell out of my car," he snarled, as quietly as possible. But it was loud enough that Bruce soon got into the action. He trotted suspiciously around and around Junior's creamy Cadillac. After depositing a half-pint of dark yellow urine on Junior's expensive and beloved hubcaps, Bruce began to howl loudly.

"Will you *shut up!*" Junior wailed.

"I will not," said Thelma, and began to weep.

"I was talking to the *dog*," Junior groaned, and tried to calm his wife. If Thelma caused him to lose his funeral business, so help him God, Junior would kill her. He'd have no place to lay her out, granted, but he would kill her.

"I said I was talking to the dog," Junior said again. "Quiet down now."

"See?" Thelma bleated. "I can't even tell when you're talking to me, or to a dog!" When Albert Pinkham came outside to check on the commotion, Thelma was weeping loudly.

"What's going on?" Albert asked as he calmed Bruce's barks with a few loving pats.

"Nothing," Junior said, and yanked Thelma out of the Cadillac by her bony arms. If he had known what was going to eventually develop, he'd have pulled her back into number 1 before she had the opportunity to become hysterical.

"My wife jammed her finger in the car door is all," Junior explained, winded. He dragged Thelma by the arms over to the cement sidewalk and waited to catch his breath.

"Therefore, she can't *walk?*" asked Albert, as he and Bruce watched the citified goings-on. If he lived to be a hundred and ten, Albert Pinkham would never figure metropolitan folks out. Nor would he want to.

"I want my television set!" Thelma screamed. "Give it back! Give it back!"

"What?" asked Junior, startled.

Albert Pinkham had seen fussy tourists in his day, as had Bruce, but here was a grown woman weeping crazily and kicking her feet to the high heavens on his blessed cement walkway because he, the proprietor, had seen fit to keep the modern nuisance of television out of his establishment.

"I live to learn," Albert muttered as he watched the fracas.

"I want my TV!" screamed Thelma. She knew very well why Junior had dragged her all the way into the northern hinterlands and then plopped her into a primitive motel room. He was jealous of Bob Barker. And Thelma would have driven back downstate, would have driven with the incoming dawn all the way to Portland, to Bob, had it not been the keys to her little yellow Corvair she had been trying since 7:00 A.M. to insert into the Cadillac's ignition.

"I can rent you a radio," offered Albert in what he thought was a burst of generosity. He didn't want to kick these nitwits out again, at least not during the dry times he was experiencing. "Same price as a hot plate," Albert said. "Buck fifty a day."

Junior ignored the offer and instead concentrated on pulling Thelma across the walkway. He'd left the door to number 1 ajar, and now he kicked it wide open.

"I'd watch what I kicked," Albert said, as sternly as he could risk.

Junior backed into the room, his arms firmly locked around Thelma, his eyes at all times on her flailing feet.

"By the way," Albert said to Junior, "there's the matter of Miss Tessier's bill."

As the color drained from Junior Ivy's fleshy face, Thelma hooted with laughter.

"My God!" she roared. "You mean she charges him?"

Junior thought he had dropped Thelma, but when he emerged from his three-second blackout she was still in his arms.

"I'll be right back," he said to Albert. Then he kicked the door shut in the owner's face.

"I'd watch what I kicked," Albert warned again as Bruce growled. Then they went back into the house where Bruce could chew on the ham bone from last night's boiled dinner, and Albert could read the *Bangor Daily News*.

Junior got Thelma undressed. He fumbled through his shaving kit and came up with the little bottle of sleeping pills Dr. Phillips had given him for emergencies such as this.

"Keep her off the Valiums, whatever you do," he had told Junior. "But see she gets some rest. Give her a couple of these only if necessary."

By the time Junior came back with a glass of water, Thelma had already passed out and was snoring loudly.

"What the hell do you mean?" Junior spit the words into Albert Pinkham's astonished face. "Where did you get that name? Who put you up to this?"

Albert stepped out on his front steps, closed the door behind him, and surveyed Pearl McKinnon Ivy's son with a cold, steady eye.

"I'd calm down if I were you," Albert suggested, a bit of April's ice in his words. "Now just what is it you want to know?"

"Who told you my secretary's name?" Junior hadn't calmed down.

"She did," said Albert. "Who else? She also said that since this was a business trip, you'd be paying her motel bill."

"I don't believe you," Junior said, and leaned back against Albert's beige house.

"Then why don't you ask her yourself?" said Albert, and pointed to the car that had just roared off the main road and pulled to a squeaking halt in front of the motel. Junior felt his breath catch up fast in his chest, as though a heavy punch had been thrown there. It was the blasted old Buick, with Monique behind its wheel looking more prim and proper than he'd seen in ages. Junior saw Cushman's Funeral Home disappearing on an ice floe, far down the thunderous Mattagash River.

"Jesus H. Christ," he muttered, as Marvin Randall Ivy III, his own son, Randy, popped out from the passenger side with a bottle of Coke in his hand.

"Hey, Dad!" Randy squeaked, his eyes bristling red from his own leafy sedative. He scratched his crotch heavily, rearranging a few of the living burrs he'd brought from Portland. "Like, you're not gonna fuckin' believe who I ran into, man."

$\mathscr{S}$ICILY AND PEARL
RATTLE THE GHOSTS IN THEIR
CLOSETS: BOY MEETS GIRL

....

"In Mattagash, A.A. means Avon Anonymous. You ever seen how addicted some women is to that stuff?"

—Bob Mullins, Edna-Bob's husband

"HAVE YOU NOTICED ANYTHING STRANGE AROUND THE OLD homestead?" Pearl asked Sicily. They sat together in Sicily's kitchen, catching up on the happenings in their lives. It had been years.

"Strange?" asked Sicily. "Not that I know of, but to tell you the truth, Pearl, there's been so much strange stuff happening right here under my own roof that I doubt I'd be able to recognize strange elsewhere."

"I see," said Pearl.

"What do you mean by strange?"

"Just strange," said Pearl.

"Good Lord, Pearl, I'm glad you're here," Sicily said. "I'm about to go straight through the roof. What am I going to do?"

"I don't know if there's anything you can do," said Pearl. "I remember how I felt when Junior married Thelma."

"How *is* Thelma?" Sicily inquired.

"Don't ask," said Pearl.

"It's impossible to talk to Amy Joy," Sicily said, and stared at her hands. "The past few days she's been in and out constantly, getting things ready at the church, picking this up, dropping that off at the gym for the reception. She's like a chickadee."

"A chickadee," thought Pearl. "That's close. Real close."

"So help me, Pearl, I've thought of everything from giving him poison to offering him money. But the truth is that I don't have enough of either one."

"Poor Sissy," soothed Pearl. "What heartache our children can bring upon us. But you don't know the half of it yet. Believe me," she said. "Thelma's added twenty years to my life. You'll see."

Sicily stared at her sister. It was a habit Pearl had developed early in life, of consoling someone by making them feel even more wretched. But Sicily did not comment on this. Now was not the time to get Pearl's dander up, to cause any sisterly warfare. Sicily needed all the troops she could get.

"And she's not even, you know," said Sicily, "in the family way or anything. I checked the wastebasket in the bathroom and I know this for a fact." Pearl grimaced at this activity. Sometimes it was better to be the mother of a son, even if that son was liable to drag home the likes of Thelma Parsons.

"I tell you," Sicily vowed, "I'm at my wits' end."

"Well," said Pearl. "What's his family like?"

"Who knows?" Sicily shrugged. "From what I understand they're no happier than me about it, although I can't imagine why. But Amy Joy told me that Jean's mother is all bent out of shape." Sicily paused. *Bent out of shape.* What next would she pick up from Amy Joy besides high blood pressure. She felt her pulse. It was thumping wildly.

"This has actually caused me some physical illnesses," said Sicily, sadly. "I don't know how much longer my bladder can hold out, or if it'll ever be right again. All night long I'm tramping to the bathroom and that's just for a few drops."

"What was it you came down with when Marge wouldn't let you marry Ed?" Pearl asked, her brows knitted in question. Sicily paused, then took a deep breath. After all these years Pearl McKinnon still had a bone to pick, and worse yet, she was turning into the spitting image of Marge.

"I didn't *come down* with anything, Pearl," said Sicily sternly. "Good heavens. You'll make me sound like a hypochondriac."

"Well, what was it, then?" Pearl pushed. "I remember it was some stunt. Well, no, I didn't mean stunt, what I meant to say was, oh, what was it?"

"I bought a bag of rat poison," Sicily said at last.

"Rat poison!" Pearl laughed heartily, and squeezed Sicily's hand as though they were sharing the joke. "That's it! And you stayed in your room, not eating a bite of food. And every time Marge checked the bag, she noticed more poison gone! What did you do with it, Sissy? Did you throw it out the window at night? Did you hide it in your chamber pot? Marge and I never could figure it out."

Sicily's eyes turned into hard, round beads. Pearl saw this and eased the hilarity.

"How old was you when you imagined you saw that woman-ghost?" Sicily inquired. Pearl stiffened at this question.

"Imagined?" she asked Sicily, and thought for a moment. "You mean to tell me, after all these years, that you never believed me?"

"Well," said Sicily. "I mean, for heaven's sake, Pearl. What was it you claimed she asked? 'What time is it?' That's pretty farfetched. Ghosts don't care about time."

"Claimed?" asked Pearl.

"Did I say claimed?" Sicily looked surprised.

" 'Are you my child?' " Pearl's teeth clamped together so tightly her jawbone ached. "She said 'Are you my child?' Now what in hell is wrong with asking that?"

"Oh, nothing," said Sicily. "Except that you weren't her child and it would seem like any self-respecting ghost would know that." At Pearl's sharp intake of breath, Sicily made herself busy at the sink.

"Speaking of children," Pearl said mildly, "how many do you suppose Amy Joy will have? Them Catholics, remember, end up with families as big as baseball teams. We're talking a busload. And the kids all look like little dachshunds."

Sicily blanched and leaned against the sink. Perhaps she should ask Pearl how Junior's oldest daughter was, the one with the crotch problem, even in public. Or maybe she could let it slip now, instead of after the wedding as she'd planned, that Winnie Craft had turned up on Sicily's sofa one day not so long ago with a clipping from the *Portland Telegram*. Surely the Marvin Randall Ivy III of Portland who was arrested on marijuana charges must be someone else. Surely, Sicily would tell Pearl, Portland must be chock full of boys named Marvin Randall Ivy III. But before any more bickering could be done, Amy Joy tramped through the kitchen with Lola Craft at her heels.

"Hi, Aunt Pearl," she said.

"Hello, Amy Joy," said Pearl. "Boy, don't you look like the blushing bride." Pearl glanced quickly at Sicily, who frowned.

"This is Lola," said Amy Joy. "My maid of honor."

"Speaking of such," Sicily said, "I told Amy Joy she should ask Junior's daughter, the oldest one, to be a bridesmaid. But then we realized the dress probably wouldn't fit her right, what with the way she's built. What do they call that malady, anyway?"

Pearl cringed. Amy Joy went on through the living room and up the stairs with Lola Craft.

"That's a complete lie," she told Lola when they were out of hearing distance. "I've no idea why she said that."

◆　　◆　　◆

Pearl and Sicily were back on better terms by the time the Ivys officially gathered at Sicily's house for a visit. It was to be a joyous time, a lull before the hectic wedding, when the bride and groom could spend a few hours with their own families before they bade them adieu. It was Saturday afternoon. Jean Claude would be off enjoying the stag party given by his brothers. As female stag parties were still light-years from Mattagash, Amy Joy had planned her own merriment at home.

"We got pizza now in this part of the world," Sicily bragged to Pearl's family. Marvin, Junior, and Thelma sat on the sofa where Jean Claude had so cleverly danced just the evening before. Pearl filled the recliner and Randy sat angrily on the bottom step of the stairs, now free from vomit. At each opportunity his fingers found their way up to his crotch and he relieved some of the itch, which was constant now. Junior appeared to be more pale and tense than Thelma, who had awakened from a well-needed sleep only an hour earlier, remembering nothing about secretaries at the Albert Pinkham Motel. Lola Craft appeared again, having sullenly promised Amy Joy she would.

"I have to," Amy Joy said, when asked why she was spending her last Saturday night on earth as a free woman with her mother and those Portland relatives.

"They're icky," protested Lola. "Let's stay up here in your room and drink this." She pulled a bottle of already mixed screwdrivers out of her overnight bag.

"I know they are, but Mama is crazy enough as it is," Amy Joy said, and examined her silver streaks in the mirror. "I don't want her to go off the deep end at the last minute. And this get-together is her idea. Do you like this lipstick shade?"

What Lola really liked she discovered as soon as she and Amy Joy descended the stairs into Sicily's living room.

"Hey," said Randy, as Lola sat a step above him. "How's it goin'?" He scratched heartily.

"Okay, I guess," Lola laughed. My God. A *city* man!

"Amy Joy," said Sicily. "What do you think of sending out for pizza? Pearl can hardly believe we got pizza up here in Mattagash."

"You gotta order at least five big ones or they won't deliver," said Amy Joy. "And you gotta buy your Pepsi at Blanche's Grocery here in Mattagash."

"On holidays," said Lola Craft, "you have to place your order a day early or you don't get nothin' delivered."

"Sometimes it's cold 'cause it comes all the way from Watertown," said Amy Joy. "You gotta put it in the oven all over again."

"On New Year's Eve you can forget it," said Lola. "Petit Pierre's Pizza will only deliver around Watertown 'cause they get so many calls they can't handle them all." She looked at Randy and blushed.

Junior had listened to all of this. My God, the territory was crying out for a little pizza competition. It was true that his mother had once wanted to combine the funeral home with a beauty salon and everyone had laughed, but a pizza joint, well, that was a hearse of a different goddamn color.

"Well, we'll order five large ones, then," said Sicily, a bit embarrassed. No matter how hard she tried, she always came off looking like a country mouse in front of the citified Pearl. "Get them with the works, Amy Joy, and whoever doesn't like whatever can pick it off. Yes, Pearl, we get pizza delivered right to our own front door."

"You ever get stoned?" Randy whispered to Lola Craft.

Not much further was said among the gathered. There had been more laughter, a veritable surplus of gaiety, when they had gathered that rainy September day in 1959 to plan Marge's burial. Now spring found them back at Sicily's, thawed out from a long winter, ill at ease with themselves, and without much merriment for the occasion. Sicily was numb with pain over the nuptials. The Ivys didn't care if Amy Joy married an Arab. Junior was numb with disbelief at seeing Monique Tessier in Mattagash. Thelma was numb from the Valium. Pearl was between fear over seeing ghosts the night before and anger that Sicily disbelieved her. Amy Joy was full of a bride's tension, and the small warning voice of logic, which rarely spoke to her. Marvin eyed Pearl and Junior and Thelma and wondered what would happen to his family if anything should happen to *him*. Randy and Lola eyed each other: It was one of those rare things that could only happen in movies or in Mattagash, Maine. It was a case of love at first sight. Lola finally looked away, and when she did Randy took the opportunity to rake his fingers quickly across his genitals.

"How long does the pizza take?" Marvin asked.

"Well, it's thirty miles away," said Sicily.

"One or two hours," explained Amy Joy. "They get a lot of orders and they can only put so many pizzas in the oven at one time."

"But it's better than nothing," Lola Craft broke away from Randy's gaze to say. "We was all getting real sick of Chef Boyardee pizzas up here in Mattagash."

Sicily cringed. The group waited numbly. *One or two hours.* Sweet Jesus.

"Winnie Craft tells me that Vera Gifford, you remember her, Pearl," Sicily reminded, "dragged out all her Christmas lights last night and lit up her entire yard. They even stuck up that awful Nativity scene."

"What?" gasped Pearl.

"The Giffords is crazy," Lola turned away once more from Randy to report to the group.

"But *Christmas* lights?" asked Marvin. "Why?"

"Don't ask," said Sicily. "Everyone in town knows that Goldie Gifford, across the road, bought about a thousand boxes of lights when they went on sale after Christmas. Why Vera is the one doing the lighting up I haven't the foggiest."

"They're always up to something," Lola said, and giggled daintily as Randy touched a finger to the toe of her sneaker.

"Wasn't Vera a cousin to Chester Lee Gifford?" Pearl inquired of Sicily. Another thorn in Sicily's side. What Pearl was really saying was "Oh yes, I remember the last time that little Amy Joy took it into her head to get married, to a *Gifford.*" When, oh when, would the pizza arrive?

"Yes," said Sicily, looking out the window as evening swept over the Mattagash River valley with a cold rain that threatened snow. "She was his first cousin."

"I thought so," said Pearl. She and Sicily locked eyes. A silence fell between the sisters. Pearl decided to make a move to break it.

"Christmas decorations in April," she said with disgust. "What will the Giffords do next?"

"Oh, I don't know," said Sicily, as her stomach growled with hunger. "Maybe they'll start seeing ghosts."

RED RYDER DOESN'T HAVE A DOG'S CHANCE: GOLDIE RALLIES HER CHILDREN

....

I'm Nobody! Who are you?
Are you—Nobody—too?
Then there's a pair of us! . . .
—Emily Dickinson

RED RYDER, THE PUPPY WHO HAD BECOME THE RESIDENT DOG
at Pike and Goldie Gifford's house ten years earlier, picked himself
up from the creaking front porch and ambled down the long drive.
He had waited hopefully for the kids, whining at the bottom of the
steps until Goldie shooed him away.

"It's Saturday, Red Ryder," she told him. "They won't be up for
a couple more hours."

At the bottom of the long Gifford drive, Red Ryder brought his
hind leg up and clawed heartily at a single flea on his bony side.

The claws dug in deep, never having even heard of clipping, and some of the tension encased in the itch was relieved. Red Ryder spied a cat walking precariously on Vera Gifford's front porch and wondered whether the chase would be worth it or not. Deciding against it, he ambled on down the road.

Being a Gifford dog had its ramifications in Mattagash. That week alone Red Ryder had had thrown at him, by the descendants of the old loyalist pet owners, a high-heeled shoe, a torn sneaker, a Pepsi bottle, a yellow rubber ball, an Orange Crush pop bottle, a garden hose nozzle, three pieces of firewood, rocks of all sizes, a broken hairbrush, and a tiny purple Gideon Bible, which flew at him like a large plum.

"Lord, it's Pike Gifford's old dog," he had heard said a hundred times. "Run it off before it infects the whole place." Such things Red Ryder had grown used to. And he didn't mind. As soon as the tossed torpedo made contact, careened off into the bushes, and the pain of it subsided, he was off again, wagging his tail, oblivious to the discourtesy.

It was in front of the Craft residence that Red Ryder stepped back to avoid a rather large rock that Winnie had found near her front steps and heaved at him.

"You go back to Giffordtown!" she shouted, and then went inside her house and slammed the door, taking Poo Poo, her poodle, with her. Poo Poo would have preferred to stay outside. She and Red Ryder had sniffed beneath each other's tails many times and had taken pleasure in such actions. But Poo Poo sensed a social taboo in the friendship she had with the Gifford dog, and merely watched the turn of events through the glass of Winnie's front door.

Red Ryder turned away from Winnie Craft's large rock and into the path of a rumbling pulp truck, which hurled him quickly into the ditch. The trucker, Donnie Henderson, kept on his way, needing to get in as many loads that day as possible. Trips meant money. A dog was a dog. Besides, that was a Gifford dog. If it had been that queer little cotton ball that Winnie Craft worshiped, it would be a different matter. Donnie Henderson kept on, with his heavy load of pulp, for Watertown. Red Ryder lay on his side in the ditch of the only road in Mattagash and breathed painfully for a half hour until he died.

For a few hours afterward, as he began to stiffen in death, bemused residents drove by and saw what Poo Poo was keeping a watchful eye on.

"Looks like the Gifford dog got it," Amanda Henderson said to Mary Mullins.

"It's probably better off," said Mary. "It was flea-bitten to the high heavens."

"Good Lord, Pike Gifford's old dog," said Peter Craft, on the way back to his filling station. "They'll probably serve that up on a platter tonight."

Red Ryder lay on his side in the ditch of the only road in Mattagash and, as usual, paid no mind to the social barbs being tossed at him like bones. It was a phone call from Goldie's sister that brought the news to the owners. They filed out of the house as though they'd heard a fire alarm and raced the quarter of a mile down the road to where the body lay. Little Pee stayed home, although it was officially his dog. Only little kids and girls would enter such an emotional fracas, he decided, so he stayed behind, but when they were safely gone he cried aloud and hit his fists into the dirty pillows of the front porch bed.

Goldie, Priscilla, Hodge, Missy, and Miltie gathered around Red Ryder in a solemn circle, each sensing, even little Miltie, that there was some kind of justice in this. They were Giffords, after all, and all things, even things that were rightfully theirs, should be taken from them. Missy threw herself down on the body and buried her face in the tangled fur.

"Poor Red Ryder," she sobbed, then, "Good dog. Good boy." Other hands searched the fur, patted the head, positioned the tail comfortably behind the body. They had had him from his puppy days and he had never once minded being theirs. This was the thought that ran unspoken through their minds. Red Ryder was all theirs. He loved *them*, not Amy Joy Lawler. Not Lola Craft. But them. Missy. Miltie. Little Pee. Priscilla. Hodge. Pike and Goldie Gifford's kids. Now, like a chance from the future, like an opportunity, he had been taken away from them. Goldie pulled her children into the circle of her arms as if they were tiny ducks. She rounded them up and held them, made sure she touched each one.

"Listen," she said, her voice ragged. "Old Red Ryder wouldn't want us to cry like this. He had a real good life with you kids and he loved every one of you." She gathered them tighter. Missy's sobs were now uncontrollable and Miltie had hidden his face in the crook of Goldie's arm, which was growing wet with his tears. Priscilla stood stunned, unable to cry.

"Why didn't whoever hit him call us?" she asked Goldie.

"Nobody in this town owes us a damn thing," said Goldie. "Nobody. If you can remember that, maybe one day you can get the hell out."

They pushed Red Ryder aside, gently, farther down into the ditch, where he could have some privacy from Mattagash in his death, and then they walked solemnly home.

"I'll bring Little Pee back with Miltie's wagon to get him," Goldie promised. "We'll bury him on the hill where he can always be close to you." All five held hands, even Hodge, who had at first been embarrassed but soon gave in to the feeling of power he felt surging up from his wrist. They were a *family*, and no one could take that from them. They felt the link to Mattagash as they walked. They came from the earliest settlers, too, just like the McKinnons and the Crafts. Hell, they were related fifty times over to everyone in town. Who, then, had decided that they would be the black sheep?

"And don't think for one minute," Goldie said at the bottom of the hill, "that Little Pee ain't feeling none of this. He's cried his heart out by now. I just want all of you to know that. I want you to know that we're a family, and a family shares stuff."

They climbed the hill rigidly, Miltie dragging back on Goldie's hand, Priscilla awkward and aloof. She had been a baby with Red Ryder and now he was dead. And she was, too, in a way. She had breasts now, and wild thoughts about boys, and was longing for her menstrual cycle, not knowing its inconvenience. Now she wished she had guarded Red Ryder every inch of the day. Had catered to his every whim. And in her sadness she felt a vague longing, a sense that she should have guarded her childhood in such a fashion. They would both be safe now if she had, she and Red Ryder. They would be careening through the April fields, waiting for the river to warm for a swim.

"Another thing," Goldie said, and halted halfway up the drive. Her children stopped silently around her. "I want you to know that I love you, each of you, equally. I want you to know that I'm proud of you. That I believe in you. I want you to know you're just as good as anybody else you'll come across in your lifetimes."

The moment was awkward among them, but then the procession began again its climbing, up, up, up, as if the Gifford hill were some awful social ladder they were forced to ascend. The moment was awkward, but each child came away from it with a small item of respect, the first of its kind, and although they did not realize it at the time, none of them would be sorely burdened by it.

Vera watched the long line of humans climb the hill.

"Goldie looks just like the Pied Piper," she said to Little Vinal, and then slapped his hand as he reached a finger into her frosting bowl. She had rubbered in on the fatal phone call and knew what had happened.

"They're boo-hooing more over that old dog than they did when Grammie Gifford died," Vera said, and let the curtain relax.

◆　　◆　　◆

Shortly after Red Ryder gave up the ghost and was safely buried on the Gifford hill, Irma arrived home for the weekend. She had barely had time to toss her purse onto the sofa and grieve the loss of the family dog when Goldie pulled her aside.

"Don't ask me why," she said. "But I have the need to express myself." Goldie held up a handful of Christmas lights which Irma recognized all too well, having sold them to her.

"What's going on here?" asked Irma, and breathed on the heavy lenses of her glasses. "Aunt Vera's yard is all decorated for Christmas, too. Have you people gone stark raving crazy?"

"This is only partly for your aunt Vera," said Goldie. "This is for the kids. It's for old Red Ryder. Let's go."

It was past five o'clock and growing colder, so they dressed in heavy socks and sweaters and scarves and mittens and went out to cheerily decorate their home and yard. Even Little Pee finally left the kitchen window and came outside to help once he heard laughter and recognized what appeared to be real family camaraderie. It was strange for all of them to be caught up in a sort of celebration with Red Ryder just dead, yet it seemed right somehow.

There were strings of lights everywhere. Goldie had planned to show reserve when she decorated the tree that December, so as not to rile Vera or any of the other women who had fared so poorly at the sale. But this wasn't December. It was April. Goldie Gifford and her kids were a family. Families could do what they wished, as long as they stayed together. And it's true that a frenzy caught Goldie up in its clutches. She couldn't seem to stop decorating. Irma felt the same way, except for her the experience was almost a mystical one, stemming from the fact that with the weak muscle balance in her forever wandering eyes she saw, without her glasses, double. And temptation caused her many a time to take those spectacles off and behold the wonders. Just a slight tremor from the wind could make it all appear to be some dazzling light show. The kind they have in Las Vegas.

"How do you think that tree over there would look if we was to light it up, Prissy?" Goldie would say. Or, "Tack some lights around that window, Hodge."

By nightfall the entire hill where Pike Gifford's house sat on the cold earth was ablaze in lights. There were strings around each and every window of the house. They covered the doors and eaves. A bright string of mixed colors ran from the front porch out to the garage, circled the door, lined the eaves, and lit up every illegal tire from Mattagash to Watertown. The mailbox was wrapped in lights. There was not an extension cord or an outlet in Goldie's house that was not working severe overtime.

"Thank God it *isn't* Christmas," Vera said, looking up in astonishment at the hill afire in color. "If Santa was to fly over that mess he'd think for sure it was New York City. He'd probably end up spending the holidays in Canada with the Quebecers."

Pike Gifford rolled a tire up the hill from Vinal's and stashed it with the others in the garage.

"Nice job," he said to Goldie as he surveyed the network of lights. "Good work," he said to the kids, and hiccuped. They giggled. Pike teetered a bit, dazed by the splash of colors, as he reached for the doorknob. It used to be just past Thanksgiving that folks started looking forward to Christmas. Now Easter was barely over and they were already at it. So be it. Pike Gifford would not interfere with the social workings of the world if the world did not interfere with him.

When the job was finally finished, Goldie and Irma and the other children came in, chilled to the bone but satisfied with the creations they'd left behind in the soft cold rain that was beginning to patter upon Mattagash. And they had left Red Ryder securely buried in the little mound that pushed up from the bank of the old river, beneath the clutch of jack pines, where he'd want to be, in the animal graveyard.

"Do you think the rain will turn to snow?" Irma asked, glancing out the window at the wet Christmas lights still blazing.

"Who knows?" Goldie shrugged. She made a large pot of cocoa, and Irma popped toast out of the toaster until she had buttered a foot-high stack. The children could dunk toast into their cups of cocoa. They could tell ghost stories. Goldie promised them this. And Goldie knew that when bedtime rolled around, when the children crawled into their flannel pajamas and said their prayers for Red Ryder, they would understand some things about themselves. They were Giffords, but they were as good as the McKinnons, and the Crafts. And they were a family who owned more Christmas tree lights than any other on the planet Earth.

"Is Santa coming tonight?" Miltie asked, wide-eyed, and laughter careened out the door of Pike Gifford's house on the hill, unheard by the rest of Mattagash.

"He just might," Goldie said, and rubbed Miltie's curly head.

$\mathscr{S}$AINT CHRISTOPHER

FLOPS IN MATTAGASH: THE GIFFORDS

GIVE NEW MEANING TO

VENI, VIDI, VICI

....

Frost heave: *Geol.* an uplift in soil caused by the freezing of internal moisture.

—The Random House College Dictionary

Pothole: that which makes you long for the horse and buggy.

—Donnie Henderson

SATURDAY EVENING FELL WITH FAT DROPS OF RAIN THAT HAD old-timers predicting that nature just might splatter them one more time with a blanket of white before she let them go headfirst into spring. The temperature dropped sharply to the low forties and threatened to dip further as night came calling. The road that followed the river out of St. Leonard and into the heart of Mattagash was coating itself with a thin, slippery shield as it snaked through Giffordtown, past Vera's and Goldie's houses, down a small swoop of hill where Alphonse Gifford's house leaned on its haunches, and into the main cluster of homes, which clung to the bank in a paranoid frenzy.

An occasional yard light belonging to a Craft or a Fennelson bit into the blackness of the road and lit it up in small patches. These were the marks of the upper class, these pole lights that came alive with nightfall and died a slow death with each dawn.

"Fifteen dollars a month," the owners could think smugly to themselves as they drove into their well-lighted yards and sat silently in their cars for a few minutes to give thanks that their circumstances allowed these social lighthouses to blink out to all of Mattagash: *Fifteen dollars a month. Fifteen dollars a month. Look what we got! Where's yours? Where's yours?*

If the Crafts and Fennelsons and Sicily McKinnon Lawler preferred to light up their yards and therefore their financial circumstances, the Giffords felt differently. The last thing Vinal or Pike wanted was a well-lighted yard. A bright circle of illumination was not the perfect place to drag a freshly killed deer. Not in July or August, that is. It was not the most propitious place to roll a set of tires, or lug a heavy battery. And Vinal could only imagine the kind of loudmouthed reflections that would occur if a yard light were introduced to a pile of shiny hubcaps. When the Lord said "Let there be light," and saw that it was good, it was not Vinal and Pike Gifford he had in mind. Yet on the Saturday evening before Amy Joy Lawler's wedding, both Gifford yards were ablaze in prisms of light never found on the pages of Genesis. The wet road that looped down the hill and into Giffordtown was beaded with green, blue, red, yellow, and white drops, like splattered paint on the pavement. On both sides of the road, the bedecked Gifford houses put on a light display heretofore unknown in northern Maine, at least on the American side of the border. It was true the French Canadian Catholics on the other side of the river sometimes came up with illuminated Nativity scenes that rivaled the Mormon Tabernacle Choir in their numbers.

"Who are all those people crowded around Mary and Joseph?" Sicily once asked Amy Joy, as they took a holiday drive through Rivière du Loup, Quebec.

"Relatives," Amy Joy had answered.

"Nevertheless," Sicily noted, "it looks like a hockey game."

Thirty miles away, at Petit Pierre's Pizza, fifteen large pizza pies were loaded onto the front seat of the Ford pizza pickup, which had a large pizza painted on each door. Beneath the thick red letters which proclaimed PETIT PIERRE'S PIZZA, was the slogan "A Pizza for the People." Behind the wheel was Freddy Broussard, Pierre's only son, who handled all the long-distance deliveries and was heir apparent to the pizza throne. Freddy also looked out at the world through eyeglasses made heavy by their loaded prescription. Freddy's eyes were 20/60. This may have prevented him from becoming a fighter pilot at Loring Air Force Base, as had been his childhood dream, but it had drawn him closer to the new clerk at J. C. Penney's. Holding each bill close to her face for inspection, Irma Gifford was slow but reliable as far as the J. C. Penney manager was concerned. But to Freddy Broussard, who had watched for days from among the men's handkerchiefs and socks before daring to speak to her, she was a large-eyed wood nymph, a river goddess, a nearsighted yet lithe vision among the long cool aisles of sundries. The music of her cash register, as it clicked, popped, and pealed was pure minstrel music to his ears. They were meant for each other. They saw the world through the same eyes, so to speak. They would be happy for life as long as they had glasses.

When the call for pizza came from Mattagash, Freddy slipped into the back where Petit Pierre couldn't hear him. His father would be outraged to learn that his son was courting a Mattagasher, an English-speaking, low-life Protestant. It was true that Freddy himself had only a slight trace of French accent left, but what counted was in the blood. In the blood, as far as Petit Pierre was concerned, Freddy spoke only French.

Irma came to the phone. Yes, of course he could visit her after he made his deliveries. He would take her riding over the potholes and frost heaves in the Ford pizza pickup. They could sit with the motor running, winding down the windows every half hour so they wouldn't be carbon-monoxided together, although Freddy found that notion romantic. Perhaps if Petit Pierre wouldn't give his blessing and his pizza empire to Freddy and Irma, they would venture into a suicide pact. They would hurl themselves blindly, again so to speak, from the Mattagash ledges into the thickly swirling Mattagash River. And they would never be found. Oh, two heavy-duty pairs of prescription eyeglasses might wash ashore the following spring, but the flesh and blood that bore them upon their noses would be gone forever.

Freddy spun away from Petit Pierre's Pizza in a thick cloud of aroma conjured up by fifteen hot pizzas. He had six to deliver in St. Leonard, on the way. Nine more would end up in Mattagash. Winnie Craft had let everyone know that five pizzas were ordered by Sicily Lawler's wedding party, so if anyone wanted a single one delivered they would be able to get the delicacy. Winnie ordered one. So did Sarah and Bert Fogarty. Then Winnie called her nephew Peter Craft at his filling station to tell him the good news. Peter's wife quickly ordered two, one to be eaten for supper, one to be frozen for the shortage that was sure to follow.

Freddy sped past Sheriff Roy Vachon and his patrolman Wayne Fortin, who were cruising the rainy streets of Watertown. Freddy Broussard left dark wet tire marks behind him as he leaned forward over the wheel, trying desperately to see beyond his own thick glasses as well as the windshield, and sped with his precious cargo over the crooked, slippery, bumpy road to Mattagash. To Irma.

He had delivered all six St. Leonard pizzas by the time the big hot dog sign at Henri Nadeau's Quick Lunch and Gas loomed into sight. Freddy reminded himself to check his gas gauge. A quarter tank. He'd better fill up. The Mattagash round-trip would be sixty miles, and if Irma consented to go riding they might need gallons more. As Henri pumped the Ford's tank full, Freddy Broussard leaned back against the seat and contemplated the weather, love, and the heavy perfume of pizza. It was turning colder and the rain was fleshing up into what looked like sleet. He reached a hand out to the passenger seat and found the small bouquet of flowers, fresh from their container in the floral cart at the Watertown IGA. Imagining Irma's sweet smile of surprise when he presented them to her, Freddy Broussard did not see the sleek black shark slide in below Henri Nadeau's gas tanks. The Plymouth's fins were wet from the ocean of the night, and it sat silently, Henri's Budweiser sign blinking red against its shiny black skin. When the pizza pickup left Henri Nadeau's yard, the shark was following.

"He wouldn't be this far from Watertown unless he's got at least five," Vinal Gifford said to Pike, whose mouth watered.

"How do we stop him?" asked Pike. He could almost smell the scent, the innocent trail his prey was leaving behind.

"First we gotta pass him," said Vinal. "Then we'll think of something." The black shark slid out of the pickup's wake as Vinal floorboarded it. The Plymouth rocked dangerously, the frost heaves tossing it up on the waves of the road, the potholes battering the frame, rattling the fenders. Freddy Broussard inched over on the narrow road to let the leviathan pass. He shivered as two pairs of beady eyes stared out of the front seat at him. Then the Plymouth swam away from him, off into the black night, and was gone.

At the WELCOME TO MATTAGASH POPULATION 456 sign, the Plymouth screeched to a halt. It was best to commit a crime within the confines of one's own township: The Giffords loathed the notion of extradition. Vinal and Pike got out and slammed their doors. The sound echoed out into the rapids of Mattagash Brook, where it joined the Mattagash River. One clear day, or maybe it was a rainy, sleety day, an ancestral Gifford had made that same river trek as had the earliest McKinnons, and this was still the old river. But Vinal and Pike had no sentiments for yore, not while they were able to sniff pizza in the present.

"This keeps up and it's gonna snow," Vinal said, and tugged his jacket collar about his neck.

"This is our shortest summer so far," said Pike.

"I've seen shorter," Vinal muttered.

Within minutes the happy headlights of the Petit Pierre's Pizza pickup shone through the mist and lighted up the faces of what appeared to be mountain men, standing in the middle of the road and waving their arms frantically.

"Oh my God," Freddy thought. He instantly reached a hand up to touch the Saint Christopher medal he wore around his neck, the one his mother had given him when he began making his long-distance deliveries. It was meant to protect him from Mattagash, that wooded area of wild men and moose and black bear. Being the patron saint of travelers, Saint Christopher might be able to save Freddy Broussard, but he couldn't vouch for the pizzas. "Holy Tabernacle," Freddy muttered, suddenly remembering his French expletives. He pulled cautiously up to within a foot of the men, rather than run them down. Vinal Gifford came around to the driver's side and tapped gently on the window, which Freddy begrudgingly rolled down.

"Don't be alarmed," Vinal Gifford said with authority. "This is a test. This is only a test." He had heard this statement from the emergency broadcast system many, many times during his long career in front of the television set.

"What?" asked Freddy. "What do you guys want?" Rain had swept onto his lenses, but he could see the faces very well. He would remember those faces in detail, in case he needed later to look at mug shots.

"Well," said Pike, who had stepped behind Vinal. "What've you got?"

"Just pizzas," Freddy choked out.

"Pizzas?" Vinal was disgusted. "We were told this here was a gold shipment."

"No," said Freddy, in a near panic. He had read that in life-and-death situations such as this, the smart thing was to simply tell a thief, "Here, take all my money." But how could he tell thieves who expected pure gold, "Here, take all my pizzas?" Freddy's Adam's apple seemed to be growing inside his throat, choking off his wind.

"No," he managed to spurt again. "I'm the pizza man."

"Pizza man?" asked Pike. "You mean to tell us you ain't the gold man?" Freddy shook his head in pure terror.

"Well," said Vinal. "Do we kill him, partner?"

"Nah," said Pike. "Pizzas is better than nothing. We're real disappointed, mind you," he told Freddy. "But we'll take them pizzas."

"You don't happen to have any pop with you?" asked Vinal. He was about to lean his head into the pizza pickup when Freddy Broussard laid a heavy boot on the gas pedal and whizzed away from the ill-shaven faces in his window. His mother had told him about the wildness still pumping in the blood of some Mattagashers. Freddy and Saint Christopher wanted no part of it.

The Giffords were stunned. Never had they, singly or as a duet, been so insulted. Who did this little four-eyed Frog think he was dealing with, for Chrissakes? And where did he think he was? New York City? Did he think he could jump onto one of them fancy moving stairways and disappear? Or into one of them buses that runs underground? Did he think he was going to find a *crowd* to hide amongst? You can't run away in Mattagash, Maine. You'll wind up staring straight ahead at the end of the road. It's kaput, unless you're a goddamn crow. He would have to turn around eventually. His pizza might be cold by then but, by Jesus, he'd be back. Pike and Vinal could take the cold pizza home, the way their ancestors might have done with partridge, or a fine mess of trout. They could take the pizza home to women who would stoke the oven, if not the hearth, and make the pepperoni all warm again, the crust crispy. A man did what he had to do to keep food on the table for his family. Game was game.

"What if he delivers them first?" Vinal asked the awful question.

"Let's get him!" cried Pike. The Plymouth screamed out of the ditch, swerved on the wet road, righted itself, and gave pursuit. The fins shook and the mud flaps spit off the April grime and then stayed airborne. The car came upon the hapless taillights of the pizza pickup, which was weaving badly. Freddy did not know this treacherous road under normal circumstances. At times he felt sheer weightlessness as a frost heave thrust him heavenward off the road. But then he was reminded again of being earthbound when his front wheels hit the lurking pothole. Pizzas bounced painfully about the interior. Freddy looked in his side view mirror.

He could see the teeth of the Plymouth's grille nipping at his heels, could see the fins cutting through the black night, the beady eyes of the headlights. What kind of feeding frenzy was this? Freddy pushed the accelerator further. Sixty miles an hour on these bumps and curves! He might as well be piloting an F-14 after all. That would be safer, it appeared, than delivering pizzas. There was no way he could lose the attackers and yet he couldn't go faster. The Plymouth-shark behind him seemed oblivious to speed as it swam above the road.

On the small hill that swooped down to Giffordtown, Freddy thought he might have a chance to make it to his delivery. There, he could rush inside and phone the sheriff back in Watertown. There was no doubt that these mountaineers meant to kill him. Why else would they pursue him? For his *pizzas?* But as he left the hill and followed the sharp turn into Giffordtown, he was not at all prepared for the light show that awaited him. He knew Irma's house must be nearby. She had told him three miles above the sign, on the right, a long drive up to the house on the hill. Freddy saw no hill. He saw no house. His weak, wretched eyes were bombarded with a dazzlement of blinking colored circles which soon formed squares and triangles as his muscles strained further.

"Holy shit!" Freddy Broussard lamented. What was this? Some kind of pizza ambush? Mesmerized by the lights coming at him from Vera's yard, and from the Disney display at the top of Goldie's hill, Freddy hit a large frost heave which insisted the pizza pickup spin mercilessly out of control. The passenger door opened and pizza boxes, all remaining nine of them, fluttered like huge playing cards about the colored roadway. Freddy's heavy glasses flew from his face and bounced onto the floorboards. The pizza pickup came to an abrupt stop in the ditch of Mattagash's main thoroughfare.

Freddy Broussard staggered out into the blinking lights that surrounded him, his arms high above his head, his glasses on the floor of the truck. So this was what it felt like to be shot down in enemy territory. He had always wondered.

"I give up," Freddy was panting, his retinas on fire with holiday fervor. "I give up," he again offered plaintively to the approaching black Plymouth, but there seemed to be no takers. Instead the shark rolled slowly along until it reached Freddy's side. The passenger door opened spookily, slow motion to Freddy's grainy pupils.

"This is it," Freddy Broussard winced. "This is where I hear the gunshot." He covered his ears and hoped the bullet would find his heart immediately, hoped he would not lie writhing and bleeding among the strewn pizzas on the red, blue, green, yellow, and white road into the wilderness. Mattagash, Maine. What a horrid place to give up the ghost, to say one's last goodbyes. Especially if one was French Catholic. His chance of getting last rites, Freddy knew, was slim. One had a better chance of getting a pizza delivered to Mattagash than a priest. Even on Sunday the tiny gathering of Catholics in the tiny Catholic church had to wait hours for the priest in Watertown to save all the French-descended souls he possibly could before he gritted his teeth and drove the thirty miles to try his luck on the Scotch-Irish flock.

Freddy decided that if he was going to die among Protestants, without last rites, he might as well get on the best footing he could with his Maker. The Act of Contrition would be a start. Freddy held his chubby ears to squelch the bullet's roar and chanted, "O my God, I'm heartily sorry for having offended Thee, and I detest all my sins."

There was no gunshot. Instead a hairy wrist poking out of a red and black lumberjack's coat dropped down beneath the Plymouth's door and grabbed one, then two pizza boxes.

"Because I dread the loss of heaven and the pains of hell," Freddy whispered. The shark rolled ten feet past him, again the passenger door opened, the hand scooped up another pizza, and then disappeared back into the car. At the panicked Ford pickup, the car stopped again and one more pizza went into the belly of the shark. Had Freddy been able to see, he would have read I BRAKE FOR BLACKFLIES on the back bumper. Then the Plymouth was swallowed up by the sleety Mattagash night.

Donnie Henderson was the first to stop, two minutes later, and offer assistance.

"Please call the sheriff," Freddy pleaded. He was alive. He had come close to death and survived, and life would be only exhilarating from now on. He leaned against the truck and reveled in the Christmas lights. He understood suddenly. Christmas lights in April. *Why the hell not?* It was pure metaphysics at work here between the Gifford homes. Freddy Broussard might never wear his thick eyeglasses again. Perhaps he would always descry the world as he did now, gazing up Goldie's fiery hill, prismatic blurs floating in the air. Was this the secret poets had discovered? Did the world's greatest thinkers know this little trick of the eyesight?

"This must be the same stuff that Timothy Leary saw," Freddy decided.

At Vera's house small heads appeared like candles in all the windows. Vera's own face dominated the window in her front door. At Goldie's no one was the wiser about the fracas at the hill's bottom. They were still busily sipping cocoa, telling Red Ryder stories, and begging Goldie to pop them popcorn for the Saturday night movie.

◆　　◆　　◆

"Christ, I wish we could eat first," Sheriff Roy Vachon said, when he received the call to arms. He had been ten minutes away from going home to a hot supper and leaving all potential skirmishes to his subordinates. His stomach growled suddenly in agreement.

"I don't suppose we can though," said Patrolman Wayne Fortin. "There's evidence all over the road. Dogs might eat it."

Two dozen Mattagashers, on their way home to their own suppers, had parked their cars along the road in Giffordtown and stood idly about to enjoy the excitement, which was rare in that neck of the woods. The sheriff arrived in a swirl of blue siren light, which looked purplish and meager next to the Christmas bulbs, and not at all as dramatic as he had hoped. Sheriff Roy Vachon was not pleased to be summoned to Mattagash. It wasn't just the notorious Giffords who kept law enforcement officers of northern Maine weary. One never knew what to expect from all those Scotch-Irish descendants on a hard-drinking Saturday night.

"There's Petit Pierre's Pizza's pickup." Patrolman Wayne Fortin spat out the tongue twister. He carried his official bullhorn, in case the pizza thieves were holed up and had to be coaxed out. When he saw the crowd gathered, Wayne was glad to have the accoutrement. The Mattagashers might break formation.

"Hey, Deputy, you gonna do some cheerleading?" a man called out from the crowd, and Patrolman Wayne Fortin blushed red to hear the laughter.

"Hey, Barney Fife, did you put your bullet in your gun?" another yelled.

"Ignore them," advised the seasoned sheriff.

Before questioning Freddy Broussard, Sheriff Roy directed the deputy to watch the crowd. Patrolman Wayne was aghast to see people opening boxes and testing bites of pizza. He aimed his bullhorn at the diners.

"Please do not eat the evidence!" he bellowed at the spectators.

"Is there a vegetarian one here?" a teenaged girl with acne asked the patrolman.

"Sheriff, they're eating our evidence," Patrolman Wayne whispered into Roy's ear.

"Well, go over there and stop them, Wayne," the sheriff said. "They won't eat *you*, for crying out loud." Patrolman Wayne wasn't so sure. He had heard all kinds of stories about Mattagashers. He leveled his bullhorn again.

"People," he pleaded, "go to your homes. This is police business."

"You cops got a hand in the pizza business, too?" Donnie Henderson asked.

"If somebody'll go to Blanche's Grocery," another man shouted, "I'll buy us all two six-packs of pop."

As Sheriff Roy Vachon questioned Freddy Broussard, he spied something near his left foot. It was round and red. It lay like a tiny planet that had been hurled out of its orbit by some cosmic catastrophe. It was round and red as Mars, and it looked delicious. Roy's stomach growled, urging him on. He bent over suddenly, to Freddy's dismay, and plopped the thing into his mouth.

"Pepperoni," he said to the disbelieving Mercury of pizza. "Now just how many Giffords, ah, suspects, were there?"

"You get me a lineup," Freddy declared, already beyond his spiritual phase and now angry. He sought his glasses on the pickup's floor and slipped them on. "I can pick those two shaggy faces out of any lineup."

After Donnie Henderson laughed heartily and then pointed up Goldie's iridescent drive to the top of the hill, Freddy Broussard finally knew which house was Irma's. She let him in and accepted the crushed bouquet of flowers with the tiny IGA sticker. All the little Giffords lined the stair steps like potted plants and sat there quietly to view the stranger. When he gave Irma the flowers, a volley of hoots and whistles rang out.

"Go back upstairs and eat your pizza!" Irma insisted. "Come meet my father," she told Freddy, as she got her sweater and purse.

"Speaking of fathers, I need to call the shop and tell my dad what's happened," Freddy said, at Irma's heels. "He needs to let our customers know I won't be delivering." Freddy Broussard stopped short in his tracks. His eyes grew even larger behind their tiny windshields. Pike Gifford was sitting on the sofa in front of the television, his socked feet resting on a worn footstool. A pizza smiled happily in his lap. PETIT PIERRE'S PIZZA, the letters on the box shouted at Freddy. "A Pizza for the People." What was it he had told Sheriff Roy Vachon, just moments ago? "I can pick those faces out of any lineup."

"Daddy likes your pizza so much he and Uncle Vinal drove all the way to Watertown to get some," Irma was pleased to announce.

"Piece of pizza?" Pike Gifford asked his potential son-in-law, and held out the box.

"No sir," Freddy finally said. "Thank you, though." His tongue was thick in his mouth, his throat dry.

"If I'd knowed you was coming right to my door," Pike said, and winked, "I'da got you to deliver this."

 POTPOURRI IN THE PINES PRIMEVAL: GABRIEL ENTERS THE CONSTITUTION STATE

....

> This is the forest primeval, but where are the hearts that
>   beneath it,
> Leaped like the roe, when he hears in the woodland the voice
>   of the huntsman?
>
> Ye who believe in affection that hopes, and endures, and is
>   patient,
> Ye who believe in the beauty and strength of woman's
>   devotion,
> List to the mournful tradition, still sung by the pines of the
>   forest;
> List to a Tale of Love in Acadie, home of the happy.
>
> —H. W. Longfellow, *Evangeline*

WHILE THE DISAPPOINTED GATHERING AT SICILY LAWLER'S HOUSE was eating hastily made tuna salad sandwiches, another sort of celebration was taking place, thirty miles away, at the Cloutier home in Watertown. Several bottles of booze decorated the kitchen counter, paper plates lounged about with sandwiches, crackers, and chunks of cheese. Chips seemed to be everywhere, in bowls, on chairs, crumbled on the floor. The house was full to overflowing with just a few friends and Jean Claude's immediate family. The six brothers were there with wives or girlfriends in tow. The three sisters arrived with their husbands. Jean's good friends, the altar boys of childhood, had arrived with their dates. A record player boomed from the living room, where half of the revelers danced so that the other half could sit. After an hour of musical entertainment, two records surfaced in what might be considered a survival of the fittest, and they were played alternately for the remainder of the night. Old Mr. Cloutier preferred *A Potpourri of Cajun Tunes* by Joel Sonnier, while the younger family members insisted on *The Best of Creedence Clearwater Revival.* All evening the musical atmosphere went from "Allons danser, Colinda" to "Oh, Lord, I'm stuck in Lodi again." From "Louisiana Man" to "Bad Moon Rising."

Jean Claude stopped once during the party to wonder why his family was happily stomping up a storm the night before his wedding. It was no secret that the Cloutiers as an entity disapproved highly of his marriage to Putois Lawler. The Cloutiers were far from being uppity-ups in Watertown. It was true many of the French-speaking Americans there had sent their children away to good colleges where they had cleverly learned to disguise their French accents. And they had come home to Watertown and settled down to take up whatever professional activities they'd learned with barely a vestige of their former French influence peeping out. These *this, that* types looked down on the all-out *dis, dat* reminders of the old French-Canadian settlers who had inched their way to the border, and then across the border into the United States of America. A few people were wise enough to be proud of this heritage, to strengthen the link with their Canadian and French ancestry. But in 1969 few French accents were heard on radio sets, or on television sets, and few politicians running for Maine's offices had last names that spoke of other than English or Scottish or Irish ancestries. In 1969 the *these, those* French descendants of Watertown, Maine, tended to look down their inherited noses at the *dease, dose* members of the community. The Cloutier family fell into the latter category, but by no means were they considered Giffords. The French equivalents to the Giffords were also abundant in Watertown. They were the ones who slipped through the windows of the KC Hall and stole a case of vodka. They attacked the Watertown drive-in with a chain saw, felling the large picture screen into the grassy field and crushing twenty speakers in the process. They brawled at one of the three drinking establishments. They rarely worked. Thanks to a religion that forbids birth control their houses swelled to the rafters with children. The Cloutiers, on the other hand, were a hardworking family, loyal to their roots, their God, and most of all, their family. And they looked down *their* inherited noses at any living soul from Mattagash, Maine, Catholic or not.

"Put back on dat *Potpourri* guy," the elder Cloutier insisted, and when the strains of "Jolie Blonde" lit up his ears, his boots went to work dancing. There was no scheme to the footwork. It was simply a lot of heavy foot stomping intermixed with an occasional gyration and a stream of perspiration from the forehead. Mattagashers were sometimes afraid to go out on the dance floor at the old Newberry store, now the Acadia Tavern, when these Frogs were hoofing up a storm.

"They're gonna take us all through the floor one night," Peter Craft once complained to Donnie Henderson, as they ordered more beers knowing that their wives were staring down the crooked road to Watertown at that very minute and wondering where they were.

Unlike the uptight Scotch-Irish of Mattagash, the French people from Watertown loved to have a good time, a genetic trait from *their* old settlers, and they loved to have it, of all places, in public, a dirty word to the McKinnons and Crafts, who were more used to closets for such practices.

"I'm chaud," Jean said to his mother, intermixing his French and English, as more and more of the new breed were learning to do. *Franglais* they called it. "It's hot," he said, and she took her handkerchief out of her dress pocket and wiped his brow, arranged the dark wet curls. How could she let this beautiful child, her baby, end up married to a Mattagasher? She could not. Mrs. Théophile Cloutier, Genevieve to her friends, could not allow such a thing.

"Where's Guillaume?" Jean Claude asked his mother. His brothers Guillaume and René had driven all the way from their new home in New Britain, Connecticut, where a community of French-speaking Americans from northern Maine had gathered to work in factories or in construction. Frogtown, it too was called by locals, and was only fifty miles away from New Milford, known as Little Mattagash, where the sons and daughters of the old settlers had chosen to congregate. Connecticut was like the last step of some social underground railway that carried off the dissatisfied young of Aroostook County in uppermost Maine—they had only the woods to turn to for a living if they stayed on their ancestors' soil. A relative in New Britain or New Milford was always glad to take in the transient souls who finally gave up their chain saws for the shiny tools of some factory. But these souls longed for the weather-beaten WELCOME TO MATTAGASH and ST. LEONARD and WATERTOWN signs, and for the first year or so they made the eleven-hour drive often, eleven hours straight up to the northern tip of Maine. But the city slowly claimed them, and being lonesome was not as bad as spending all those hours in a car. Homesickness eventually went away like measles or chicken pox. Their children grew up with only a trace of French accent, or the old Irish brogue, and no interest whatsoever in the cold wooded area that had once harbored their parents. By the next generation the accent, like the homesickness, was completely gone.

"He's gone to gas up the car," Jean's mother answered him in French. "St. Rose is a long way." They were, the brothers and the altar boys of old, taking Jean Claude to St. Rose, Canada, where the strippers from Montreal abounded, and where the management didn't mind if a full-blooded French-speaking all-American boy of Canadian descent rubbed a leg or tweaked a nipple, as long as he flipped a few pink Canadian two-dollar bills onto the stage.

"St. Rose!" Jean Claude said to Guillaume, when he returned with a full tank. "Vierge!

"You doan find no virgin in dat place," said Guillaume, who had been earnestly trying to dispose of what he considered his rustic, country French. The English of the big city would be better, Guillaume decided, for a man who was on his way up to one of the foreman positions of O'Donnell Brothers Construction Company in New Britain. Everybody in Connecticut called Guillaume, at his own insistence, Bill.

"Put on dat *Potpourri* man, tank you," Mr. Cloutier shouted and the house rocked with dancing. It was almost ten o'clock before the brothers and altar boy friends, traveling in three cars, set out for St. Rose's new discotheque. Jean's mother and father hugged him tearfully.

"Demain à ce temps je serai un homme marié," he said to his parents. This time tomorrow I'll be a married man. They nodded, and his mother hugged him a second time. Then his sisters kissed him. He climbed into Guillaume's Chevy super sport with the bright blue Connecticut license plates, of which the whole family was proud. It told of their son's rise in the world, among the godly English, in Connecticut, THE CONSTITUTION STATE. The Chevy sped off, its 440 engine rattling its power beneath the hood. On the return trip they would cross the border into the United States at Madawaska, fifteen miles from Watertown. Where they crossed the border depended on what time of day it was and therefore which customs officer would be on duty. They could be regular nice guys with a job to do, or they could be power-hungry little men in official suits, born too late for Hitler's gestapo. Jean Claude had seen much of both types in his days of border crossing, and driving fifteen miles out of one's way, even if it was three o'clock in the morning, could be well worth the trip.

The second car pulled out and followed Guillaume into the wet night. All the women remained behind to finish the party at the Cloutiers'. St. Rose was no place for them. They might see their men do things that would bring tears to their eyes.

The third car lingered. Jean's brother René came out carrying a suitcase in each of his large hands and tucked them both away in the trunk. Even if the customs officer did ask to look through the suitcases, Guillaume's car would already be safely on its way to St. Rose, and Jean Claude woud suspect nothing.

"His money." The old woman was teary-eyed. She gave René an envelope. "Keep him down there," she said to René, and kissed him goodbye.

"Once he's thinking straight"—René spoke French back to them, and discovered that in just a short year of living in Connecticut he was already struggling to remember his native language—"we'll bring him back for his car." Mr. Cloutier took his hand and shook it.

"Take him to that French bar where you and Guillaume go, down there in New Britain. Introduce him to a nice French girl," the old man advised.

"Get him a good job," the mother said. "He'll be better off."

They watched René drive away in Eloie Thibodeau's old black Pontiac with the bland, unsuccessful MAINE, VACATIONLAND on the plate. What was that compared to THE CONSTITUTION STATE? They were giving Jean Claude, as his wedding present, a very important trousseau. They were giving him Connecticut.

The three sisters stood with the parents on the front steps, which were sagging with the memory of too many Watertown snows. On-the-border winters. The family waved goodbye until even the sound of the car died away, and then they went back inside the old house. Aunts and uncles had arrived at eight o'clock. Even though everyone knew there would be no wedding, it was a shame to let a good party go to waste.

"Put back on dat *Potpourri* guy," Old Man Cloutier wiped the tears from his eyes and requested.

◆　◆　◆

Jean Claude drank all the vodka that his brothers and friends put in front of him. His stag party was a major success. He developed a particular interest in a brunette stripper who called herself La Petite Hirondelle. The Little Swallow. Guillaume and René drank 7-ups, which looked enough like vodka, but the rest of the large group saw no reason to drive all the way to St. Rose and stay sober. Besides, whether he knew it or not, this was Jean Claude's going-away party.

"Tabernacle! Look at dem buns!" Eloie Thibodeau shouted, and grabbed the fleshy cheek of one stripper's rear. That was the last line of poetry Jean Claude heard. The next thing he would remember was sitting up in the backseat of the magnificent new Chevy super sport, ten o'clock Sunday morning, and asking his whereabouts.

"Almost to Mass," said Guillaume, and lighted a Canadian cigarette, a DuMaurier. He would need to smoke them all, rather than be seen back in New Britain with a reminder of his heritage.

"Où?" Jean Claude asked. "Where?" *Mass?* He couldn't go to church as hung over as he was.

"Massachusett," said René, forgetting the *s*. He would need to start remembering such things, now that he was headed back to the land where *s*'s were never forgotten.

"Massachusett?" said Jean Claude, and lay back on the seat. "Chalice!" he said. He was on his way to the Constitution State.

PEARL OF ARC HEARS
A BANSHEE IN THE SUMMER KITCHEN:
THE WEDDING GUESTS ARE
ALBATROSSES TO THE
ANCIENT MOTELIER

....

Banshee: *Irish and Scottish folklore.* A female spirit believed to wail outside a house as a warning that a death will occur soon in the family.

—*Webster's New World Dictionary*

SUNDAY MORNING FOUND PEARL MCKINNON IVY STARING OUT OF her bedroom window with dark puffy circles beneath her eyes. There had been voices again in the summer kitchen, lilting and ghostly. She had even nudged Marvin awake and asked him to listen.

"There's nothing," he said, and rolled onto his portly side and was soon snoring. Pearl lay awake staring at the ceiling and pondering her sanity. There they were again, micelike and muffled: scampering noises and whispers, coming from the old summer kitchen. Marge, no doubt, rifling through the dusty trunk in search of her love letters of another era, of a golden time. How soon before she put two and two together, assuming ghosts could add, and came clawing at the back door for an explanation?

"I want my letters!" Pearl could hear the April wind whistling about the eaves. She would have to tell Sicily. Sicily would be in danger, too, as she was half responsible and, by God, Pearl would not hesitate to let Marge's ghost know this tidbit. All night long she had lain awake to the tinny voices of those old lovers, Marge and Marcus Doyle. Were these voices in her head? Pearl shuddered to think that she was on the short road to another breakdown. But she had heard bees, thousands of them, during that first lapse with sanity, when Marvin decided to become an undertaker instead of a lawyer. Maybe the voices were divine. Look at Joan of Arc. She'd heard voices and she ended up burning at the stake for them. Pearl shuddered again. She could envision herself tied to a large pine tree while the good wives of Mattagash circled around her with cigarette lighters. But again, that little Joan of Arc was French, so God only knows what she was hearing. Extraterrestrials, maybe. And Pearl decided that if God had wanted to talk directly to her, he would have chosen the quiet streets of Portland, Maine, to do so and not have waited until Pearl was back in Mattagash. Yet Mattagash was where she wanted to be, if the supernatural world would just leave her alone.

"I'm home," Pearl said. "Even if it is haunted."

•   •   •

Sicily Lawler had spent a restless night with her own tortured dreams. She was sitting on the sofa in her brightly colored living room and thumbing through a scrapbook of her grandchildren, the offspring Amy Joy and Jean Claude were sure to bequeath to her in her old age.

"They were all frog-legged," Sicily remembered. "Poor little tadpoles," she whispered, and squeezed her eyes shut, in hopes that the horrible pictures would dissipate.

Downstairs in her kitchen Sicily was shocked to see a virginal

layer of snow spread out over Mattagash. If that wasn't a sign from
Providence to call off the wedding, what was? She heard Amy Joy
stirring about in her bedroom, in the very room where she had
grown and blossomed into womanhood. There were a few weeds
poking out here and there, granted, but there had been a blos-
soming. How sad to think that short French fingers would close
around the stem and pinch out the life. Nip Amy Joy in the bud.

"I always thought this would be one of the happiest moments in
my life," Sicily thought, as she patted Puppy's furry head. Maybe
Amy Joy would have met her Prince Charming right here in Mattagash. After all, the Kennedys came down the Mattagash River
once. And so did Jane Wyatt, from *Father Knows Best*. All the
actress wanted when she came ashore was an honest-to-God place
to pee, and she had trudged up the riverbank to Norton Gifford's
lean-to house. Of all the god-awful places to come ashore! And Rita
Gifford had led her to the indoor chamber pot and instructed poor
Jane Wyatt to toss the little yellow tissues she had in her purse
into the empty hundred-pound potato bag leaning against the door
for such inconveniences. But maybe Jane Wyatt would have
trudged up the hill at Sicily Lawler's house, and Sicily would have
handed her a glass of lemonade, and Jane would say that she knew
just the perfect young man for Amy Joy. A young man far, far away
from Mattagash. Maybe even a movie star.

"I could be having one of them things called brunches with a
Mrs. Rockefeller or a Mrs. Kirk Douglas, those snazzy people who
have more Rolls-Royces than they do children." Sicily imagined
several such cars, sleek and shiny, pulling up to Albert Pinkham's
motel, the wedding entourage. Sicily would say clever things like
"Charmed" when the Vanderbilts introduced themselves and she
would even curtsy in respect. Yet here was Amy Joy marrying into
a family of the French persuasion whom Sicily had not even met.
And if Sicily curtsied to one of them, it would be so that she could
gaze at them eye to eye.

"Little heathens," she muttered, and put on some water for tea.
As the coiled burner grew red and the water began to pop into
tiny bubbles, Sicily contemplated her fate. She missed Ed terribly

on this morning of all mornings. If Ed had been alive these past ten years, Amy Joy would have progressed differently along life's highway. Right now, as far as Sicily was concerned, Amy Joy was in the ditch.

"She's left the road completely," Sicily mused. She nipped at a hangnail, and stared out at the dazzling white. She would need to iron her dark blue suit, the one she wore to Dorrie Fennelson's wedding. She would not waste money on another dress for such a sad occasion as her own daughter's wedding. She *would* wear the bouquet that was sitting in her refrigerator. Amy Joy had bought it the evening before and now it was perched atop a dozen eggs, next to the orange juice, with its little green "IGA grocery item" sticker. Pearl had worn black when Junior married Thelma Parsons, but Sicily had always fought the psychological, inward battle and left the boisterous ones to Pearl. She wasn't sure yet what it was, but on the snowy morning of her daughter's wedding she knew something had to be done. Maybe she could fake a heart attack at the church, but no, Amy Joy had said she'd had it *up to there* with Sicily's organs. Maybe when the minister asked if anyone had any objections Sicily could stand up and ask, "Where should I begin?" She had even thought of lacing Amy Joy's Pepsi last night with sleeping pills, hoping she'd sleep all the way past 7:00 P.M. on the day of her wedding. But Sicily was afraid she might use too many pills. Amy Joy would stay sleeping forever and Sicily would go to jail for life. Although, compared to having Jean Claude as a son-in-law, Sicily *could* imagine herself knitting boxes of mittens, crocheting a cellful of doilies, painting every paint-by-the-numbers picture in the state of Maine, and being perfectly happy. Except that she would miss Amy Joy terribly, just as she would miss her after today. Twice during the night Sicily had left her own warm bed and tiptoed down the stairs to stand outside her daughter's bedroom door. Only when she heard the regular whistles of breath coming and going from Amy Joy's chest like little trains did Sicily find contentment enough to go back to her room.

"This is her last night in my house as a child," she thought. "At least as my child. This is the last day of her youth," Sicily decided, forgetting that twenty-four years old meant beyond spinsterhood in Mattagash. Twenty-four years old and still single meant *Twilight Zone*.

Sicily plopped a tea bag in her cup and splashed hot water on it. There were still several hours before the catastrophe. Maybe something unforeseen would happen. Maybe there would be an earthquake. Few people realized that the state of Maine had as many faults as other states, so to speak. Sicily had read that the whole state was perched over a dangerous fault. Not just folks in California could brag about the earth shaking the bejesus out of them. But the last real big quake had been in 1911, and Sicily realized she'd need more than a slight tremor to disperse the Frogs from Watertown.

"Please, Jesus," Sicily begged. "Give me a plan!"

• • •

They had been at Albert Pinkham's establishment for only two nights and already he was at his wits' end as to whether he should toss them out again, or swallow his anger and pad the room bill. There had been a constant parade of Ivys to his door demanding everything from writing paper to postcards to an ice bucket. An ice bucket, for Chrissakes! And there was the Mattagash River bank piled to high heaven with cakes of ice so big they'd make your head spin!

"Here," Albert had said, and offered Randy Ivy a plastic Tupperware bowl and an ice pick. "Now you go down through that little patch of trees to the river and you chisel off all the ice you'll need in your lifetime. Get enough for the whole family."

"Balls!" Randy had looked through bleary red eyes and told Albert. "You mean you ain't got ice in your fridge, man?" "Does this look like an igloo?" Albert demanded, and slammed the door in the boy's face. Albert had never seen dogs pay so much attention to their genitals. No one in Mattagash acted as crazed as Randy Ivy, except maybe Bill Fennelson, Junior, and he had a good reason. His mumps had gone down on him. And there was something else. Albert was smelling funny smells coming from number 4. As if someone had poured gasoline on old socks, then set them on fire. He was keeping as close an eye as he could on the comings and goings in number 4. Lola Craft was one of the comings. A real strumpet, that one. What his mother would have called a fallen sister. And if Winnie Craft were to hear such talk, which was circulating the entire town of Mattagash, it would most definitely take the wind out of her gigantic sails. Winnie Craft would be permanently beached with that kind of news.

A slight knock jarred Albert back to the troublesome present, and he peered through the curtains directly into Thelma's pale, peaked face. She had already been there *five* times that morning. Albert had blazed that number into his brain. Three times she had whined and lamented that there was no breakfast to be served her in the privacy of her room. Breakfast in her room!

"Are you a queen or something?" Albert had asked the confused presence before him. "No? Sorry. We only serve queens breakfast in bed."

Once, she had come for postage stamps.

"This ain't the post office, Miss Ivy," Albert had calmly explained. "You drive to St. Leonard on Monday and they'll sell you all the stamps your funeral parlor money can buy." He didn't care if he insulted her one bit. She was too dazed to notice anyway.

"Funeral *home*," she had told him. "We are not a *parlor*. We don't give *massages*."

"I'll give you a *slap*," Albert thought, but said nothing. Now here she was again. Albert opened the door. He would never be able to vacuum and then make up the bed in number 2, the bridal suite, if these niggling sandwich eaters kept up their abuse.

"What is it now?" he asked, trying desperately to keep that dangerous Scotch-Irish blood pressure to a muted roar.

"Do you have dry-cleaning service?" Thelma asked, as Albert slammed the door in her puny face.

•   •   •

Junior knocked lightly on the door to the pink room and Monique Tessier answered.

"Well, if it isn't an old friend of mine," she said.

"Just what are you doing way up here?" he slipped into the room to ask her. He had no desire to run face-to-face into Randy, next door, although he had not seen much of his son since they'd pulled into Mattagash. Randy had asked for a Bible and then retired to his room.

"It's a free world," said Monique Tessier. "I guess I can go where I want."

"The hell you can," said Junior. "This isn't the world. This is Mattagash, Maine. You're looking for trouble."

"You got any?" asked a sultry Monique, and slipped a cigarette from a new pack.

"This won't work, this little stunt," said Junior. "Thelma already knows about you. The old man knows. I'll just tell them the truth. You followed me here against my will."

"What will you tell them about this?" asked Monique, and in an instant she had slipped her sweater over her head and stood surrounded by pink walls, braless, brown from the sunlamp she had been lying beneath on her living room floor since December.

"Oh my god!" said Junior and covered his eyes. He tried to think of something else, of his son Marvin Randall Ivy III, in the very next room, maybe reading Leviticus at that very moment. *And the man that committeth adultery shall surely be put to death.* "Oh sweet Jesus," Junior moaned. He could not forget them. Their images danced beneath his closed lids and would not go away. He could see yellow spots now which swam into large brown nipples, and the nipples rose magnificently from mounds ripened beneath a sunlamp but genuine as hell.

"She's hypnotizing me with them," Junior thought, and imagined them swinging on the end of a string before his face. *You are getting sleepy . . . very sleepy.* He could smell her Chanel No. 5 perfume, a mixture of cigarette smoke and lipstick mingling on her breath, her breath warm in his ear. It was Neeky, these sights and sounds and smells.

"It seems like such a long time, Junie," she cooed, her hands on his belt undoing it, her hands rubbing his chest, her fingers twirling about his fleshy waist, spinning like little batons at his temples, undoing his knitted hands, undoing his marriage.

"Junie," Monique cooed.

"Deliver me, Lord," whispered Junior. "Please go away," he beseeched Monique. "Please go back to Portland."

"You don't want that now, do you?" Monique asked, and planted Junior's hands on her massive breasts. "You don't want to be stuck up here in the sticks all by yourself, do you?" Junior gazed down into her violet eyes, lavender as flowers.

"Elizabeth Taylor," he thought. And he wondered if Randy might find a passage somewhere in his trusty Bible that would exempt a weak man from time to time, when faced with a pure-blooded Jezebel.

◆　◆　◆

Randy Ivy paid no attention to the headboard next door as it bumped urgently into his wall with a calculated rhythm. He was too concerned with examining Lola Craft's navel for the hundredth time that day.

"It's fuckin' unreal," Randy said to the girl, who lay on her back, eyes glued to the ceiling. She was unused to pot, had never even smelled it until opportunity crossed her path with Randy Ivy's own twisted trail. "It's like a little Grand Canyon right here on your stomach, with little people from Ohio and Kentucky crawling around the rim, takin' Polaroid shots. I'm talking eerie, man."

"What about yours?" said Lola. "Let's look at yours for a while." She tugged up Randy's T-shirt. "An outie!" she screamed in delight.

"Yeah," said Randy. "We're talking pyramids in Egypt now. We're talkin' fuckin' camels walkin' around mine." Randy pulled off his jeans and then helped Lola off with her own. Lola was better than Leslie Boudreau. With Lola he was a city man. He was in charge.

"Let's dance naked," he said. "Like natives." Lola squealed.

"I gotta go help Amy Joy get ready," she said. "Besides, Mama thinks I spent the night there. She might phone about something and want to talk to me."

Randy leaned down and stuck his tongue in her navel. Lola pulled away in hysterics.

"That tickles!"

"I'm filling up the Grand Canyon," Randy said. "I'm a big wave wiping all them little tourists away. Come here, little canyon." He chased Lola about the room with his tongue stuck far out in pursuit. They fell on the bed and Randy pressed his groin hotly against her stomach. A few more nits loosed themselves. It was the first genuine case of crabs to hit Mattagash, Maine, and the culprits were ready. They'd had a terrifying and tightly squeezed ride all the way from Portland, after leaving the amorous affections of Miss Leslie "Boudoir" Boudreau. They had been jostled, raked, and poked. They had managed the extra pressure of the potholes and the frost heaves, as well as Randy's lack of social inhibitions. But they had survived, a testament to their evolutionary durability. Now, like burdocks, like the cherry pits that robins eat only to shit them over new territory, thus spreading the silky cherry blossoms, the crabs lined up. They marched around the scrotum, dodging the rake of Randy's fingers that suddenly came at them. They arranged themselves in mindless formation. Their nits loosened from Randy's curly pubic hairs and reached up like the sticky hands of small children. This was nature. They weren't as cute as kittens, but the crabs were entitled to their chance. When Lola Craft pulled herself up from Randy's warm embrace, she took some little visitors from Portland with her. Another kind of houseguest.

"Randy?" Lola stopped at the door and looked back.

"What, babe?" Randy's scrotum felt as if acupuncturists were at work.

"Were you serious about taking me back to Portland with you?"

"Fuckin' A," said Randy. "And soon. We're almost out of dope."

♦　♦　♦

Amy Joy Lawler could not look at herself in the mirror at first. She was afraid to stare into her own eyes, at the truths which might be lying there, waiting like mousetraps. Planning a wedding was one thing. Following through with it was another. It was as if the plans kept your mind off the consequences. Now here she was, all the invitations sent, the corsages bought, the food dishes assigned as to which neighbors would bring what, a kind of community catering of casseroles, sandwiches, and pastries. The Mattagash gym was heavily decorated with pink and white carnations made from boxes and boxes of Kleenex tissue which Amy Joy had delivered to the lower grades at Mattagash Grammar School. This tiny work, by scholarly hands, was usually reserved for graduation exercises, but everyone made an exception in Amy Joy Lawler's exceptional and oligarchic case. Peter Craft had picked up the three cases of pineapple juice so that his aunt Winnie could make Tropical Islands Delight punch, although the snow filtering down over Mattagash would make it difficult for locals to stop shivering long enough to appreciate a taste of the tropics. And of course, Sicily's wedding dress had been altered for the occasion. Amy Joy pulled the gossamer dress from its plastic bag and looked at it. The dress. This would be another clincher for Sicily. But it was *Amy Joy's* wedding, and that made all the difference. She hadn't starved herself for almost two months for nothing. When Nora Henderson did the alterations following Amy Joy's instructions, the dress had gone in as a floor-length and come out as a mini. Sicily would just have to understand that for the first time in her life Amy Joy had legs that were not bulging with fat and dimples. This would be the last time, as a single woman, she would be able to show off gams such as these. And she intended to go out of spinsterhood in a blaze of glory, of glorious snowflakes, her legs clad in white hose and covered with tiny white roses. Let Sicily drop dead in her pew. It was 1969, not 1931, when the dress had first been used to lure Ed Lawler into an unwanted wedding. Amy Joy had heard Aunt Marge drop a few barbs about Sicily's indoctrination of the schoolteacher from Massachusetts who would become her father. She fingered the cobwebby lace of her mother's wedding dress, now a third of its former length. Amy Joy had asked Nora Fennelson to save the amputated material in case Sicily had a hypochondriac fit of some sort. Amy Joy also realized that by the time her own daughter chose to wear the dress, styles might have changed again.

"I want the train as long as possible, though," Amy Joy thought, and ran her fingers along the eight-foot wake of lace. She wished the weather hadn't turned into such an enemy on her wedding day. A white, lacy mini dress and rose-clung hose somehow clashed with all that snow. Amy Joy was thankful she had chosen a silky purse as "something blue." In reality it was something to carry makeup in, and blue was the first color she scooped up out of the spring grab-bag sale of pocketbooks at Mademoiselle Nicole's in Watertown. She put the dress quickly away, under its brown plastic wrapper, when Sicily knocked on the door.

"Amy Joy?"

"What?"

"Can you open up a second?" Sicily asked, and her daughter did so. Sicily was standing in the doorway with circles under her eyes and a slice of buttered bread in one hand, a bottle of Pepsi in the other. Amy Joy smiled.

"You can be the sweetest thing when you want to," she said.

"I figured this might be the last time you ever ate your specialty in my house," Sicily said. "In *your* house."

"I've only been putting the butter on one out of every four times," said Amy Joy. "But I don't suppose if I eat this butter now that it will show up by seven o'clock." She took the Pepsi and the bread and beckoned for Sicily to come farther into the room.

"What's this, anyway?" Amy Joy asked, and waved the bottle of Pepsi. "I thought you hated to see me drink this. You said my front teeth would drop out before I was twenty years old."

"Well, it's not exactly that bad, Amy Joy, dear," Sicily said. Oh, how she wished her teeth *had* fallen out! Jean Claude wouldn't have given her the time of day then, and Sicily could always find the extra money to get her daughter a new set of choppers later on. When she was about fifty. "It's just that I always thought you drank too many of them. You had a bed-wetting problem as a child, which I'll never forget. And then there's that peculiar sound you make when you drink Pepsi." Sicily frowned as Amy Joy sucked up some Pepsi. Oh Lord, but she would let the child stack cases and cases of the blasted sticky stuff all through the house and never complain again if only she would back out of this fiasco.

"What peculiar noise?"

"Nothing, dear. How are you feeling today?"

"Why?"

"Well, I mean, this close to the big moment and all."

"Nervous," Amy Joy admitted. "How did you feel?"

"Nervous," said Sicily, and for a few seconds they smiled at each other, sharing a warm moment, a hard-found answer to a secret only brides could know, a secret about the fragility of human beings. Mothers knew that daughters were sure to feel it. Daughters were surprised to learn that mothers knew such things. A moment was shared, and a warm, delicious silence fell between them.

"Oh God, please don't marry that Frog!" Sicily pleaded.

"Get out!" said Amy Joy. "I mean *now*."

"But, Amy Joy, you're ruining our lives!" Sicily screamed.

"*Our* lives," Amy Joy snorted. "Will you listen to you? Lola Craft is coming over to fix a few French curls on the top of my head and I'd prefer that my maid of honor not see you throwing one of your world-famous conniptions."

"This isn't a conniption!" Sicily screamed. "This is an emergency! Besides, what honor? There's no *honor* in this, and I doubt seriously that Lola Craft is still a *maid!*"

"You're making a fool of yourself," Amy Joy said, and turned to face her vanity mirror. There it was again, catching her unaware, the pitiful face of childhood, longing to stay where it was.

"*I'm* making a fool of myself? All of Mattagash is laughing so hard it sounds like the ice running. Even the Giffords are laughing."

"What has Mattagash got to laugh at, anyway?" Amy Joy asked, and sprayed a long silver streak down the right side of her hair. She hadn't planned to apply this now, only after Lola had planted a small band of curls high on her head. The decision to do so prematurely was to heighten the effect such an action would have on her mother, not on her hair.

"Oh sweet lovely Savior," Sicily stammered, and leaned weakly against the door jamb. "Is this to mean you plan on wearing those signal flags to your own wedding?"

"Affirmative," said Amy Joy.

"Is this to mean that I'll see those silver banners hovering there as my beautiful wedding dress comes into the church, scraping the floor?"

"Not exactly," said Amy Joy.

"I wish now you'd joined the air force," Sicily said. "I wish you hadn't been so overweight that they couldn't have shoved you into a uniform, put you aboard some bomber, and dropped you somewhere over Texas."

"Why don't you just stay home tonight?" Amy Joy snapped, and threw her hairbrush against the wall. "I don't want you at the church, or at the gym, anyway!"

"Oh, is that right, missy?" Sicily grabbed the plate that held Amy Joy's small yellow field of hay. She reached for the Pepsi bottle, but Amy Joy whisked it away from her grasp.

"Well, you might be jumping outta the frying pan into the fire. We'll just see. And don't expect to see me standing in the open door when you come squalling back home."

"I don't," said Amy Joy, and took a large gulp of soda pop. "I expect you to be snooping from behind the curtains, or rubbering on the phone."

"We'll see," said Sicily. "We'll just see. You're gonna cry your eyes out to come back home."

"Negative," said Amy Joy.

$\mathcal{M}$AY DAY! MAY DAY! MAY DAY!:

GOSSIP IN THE HOUSE OF WORSHIP

....

> Thou still unravish'd bride of quietness . . .
> Who are these coming to the sacrifice? . . .
> What little town by river or sea-shore . . .
> Is emptied of this folk, this pious morn?
>
> —John Keats, "Ode on a Grecian Urn"

WEDDINGS ARE ALMOST AS POPULAR AS FUNERALS IN MATTAGASH, Maine, and just as no one discriminates against a corpse, no one cares whether the bride and groom are an attractive couple, or whether they are well liked. All one really cares about is whether *she's* pregnant and how happy *he* is about the whole deal. But Amy Joy Lawler, the missionary Reverend Ralph C. McKinnon's direct descendant, about to marry a French Catholic added a distinct twist to the ceremony. Everyone in Mattagash was overly curious to see how happy Sicily appeared throughout the whole affair.

"Poor thing," Winnie Craft had gossiped to everyone. "She's been practicing smiling all week."

Two inches of late snow had come down upon Mattagash during that Saturday night. It covered up the frozen pepperonis and left-over pizza crusts, which held the teeth marks of several local dental structures. It covered up Freddy Broussard's tire marks where he'd had his rendezvous with death during his flight from the marauding Giffords. It covered all of Goldie's Christmas lights and promised to enhance the decorations further when evening fell and electricity surged through them once more. Snow buried the crinkly autumn leaves still clinging musically to the cement walkway circling Albert Pinkham's motel. It painted the creamy Cadillac a cool white. It piled playfully on the new mound in the old animal graveyard on Pike Gifford's hill. It heaped itself in fluffy lumps atop the outdoor pole lights in five of Mattagash's finest yards. It built up into a neat pile on the seat of Little Vinal's blue bicycle. It dusted the frozen leaves of Vera's premature tomato plants like a cold fertilizer. It turned black-shingled roofs into white ones and ate up the tar of the road. Only the surging Mattagash River was a match for the snow, as it gobbled up the helpless flakes and grew a little larger and mightier. By the time noon arrived and several cars had spun their way to Watertown, or St. Leonard, the dark tar had emerged once more. By six o'clock, when Floyd Barry, the minister from St. Leonard, fitted his key into the door of the Mattagash Protestant church, several fat flakes were coming down again. By six-fifteen, all the ringside pews at the church had been filled, and all the automobiles catching snow out in the large yard had on their back-seats colorfully wrapped presents of pillowcases, sheets, towels, irons, ovenware, blankets, toasters, potholders, lamps, candy dishes, cutlery sets, and a host of other housewares for two young people venturing out into matrimony.

The family pews still eagerly awaited the arrival of the relatives. Mattagash was anxious to get a good close-up look at Pearl Mc-Kinnon Ivy, gone now for over forty years. And it wanted to get a good look at that string of undertakers she had tied herself to down south in Portland.

The few Catholics stood about the entrance door, allowing Protestants the honor of sitting upon the chairs of their religion. They would take the leftover seats. Whispers fluttered like birds, like shimmering snow buntings, up and down the aisle, in and out of pews, around the IGA flowers arranged in plastic vases at the altar. Gossip flew like snowflakes. *What will Sicily do? What does Amy Joy's dress look like? Are the Frog relatives coming? Does Pearl McKinnon Ivy look as old as she should, or has she had one of them city face-lifts? Will Lola Craft make a boy-crazy fool out of herself when the Frenchmen arrive? Will Amy Joy wear those ridiculous silver streaks? Will Sicily cry?* Oh, but weddings were almost as enjoyable as funerals, as delicious, as enduring.

"What a darn shame it had to snow," Dorrie Fennelson said, actually Dorrie Fennelson Mullins, but she had been married just eleven months and this new name hadn't had enough time to settle down in the memory banks of the locals. Dorrie Fennelson, Amy Joy's childhood friend, rocked her new baby.

"I really thought spring was here for good," said Edna-Bob Mullins, Dorrie's mother-in-law. "Looks like she tricked us."

"The old-timers called this a sheep storm," said Girdy Monihan. "That's when their sheep'd be out grazing and suddenly, with no one expecting it, it'd snow again. They used to lose most of 'em."

"I lost all my daffodil bulbs," Edna-Bob said, as though they were more important than sheep. Edna-Bob had been given her burdensome appellation because there were two other Ednas in Mattagash, that being a popular name back in the teens when all three were born. This Edna's husband was Bob, so she was distinguished from Edna-Ray, and Edna-Jim. The same was true of Martha-Will and Martha-John. It had served well for Sarah-Albert, now divorced from Albert Pinkham and living in New Hampshire, and for Sarah-Tom. If these women had minded the maleness of this roll call it wouldn't have mattered. The town did the naming, and there was no stopping the machine.

"How low did the temperature drop last night?" Edna-Bob Mullins asked.

"Lola Craft is running after Pearl McKinnon's grandson," said Girdy.

"Lord!" said Dorrie, and rocked her cooing baby on her knee. "Have you got a real close-up look at him? I think he's on some kind of chemical."

"His mother takes medication twenty-four hours a day, so it's no wonder," said Girdy.

"Who told you that?" asked Dorrie.

"Winnie said Sicily told her, and then asked her not to tell."

"Good luck with that," said Dorrie.

"They're all packed into Albert's motel like a bunch of big shots," said Edna-Bob. "They could've easily stayed with Sicily, but you know how Pearl McKinnon always had to make a big time of everything."

"She made Sicily open Marge's old house, and even had a telephone hooked up," said Dorrie, and hoisted the baby up to her shoulder where it burped loudly. "Them Gerber carrots make him do that," Dorrie explained, then added, "I can't wait to see poor Sicily's face today."

"All show," said Girdy Monihan. "Pearl McKinnon is my age and I know. She's always been all show. And a real clotheshorse to boot."

"I wonder what Ed Lawler would think of all this if he hadn't gone and shot himself," Edna-Bob said.

"You know," said Dorrie, "I barely remember him. And you'd think I would, him being our principal and all."

"At least Sicily ain't seeing Chester Gifford walk in as the groom," said Edna-Bob.

"Weren't you and Amy Joy good friends back when she was chasing Chester Gifford?" Girdy asked Dorrie. •

"I suppose we were," said Dorrie quickly. "Good Lord, can you imagine Chester Gifford here today?" Dorrie belly flopped the baby across her knees and it farted loudly, a social comment on the Giffords perhaps, bringing laughter in the church, and a deep redness to Dorrie's face.

"How old would Chester be now?" asked Edna-Bob.

"Early forties," said Girdy. "He was born the same summer as Ernest Fogarty. Remember Martha's breech birth?"

"I can't wait to see poor Sicily's face," said Edna-Bob.

The menfolk launched into a different kind of conversation, a sort of occupational gossip.

"Is that Jonsered chain saw any better than the Partner?" Donnie Henderson asked Teddy Monihan.

"Not much," Teddy answered. "Leastways, I can't see any difference in my paycheck."

"Who you cutting for now?" asked Bob Mullins.

"Old Man Henley," answered Kevin Craft. "Who else?"

"I lost another skidder chain," said Amory Hart. "I think there's elves in the woods."

"I lost a chain saw and a toolbox," said Teddy Monihan. "I'd come right out and say the woods is full of Giffords and leave the elves alone."

"It's getting harder and harder to make a living nowadays in the woods," said Teddy Monihan. "The upkeep on my equipment alone is about to send me under."

"Well, if the Dickey-Lincoln dam project ever comes through," said Amory Hart, "this whole area'll be underwater and we'll all be eating sandwiches in Connecticut."

"That dam ain't never going through," said Bob Mullins. "That dam's been in Congress for years, and it'll be in Congress long after you and me is gone."

"Harder and harder for a man to make a decent living," said Teddy Monihan again. "Makes you kinda understand the Giffords."

"Whose Cadillac out front?" asked Bob Mullins.

"Belongs to Pearl McKinnon's son. It's been parked out in front of Albert's place." Amory spit softly on the floor and then covered the foamy little mass with his shoe.

"Albert must be enjoying that," said Bob Mullins, and the men shared a knowing smile.

"It was him owned that green Packard that Chester Gifford wrecked. Remember that?" asked Donnie Henderson.

"Must be hard on gas, a fancy car like that," said Kevin Craft.

"They can afford it," said Donnie Henderson. "They got caskets stuffed full of money back in Portland."

"I wonder how he likes the potholes and frost heaves," Bob Mullins said. "That must be like sailing on the *Titanic*."

"This weather keeps up and we'll be having winter all over again," said Amory Hart. "I heard on the radio this morning that it's been twenty-five years since we had a May snowfall."

"The way I figure it," said Teddy Monihan, "if they put that Dickey-Lincoln dam here and mess up the climate, Maine is gonna start gettin' Florida, and Florida's gonna start gettin' bullshit." Everyone agreed.

By six-thirty the small Protestant church was bulging with new shoes, new neckties, new gloves, new dresses, new coats, new purses. The cars outside, with their prettily wrapped presents which would end up on the gift table at the gymnasium after the wedding, were slowly crusting over with soft snow. Energetic boys, wishing to be outside frolicking among the new flakes, were given stern looks by their mothers. Young girls tittered about their dolls and discovered each had dressed her Barbie in a splendid wedding gown for this special occasion. As all potential baby-sitters were in attendance, Mattagash babies were compelled to come along with their mothers. There were five babies, two sleeping, one laughing at his mother's tickling fingers, one staring with the blankness of newborn uncertainty at his father's yellow "Partner chain saw" cap. The fifth baby was Dorrie Fennelson's, and he was crying loudly and annoyingly, unaware of the circumstances. The only other wedding he had been to was his mother and father's.

When Pearl, Sicily, Winnie Craft, and all the Ivys filed in and took their places in the front pew, a constant drone of words hung over the crowd. The finely tuned gossip buzzed in the old church. *Look how heavy Pearl McKinnon's got. Heavier than she was at Margie's funeral. Ain't her son fat? The whole family's stuck-up. Is that her son's wife? Did somebody drug her or something? Look at the grandson's eyes. My God, that daughter-in-law's got some kind of animal around her neck! Is it a groundhog? A beaver? Is it alive? What will them people do next? Is Sicily gonna pass out?*

When Monique Tessier slipped in the front door and was given a seat by an enchanted high school boy, the gossip shifted gears and modulated. *Who is she? She ain't from Watertown.* Monique took off her heavy winter coat, a burdensome accoutrement that would have already been packed away until next winter had she stayed in Portland. She wore a light blue woolen dress with a gossipy neckline. *Oh good Lord! That woman ain't wearing a bra! Has she no shame? The potholes will teach her a good moral lesson. She looks just like Elizabeth Taylor. Oh, who do you even suppose she is!*

By a quarter to seven, when none of the Watertown participants in the wedding had shown up, the gossip modulated again, into a shrillness that was bouncing off the walls inside the tiny church.

"Where are they?" folks whispered, and then pointed to the empty front pew on the groom's side.

"Probably took a wrong turn and ended up in the swamp," Donnie Henderson said to Bob Mullins. "You know how Frogs are!"

Sicily and Pearl spoke briefly to each other, stirring up even more interest behind them. The waves of whispers beat as steadily against the beams of the Protestant church as the ancient river, which had brought the beleaguered ancestors of all gathered.

"Did our ancestors come here to worship God as they wanted to?" Amy Joy had asked Sicily, one Thanksgiving Day when she'd just returned from a school play about the vicissitudes of the Pilgrims.

"Pine trees," Sicily had answered her daughter. "They come here for pine trees."

Lola Craft had loaned Amy Joy her red floor-length maxi coat to wear over the mini wedding dress and then she had driven her to the back door of the Protestant church in the Crafts' big 1968 Oldsmobile, which had been the most respected car in Mattagash until the Cadillac breezed in. In Floyd Barry's office Lola had pampered Amy Joy's curls and inspected the silver streaks.

"Your makeup looks real good," she assured the bride, who was squinting into the tiny mirror of her compact.

"What time is it?" asked Amy Joy.

"Six-fifteen," said Lola. "You nervous?"

"Affirmative."

"Me too."

"Is everyone out there already?"

The maid of honor came back from peeping out at the flock from behind the curtains to report to the bride. It was Lola's bridal task to be of any service to Amy Joy, to help ease her stress. And one day Amy Joy, as matron of honor, would cater to Lola's every temperamental nuptial whim.

"Jean Claude's family ain't here yet," said Lola.

"Is *he?*" asked Amy Joy.

"Nope. At least I can't see him. Randy's in the front row, though." Lola beamed. When she married Randy, her matron of honor would also become her first cousin. It didn't matter that she and Amy Joy were cousins a hundred thousand times already, back there in the entangled generations of their ancestors. This was a straight-out, *noticeable* relationship.

"Did you talk to Jean Claude today?" Lola asked.

"No," said Amy Joy, and began nervously to finger a silver streak of hair. "It's bad luck for the bride and groom to see or talk to each other the day of the wedding."

"I thought it was bad luck to see each other," said Lola. "I didn't know about the other."

"It's both," Amy Joy said with authority.

"Whew!" said Lola. "Good thing it ain't me and Randy getting married today. I'da blown it. I didn't know it was both see and talk."

"I talked to him last night, just before his stag party." Amy Joy opened the small overnight case she'd brought with her. It held her high-heeled shoes. She'd worn sneakers so as not to slip and fall on the snowy steps. It also held makeup, pantyhose, spearmint gum, the Clairol silver spray, and two Pepsis.

"You want one of these?" Amy Joy found her bottle opener and pried the cap off her bottle. "It'll calm your nerves."

"Naw, I don't guess so," said Lola. "Not unless you got a bag of peanuts to dump in it. It's real boring without peanuts."

"No peanuts," said Amy Joy. "How do I look?" She slipped off the maxi coat and posed heartily for Lola. The maid of honor caught her breath.

"Beautiful!" Lola Craft gushed. "I mean, to the max!"

Amy Joy smiled. It felt wonderful to have slimmed down some. It would surprise the whole congregation greatly when they saw her. It was a perfect exit from Mattagash. Although she'd never been more than thirty pounds overweight, Amy Joy had heard the fat jokes for years. There were plenty of girls in Mattagash lots fatter, but she was a McKinnon's daughter, and so eyes were more heavily cast upon her, tongues lashed her name around more often than others. What a curse it was to be a member of the upper class!

"What time is it?" Amy Joy asked.

"Six-thirty."

Amy Joy drank her Pepsi and stared at the pile of letters on Floyd Barry's desk. A small calendar on the wall warned *The Lord Giveth and the Lord Taketh Away*.

"Indian giver," Amy Joy said, and helped herself to a long noisy drink of Pepsi.

"Not a sign," said Lola, winded, returning with the latest bulletin. "The church is almost full, but so far I don't see anyone from Watertown, or Jean Claude. Mr. Kenney is asking when you'll be coming around to the front door so he'll know when to be ready."

"Well, at seven sharp, I guess," said Amy Joy. Her hands had begun to shake. She was cold in the mini dress, and Floyd Barry's office offered little warmth on such a chilly May first. But it was another kind of chill that was inching its way up her legs and arms, a small terror yet undefined. And there had been bad dreams the night before. She had heard a gun fire repeatedly *Bang! bang! bang!* yet she couldn't see it, or see who was firing it. She'd dodged bullets all night long and now here she was, feeling as if she were about to face a firing squad. Thank God for Pepsi. She slugged hard on the bottle.

"What do you suppose is keeping them all?" Lola asked nervously.

"The weather," said Amy Joy.

"The weather." Lola nodded agreement.

"That road is hell-acious even in the summertime."

"Hell-acious," agreed Lola. "Can I have that Pepsi now?"

"Help yourself," said Amy Joy. Her shoes had suddenly begun to hurt.

"It was real sweet of Mr. Kenney to give you away," Lola said, after her second nerve-calming sip.

"His being the school principal is kinda like representing Daddy," said Amy Joy, and tears came quickly to her eyes. *Daddy*.

"I don't suppose we should call?" asked Lola.

"No, I don't think so. Even if his mother threw a Catholic fit, Jean Claude would still come."

Amy Joy sat down by the window and looked off into the white snow, which was coming along more steadily, the flakes growing into larger patterns of themselves. She could be pulled into the snow, if she let herself, could be hypnotized enough by those unique snowflakes to go right out into it, in her snowflaky mini dress, and curl up under some fat old jack pine, let it cover her completely so that not even the little roses on her stockings could be seen. And if she did, she would get sleepy and this cold chill would vanish.

"What time is it?"

"Five minutes to seven." Lola's hand shook as she held her wrist out to read the watch's numbers.

"Give me the phone," said Amy Joy, when Lola returned from a final report that the bridegroom appeared to be a no-show, as did his immediate family and friends. Amy Joy dialed the number slowly, making sure, very sure.

"Al-lo?" It was one of his sisters. His sister! Why wasn't she on her way to Mattagash?

"Is Jean Claude there? This is Amy Joy. He's not at the church yet and we're getting a little nervous." The words burst out of her parched throat. She'd met his sisters once, at the Acadia Tavern, and she had been treated rudely by them.

"Jean Claude is very sorry, him," the sister said. "But he's go to Connecticut to work with René and Guillaume."

"What?" Amy Joy gasped. "What are you saying?" The door to Floyd Barry's office opened and Sicily appeared.

"Amy Joy dear," Sicily began, but Amy Joy silenced her with an upraised hand.

"What are you saying?" she asked the woman who should have been her sister-in-law in a few minutes.

"He's not get marry, him. He's go to Connecticut last night with Guillaume and René."

"Oh," said Amy Joy, and the word trembled. "Why didn't you call me this morning and tell me?" *Why didn't Jean Claude call her?*

"Mama, she say, let him get down dere firss."

Amy Joy thought about this. What did they imagine? That she'd rally the police in three states to bring him back?

"Thanks a lot," she said. Her voice was thin and vague. She was dreaming. She must be dreaming. Oh please God, please Ed Lawler, please Chester Lee Gifford, please Aunt Marge, please all the spirits and ghosts and gods out there in the realm where all the answers lie to all the really big questions, please tell her she's dreaming.

"I'm going to throw up," she thought.

"Oh my God!" Sicily screamed. Amy Joy laid her head back against the wall and closed her eyes. *Bang! bang!* she could hear the bullet again, the lonely bullet from the unknown, dreamy gun.

"Oh sweet Jesus, what have you done to my wedding dress?"

Sicily's scream may have been heard out in the church, but chances are it was not. At least it was never mentioned among the volumes of mythology which grew out of The Day When Amy Joy Lawler Got Stood Up. They said other things, the carriers of this tale. They mentioned the frantic waiting by the guests. They mentioned the tired pacing of principal Robert Kenney at the back of the church, until he'd worn the varnish off the floor. They spoke of Sicily twisting and turning in her chair and finally disappearing behind the thick red curtain which led to the back office. They heard voices rising and falling back there. The truthful messengers of this tale would say the words were indiscernible, muffled, lost to posterity. The less truthful would say that Amy Joy was crying her heart out, and swearing in French to boot. This wasn't true. This was one of the threads of *possible truth* that attach themselves to a good strong mythology, a long-lasting legend, and hold on.

"I said what have you done to my dress?" Sicily wailed again. "Where's the rest of it?"

"There won't be a wedding," said Amy Joy softly. "Jean Claude is in Connecticut." Sicily stopped ranting and let this tidbit settle in.

"Actually, dear, the dress don't look that bad."

Floyd Barry knocked on the door.

"Seven-ten," he said cheerily. "Are we running a little late?"

"It's off," said Amy Joy. "Would you tell everyone?"

If the wedding had gone on, it would have given birth to much speculation and much replay over the next few months. Everyone in Mattagash knew how unhappy Sicily Lawler was with the situation. They knew that Amy Joy was dieting heavily to pare the plumpness off her God-given body for reasons of pure vanity. They knew her innermost secrets as she plodded toward her wedding day. Lola Craft, whom she regarded as her very best friend, told all to everyone. Lola liked being the possessor of unknown facts. It gave her some much-needed personal attention for a few fleeting minutes. And everyone in Mattagash said Lola couldn't help it anyway. It was in her genes, thanks to her mother, Winnie.

The wedding would have had monumental effects anyway, but to have Amy Joy Lawler stood up, like a lamb at the altar, was beyond the wildest expectations of any sports crowd.

"I think I'm going to die," Amy Joy said, and placed her hand on her heart. Later, Lola reported this item faithfully.

"She put her hand right on her heart when she said it," Lola would widen her eyes and say. But Amy Joy did not cry out, "Jean Claude, please come back!" as Lola reported, for sensationalism alone. What she truly said, what would be lost to the annals of gossip in Mattagash forever, was, "Is Dorrie Fennelson out there?"

"Yes, she is, and she brought that colicky little brat," Lola answered. "You two have hated each other for a long time, ain't you?"

"Affirmative," said Amy Joy.

By the time Lola had backed the car up to the office door to carry Amy Joy and Sicily home, the crowd had spilled out of the church and was standing curiously around, as snowflakes piled up like rice thrown on their heads. It was already decided that, since all the women had contributed the food waiting down at the gym, there was no need to waste it. They would take the numerous gifts home first, so that the Giffords wouldn't get them. They would leave them wrapped and ready for the next foolish couple. "You might as well tell them to go to the gym and enjoy themselves," Sicily said to Floyd Barry. "They're gonna anyway."

When the long red maxi coat ran from the office door to duck into the Oldsmobile, there were cries of "There she goes! There's Amy Joy!" And then the car disappeared, with Amy Joy covering her face in the backseat, like some reluctant star of the old silver screen. They disappeared into a snowy spring day, into the mind of every Mattagasher watching with mouth agape, into the very heart of the new legend.

A LITTLE NATIVE CRUCIFIES THE NATIVITY SCENE: ANGELS ON THE YELLOW BRICK ROAD

....

Oh who is that young sinner with the handcuffs on his
    wrists?
And what has he been after that they groan and shake their
    fists?
And wherefore is he wearing such a conscience-stricken air?
Oh they're taking him to prison for the colour of his hair. . . .

Now 'tis oakum for his fingers and the treadmill for his feet,
And the quarry-gang on Portland in the cold and in the heat,
And between his spells of labour in the time he has to spare
He can curse the God that made him for the colour of his
    hair.

      —A. E. Housman, "Oh who is that young sinner"

A FEW MINUTES AFTER SEVEN O'CLOCK, WHEN AMY JOY WAS BEING chauffeured from the church still a single woman, Goldie Gifford threw the switches to all her magnificent lights and the Gifford hill rose up in a swirl of color to meet the pelting snow. The wedding would last almost an hour, so Goldie told her children they must have their water heated for the galvanized bathtub upstairs and be bathed no later than six-thirty. They were to *keep clean* until eight o'clock, and then they could walk safely together to the Mattagash gym a mile away and attend the reception. Once there, they would, or so help her they'd be in trouble, *behave themselves*. This would give Goldie and Irma enough time to heat their own pans of water and leisurely bathe themselves without curious little eyes peeking around corners or into windows.

Irma had toted the large pans of steaming water off the stove and up the stairs until her thick glasses were steam-ridden. Now she was in her own room, bathing. Goldie would get the tub, Irma promised, no later than seven-thirty. Then at nine o'clock the two would thumb a ride over to the gym with Goldie's sister Lizzie. The celebration would be in full swing by then and Goldie would not feel so uncomfortable walking in before the condescending eyes of Crafts and Harts and Fennelsons.

Miltie, Missy, and Hodge were indeed bathed and ready by six-thirty. Under direct orders to keep clean, Miltie grew impatient with *The Wonderful World of Disney* on TV. He sought out Goldie in the kitchen.

"Mama, can we decorate inside the house, too?" he pleaded.

"Oh, honey, I don't know," Goldie started to protest. "I think we pushed about as far as we should. People'll think we're crazy as it is."

"Aunt Vera's crazy, that's who," Missy shouted from the living room.

"Pleeeeeeease." Miltie tugged at Goldie's hand. She looked down at her youngest child's face, already losing the soft roundness of babyhood. Would it happen overnight, as it had with the other children? Would Goldie get up one morning soon to find in horror that her baby was gone, a little man in his place? A few more Christmas decorations wouldn't hurt.

"Okay," said Goldie, "but just a few." She brought a small box down from the attic and opened it up. There was a little plastic cone centerpiece, and numerous shapes and colors of extra bulbs for the outdoor tree. In the bottom of the box was the small Christmas angel, the one Goldie had bought from the old woman in Bangor. She removed the red tissue paper carefully. The angel's small face looked up at her. This was Goldie's secret angel. There were things about this angel she would tell no one, not even her sister Lizzie. Just Goldie and the angel knew *some* things.

While Goldie pondered the best place for Miltie to display the pale cherub, the telephone rang.

"Will one of you kids git that?" Goldie shouted into the living room.

"It's Uncle Vinal, Daddy," she heard Missy say. "He wants to talk to you."

"Vera's on her way up the hill," Vinal said to Pike. "It seems Little Pee massacred them puppets she's got in the front yard. She thinks Goldie put him up to it."

"I see," Pike said, businesslike. For all the family knew, the two patriarchs were discussing hubcaps and tires.

"I don't know about you, Pike," his brother said. "But I say we let them two git it all out of their systems before the reception."

"I'll bring that wrench down tomorrow," Pike said cryptically into the phone. Goldie heard him plunk the receiver down and tell the kids to flick the station to a rerun of *Bonanza*. Then she heard him flop out on the couch.

"It's the one where Hoss gets shot and almost dies," Goldie heard Pike say loudly to the children. Seconds later, a knock sounded heavily on the kitchen door. An angry battering. In the living room, Pike winced. *He* wouldn't want to be at the other end of Vera's wrath. He'd prefer the sheriff from Watertown any day.

Goldie went to the door and opened it a crack, not because she was expecting Vera, but because all day long the wind had been picking up small tufts of snow piled on the porch and tossing it inside each time the door opened. Little Pee had promised several times to shovel it away, but he had disappeared after supper and Goldie hadn't seen him since. She opened the door a crack and saw Vera Gifford Gifford in only her housecoat and Big Vinal's winter boots.

"Did you put him up to it? Did you?" Vera was shouting. "Who give him that can of spray paint, anyway? And where'd he get that hatchet?" Vera was trying to open the door and Goldie was holding it with all her might, as they'd done earlier that January. Only now there was a four-month-long pent-up torrent of anger pushing with Vera.

"Who are you talking about?" screamed Goldie. She was wondering why Pike didn't come to her rescue. But she dared not turn her head to look, for fear Vera would find the sudden strength to break the door down. Instead she shouted, "Pike! Pike!" But her husband didn't answer. The children ran to the stair steps, like mice, to watch the goings-on.

"My three wise men are strewed up and down the road!" Vera railed. "He pulled the head completely off Joseph! And you ought to see what that little pervert done to the Virgin Mary!" The thought of her dead figurines renewed Vera's anger. She heaved heavily on the door and Goldie, without Pike to help her, was pushed back until Vera was able to reach one arm inside. She caught Goldie's thick hair in her hands and pulled her out into the cold, colorful night. Goldie still had the little angel in her hand, but she dropped it when her feet hit the wet snow on the porch and slid under her. Vera, with one hand still buried in Goldie's hair, used the other to throw a few well-aimed punches to the face. Goldie tried to fight back, but she couldn't seem to push the bigger woman off. Vera was now straddling her, and Goldie felt fingernails scraping across her cheek. She turned her head sideways to avoid the lashes, and that's when she saw her, lying on her back in the snow. Lying with her two blue eyes staring up to heaven, as snow came down to fill them. Goldie's Christmas angel. Full of sadness and secrets.

When the torrent of anger rose up in Goldie, she remembered that it had not been a smashed pencil box, all those years ago, that made her hate Vera. It had been something else. And she remembered what she had always tried not to remember. She remembered the day at school, when she was ten years old and a tomboy, but suddenly bleeding like a woman. She had heard the elusive stories and vague reasons for this blood from an older girl at school. But she wasn't sure. She couldn't ask her mother, who was more interested in the long line of shaggy men who passed through her bedroom than in her children. Goldie felt as if her body had broken, and she was bleeding from it. She was sure there was a little red wound inside her, seeping. She had rolled up bathroom tissue at school into a small pad the first day. That was the day she looked down and saw her panties spotted red, as though little roses were growing in the crotch of them. The flow was very light, as it is the first time it comes to small bodies. It was a small flow, but it required attention. That night at home, Goldie found an old sheet her mother had thrown under the sink to be cut into rags, and with a pair of scissors she cut a few small strips from it, which she shaped into pads. Then she sneaked the tissue pad from school outside, wrapped securely in a newspaper, and when no one was about, she dropped it down one of the holes of the outhouse. She crumbled pages of the Sears Roebuck and tossed them down onto the newspaper. She needed to be sure. And that's how she safe-guarded her awful secret for years, until she married, until she was in a house of her own. Her mother never asked once if she had any questions about her body, about the upheavals it was sure to go through on its way to womanhood. Still, Goldie might have grown into this new knowledge of her body with unashamed cer-tainty if it hadn't been for that day at school, the second day of her trauma. That was when the little homemade pad sneaked its way up the back of her panties as she was playing Red Rover. She simply hadn't thought about belts or pins, or such things. She was ten. That's all she wanted to be. She had been dared over by Vera to the enemy side. She had been dared to break the clasped hands of the opposite team with her body, which was already broken. And she had run with all her might, had given it her very best, only to be stopped by Vera's strong grasp of another girl's hand. Goldie was a captive of Vera's team. As she hurried to take her place at the end of the line, the little pad slipped out of her panties and fell limply on the ground. Goldie felt lighter suddenly, but she didn't miss the pad. She had forgotten it the way some women forget pocketbooks. Vera noticed it first. Vera grabbed it up, held it high over her head. Vera, who was fourteen and over the shock of it. Vera, mature, held it up to the others. "Look who's a woman now!" she had shouted. Goldie looked up at it as if it were Jesus on the cross, as if it were a little red comet streaking the sky. When the pad was suddenly on the ground, there was no denying it was hers. She felt her compatriots—the very girls she'd run across the field *for*, the reason she'd lost the awful thing in the first place— swarm up behind her. Those who didn't know what it meant stood before it, all open mouths. Those who knew, those who were shell-shocked at thirteen and fourteen, pointed and giggled. Goldie looked at them all. Their faces were flushed, as if they'd been fighting a war, not playing. Then she looked up again at the folded sheet, in need of a bleaching, with its thin curvature of blood. It looked like a bottom lip. Like a half-smile, laughing. Like a baby's grin. And Goldie was embarrassed of her breasts, which had begun to push out from her chest and hurt her. She was embarrassed of the awful malfunction in her body. And for years afterward, when she bled she felt it was her heart bleeding. It was her heart crying out for the old days of tree climbing, and hopscotch.

Now, on the snowy porch of her womanhood, Goldie reached up for Vera's mouth because it was red and gaping before her. She reached for Vera's bottom lip, as if it were the thin trace of blood Vera had stolen from her, a lifetime ago. Goldie wanted to make blood come out of that lip, to make it hurt. She wanted to take it back, as she couldn't do that day in the school yard when Vera was fourteen, and tall, and holding it over her head like the Statue of Liberty. And now Vera was crying like a baby, and Goldie let go of the torn lip. She let Vera put her hands over her mouth to cover it—something Goldie had wanted to do when she was only ten and standing naked in front of those girls, girls who would become the women she would meet every day in Mattagash for the rest of her life. She had wanted to hide her womanhood because it was a cut, a sore, and even though she was only ten, it had set out to hurt her.

Vera was sobbing above her now, and Goldie pushed her off and onto the white snow on the porch. She touched a finger to the scrapes on her face where Vera's nails had dug away the top layers of skin. There were little bloody lines there now, like tire tracks on snow. She brushed away the spit and some blood from the corner of her mouth. One of her front teeth felt horribly loose. She had bitten her tongue and it throbbed wildly. Vera was pulling the torn housecoat about herself and trying to stand up in Vinal's huge boots. Goldie picked up the Christmas angel. It was wet with snow but undamaged. She held it gently in her hands as if, like childhood, it could break at any moment.

"Now you go on home," she whispered through her swollen lips to Vera. "You go on down the hill." Missy and Miltie were crying and pulling at Goldie's arm. Irma ran to the door, wrapped in a bath towel, and shouted, "What's going on?" They helped Goldie to her feet, and then they all stood still to watch Vera go back down the snowy hill. Popeye nipped at her boot heels, thinking the unsteady gait and all the racket meant that Vera wanted to play. Goldie closed the door behind them. She could hear Pike's snores floating in from the living room. "He knew what was going to happen," Goldie thought. "He knew from that phone call." Her children stood quietly around her like little rabbits, their ears leaning forward.

"I want all of you to go to that reception and have the time of your lives," Goldie told them. "But don't let me hear word that any one of you did one thing you shouldn't. And if you see Little Pee over there, you send him home. You tell him I mean it this time."

"Are you sure, Mama?" Irma asked, her big blurry eyes trying desperately to focus without her glasses. "It doesn't really seem fair. I mean, for us to go."

"I'm sure," said Goldie. "I've never been more sure of anything."

When Irma was ready, Goldie watched her load the children into Lizzie's car. The snow's intensity made Goldie leery about letting them walk, so Lizzie came by early in her swooping big gray Ford to whisk them down to the gym.

Goldie stood over Pike's body on the sofa. His mouth was wide open, displaying several cavities on the inner ridges of his teeth. His face was puffy with alcohol, and he needed a good clean shave. Goldie stood and looked down at him.

"I *will* divorce you," she said. "I *will* save my children from you."

"Huh?" Pike grunted himself awake and looked at his watch. "I gotta meet Vinal," he said, and brushed past Goldie, ignoring her black eye and swollen lip. She heard the front door slam.

Alone with the Christmas angel, her face on fire with the bruises Vera had put there, Goldie straightened the gossamer angel's-hair wings, reshaped the little pipe cleaner halo, smoothed the lace dress. She thought of Amy Joy Lawler, probably already married by now. And she thought of the little old woman who had sold her the angel. She wondered if that was how the old woman herself might have looked on her wedding day, like a poor little angel, with such a sad face. An angel trapped in Christmas forever. Trapped, forever, for the holidays.

"People should be able to be different if they want to," Goldie said. "People should be able to change their lives. If they want to." And she packed the angel away. She would wait this time for the heat of July, until the Fourth maybe, and then she would bring her back out into the sunlight. Goldie would let her stand in her little dress on the top of the television, regardless of what all Mattagash said, regardless of how hard Vera laughed at the bottom of the hill. And then Goldie thought of the little dish she had held in her hands, all those years ago, at the old woman's house, the dish with the sad Christmas scene.

"It was Christmas Eve," thought Goldie. "And it was the old woman's house, all gray and lonely. No one was coming. No children. No fat silly man in a sleigh." And she wondered if the old woman was still alive.

Goldie stashed the angel away in a dark corner of the attic. Then she fixed herself some Taster's Choice and went to the window to stand. Her Christmas lights were ablaze in the snow, all the trapped diamonds brought to the surface and glittering. She wondered if Amy Joy was happy tonight, and hoped that she was. Amy Joy had been less mean than all the others. And Goldie also wondered if the old woman's house was still standing, if she was still there inside, turning out treasures in her little factory. She could go there and live all her life and be happy, just helping the old woman. She would be like one of Santa's elves. And Goldie would take all her boxes and boxes of Christmas lights and she would light up the whole place. She would light up the doilies and Easter eggs and cats. She would light it up like Disneyland. Or the North Pole. Someday, when Lizzie had an itch to travel, and Goldie had a few extra dollars to tuck inside her bra, she would go back down there. Just to see.

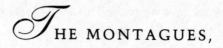

THE MONTAGUES, McKINNONS, CAPULETS, AND CLOUTIERS SHUN THE BALL: A GOOD TIME IS HAD BY THE REST

....

"Welcome, gentlemen! ladies that have their toes
Unplagued with corns will have a bout with you:
Ah ha, my mistresses! which of you all
Will now deny to dance? She that makes dainty,
She I'll swear hath corns. . . .

You are welcome, gentlemen! Come, musicians, play.
A hall, a hall! give room! and foot it, girls."

—William Shakespeare, *Romeo and Juliet*

THE MATTAGASH GYM WAS WELL DECORATED. BEHIND THE bridal table hundreds of pink and white Kleenexes, shaped into papery carnations and held together with bobby pins, had been taped to the wall. The real flowers, the IGA carnations, had been saved for the three vases that sat on the long bridal table. This was the same table on which Amy Joy had eaten her meals for three years of high school. Her freshman year she was forced to attend school in Watertown until Mattagash finally built their own in 1961. They added a few classrooms and then the huge gymnasium on to the grammar school of which Ed Lawler had been principal. Mattagash students would take great pride in this. They had been lost among the strange and sometimes snobby ways of the Watertown students. But after 1961 they would even have their own basketball team, and baseball team. And there would be a place for wedding receptions if one could pay the ten-dollar rental fee. There was no longer any need to fill someone's living room and kitchen to bursting when a wedding reception needed a place to be born.

No one remembers now why, but for what seemed centuries Winnie Craft, Claire Fennelson, and Girdy Monihan had been serving the punch at all socially acceptable receptions. They hovered about Winnie's cut-glass punch bowl like fat hummingbirds, pouring, stirring, refilling. Ed Lawler had often thought of them as the three witches from *Macbeth*, but this was not an insight he could share, Mattagash being most suspicious of Mr. Shakespeare and his ilk.

"A real dirty mind, if you ask me," Marge McKinnon had said of the bard almost sixty years earlier, after hearing old Flora Gumble read *Romeo and Juliet* to the eighth-grade class. This statement squelched any hopes for *Hamlet* or *Othello*. It was Shakespeare's first introduction to Mattagash high society, and his last.

The three-piece band from St. Leonard had already been paid their fifty-dollar fee to provide a night of musical entertainment. They twanged in a barrage of flats and sharps and out-of-tune tunes, totally unaware that the bride and groom were not present. Nor were any other members of the House of McKinnon, or the House of Cloutier.

Lola pulled Randy onto the floor, anxious to show him off to Traci Monihan, Debbi Fennelson, and her first cousin Sheila Craft. Cradling her head in the pimply crook of Randy's neck, Lola peered over his shoulder to scan the faces watching. There they were. *Debbi. Traci. Sheila.* Modern names compared to the *Myrtles, Marges,* and *Ednas* of the generations before them. Television and magazines had tossed aside the old-fashioned appellations and had brought to Mattagash names the old settlers had never before heard spoken. Names that ended in, good Lord, the letter *i*. These girls were the new breed now, and as they watched Lola dance, they exchanged smirking glances and barbed comments. Lola knew what it meant. They weren't going to look one bit impressed with her rich city catch. They weren't going to give Lola that kind of satisfaction for free. Yet Lola knew that if one of them had been lucky enough to snag Marvin Randall Ivy III, she'd have done so without a second thought. Then it would be Lola's turn to lean against the wall of the Mattagash gymnasium and feign utter disgust towards the bachelor-in-residence.

"I wouldn't touch him with a ten-foot pole," Lola heard Debbi Fennelson say, as she and Randy danced by.

"Sour grapes," Lola said to them, and Randy tilted his head back to look at her. His eyes appeared to be in need of a good bleaching and then perhaps an ironing.

"What?" he asked Lola.

"Nothing. I was just saying hello to some ex-friends."

"I'm down to my last joint," said Randy. "Something has to be done. I can't take this place straight. It reminds me of Bedrock on *The Flintstones.*"

"What are you going to do?" Lola asked.

"Well," said Randy, "first we're going to kill the other half of your pint of vodka." Lola giggled. She and Randy would have a full rollicking life together, she knew. Already they had spiked their punch glasses, when they thought no one was looking, with the bottle Lola had hidden in her bulging purse. Being a native, she should have remembered that someone is always looking in Mattagash. They were far from the only ones to indulge in such a manner, but Lola and Randy were much too conspicuous, a fault frowned upon since the first early settlers began hiding jars of liquor in summer kitchens during the winter months, and in barns during the summer months. This combination of religion and climate still held honesty in fast check among the latter-day settlers.

Winnie Craft was keeping an approving eye on the dancing pair. She was the only one Lola cared to deceive. Like the rest of Mattagash's youth, Lola had given up the old ancestors' notion of *flaunt not,* but she still wanted no part of Winnie's endless lectures. When Winnie ducked back into the kitchen for a refill of punch Lola sneaked the bottle out of her purse. She filled the two glasses while Randy stood in front of her, shielding the act from the rest of the crowd with his skinny body.

"Lola just poured whiskey into her punch," Girdy Monihan whispered to Claire Fennelson.

"Poor Winnie," said Claire, "to have that wild boy hanging around." Claire wished silently that Debbi had been quicker than Lola to secure what Mattagash was now referring to as a billionaire's son.

"We could go get the janitor while Winnie's gone," said Girdy. "But I suppose there's others doing it, too."

"I suppose," said Claire, and scanned the crowd for a glimpse of Debbi. She had known Girdy Monihan enough years to recognize a hint when it was thrown at her. Who was Girdy to talk, Claire could have said but didn't, when everyone knew Girdy's own daughter had smoked herself into a cancerous grave, just like a *man* would do, spitting and hacking up blood while Girdy assured everyone it was infected wisdom teeth.

"Then," said Randy, "you're gonna drive me to that piece of shit they call a motel."

"And?" Lola whispered, thinking Randy had lovemaking in mind. She was as sultry as any of those women she had seen on the big screen at the Watertown drive-in.

"Then I'm gonna get my old man's spare car keys," said Randy, and swirled Lola around.

"*And?*" Lola was breathless.

"And then we're going for a little spin in the Caddy."

"Oh God!" Lola gushed the way no movie woman ever would. But then, *they* had seen their fill of Cadillacs. She could only hope that Debbi and Traci and Sheila would have their noses pressed like little dogs against the window of the gymnasium front door as she and Randy sped past in the creamy, dreamy Cadillac.

"Where we spinning to?" asked Lola.

"Portland," said Randy. "I've had it with Prick City."

◆ ◆ ◆

Albert Pinkham made several trips out to his snowy pickup to nip from the bottle of rum he'd hidden beneath the springs, and to let Bruce out to pee yellow holes in the white snow. Let others keep an eye on their wristwatches and their drinks, men who had to be up by five o'clock and at work in the woods by daylight. Albert Pinkham was a free man, not just from Sarah Pinkham but from the occupational burdens suffered by his fellow Mattagashers. And the knowledge that the bridal suite, which had been paid for in advance, would be vacant all night long made him smile. Albert liked little inconsistencies such as that. He patted Bruce, who had curled back up in a neat bundle on the front seat. Bruce hated to miss special occasions.

"You having a good time, old boy?" Albert asked his companion. "You having the time of your life, Brucie?"

Bruce might not be having such a monumental time, but he could sense that Albert was, and he leaned away from Albert's thick rummy breath and whined softly.

"Sometimes you're as bad as Sarah," Albert said to his dog, and tipped back the cold bottle of rum, which would warm his insides in an instant.

◆ ◆ ◆

Monique Tessier had been forgotten by the gossips back at the church after Amy Joy had handed them such a platter of emotional goodies. But her reentrance at the Mattagash gym, in her sleek blue dress, brought back a wash of curiosity. Just who could she be? She was no one's relative, it was determined, after questions ran like electricity among the Crafts, the Fennelsons, the Monihans. Some data did pour in when a Henderson remembered seeing her at Blanche's Grocery buying long skinny cigarettes, the kind women in TV commercials tended to smoke. And then someone from among the Harts remembered seeing a big beige Buick in Albert's driveway, and a woman getting into it. Martha Fogarty was almost positive this woman was related to the Ivys, since she'd seen Randy Ivy getting a ride with her from Blanche's. Information was passed more frequently than cake and punch. When pudgy Junior Ivy appeared at the gym, peering nervously about, suspicions were confirmed. Maybe she was a cousin or something.

"She don't look like a cousin," said Edna-Bob.

"She don't look like any member of a family," said Girdy. "Not even a distant relative."

When Albert Pinkham reappeared, a slight slur to his words did not stop him from delivering the missing piece of the puzzle.

"Yup. She's staying at my place, all right," he told the women who inquired. Not that it was any of their goddamn business. But Albert was in a congenial, rum-inspired, and neighborly mood. He would offer even more than they'd asked for.

"She's the Ivy secretary, here on business." A secretary! Good Lord, but what woman who wasn't going to be a housewife would be anything other than a schoolteacher! Schoolteachers were necessary and they were inward types. Secretaries *flaunted*. Real *floozies*.

"I saw you leave and I figured you'd be here," Junior whispered to Monique. "I'll meet you outside in five minutes."

"Why?" asked Monique. She could tell he was angry. "I just got here. I intend to have some fun."

"Monique, *please*." Junior's attempted ventriloquy, to convince the locals he was not talking to *this woman,* was for naught. Besides, Monique was openly conversing with *him*.

"Monique, you've got to leave this godforsaken town before the old man sees you."

"Let him."

"No, don't let him," Junior snapped. "You've no idea the jeopardy you're putting my career in by turning up in Mattagash." Monique had to bite her tongue. Did he have any idea the kind of jeopardy *her* career was in?

"I knew your family wouldn't be here, not after what happened back at the church," said Monique. "But I'm bored, Junie. I need a little excitement."

"Portland's the place for excitement," Junior muttered. "Not Mattagash, for Chrissakes."

"Are you trying to tell me you've forgotten this morning already?" Monique throated the words. No, of course Junior hadn't. As a matter of fact his genitals tingled at her reminder. But enough was enough. Sex was a temporary thing, but his own funeral home would last forever.

"This morning was a mistake," said Junior. "And I shouldn't be seen here with you now, Monique. I tell you, you gotta leave town."

Monique's face flushed red as she slipped her woolly winter coat back on and grabbed her purse. Junior pretended not to see her go.

"Hello, I'm Junior Ivy, Pearl McKinnon's son," Junior said to several people, who already knew very well who he was. "Nice reception," Junior told Winnie, Claire, and Girdy, who were huddled like the three Fates around the punch bowl. Spacing his departure from Monique's by ten minutes, Junior felt, would be enough to dissuade any suspicions. He forgot his own warning to her back in Portland. *You can't lay low in Mattagash. In Mattagash, D-Day would've flopped.*

Outside, the snow was still falling in thick flakes. All the cars belonging to the gatherers were white things, a yardful of small beached whales. Junior found the Cadillac. In just the short time he'd been inside, the windshield had acquired a thin blinding film of snow. Junior wiped it away.

"This is like the goddamn Arctic," he muttered, and ran a gloved hand across the back window as well. Then he wiped the side windows. He didn't notice, what with snow clinging to the tires, that his lovely hubcaps were gone.

"Junie?" A ghostly voice, snow-filled and downy, came out of the shadows of the gymnasium and beckoned him. There she was, snowflakes clinging like little doilies to her hair, her shoulders glistening with wet, her blue coat turned purplish under the school yard light. A snow nymph, this voluptuous secretary, a snow goddess whose tiny footprints in the gymnasium yard would lead to some mythical birthplace, a mountaintop, a clamshell, the Ocean Edge Motel in Portland, Maine.

Junior followed her over to the Buick, now buried beneath a thin blanket of snow.

"You've got to leave town when the snow stops," he pleaded.

"Please," she said. "Just talk to me. I'm so lonely tonight. Weddings do that to me, even when they don't take place."

Junior sat in the passenger seat, as he'd done that afternoon in Portland when he'd tried to cut the cord and loose himself. Monique started the car, then let her cold fingers trace his cheek, the neckline of his shirt, his pouting lips. Junior felt that tingle again, more a quiver, a quick streak of electricity coursing through him. He was a fat fish flapping on shore, and Monique knew it.

"If I have to remind you every ten minutes of your life," Monique whispered, "about what you're giving up, then I will." She leaned forward and licked her tongue about his Adam's apple. A snowy shiver went through Junior as goose pimples sprouted on the surface of his skin. Monique put her hand on the hard lump beneath his zipper.

"Oh God," Junior moaned. "Remind me. Remind me."

Ten minutes later Junior pushed himself up and looked down on Monique where she lay in the backseat, her hair splayed about on the upholstery. Snow blinded all the windows of the car.

"It's like being in a white cave, isn't it?" Monique asked. "A snow tunnel." Junior said nothing. He'd done it again. He'd been led by his penis, as though there were a ring in it, across the snowy school yard, into the old Buick, and then into the spongy backseat. He was no more than a high school boy with menacing hormones. He was a tethered bull. Maybe his father was right. If Junior didn't get his rabbit raisins into a meaningful pile he would never become the entrepreneur he wished to be. After the fact, Junior was able to look at Monique with complete objectivity.

"This has got to end," Junior said. "I'm gonna have to get my family together and concentrate on them *and* business." Monique was huffed. How dare he, after they'd made such eloquent, albeit rapid-fire, love? She wished she could take it all back, as though a sexual encounter were akin to a cup of sugar, or a borrowed book. But she couldn't. Once again, he'd used her.

"Junie?"

"No, Monique." Junior zipped his pants up, over the large ball of his stomach. "If I have to have a heart-to-heart talk with the old man tomorrow, I will."

"What do you mean?" Monique wished greatly to slap his chubby face as hard as she could. But that would be a blunder. She knew very well that Marvin Senior had dragged his son all the way to the god-damn-awful ends of the earth to break the spell she had cast over him.

And she also knew that absence made the heart forget, especially in Junior Ivy's case. Food seemed to be the only constant there.

"I mean when we go to the funeral home tomorrow in Watertown I'm gonna tell him how you came up here without my permission. I'm gonna tell him before he sees you and gets the wrong idea. I got a business at stake here."

Junior knew Monique was seething when he got out and slammed the door. Let her seethe. He needed to discover some way to circumvent her sexual power over him. Maybe he should buy a few girlie magazines and a box of tissues to keep in the men's rest room at the Ivy Funeral Home. A trip to the bathroom every few hours would help keep Monique's charms on ice. Or better yet, he might get one of those blow-up dolls, anatomically correct but without all the hang-ups real women have. Blow-up dolls don't take Valiums or chase men from one end of Maine to the other in battered Buicks.

"Now I mean it," Junior said when Monique rolled down her driver's window and looked sadly at him. "I will never get inside your car again, so don't plead."

"Who's got your car?" Monique asked, instead of pleading.

"What?" Junior spun around in time to see the creamy Cadillac swirling out of the snowy yard. "Don't!" he screamed. My God, what kind of awful déjà vu was this? Could he never visit relatives in Mattagash without having his car stolen or, worse, wrecked? Junior had lost a delicious Packard to Chester Lee Gifford, who demolished it badly enough to die in it. Chester Lee totaled himself the night he totaled the car. Junior ran, with his belly jiggling and his breath coming in short grunts, as far as the road, but he couldn't catch the smooth car. He watched its snowy taillights instead, as they disappeared around a bend in the road.

"Excuse me," Junior said, and rapped on Monique's window. "Would you give me a lift to my mother's house?"

•   •   •

The Plymouth-shark sat quietly in a dimly lighted corner of the school yard. A smothering of snow had colored the immobile shark white, and now its great eyes gazed out at the rest of its species with deep interest. Pike and Vinal Gifford were embarrassed at the meager pickings that lined up in the Mattagash High School yard. The cars were almost all local ones, with dull and dented hubcaps, with snapped aerials, with tread-worn tires. These slim pickings had helped years ago to shape Vinal and Pike's personal motto: *Don't rile up the old hometown more than is necessary.* But where was the slew of Watertown cars they'd been promised? Where were all the southern relatives? Other than the four swell Cadillac hubcaps, which lay like large shiny moons on the backseat, there were no plums out there to pick, regardless of the weather. Even the old Buick from Portland had lost its hubcaps over the many years of its rattling life along the interstates and city byways. And yet Mattagash had touted this as the social event of the decade! Vinal and Pike were good enough at their trade to be vastly insulted. They had a good mind, at least together they did, to take the whole jeezly town to court for enticement, or some such thing. Advertising through the mail and by word of mouth that a wedding was to take place *which didn't* was no different from claiming a UFO had christened their new sporting lodge. To add injury to this insult, just as they were about to go back and further lighten the Cadillac of its tires and battery, it had driven away from their grimy fingertips! It was almost enough to force a man to turn over a few leaves of his life, to rethink his career choice.

"This keeps up," said Vinal, snapping open a beer and handing it to Pike, "and we're gonna *have to* cut off our little fingers for the insurance money."

SHE SAYS TOE-MAY-TOE, HE SAYS TOE-MAT, SICILY'S GLAD THEY CALLED THE WHOLE THING OFF: COPS, ROBBERS, AND BULLET DREAMS

....

Quand le soleil dit bonjour aux montagnes
Et que la nuit rencontre le jour
Je suis seul avec mes rêves sur la montagne,
Une voix me rappelle de toi.

Now when the sun says hello to the mountains
And the night says hello to the dawn
I'm alone with my dreams on the hilltop,
I can still hear your voice though you're gone.

—"The French Song," sung at all French weddings
in the valley, canceled at the Lawler-Cloutier bash

AMY JOY SAT IN THE DARK OF HER ROOM AND THOUGHT ABOUT
the past because she found the present too painful, and the future
too damning. The past was now a place of asylum, a sanctuary. So
she thought of those strangers, those loyalists of long ago, those
people of another time. They were responsible for the blood flowing
in her veins in 1969. They probably never even imagined such a
year would roll around, and yet here it was, and some of her blood
was still theirs. Amy Joy knew this from biology class. It was all a
matter of genetics, of cells and tissues and eye color, but it afforded

her a feeling she had never before experienced. She wished now that she had asked her aunt Marge questions about those faded names in the family Bible. Aunt Marge had lingered under her very nose and then died. Yet instead of giving her some undivided attention, Amy Joy had offered it all to Chester Lee Gifford. But the young were forgiven, weren't they, for cavorting with life? Chester Lee was dead now, as was Ed Lawler, the other man in her early life. They were all jumbled up together, these three, in her mind: her father, Chester Lee, Aunt Marge McKinnon. Maybe because they all died in the same rainy, leafy autumn of 1959, in a matter of days. They were faces that disappeared from her life simultaneously, these three musketeers, these buccaneers of her memory. They were paper dolls to her now, hand-linked, dead, lost forever. Just like the old loyalist ancestors who had given rise to the lot of them. Now she could add Jean Claude Cloutier to the list, to the disappearing act. But the truth was, if they were all standing before her again she would choose Ed, if she could choose only one. Her father, the only one she would ever have. How many times had she wondered why Ed Lawler had driven his car down to the Mattagash school, held a revolver to his head, and pulled the trigger? Did he hate Amy Joy and Sicily that much? Now, for the past few weeks, on nights when it was least expected, Amy Joy experienced what she called her bullet nightmare. In her dream she would be walking along the old riverbank, the childhood bank, the ancestors' river, when out of nowhere it sounded. *Bang! Bang!* Or she'd be driving in her car, driving as fast as she could toward Watertown, in what seemed like a most desperate rush to escape, her foot aching on the gas pedal. *Bang!* Lately it was happening in all her dreams, the good and bad. She felt as though an unknown assassin were stalking her, a Lee Harvey Oswald, crazily hidden behind some warehouse peak in her mind. A James Earl Ray, scraggly and evil and lurking near the motels of her subconscious. It took her days to analyze it, even a dream so obvious. It was just the night before that she'd sat up in bed, broken away from another bad dream full of noises.

"This is the bullet that killed my father," she'd said softly. "I'm hearing it time and time again. If I'm not careful, it will kill me, too." Then she lay back to listen to the orchestra of the Mattagash River, the old highway, to fall asleep again, *hoping* this time to hear the gunfire once more that had taken her father's life.

"This is his warning to me," Amy Joy had thought. "This is when I'm closest to him. When the bullet fires, I hear his finger sliding over the trigger. I can almost touch that finger. It's like we're finally holding hands."

Amy Joy sat in the darkness. She knew now that her father didn't hate her. He didn't even hate Sicily. What he did hate was a way of life from which there seemed no escape. She must be careful with the lesson, the trousseau, he had left her. She must stop crying, eventually, when it was the right time to stop. And she must *live*. There were worse things.

"I'm becoming my father's daughter," she thought.

◆　　◆　　◆

Sicily knocked for the hundredth time on Amy Joy's bedroom door.

"Please, dear," she said. "Open the door. I can't stand to hear you cry." Amy Joy made no response. "One day you'll see this as the best thing that ever happened to you," Sicily added. "Believe me. I know it's hard to fathom right now, but it's true." She could hear Amy Joy muffling her sobs in a pillow.

"Would you like a nice Pepsi?" Sicily asked.

Back in the kitchen Sicily stood and watched a whirlwind of snow circling the pole light like a swarm of feathery moths.

"If this keeps up, winter will be back," she thought.

Puppy came to the door and whined to be let inside. Sicily let him in, then leaned far out into the snowy night to listen. It was nearly three fourths of a mile up the road from her, around bends, past frost heaves and potholes, over dips and twists in the river-road, and yet Sicily could hear the music rattling its echo down the banks of the old river. Music. They must be dancing up a sweaty storm inside the new gymnasium, a structure old Nellie Monihan, who had passed her pessimism on to her daughter Girdy, had predicted would be the downfall of the town. "The same thing happened to Rome, mind you," Nellie had said a million times until she herself fell and was buried in the prestigious Protestant graveyard.

Sicily could almost see Winnie or Girdy motion for the janitor to come with his long wooden pole, the one with the hook on it, and open the windows of the gym to let in some frosty air. She had been there a hundred times herself to see this done. And she had seen the little kids gather around to gaze up in wonderment as he unlocked those high, eagle-nest windows, little boys who went home that night promising themselves they would grow up to be janitors so that they could do such feats in the heart of the entertainment. And little girls, well, Sicily could only assume that these creatures went home with their sweaty hands locked in their mothers', hoping to grow up and marry a janitor.

Sicily heard it again, a swell of music and laughter rolling along the acoustical banks of the Mattagash, cascading, crescendoing, breaking like waves. She was not surprised to hear this. She knew that, years ago, old-timers could shout to each other from a separation of two miles and be heard. She knew that the old workhorses, trudging along in their belled harnesses, rang out like tambourines from among the gangly pines and cedars. There were all kinds of communications going on back then, before the telephone, before automobiles sprouted like weeds in everyone's dooryard, before televisions, transistor radios, and other such nonsense. Had it not been for an electric knife—yes, truly, Sicily was almost ashamed to admit it, but had it not been for a knife that *plugged into the wall*—Winnie Craft would still have the meaty part of her right index finger, the fleshy part that pushes against a pen or pencil to help execute writing. Winnie Craft had not sent out a single Christmas card since her son brought that god-awful contraption up from Connecticut two years ago, but Amy Joy had remarked often enough that this injury did not stop Winnie from picking her nose.

"Just to show off," Sicily said of the knife, and then closed the door. But it was true that something was happening to the young men and women of Mattagash, particularly the women, something she did not like. There was a silent current running among them, whispering to them, tempting them to toss down the mores of their mothers. Like the knife, it was slicing through the past, cutting it into tiny, useless pieces. Pampers were another bad sign. It was true, wasn't it, that Kevin Craft was turning up lately at town functions alone, and that his wife, Bonita, was now traipsing to Watertown every day, big as she pleased in Kevin's new Chrysler, to shop for idle odds and ends.

"Pampers and cake mixes," Sicily muttered, and searched through the pages of the *Bangor Daily* for its crossword puzzle. Even as a teenager Bonita Gifford had made the wind look tame. It was true that she came from one of those families of Giffords who were hardworking, honest folks and suffered from sharing the same last name as the renegade members. But Bonita never grew up, if you asked Winnie, or Girdy, or Sicily, or Claire. Now she was in her mid-twenties, the mother of three little children, and still acting like she led the life of Riley. Word was even circulating that she was asking for a divorce! Good Lord in heaven but Sicily knew that the only thing more damning than Amy Joy wanting to marry a Frenchman was wanting to divorce him afterward. Mattagash had guilt notions about that action that even the Catholics had yet to learn. Yet there had been two inglorious divorces already and talk of others to come.

"All my money goes to buy fancy, factory-made, store-bought diapers," Kevin Craft had once complained at Blanche's Grocery. Blanche refused to carry the controversial item, giving Bonita the excuse to gallivant all the way to Watertown for them.

"They're designed by real engineers to catch as much baby shit and pee as they possibly can," Kevin had lamented. "And then Bonita rolls 'em up real nice and throws 'em out in the garbage so I can take 'em to the dump."

And Sicily knew that without the automobile's sudden availability to all, and without the devilish telephone, Amy Joy's romance with Jean Claude Cloutier would never have gotten off the ground. Before these inventions folks kept apart naturally, stuck like birds to their own kind. It hadn't been so many years ago when the old river provided all the entertainment that was needed. In summertime the inner tubes from worn-out tires would go into the water as small, airy boats, and children could fish until dark, or swim to a small heart's content. There was sledding and skating in the wintertime around a pile of slabs from the old sawmill set ablaze, or the remains of those summer tires swabbed in gasoline and lighted.

"We used to make a big pan of fudge and tell old stories," Sicily said to Puppy. "There was always someone who could remember a song off the old tube radio, and they'd teach it to the rest of us." She opened the door one more time to catch the cold rumble of warm music and laughter ricocheting along the riverbank. If you didn't know better, it could be the echo of a quilting bee straight out of the 1920s. Gee, but they were kicking up their heels at the reception, even Sicily's friends who must know how terrible she was feeling. Sicily closed the door. Before she made herself a *nice cup of tea*, she leaned back against the kitchen cupboard and closed her eyes. Puppy stared at her, his head canted, and whined. Let all Mattagash party themselves into a sweaty spring tizzy. Sicily knew some truths to be self-evident. First, the party was really hers in spirit and, second, she still had some clout with her personal deity.

"Thank you, Jesus! Thank you, Jesus! Thank you, Jesus!" Sicily whispered the words, so that her grieving daughter would not hear. Then she did a bit of the Charleston, executed to a perfect 4/4 time, a dance she had not attempted since her own wedding reception in 1931. Sicily did her twisting steps up and down the shiny linoleum of her kitchen floor. Jean Claude was right. La belle-mère was a good dancer, her.

◆　◆　◆

Pearl and Marvin were having an evening snack, with Pearl about to confess the summer kitchen ghosts, when Junior waded through the few inches of snow in Marge's old driveway and banged his corpulent fists upon the door.

"What in hell is it now?" Marvin groaned.

"It sounds like Junior," Pearl said, relieved that no snowy ghosts were beating upon the house.

"This better be important," Marvin warned. He was too comfortable in his slippers and robe to be roused on such a blustery night. He padded reluctantly to the door.

"What is it, for Chrissakes?" he asked his trembling son.

"Someone stole the Caddy, Daddy!" Junior blurted, then blushed at his schoolboy rhyme.

"Again?" asked Marvin. "Good Christ! Are the Giffords addicted to fancy cars?"

"I think so," said a winded, red-faced Junior, treading past Marvin to the telephone. "But this time I'm gonna nail the bastard!"

"What is it?" asked Pearl. Sometimes the living were more unsettling than vengeful ghosts.

"Someone stole the Cadillac," said Marvin.

"Again?" asked Pearl. She too remembered the fateful Packard.

"If whoever it is wrecks that car," Junior threatened his parents as he waited for Roy Vachon's office to answer. "If he wrecks the Caddy like that asshole did my Packard, so help me I'll kill him!"

"You won't have to," Marvin said. "The last thief killed himself."

"I don't care!" Junior shouted. "I'll kill him again if I have to!"

"Chester Lee Gifford," said Pearl. "Amy Joy's first big attempt at marriage."

"Sheriff? This is Marvin Ivy, Junior," said Junior. "I'm calling from Mattagash to report a stolen car. A 1969 cream-colored Cadillac. It's heading toward you." There was a long pause as Junior listened to Roy Vachon. Pearl and Marvin squeezed in close to his ear for immediate information, but Junior turned away from them, cradling the phone.

"This has happened before," Junior said. "In 1959. Chester Gifford, from here in Mattagash, stole my Packard and wrecked it. And you can almost bet that it's another Gifford driving this time, too. I want that car, Sheriff, before it happens again. What? What do you mean, can't I keep track of my cars?"

◆   ◆   ◆

Randy Ivy pulled into Watertown's limits and passed the old customshouse looming on the left, marking the entrance into Canada,
where the friendly sign announced BIENVENU! But Randy declined
the invitation, and Canada slept on, its lights curled along the other
side of the river like little stars, unaware that Lola and Randy and
their nits could have swung a left onto the steel-green bridge and
invaded their territory.

"I got two sisters who'll just love you," Randy was telling Lola,
as Roy Vachon pulled out from the shadows of the customshouse
and blasted the creamy Cadillac with a wave of flashing blue light.

"Balls!" said Randy. "It's the pigs!"

"The what?" screamed Lola, certain they were being chased by
hogs from Watertown's immense and smelly hog farm.

"Cops!" Randy explained. "Did I tell you that I lost my license
last month?"

THE LAST BARN BUILDER, YO·HO·HO, AND A BOTTLE OF RUM: BRUCE SEES DOG DAYS IN MAY

....

"I predicted this mess when they took the snow fences down too early. We'll be lucky if an avalanche don't bury us all. Forever."

—Girdy Monihan, town pessimist, to fellow punch servers at Amy Joy's wedding reception, May 1, 1969

ALBERT PINKHAM DROVE THE THREE HUNDRED YARDS FROM THE Mattagash gym to his home/motel in a zigzaggedy line, doing his best to follow the last set of tire tracks before the snow filled them in. It was just after eleven, but he had abandoned the party an hour earlier than everyone else. The full effect of the rum, the sweaty closeness of dancing bodies all around him, the reverberating gossipy words of the women, had caused a notion to go to his brain. There was a very good chance, Albert realized, that he was drunk.

Back at the gymnasium door, Albert had steadied himself to gaze around at the snowy lumps in the yard, the camouflaged pickups. There were only six pickups parked about, with their hollow boxes filling up quietly with snow. The rest were cars, and even though he was smoldering with Puerto Rican rum Albert Pinkham could still tell snowy pickups from snowy cars.

Bruce watched the road carefully. Albert knew that if he veered too far to the dangerous right Bruce would bark loudly and snap him back to attention. But he managed to keep the weaving pickup on the twisty road that wound away from the gymnasium and on toward the welcoming Albert Pinkham Motel sign, now layered in thick snow. Warm yellow lights burst out of number 1, the Ivy castle these past few days.

"Spoiled sons of bitches," Albert muttered to Bruce, and pulled the trusty rum bottle from its wiry nest beneath the seat. He sucked a long fiery drink from it, then passed the bottle over to Bruce, who turned away from the smell of it to stare out the window at the snow-tipped trees.

"Oh, excuse me," said Albert. "I forgot. You don't drink." Albert snorted laughter through his nose and Bruce whined expectantly. He had seen Albert Pinkham, his master, in such condition only a dozen times in their ten-year relationship. Sparse as they were, Bruce disliked these times immensely. Once, Albert had even passed out on the sofa, after Kevin Craft's marriage, before filling Bruce's water bowl and leaving him a healthy serving of chunky IGA-brand dog food. There was no doubt about it. When Albert Pinkham got drunk, Bruce was subjected to a dog's life.

"The old barn builder," Albert whispered. "Ain't no one anywhere today can build a barn to match the ones that old son of a bitch built." His eyes misted. "Ain't no one even wants a goddamn barn anymore." He struggled with the door handle, and the door flew open so smoothly that Albert teetered out after it. He launched headfirst into the snow, where he felt the quick, heavy impact of the ground against his temple. It didn't hurt a goddamn bit.

"But it's gonna hurt like hell in the morning," Albert joked to Bruce, who had jumped, whining, to the rescue. Bruce licked his owner's face, licked away the fragile flakes and the little red trail of blood that had popped like a spring from beneath the skin of Albert's temple.

"Ha ha," Albert giggled, and tried to lift an arm to push the dog away. "Ha ha ha. Bruce, don't, boy! That tickles like shit."

"Oh, Mr. Pinkham," a voice rang out from across the yard. "Yoo-hoo!" It was Thelma Ivy, leaning precariously out of number 1. "Mr. Pinkham, we'd like breakfast in our room tomorrow."

Even in his stupor, Albert was aghast. How many times that day alone had he asked Thelma Ivy to show him, on the Albert Pinkham Motel sign, just one place where it said restaurant. The woman must be brain-dead.

"Anything you want, Miss Ivy," Albert lifted his head to say. "We aim to please."

"Continental, if you don't mind," said Thelma, who seemed not at all surprised that the proprietor was flat on his face.

"Continental. Oriental." Albert waved his arm. "You just name it."

"Thank you," said Thelma, and disappeared back inside number 1.

It was ten minutes later that Albert Pinkham adjusted his key into the lock of his door and swung with it, as it flew open, into his own warm kitchen. He had left the bottle outside, in cold shards on the ground next to his spill. He had another one, by God, the one that deer hunter from Boston had given him. Albert found it on the bottom shelf of the cupboard and broke its seal.

"Here's to you, you city son of a whore," Albert toasted the donor of the blessed bottle. "You couldn't hit an elephant in the ass at ten feet," he added. Bruce ran to the sofa as Albert staggered to the kitchen drawer and slid it open. There beneath the nickels and pennies, the pencils and paper clips, was the tintype of the old barn builder. More of his face was missing now, wasn't it? Albert tried to focus. A bit of the right cheekbone was gone, almost the entire left pupil, a good part of the nose. The old barn builder was disappearing by the second.

"Please come back," Albert whispered, but the tintype didn't answer. Only Bruce whined a pitiful response. Albert laid the picture down on the table and then opened his refrigerator. He took the carton of eggs, eight of them still growing out of their paper cups. He took the half pound of bacon and a bottle of orange juice. From the cupboard he added a loaf of white bread and a can of Folgers coffee to the larder. He staggered to the door, Bruce following out of sheer curiosity.

At Thelma's door Albert kicked viciously. If Junior Ivy could kick doors, by Jesus, Albert Pinkham could too. Thelma opened it. Expecting Junior at any minute, she was still in her housecoat. Her eyes were lined with her trademark dark circles and her hair fluttered in unruly wisps.

"Lord love a duck," said Thelma, as Albert kicked the door wide open. She screamed lustily, then ran back to cower on her bed.

"You want breakfast in bed, miss?" Albert said, in his best proprietor's voice. "Well, by Christ, the Albert Pinkham Motel is here to serve you." Then, amidst the shrill echoes of Thelma's screams, Albert splattered the room with eggs. They ran like mutant daisies down the walls. He slung all the slices of bread, large snowflakes, at Thelma before he opened the orange juice and poured it about on the floor. Thelma clutched a pillow to her head. The bacon buzzed above her, stuck to the wall like strips of brown tape, then dropped to the floor, pale gooey snakes.

"Coffee?" Albert asked with a roar. The grounds came at her, a brown swirling snowstorm, an Okie dust storm, stinging and whipping its way across the room. Thelma was thankful that she had not been so quick to give up her Valiums that day, despite her promise to Junior.

"Enjoy," said Albert Pinkham.

He stepped out onto his cement walkway, an engineering idea that had occurred to him after seeing Atlantic City's famous boardwalk on TV. He looked at number 2, the bridal suite, with snow piled up on its knob, with nothing but silence coming from the box springs within. A wave of loneliness washed up inside Albert

Pinkham, mixed with a little nausea. He followed the building, as though the shingles were braille characters, around to the back, to where number 3 blared its yellow light out at him.

"Violet," Albert whispered. Bruce was not there to whine in memory with his master. He had stayed behind in number 1 to helpfully clean up the strips of bacon from the floor.

Albert knocked gently and Monique Tessier, half expecting the ubiquitous Junior, opened the door in a gossamer yellow negligee, which glowed around her shapely body like a golden aura. A heavenly halo.

"Violet?" Albert pleaded to this vision, this sun goddess. All he wanted, he tried in vain to tell her, was what she'd promised him that autumny afternoon, ten years earlier, as the red and orange leaves of a dead year piled like colored rain on the roof.

"Mr. Pinkham!" Monique scolded. Her eyes were large as her nipples. Albert could barely decide which he should gaze at as she spoke. "You're drunk!" Monique tried to close the door again, but Albert's work boot lodged itself snugly into the crack.

"Please, Violet," he said. "They're all gone now. Sarah, Belle, Mama, Daddy."

"I don't know what you're talking about!"

"Granddaddy's gone, too." Albert said. "I'm the only one left now, Violet." He reached a thin arm inside the crack of the door and touched Violet's velvety one. She was warm, cozy as autumn. She was on fire, with pink walls flaming all around her, with rose petal walls looming.

"I need you," Albert said. "I only want what you promised." Monique Tessier opened the door.

"Come in," she said, and stepped aside. Albert had difficulty lifting up his heavy boots although inside them his feet felt light as a dancer's. His legs, however, were heavier than the trees he had refused to cut, all those years ago. He staggered past Monique Tessier and into number 3.

"Thank you, Violet," he said, as Monique brought a J. C. Penney fake-brass table lamp down with genuine force on Albert Pinkham's troubled head.

Albert fell out across the floor of the room, seeing only pink stars in his last seconds, knowing only that Violet LaForge, *the slut*, had tricked him again. Monique Tessier held a hand to her mouth. It occurred to her that perhaps she had been a tad too hasty. Perhaps the motel owner was richer than he purported. She was reminded of newspaper stories about country bumpkins who had buckets of gold stashed in their wells, or beneath the shit piled up in their outhouses. Crusty old men who slept upon mattresses stuffed with silver dollar certificates. But no, surely every single female in Mattagash would be in heat for Albert Pinkham if this were true. Junior was right. This was not a town in which one could successfully stage a secret.

"Mr. Pinkham," Monique said, hopefully, and pushed her toe against Albert's side. "Are you alive?" She tried to pull him, by one booted foot, out of her room. But Albert's drunk body had settled inside its bones with the same certainty as the massive ice chunks along the Mattagash River. Albert was pure, dead weight.

Monique was about to panic. She feared what Junior would think if he found Albert in her room. She was close, very close, to securing Junior for her own, and then, by God, money would fly.

"Please leave my room," Monique said loudly, in case even the snowflakes were Mattagash spies. "Now!" she warned. A rattling sound broke out of Albert's mouth, followed by a small waterfall of spit.

"Oh Christ!" said Monique, and looked away from this unconscious symphony of Albert's body.

Something had to be done before Junior returned from reporting the Caddy missing. Monique pulled on a sweater and a pair of sweat pants. She put on her ankle-high boots and trod next door to Randy's room. The light was off, but then, Monique knew, all of Randy's lights were out these days. He hadn't even questioned her vacationing in Mattagash at the same time as the Ivys. Poor Randy. There was no response to her knock, and there were no tell-tale tracks going into the room. Even the *snow* was a gossip bag in Mattagash, Maine.

Monique returned to number 3 only to find Albert Pinkham still unconscious on her floor. But she had formulated a plan. Women without *means* always have *plans*. She wrapped a white bath towel about her head, hiding her luxurious chestnut hair, and pinned it snugly. She dug in her purse for her sunglasses and plopped them over her lavender eyes. She looked at the ghoulish image in the mirror. Mysterious, *yes*. Deathly, *maybe*. Elizabeth Taylor, *not on your life*.

At number 1 Monique was saved the problem of knocking on the door. It was wide open, allowing a trail of wind-blown snow to cascade into the room. Having consumed a half pound of bacon, Bruce bounded past her, in search of what might be left of his master. Monique was aghast at the condition of Albert's second most-rented room. It was in a culinary shambles.

"Hello?" Monique said huskily, in her best Marlene Dietrich voice. No one would notice a secretary's *funeral home cadence* in the old star's lilting drawl. "Anybody home?"

When no one answered, she stepped inside. She could hear mouselike noises coming from the bathroom. She crept over the bread and splattered eggs and peered around the corner at Junior's wife, who was leaning against the washbasin. Thelma Parsons Ivy had just washed a couple more Valiums down and was beginning to feel a calm settle about her stomach and her senses. So what if Albert Pinkham had assaulted her with breakfast items. He was only expressing himself in a most creative way. Men should go to war in just such a fashion. Women could clean up behind them. Live and let live, Thelma Ivy would be the first to intone.

"Hi there," Monique said, and Thelma heard the throaty words bounce off all the noisy bathroom acoustics. She looked up to see a person in dark glasses and a terry-cloth turban peering at her with great interest.

"Ahhhhhhh!" Thelma screamed, and threw Albert Pinkham's water glass, one that had been happily filled with jelly just months earlier, into the bathtub. The glass bounced twice before it broke in a crescendo of tinkling tones.

"Ahhhhhhh!" Thelma screamed again, and covered her eyes.

What kind of creature was this, what kind of old Mattagash snow-demon had come up from the deep, icy riverbed to taunt her.

"Don't be afraid," Monique assured her, the voice still huskily Hollywood. "I'm your neighbor. Around back."

Thelma stared at her with suspicion. No one said this was Mr. Rogers' neighborhood, but she knew this woman, didn't she? Where had she seen her before? Was she one of the models on *The Price Is Right? Let's Make a Deal?*

"What do you want?" Thelma asked.

"I need you to help me," said Monique. "Mr. Pinkham has had an accident in my room."

"He had one here, too," said Thelma.

"Can you come help me get him into his house?"

Suddenly Thelma knew, with Valium certainty, what was in the snowy social air. A spy! Junior had sent some Mattagash spy to test her. Well then, let the games begin. She would simply dust the snow off the gauntlet and take that sucker up.

Back at number 3, Bruce was sitting at Albert's head and whimpering sadly.

"You take that leg and I'll take this one," the spy in the turban instructed Thelma. Bruce growled in disapproval and startled Thelma so that she dropped Albert's foot.

"Be careful," she warned herself. "Try to remember that this is a test. This woman is a spy. This dog could be one, too."

"Okay now. Pull!" Monique said, and Albert's body moved off the floor of number 3, over the hump of the doorway, and out onto the cement walkway. Bruce soon realized that these ladies were motel allies. He anchored his teeth in the arm of Albert's jacket and assisted the tugging.

"Let's turn him on his back," Monique suggested. "Or we'll rub all the skin off his face." Thelma wasn't so sure that a little natural cosmetic surgery for the motelier was a bad idea, but she helped turn Albert anyway. They were a *team*, the woman in the turban and the woman on Valium. They dragged Albert Pinkham across the snowy expanse of his motel yard and up the steps of his house.

Behind them, on the white ground, they left a wide trail, a track, as though the tired workhorses of old, the ghosts of those horses, were back at work yarding out long pine logs and leaving ephemeral trails in the snow.

Pausing for breath on the porch steps, Thelma looked at Monique Tessier's finely shaped nose, which poked out beneath the sunglasses. Oh, *where* had she seen this strange woman? They pulled Albert Pinkham into his own kitchen.

"We can't lift him, so let's leave him here on the floor," Monique said. "At least he'll be warm until he sleeps it off."

"Well," said Thelma, "we could've left him outside. It's stopped snowing." Monique stared at Thelma.

"Poor thing," Monique thought. "She probably hasn't felt cold in years."

As Marvin Senior drove Junior into the white driveway of the Albert Pinkham Motel, his car lights caught two women in the act of making their way across four inches of new snow between the house and the motel. One had a bath towel on her head and was wearing dark glasses. The other was Thelma.

"What the . . . ?" asked Junior.

"I'm not even going to ask," sighed Marvin. "I've got a long day tomorrow. *You* handle this."

Back on Albert Pinkham's floor the snores were rolling evenly out of the grandson's mouth, while on the table, on the tintype, the grandfather's hollow eyes picked up the beam of light that raced around the room as Marvin Ivy turned his car in the driveway. What was left of the lips still curved upward in an old smile, a memory of the log drives and the first burly lumberjacks. The grandfather's hands were limp from the last barn ever built in Mattagash with style. Albert Pinkham was right. A way of life was disappearing.

THE PINES ARE ALIVE WITH MUSIC: BEING A GIFFORD MEANS NEVER HAVING TO SAY YOU'RE SORRY

....

Folks in a town that was most remote heard . . .
Lay he, yodel lay he, yodel lay he ho.

—"The Lonely Goatherd," Oscar Hammerstein II,
The Sound of Music

IT WAS ALMOST 1:00 A.M. WHEN ROY VACHON SIGNALED A TURN into Albert Pinkham's motel and steered the Watertown sheriff's car into the unplowed drive. Behind him, happily ensconced in the driver's seat of the exotic Caddy, was Patrolman Wayne Fortin. On the thirty-mile drive to Mattagash, Wayne had turned every knob and button he could find on the magical dashboard of the magnificent car. He felt very much like Captain Kirk of *Star Trek*, as he sank down into the cushiony seat and stared out the window at places no sensible man had ever gone before. *Mattagash*. But

Roy Vachon had no choice but to drive Lola Craft home after he put the car thief safely in jail. There was only one cell in the Watertown jail and Lola was, after all, a female.

"You understand, of course, Miss Craft," Roy Vachon warned her, "that you're what is called an accomplice."

"I've been called worse," Lola bleated, thinking of what Winnie would say when she found out. Lola had burst into tears when she first saw the blue light swirling around in the snowy night behind the Caddy, and had stopped only long enough to give her name, begrudgingly, to the Watertown sheriff.

"Since I've got to drive her home anyway," Roy Vachon said to his patrolman, "you might as well follow me in the Cadillac. I got a feeling that asshole from Portland is gonna ring our phone off the hook until he gets it back."

Wayne Fortin hated to return to Mattagash, even to drop off the Cadillac. But the notion of driving one of those babies for thirty miles took the nervous edge off the situation.

"Okay," Wayne Fortin had said to the sheriff. Then he had gone into the tiny cell where Randy Ivy pressed his oily face against the bars. When prisoners did that—and prisoners to Wayne Fortin had been only drunks and petty thieves in the past—they always reminded Wayne of babies pressing their faces against the wooden bars of their cribs. There was something to this poetic criminal information and one day, when Wayne Fortin figured out exactly what it was, he would write a best-seller and make a zillion bucks.

"We'll be back in an hour or so," he told the baby-faced prisoner.

"You don't understand," Randy Ivy had beseeched for the hundredth time that night. "The car belongs to my old man."

"Sure," said Wayne Fortin. "And my old man owned the *Titanic*."

"I'd believe it," Randy had grunted. "You probably helped him build it."

"I'd watch it," Wayne warned, and pointed a stern finger at Randy.

"Look, man," Randy had said back, through the lonely bars. "My name is Marvin Randall Ivy *the Third*. My old man is Marvin Ivy, Junior. Just call him up and ask him."

"Then why can't you show us any identification?" Wayne asked cheekily.

"I'm a goddamn *kid!*" Randy wailed. "I ain't got any identification. I used to have a license but a judge took it."

"I can see why," said Wayne Fortin, as he paused to stare into the bloodshot eyes of the prisoner. His haircut alone reeked of nonsocial behavior. Even the tiny red pimples about the chin and forehead looked guilty as hell. People who had titles such as Little Snot-Snot the Third, people who had numbers tacked after their names, didn't look like this kid. Rich kids didn't have pimples, for crying out loud. Their parents paid so many dollars per blackhead to have famous doctors come over from Sweden, where there's cures for everything.

"If your name ain't *Gifford*," Wayne Fortin had said to his captive, "then mine ain't Fortin."

"I know your name ain't Fortin, you boob!" Randy had screamed after him, exciting all his pimples. "It's *Fife. Barney* Fife!"

Now in the comfortable seat of the Cadillac, Wayne Fortin watched Roy Vachon's breath coming out of his nostrils in cold puffs as he knocked on the door of number 1. Wayne seethed. The pimply little SOB. What rankled him more was that it wasn't just Mattagashers who likened him to Andy Taylor's deputy from Mayberry. Even his own cohorts in Watertown were guilty of such. He'd been listening to these insults for the entire two years he'd been on the force.

"How's things in Mayberry?" Walter Cormier asked him once, and all the men gathered around the pool table at the Watertown Hotel had broken into hysterical laughter.

Wayne Fortin slid out from behind the wheel of the expensive Cadillac.

"I'm a victim of TV," he sighed to himself, and handed Junior Ivy the keys.

"Which Gifford was it?" Junior was asking Roy Vachon, as he

ducked his head into the car and gave it a quick checkup. It all seemed to be there.

"We don't know yet," said the sheriff. "He refuses to give us his real name."

"Your hubcaps are gone," said Wayne.

"The son of a bitch," Junior snarled, and kicked the front tire. "He's a lucky man there ain't a scratch on this car." Junior ran his pudgy hand along the smooth side.

"He had a girl with him," the sheriff added. "We'll get his real name if we have to take fingerprints. But I've learned that a so-bering night in jail serves well enough to jar a man's memory."

"I'd like to jar his *balls*," said Junior. "Was he drinking?"

"Loaded," said Roy. "And by his eyes, I suspect that wasn't all. The college kids in Watertown have begun bringing marijuana up from downstate."

"I tell you," said Junior Ivy, having navigated the circumference of the car on a slow inspection, "he's a lucky man to be in jail. If I'd gotten my hands on the bastard, well, there's no telling."

Roy Vachon and Wayne Fortin stared at the owner of the won-drous Cadillac. Maybe if he fell on someone there would be no telling how they'd end up. Mashed potatoes. Omelets, maybe. But other than that, the sheriff and his sidekick couldn't imagine this fat pale man from Portland a threat to anyone.

"Yes sir," said Junior. "He's one lucky man I didn't meet up with him first."

"You and what army?" Wayne Fortin wondered silently.

"I gotta go inside," Junior said, finally satisfied that the hubcaps had been his only loss. "I'll stop in tomorrow and press charges, but right now I'm freezing my ass off."

"Maybe in Antarctica you could," Wayne Fortin thought smugly. "But it'll take colder weather than thirty degrees to pull off a job like that."

"Whatever you say," Roy Vachon said.

"In the meantime," Junior yelled over his shoulder, "you keep that son of a bitch Gifford locked up." He was carefully retracing his deep footprints in the snow.

"That's the funny part," said Roy Vachon, as he opened the driver's door to the patrol car. "He's been trying to tell us his real name is Marvin Randall Ivy the Third."

Junior lost his balance at this declaration and stepped off his well-blazed trail into fresh snow. So help him God Almighty, but he would kill Randy deader than ever he planned to kill a Gifford.

"Yes, well," said Junior. "Whoever he is, a night in jail will be, as you said, sobering for him." Then Junior went inside number 1 and rammed his fist into the motel wall with such force that it was almost enough to bring Thelma back from one of her deep, trouble-free, Valium dreams. It was force enough, however, to topple all of Monique Tessier's well-placed lipsticks on the wooden table in number 3.

•   •   •

The Plymouth-shark was the last creature out on the snowy twisting main road of Mattagash. The river-road. Everyone else had early mornings, the men to the woods, the women to their housework, the children to school. And, of course, Mattagash's three entrepreneurs, called the three musketeers by their envious townsfolk, each had his own calling. Albert Pinkham had his motel, Peter Craft his filling station, and Charles Mullins would have his hot dog/snack stand come June. In the meantime, Charles was back at work for Henley Lumber until summertime arrived and the canoes full of noisy tourists began their city assault upon the peaceful Mattagash River. Vinal and Pike Gifford, on the other hand, simply had to hit their living room couches when the beer and lack of sleep compelled them. Vinal was addicted to two soap operas, which decreed he rise by noon in order to catch them. With that single responsibility between them, Vinal and Pike were the only souls rootless enough to be wallowing about on the road that ran past the houses of town, the darkened houses whose occupants were in bed by twelve-thirty and now asleep. Ordinarily a Sunday night would have tucked everyone in by ten o'clock, and this one would have too, if boy-crazy Amy Joy Lawler hadn't insisted on getting married May first. A *Sunday*. It was almost sacrilege. But the whole town, like a reluctant family, had given in to the whims of what they thought was a future bride. Only in Kevin Craft's house was a soft yellow light still blazing out of the bedroom, one stream of it reaching down to the black river, the other stretching out to the milky road.

"I want a divorce," Bonita Craft was telling Kevin as Vinal and Pike Gifford cruised past their house, the noise of the Plymouth's engine echoing in the dip of the road as they left the Crafts and their heartbreak behind. All of Mattagash already knew, anyway, what Bonita Craft had finally said, because what is said in bedrooms always surfaces in kitchens. No doubt Bonita Craft had told her very best friend that she intended to ask Kevin for a divorce. And Bonita's very best friend told a very good friend of her own, who wasn't so particularly fond of Bonita. No one in Mattagash is so good a friend that they put secrets away like old recipes. True, there must have been many honorable people to come and go over the years. But they are the unsung heroes who have taken their secrets with them to the grave, where they are finally safe.

"Kevin Craft's still up," Vinal Gifford had said to Pike, as they slipped quietly past on the white road.

"I hear they're getting a divorce," said Pike, and opened another beer. And then the Plymouth had ducked out of sight and left the light of the Craft house behind, left Kevin Craft himself reeling in disbelief, the last person in Mattagash to learn that, yes, he would soon be divorced.

"Stay far enough back from the sheriff's car and the Cadillac that they don't see your headlights," Pike warned Vinal, who slowed the hulky Plymouth.

At Albert Pinkham's motel the Plymouth speeded up and went past, seemingly oblivious to the excitement taking place in the motel yard as Junior inspected the car and learned that his own son, his spoiled seed, as Marvin had once called Randy, was the culprit. The shark turned around at the Mattagash bridge, closed its yellow eyes, and watched through the leafless elms in Albert's yard to see what would unfold.

As they expected, the sheriff and the patrolman left and Junior Ivy went inside and turned out the light of number 1. The Giffords knew this would happen. They were sociologists of the highest order. *This'd be a good time to get a close-up look at them tires behind Craft's Filling Station, Vinal. The Ed Sullivan Show's on tonight.* They were doctors. *This ain't caused by no inflammation of the ligaments, doc. I seriously think that lifting that stick of pulp done forced my spinal structure to absorb more stress than it can tolerate.* They were lawyers. *It's against the law to knowingly write a bad check, Pike. But they got to prove that* knowingly *part. That's the clincher.* They were archaeologists. *Look at the gas cap in that taillight! The first year that Cadillac did that was 1941.* Like writers, they followed a profession that bordered on all walks of life. Now they seemed more like concerned meteorologists, watching the soft, engulfing snow. It was no longer falling but instead spread itself like a heavy quilt from the old country on all its children, on the entire town, on the big family that had grown out of the first scraggly settlers.

"It's kinda sad Kevin and Bonita are gettin' divorced," said Pike, in one of his poetic moods. "It ain't like we're friends or anything, but it's still sad."

"Yeah," Vinal agreed. "Not only that, but she has a real nice ass. I hope it ain't true she's moving to Connecticut."

"Who told you that?" asked Pike, with great interest. True, Bonita never spoke to them, but they still felt as if they knew her.

"One of the kids heard it at school," said Vinal.

The brothers sat like awkward twins joined at the beer can. Chang and Eng on a bender. What was it Goldie had said of them? *Different shells with the same meat inside.* They sat and waited for Junior Ivy to sink like a heavy snow farther down into his fleshy dreams. They waited with their eyes on the fancy Cadillac, a much more interesting creature to the men of Mattagash than a strange fancy woman.

"You think you can jump-start it?" Vinal asked his brother, the better technician.

"Does the Pope wear a funny hat?" Pike answered.

• • •

For two solid hours Pike and Vinal Gifford drove the Cadillac, the color of sweet meringue, up and down the main road of Mattagash. They immediately helped themselves to Junior's tape deck, but were disappointed to find that the only eight-track tapes he had in the car were disagreeable to Gifford tastes.

"Take that shit off!" Vinal lamented, after Pike had shoved *Roger Williams, Mr. Piano* into the machine. "You want to ruin my ears for life?"

The Golden Voice of Mario Lanza fared no better. Vinal was disturbed by Pike's choices.

"Do I look like a fruit to you?" Vinal demanded to know of Pike, as his brother tossed *Mr. Piano* and *The Golden Voice* out the frosty window of the Cadillac.

"This looks interesting," said Pike, and held the tape closer to the interior light for proper reading. " 'I Got You Babe,' " Pike read. "By Sonny and Cher."

"Shit!" Vinal snorted. "Ain't there no country music?" But Pike was not listening. He was far more interested in the lanky picture of Cher than in Vinal's opinion of her music.

"Ain't she the spittin' image of Loretta Lynn?" he asked Vinal, who swerved the Cadillac in order to answer properly.

"Pike, please find us some musical entertainment," Vinal pleaded. "I ain't listened to anything in my life but an old car radio fading out on me every time you go around a turn or hit a pothole."

"You can pick up Boston on a frost heave," said Pike, as he rolled down the side glass and pitched Sonny Bono, along with his wife Cher, out into the night. They landed with a heavy thunk beneath a swath of baby cedars, a hundred yards from where Roger Williams and Mario Lanza were slowly being buried alive in the drifting snow.

"Will you play a tape? *Any* tape?"

"Oh Lord," said Pike. "I just hit pay dirt."

"What?" asked Vinal, trying to peek and steer.

"Julie Andrews," Pike said. "*The Sound of Music.* That's Missy's favorite movie."

"Well," said Vinal. "It ain't Kitty Wells or Loretta. But it'll have to do."

They drove countless times past the motel where the car's owner, Junior Ivy, snored in his dreams. They cruised snakily past Marge McKinnon's old house, where Pearl and Marvin slept fitfully, each tossing and turning within their nighttime dramas. They zoomed past Sicily Lawler's house, where Sicily was sleeping peacefully for the first time in weeks, and Amy Joy sat in the blackness of her bedroom and peered with puffy eyes down at the ice cakes dotting the Mattagash River, wondering what it would be like to slip beneath the freezing water and just disappear. Vinal and Pike Gifford made countless trips in their two-hour odyssey past Winnie Craft's house, where Lola sat in the bathroom, with the light out, and counted all the aspirins in the aspirin bottle over and over again as she pondered which would be worse: suicide, or Winnie's discovery that her daughter was an accomplice. The slippery Cadillac cut through the night dozens of times where Kevin Craft had built his home, a one-story modern structure, which predicted folks would start having smaller families, at least if they were going to start living in such flattened-out houses.

"Looks like a goddamn Cracker Jack box," Vinal said to Pike, as he did most times when they passed Kevin Craft's home. But Pike laughed anyway, as though hearing the analogy for the first time. The two brothers did not contemplate the darkness or the silence inside the house, where Kevin sat in the living room, turning his .22 rifle over and over in his lumberjack hands and wondering if it might be enough to do the trick.

" 'The hills are alive with with sound of music,' " Julie Andrews sang for the Giffords in her command performance, and the brothers felt warm, and good, and safe.

"Jesus," said Pike, after Vinal finally pulled over and let him have his turn behind the wheel. "This must be what it's like to drive the batmobile."

"Take it easy, Robin," Vinal teased, as the Cadillac spun out onto the road in a quick burst of snow. "If we end up in the ditch, who we gonna call to come haul our asses out?"

The Cadillac used up its tank of gas as it traversed the single, ragged road in Mattagash, past the snores and laments of the townsfolk, past the sons of bitches who had put the Giffords down for nearly a hundred and fifty years.

"I wish the old man could see us now." Pike whistled through his teeth. "He'd be some proud."

"Listen," said Vinal. "Whadda ya say, let's do this car with a little class. After all, it's only fitting for a Cadillac."

"Whadda ya mean?" asked Pike. His eye on the gas gauge told him whatever they did would have to be soon. But he liked the notion of class. And he liked the classy music. The Giffords had risen in the world.

"First," said Vinal, as they pulled up to the resting place of the Plymouth, snug and out of sight behind the Mattagash gym, "we'll take the tape deck and that tape of what's her name. Then you get the tools you need to take the radio and aerial."

"While I'm doing that," said Pike, "you take these fancy seat covers and floor mats."

"I'll pry open the trunk," offered Vinal. "He's bound to have more in there than his spare tire."

"Now what?" asked Pike, as the two brothers stood beside the naked Cadillac. Pike had just finished work on the rearview mirror, and he laid it next to the side view mirrors, in the Plymouth's trunk. "There's only the tires and battery left," Pike added. "From what I can see."

"Here's where the class comes in," said Vinal. "Here's where we give this old town a little slap in the face."

"How's that?" Pike asked again.

"First of all," said Vinal, "we need to make a quick trip home to the woodpile. Then I'll show you." Before they got back into the Plymouth, Vinal and Pike stood side by side and peed heavy yellow streams down into the snow, that natural *pissoir*.

An hour later Vinal snuggled in next to a warm, sleeping Vera, at the bottom of the hill from his brother, in the heart of Gifford-town. At the top of the hill, Pike Gifford was unable to creep into Goldie's bedroom. He had come home feeling particularly poetic and successful, and less drunk than usual. He had even slipped off his heavy boots at the bottom of the stairs and crept quietly past the other bedrooms where his children dreamed of better lives. He was happily whistling "The Lonely Goatherd" and wondering what it would be like to slip into bed with Julie Andrews when he discovered that Goldie had locked the bedroom door. Another night Pike would have kicked the son of a bitch down, would have slapped Goldie around until she cried, or he got tired of hitting her. Whichever came first. But tonight was different. Tonight he and Vinal had cruised in a fancy car, had listened to some upper-class music, had bit into and then tasted what it was like to be rich. And then, maybe because of all that, they had left the evening behind them with a sweet touch of class.

" 'Men drinking beer with their poles afloat heard,' " Pike sang under his breath. " 'Lay he, yodel lay he, yodel lay he ho.' " He went down to curl up on the car-seat sofa in the living room, while back at Albert Pinkham's motel the creamy Cadillac, sans battery and tires, lounged on four wooden blocks and looked generally miserable.

$\mathcal{T}$HERE'S GOT TO BE
A MORNING AFTER: RAVENS, COYOTES,
AND BEER CANS

....

The interstate rumbles like a river that runs
To a rhythm that don't ever slow down
As cars and trucks and time pass by
That old coyote town . . .

—Paul Nelson,
Gene Nelson, Larry Boone,
"Coyote Town"

THE FIRST CREATURE STIRRING AS DAWN CREPT IN OVER THE ragged tops of the pines to splash Mattagash awake was the northern raven. It rode the rising air currents high above the Mattagash River and gazed down on the gymnasium with its sharp black eyes, searching for shapes and angles that would register food in its brain. But all that caught its eye were several pink-tissue carnations rolling along the crusty snow in a small wind, cascading after each other until they disappeared in the clumps of dead burdocks along the riverbank. These were the only remnants of the wedding reception, except for one brown bow, which had caught in a cluster of bare hazelnut bushes by the old American Legion Hall and was flapping alone in the morning light. It had blown from Girdy Monihan's present, the one she carefully took back into her house before the reception, the can opener she would now give Peggy Mullins who was scheduled to marry in June. The raven swooped down closer. *Prruk. Prruk.* It could have been a mouse, a sparrow, a fat doughnut, but the bird's keen intelligence assured it that this was something inedible, some little knickknack left by the humans, and meaningful only to them. Its eyes caught the slow movement of a coyote, lean and hungry, which had moved to the hardwood ridge on the opposite bank to sit on its haunches and peer intently across the spring river at the town. Like the native Indian, the coyote was a lonesome relic of the past, and it moved back into the piney shadows, found a trail of fresh deer tracks, and was gone. The raven circled, still. The only car tracks near the gymnasium that had not been eaten alive by the snow were those of Vinal and Pike Gifford. The two thin lines from the Plymouth's tires lay below the bird like clothesline ropes stretching out of the gymnasium yard and onto the raggedy road to mischief. Two empty beer cans caught the first light as the raven swooped back again for a closer inspection. But the metallic creatures were useless to it as they lay beside the frozen yellow eyes in the snow where Pike and Vinal had heartily relieved themselves. With no sign of road kills along the crooked highway, the raven arched back up to the next thermal and did a series of acrobatic tumbles and rolls, then fell away in the direction of St. Leonard. Beneath its wings, inside the solid wooden houses built from the same forest that engulfed them, the people came to life.

Peter Craft, Winnie's nephew, was soon counting ones and fives and tens into the cash register at his filling station. With one hand Albert Pinkham was holding a cold wet towel against the bluish lump throbbing on his temple, and then to the large lump on the back of his head. With the other hand he dumped dog food into

Bruce's empty plate. At her grocery Blanche was stocking the shelves with pouches of chewing tobacco and heavy work gloves, her biggest sellers at that time of morning. Kevin Craft, Winnie's nephew, rolled over on the sofa, the .22 rifle lying like a woman by his side, lying like Bonita, cold to his touch, explosive. Lola Craft, Winnie's daughter, had fallen asleep fully dressed, had fallen asleep while counting aspirins the way insomniacs count sheep. After cooking greasy breakfasts and seeing their husbands off to the woods with bulging lunch pails, wives could go back to bed until six, when the children would need to be roused for school. Those few households not touched by the woods-working business stayed peaceful as five o'clock brought the first strains of daylight through the jack pines, followed by the face of the constant sun itself as it skirted the horizon and rose up to a full ball. As the woodsmen drove into the morning glare of the sun, into the heart of their jobs, their work, their forest, Sicily slept on, and so did Marvin and Pearl. So did Junior and Thelma, and Monique Tessier, who, like Marvin Ivy, had a busy day ahead of her. Even Amy Joy slept, having stayed awake, having cried, until 4 A.M. From exhaustion Amy Joy slept, but instead of wedding dreams, instead of bridal bouquets and baby carriages, she dreamed death dreams, bullets and noises, and muffled voices she could not identify. As the sun blazed up red, pulling a red morning sky behind it, the lumberjacks drove in battered pickups and pulp trucks past the Albert Pinkham Motel. They saw the fancy Cadillac beached upon hardwood blocks, without tires, without any accoutrements, and their fenderless trucks suddenly felt rich and sumptuous beneath them, and they drove on with a sudden pride in their occupations, in themselves. Sometimes, city folks and tourists left other things behind besides their trash.

It was just a few minutes after eight o'clock when Winnie Craft, who had already been on the phone for a half hour, broke down and called Sicily. Winnie wanted badly to be the first person Sicily spoke to, and by the sound of Sicily's sleepy hello, she was positive she'd beat everyone else to the punch.

"Beautiful day, ain't it?" Winnie inquired.

"It sure is."

"Looks like spring is finally here this time."

"I think it really is," agreed Sicily.

"She finally did it," Winnie said.

"Who?" asked Sicily. "What?" Winnie Craft, like most Mattagash women, parceled out gossip like puzzle pieces until at last the whole picture fitted nicely together.

"Bonita," Winnie stated flatly.

"What did she do?" asked Sicily.

"Kevin's mother called me and told me. I just barely hung up the phone from talking to her when I called you."

"What did she do?" Sicily knew, of course, or suspected, but she didn't want her info any faster than Winnie was willing to deliver it. Excitement flowed along the wires, along the gray telephone poles, between the two women.

"She told Kevin she wants a divorce," Winnie said finally, and let out a long breath.

"Well," said Sicily. "I must say I'm not surprised."

"Me neither," said Winnie.

"How's Kevin taking it?"

"Alice says he's going to Connecticut and look for a job in construction. Ain't that a shame, though?"

"Poor thing. He'll miss them kids."

"It's too bad she won't let him take them," Winnie said, and fingered the soft little hairs in her right nostril, unbeknownst to Sicily, who was usually unnerved to see this action. "She can't be much of a mother anyway," Winnie added, "or she'd think of them kids first and just grin and bear it."

"I suppose," said Sicily.

Winnie wanted desperately to hear tidings of Amy Joy and to get Sicily's feelings on the issue. Then she could happily call Claire Fennelson and say *Beautiful day, ain't it? Looks like spring is finally here, don't it? I just barely hung up the phone from talking to Sicily.* Then she could sit back with her morning coffee and let Claire beat the latest news out of her, as if she were a rug. But Sicily gave her no such relief.

"I've got a cake in the oven, Winnie," Sicily said instead. "I gotta run."

Winnie hung up the phone with a plunk.

"Cake in the oven at eight o'clock in the morning, my foot," said Winnie. How could she call Claire now? What would she say? *Nice day! Spring's here! Guess what! You'll never believe this, but Sicily's got a cake in the oven!* What if Sicily talked to Claire or Girdy or Edna-Bob first and *they* called Winnie with the breaking story? Winnie thought about this.

"I'll just tell them I couldn't care less," Winnie decided. "I'll tell them all that Sicily Lawler is my best friend and has been for years, and that I have no intention of gossiping about her, or poor little Amy Joy for that matter." Amy Joy. Maybe Lola, when she finally got up at the crack of noon, would at least have the latest scoop on the jilted bride. Winnie would just watch *Captain Kangaroo* and wait, damn it.

• • •

Junior Ivy was freshly shaved and dressed, his corpulence partially hidden in a dark striped suit, when he stepped outside his room at the Albert Pinkham Motel. He was to meet his father at Una's Valley Cafe for a good sturdy breakfast, the kind the local potato farmers put away each morning, and then together they would inspect the lucrativeness of Watertown's only funeral home. All night, even as the Cadillac was being deflowered, he had dreamed of his father Marvin dangling a big silver key over his head, just out of his reach. It was only when Junior got good footing on something solid beneath him that his fingertips reached the key and it fell into his grasp. His own funeral home! When he looked down to see what his footstool had been, he saw that he was standing on Miss Monique Tessier's back.

"If that's what it takes," Junior had told himself while he shaved, remembering the symbolic dream, "then, by God, I'll do it. I'll step on anyone I have to, especially her. And today I'll tell the old man the truth. I'll tell him I want my family back together too, like *he* wants. And I'll tell him Monique is here in Mattagash looking for trouble. Then I'll go to the Watertown police station and get that little son of a bitch out of jail. The old man won't even have to know."

Now Junior stood on the snowy walkway outside room number 1 and stared with popping eyes at what was left of his most precious treasure. He felt his heart doing the same acrobatic flip-flops as the raven had done. He sensed little firecrackers going off inside his temples. He tried to breathe deeply, as his eyes caressed the bruised body, filled the gaping holes, soothed the obvious cuts and scratches. His 1969 cream-colored Cadillac up on blocks like something you might see on television from the hills of East Tennessee. Or in a Gifford's yard. Junior sensed a bad case of hyperventilation coming on. A pickup went slowly past the motel, with Bert Fogarty and Herb Fennelson peering intently out their windows until the horn sounded rudely and the driver yelled, "Get a Ford!" at Junior. Junior's neck bristled as the small needlelike hairs stood on end. His breathing returned to normal. He had to think. This obviously wasn't Randy's doing. Randy was in jail. Not only that, Randy was an idiot. This was the work of professionals. How could Randy remove a radio, an aerial, a rearview mirror? Randy still thought cars were born all in one piece, for Chrissakes, in some goddamn huge cabbage patch, in Detroit maybe. Randy was too goddamn dismantled himself to do the same thing to a car.

"Giffords," Junior said with disgust, and the word stuck like welfare peanut butter to his tongue.

◆　◆　◆

Thelma left her place at the window and slipped into the bathroom. Now that Junior was safely out of range, she plopped a Valium into her mouth and felt it stick to her throat. She drank more water to dislodge it, as she wondered why Junior had treated his beloved Cadillac so shabbily.

"He'll have *me* up on four blocks one day," Thelma decided with warm certainty, "if I'm not real careful."

◆　◆　◆

"Need a ride?" a cheery voice rang out behind him. Junior spun around to see Monique Tessier, dressed to kill in what looked like an honest-to-God business suit. "Looks like you're having a little road trouble."

Junior bit his lip. Even though he intended to dump her, he was suddenly embarrassed for his ex-mistress to see him thusly, the mark of his manhood displayed limp, useless, before him. Rape had taken place here, and like a vengeful husband, Junior Ivy would get even.

"Yes," he said finally to Monique Tessier. "I need a ride to Una's Valley Cafe in Watertown." And for the second time since he decreed *I will never get inside your car again, so don't plead,* Junior got into Monique's old Buick and they burst off down the road like a regular married couple.

◆　◆　◆

Pearl watched Marvin drive off for his appointment with his son.

"I hope they don't buy it," Pearl thought. "I don't want Junior and Thelma so close to Mattagash. Forgive me, Lord, for even thinking it, but it's true." The phone blared loudly. Sicily.

"How are you gonna handle this?" Pearl asked her younger sister.

"Well, I've been thinking about it," Sicily said, "and I'm gonna handle it just the way Marge would. I'm gonna pretend it never even happened."

"Bully for you!" said Pearl. "And Amy Joy?"

"To tell you the truth, I think she cares more about what Dorrie Fennelson will say than the whole town," Sicily told Pearl. "But I know Amy Joy. It won't be too long before she'll put it all behind her."

"Bully for her, too!" said Pearl and laughed a deep, gut-splitting, McKinnon laugh. Amy Joy had some pioneer blood in her veins after all.

When she and Sicily finished chatting, Pearl stood for a while and watched a flock of snow buntings rise up in a graceful arc to catch the sun. They shimmered white, like porcelain birds, then disappeared. Maybe back to the Arctic, now that spring was coming.

Pearl fixed a second cup of coffee and looked out the back window at the old summer kitchen. There had been so much racket out there last night that she thought the roof might come crashing down on the ghostly revelers. Marge, Marcus Doyle, and friends. Even Marvin had finally noticed it, coming out of a deep sleep to mutter, "What?"

"Go back to sleep," Pearl had told him. "It's nothing." She no longer wanted to share the secret of the summer kitchen with her husband, but to protect him from it. It was, after all, her unearthly problem.

Pearl noticed that Marge's old curtains hung in the windows of the summer kitchen with the stiffness that comes with accumulated dust and cobwebs. As soon as spring was really here, which was soon, judging by how fast the sun was gobbling up the last snow, Pearl would venture into Marge's old domain and give it a thorough cleansing. She'd take Lestoil and Windex and S.O.S. pads to all the blasted ghosts. She'd fling open the windows and exorcise all the past sins that had occurred among the three sisters. Surely that was the thorn in Marge's side, if ghosts still had sides, which was causing her such unrest, and not the tattered love letters. She had gone to her grave with much anger in her heart, anger at Pearl and Sicily and the old reverend.

"She missed out on her own life to raise me and Sicily," Pearl thought. "And yet we never once thanked her for it." She wondered if Sicily ever did, once Pearl had run off to Portland and found refuge in the Ivy Funeral Home. Ahha! She'd said it herself. *Run off to Portland.* The very words that used to send her into a tizzy if they came from Marge's or Sicily's lips had now come from her own. *Run off.* Run away. Run from. Oh Lord, it was true. Her sisters had been right after all. But which was the better of two failures, then? Was running away any worse than being too frightened to run at all? That was the affliction that killed Marge young, at barely fifty-nine years of age.

"She was younger than me," Pearl whispered, and then shuddered. And it would kill Sicily, too, if she wasn't careful. Fear was the worst enemy of any young woman in Mattagash, in any small town. Fear of big ideas, big decisions, big towns. By the time they became older women, the fear had already turned into anger, tightening their mouths, curling their hands into arthritic fists. Even if they're not afraid to run, as Pearl ran, as Amy Joy tried to, the anger follows them. It'll go to Connecticut, to big cities like Chicago, all the way west to California. Anger knows no geographical limitations, and it needs no bus ticket.

"If she's not careful," Pearl thought, "it will kill Amy Joy, too. It's in our blood, this thing, this disease. The men used to get rid of it by beating workhorses to death in the woods. Now they run their machines into early graves. They work hard and drink hard and die hard. But women? All we can do is fight our wars with words, instead of real bullets."

She stood for a long time and traced the outline of the summer kitchen, the snow on its sunny roof already beginning to drip from the eaves, to go back to the earth, to nourish the barren soil. She herself had come back to Mattagash to be nourished. If Marvin returned from Watertown with the intent to buy Cushman's Funeral Home for his son, Pearl had a plan.

"Give the business in Portland to Junior," she would plead with her husband. "You take the one in Watertown. You need a good rest anyway. You're tired. Your health isn't that good anymore. Give the Portland business to Junior, or *give me up*."

Pearl relaxed the curtain and let spring go back about its business. When the weather was just right she would clean the summer kitchen. She would bury all her hatchets, the ones she'd been lugging down the years. She'd dispose of all the anger.

"I'm an old dog," Pearl said, "but, by God, I'm still learning some new tricks."

◆　◆　◆

"How'd you get here, then?" Marvin asked Junior, when he'd been told of the Cadillac's demise.

"I thumbed a ride from a couple of local yokels," Junior said, remembering the two men in the pickup truck. "In a Ford," he added.

"Well, once we've met with Cushman, we'll stop by the police station and make a report," Marvin assured his distraught son.

"I suppose we better," Junior said, his voice far away from his thoughts. "I got something to pick up over there, anyway." Junior stared at his father. *Please, Jesus, help me to outmaneuver this latest mess*, he silently prayed.

"I got a lot to tell you," Junior confessed softly. "I didn't want to spoil your breakfast, or upset you in any way before our meeting with Cushman. I thought it best to wait 'til afterwards."

"I appreciate that," said Marvin, and he meant it.

•   •   •

"So why are you wanting to sell?" Marvin asked Ben Cushman, once the three men had settled comfortably in the office to discuss the life of the funeral home.

"I guess you could say the winters are getting to me," Ben said. Marvin liked him instinctively. Ben Cushman was an honest man. Whatever he told Marvin about his business Marvin would believe. "They make my bones ache," Ben added. "My only child, a daughter, lives in Florida with my two grandchildren. She thinks I'll like it there." Ben smiled widely.

"I can understand what you mean about the winters," Junior prattled nervously. "The springs up here are bad enough!" Marvin frowned. You let a man belittle his own territory, his home turf, because it's his right. But you don't agree with him, and you certainly don't go one up on him. When would Junior ever learn? But Ben Cushman was the kind of man to overlook men like Junior.

"This profession continually reminds me how fleeting time is," Ben went on. "I want to know those grandkids now, not someday." Marvin agreed, although he didn't tell Ben that he considered him a lucky man to live in a different state from his grandkids. He didn't tell Ben that there were some grandkids you should never get to know.

"Mind if we look around?" Marvin asked.

"We promise not to disturb anyone." Junior guffawed as his father grimaced. So help him, but there were days when Marvin felt like waltzing Junior downstairs at the Ivy Funeral Home and embalming *him*.

"Help yourselves," Ben Cushman said. "I'll be here when you finish."

Marvin and Junior toured the chapel, and the four rooms where northern houseguests had been reposing for family and friends ever since Cushman's Funeral Home opened its doors. Even old-timers from Mattagash, who vowed never to darken the door of an establishment that made money from the dead, were hastened quietly down to Cushman's once their lips were sealed forever. What they didn't know wouldn't hurt them. Funerals were for the living anyway. There were still a few wakes taking place in living rooms here and there along the river, but this at-home notion had become quaint even in remotest Mattagash, barbaric to some.

Marvin and Junior even stopped in the coffee lounge for a quick cup before heading downstairs to the embalming room.

"We have no clients in there right now," Ben Cushman had informed his visitors earlier. "Check it out." This room was, Marvin was telling Junior, by far the most important room in funeralology.

"It can make you or break you, son," Marvin had managed to say just as a small voice broke into the conversation. As blood drained from Junior's face, as Junior's face embalmed itself, Marvin Ivy looked up into warm violet eyes, at a perfect chiseled nose, an aristocratic chin. Monique Tessier.

"I said good afternoon, gentlemen." Monique had brought forth her best business voice to match her mauve wool suit. "Mr. Cushman told me where I might find you." There was no response from either man until Junior said, in an almost inaudible whisper, "I can explain this."

"I think you'd better," Marvin whispered back. He wasn't sure if Ben Cushman had followed Miss Tessier out of his office and was standing somewhere nearby.

"Have you had a chance to have that little talk with your father yet?" Monique asked Junior. Marvin looked sharply at his son, who could see Cushman's Funeral Home disappearing like a smashed toy before his eyes.

"She's lying," Junior whispered fiercely.

"Oh, Junie." Monique's tone was merely playful. "I'll help you stand up to him. Don't be afraid."

"I tell you, she's lying!" Junior's forehead broke into a shiny sweat. Oh Christ, but where was his mother at a time like this? "The last thing I said to her when she dropped me off at Una's Valley Cafe was that I was going to tell you everything." Junior's whisper was now a hoarse croak, froggish and desperate.

"And so you *are* telling him everything," Monique purred.

"I thought you said you thumbed a ride with a couple of yokels," said Marvin.

"I was waiting until the deal was closed," Junior whined, "so I wouldn't upset you."

"Don't whine," Marvin scolded. "For Chrissakes, please don't yammer."

"He wants a divorce," said Monique, unabashedly.

"No!" Now Junior *was* disturbing the houseguests at Cushman's Funeral Home. "I tell you she's lying. She came to Mattagash on her own."

"Oh, really, Junie." Monique was patronizing. "I didn't even know that horrible place existed."

Marvin looked at Junior, who looked at his feet.

"You wait outside," Marvin said sternly to Monique Tessier. "*You*, come downstairs with me so we can straighten this out."

The embalming room was not the most perfect place for a father and son heart-to-heart. But the thick doors would afford them privacy, and most likely Monique Tessier wouldn't follow them in there. Marvin closed the door then stood, slack-jawed and steely-eyed, as he stared at his son. Junior wiped the upstairs sweat from his forehead and looked at the ceiling. Warm tears pushed out onto the crow's feet around his eyes and then rolled, unchecked, down his face.

"Don't cry," Marvin snapped. "For Chrissakes, please don't cry."

"I can't help it," Junior whined. "None of that is true."

"What the hell is going on in your head?" Marvin shouted. He slammed a fist into his palm and then began to pace around the embalming table. "I give you chance after chance after chance. I offer you a business, for Chrissakes. I pay you far more than you should be paid. *You* should pay *me*, just for letting you work for me. Do you know that?"

"I know it," Junior conceded, tears drenching his white collar. He mopped his face with his tie.

"I even let that miserable excuse for a grandson into my business to keep his dope-crazy ass out of jail!" Junior winced. *Oh Jesus, don't let him find out that his grandson's ass is in jail even as he speaks!*

"Yes sir," Junior wept. "But I tell you the woman's lying. I put my best foot forward and now she's messed it up."

"I oughtta put my best foot into your fat ass," Marvin threatened, the blue veins in his temples working like earthworms beneath the skin.

Then it happened. Everything exploded in his chest, in the interior of Marvin Ivy's pear-shaped heart. He clutched at his breast.

"What's the matter?" Junior yelled, as Marvin fought for air.

"Pearl," was all Marvin could whisper. Oxygen wheezed in and out of his nostrils as though from a small bellows. He reached a hand toward the counter, grabbed at the embalming machine to hold himself up, but his legs buckled and he went down on his knees. What he had intended to say, *take care of Pearl,* what had seemed important to him, was no longer meaningful.

"First," Marvin Ivy told himself, with clinical detachment, "they will disinfect my eyes, my nose, and my mouth with disinfecting spray, before they close them for good."

"Help!" Junior yelled, hoping Ben Cushman would hear him from beyond the thick doors, from beyond the veil of this newest tragedy. "Daddy," Junior moaned.

On his knees, Marvin was eye-level with the counter and noticed for the first time an empty McDonald's drink container, its straw at half-mast.

"My God, that's beautiful," he thought, as the yellow arches shone like halos and reached to the high heavens. Marvin fell backward, flat on his back. He turned his head and a bloody spittle ran from the corner of his mouth.

"Oh please, please, please," Junior petitioned some god, some maker, perhaps, of human beings, and embalming machines, and Big Macs.

"Then," thought Marvin, "they will raise the blood vessels and inject the preservative." He looked nonchalantly up at the table looming above him, at his son, white-faced and grieving. Suddenly, Marvin could see the old textbooks from embalming school, could see inside the covers where he had hastily scrawled "Marvin R. Ivy, Portland, Maine." There had been no need to put "Senior" back then. There had been no "Junior." There was just Marvin and Pearl, newlyweds on the short road down through life. *Take care of Pearl.* He wondered what year he had written his name thusly, what day, by God, the very minute, the very second in time.

"Time," thought Marvin. "What a foolish concept. It's all one straight, continuous line, isn't it, if names written in books over forty years ago are still dripping their ink."

"Stay right here," Junior whimpered, as though Marvin intended to skip some light fantastic out of Watertown. "I'll go get an ambulance."

"Ambulances," thought Marvin. "Noisy things." He'd heard enough of them in his life. No need to run one more by him. He felt Junior checking his wrist for a pulse, for a little encouraging word from the old ticker. There was none. There was no news to send.

"We're closing down shop, kiddo," Marvin thought. He was happy to learn that he still possessed a fine sense of humor, and that at least some houseguests go out laughing. He wished he could share this tidbit with Pearl. "Then they'll close and seal the incisions. They'll wash me, and dry me, and dress me in my finest."

Junior had seen death enough to recognize its tracks. Marvin's face had turned clay-colored, his body tones slack as yarn. As Junior took one of the doughy hands up into his own, Marvin looked down and saw the action, saw his own colorless face, his own eyes riveted on the ceiling.

"I'm sorry," Junior wept.

"Silly," Marvin thought. "I'm not there. I'm up here."

"Daddy," Junior cried, and laid Marvin's limp hand across his chest. He looked down at Marvin's blue lips, at his father's unmoving chest, at a tiny little vein on Marvin's nose that Junior had been too busy with life to notice. Marvin Ivy, Senior, was soundly dead.

"Daddeeeeeeee," Junior wailed. "Don't die with this between us."

Marvin Ivy bounced like a soft balloon across the ceiling. He looked down one last time on the body that housed his earthly son.

"For Chrissakes," Marvin thought, before he cut himself free from the idle, dream-stricken earth. Before his consciousness failed him. "Don't *yammer!*"

"He shouldn't have died like this," Junior whispered, and reached out gently to close the blank eyes. What he didn't know was what Marvin Ivy had learned in an instant, before his life had sputtered out, that it doesn't matter how you die. All that matters is how you live.

•   •   •

Monique Tessier had just finished a cup of Sanka at Una's Valley Cafe when an ambulance roared past the cafe window and into Cushman's Funeral Home. There was a mix-up for you. But Monique kept a watchful eye, as she had for the past fifteen minutes. She was quite sure either one or the other, Marvin or Junior, father or son, would come outside eventually and offer her a deal.

"Just like Monty Hall," Monique said, and smiled. To show them what a good sport she was, she might even settle for as little as ten thousand, though she hoped the Ivys would be gentlemen enough not to place her in such an embarrassing cul-de-sac by quibbling. What she saw instead was Junior Ivy hurriedly tagging along after a stretcher, which disappeared into the ambulance,

Junior behind it. Then they were gone in a flash of noise and siren.

Monique paid for her coffee and walked calmly across the street to Cushman's Funeral Home. Inside she found Ben Cushman slumped on the sofa in his office.

"Funny," he said. His hands were shaking. "Funny, but I never get used to it."

"What happened?" Monique asked. Her voice was coming from another woman, not from her. Her voice was coming from a woman desperate enough to commit blackmail.

"Marvin Ivy is dead," Ben Cushman said, and a silly noise, almost a giggle, warbled in his throat.

"I just want you to know," Monique said vaguely, wishing she could say it to Marvin, and to Junior, but saying it to Ben instead, as their proxy. "I want you to know that my father beat me for years. And then my ex-husband beat me. I didn't deserve that. I deserved something better. I deserved something nice. I just want you to know that." Then she closed the office door and left Ben Cushman sitting alone on the sofa, where just minutes ago Marvin Ivy had been talking, and laughing, and living. Ben Cushman had never gotten over the ironic suddenness of death, the boldness of it. Death had balls, there was no doubt about it.

"Well," Ben Cushman said, to any lingering ghosts who might still be close enough to hear him. "There goes Florida."

•   •   •

When he finally left the Watertown Hospital to go home and tell Pearl, Junior Ivy decided to stop weeping, as his father had only recently requested. He stood outside by the black Oldsmobile that declared IVY FUNERAL HOME, PORTLAND, MAINE on its door, another of Marvin Senior's innovative ideas. "Marvin Ivy, Sr., and Son" the letters told anyone interested, and then listed the phone number. The Son of Marvin Ivy, Sr., and Son stood next to his father's business car, which Ben Cushman had been kind enough to have delivered to the hospital, and wiped tears from his eyes. Spring had convinced everyone once more that she had arrived, and this time she had indeed. No one faulted her for this, but instead Junior could hear all Watertown welcoming her home. People in such wintry climes are more forgiving of nature than they are of their neighbors. This tenet enables them to survive the briefness of summer, the sadness of autumn, the longevity of winter, and then the sluttishness of spring. Junior could hear children caroling summer tunes from bicycles, and the high whine of road equipment above the monotones of construction workers. The bells of an ice-cream truck, on its maiden voyage of 1969, rang out like shimmering church bells in the distance, then disappeared. Across the street from the hospital's parking lot, people loaded bulging, ripping sacks of groceries into the backseats of their cars. Food. Sustenance for the body. Life was going on, yet Junior felt apart from it, an outsider, a spy on all the participants.

"My father is dead," Junior murmured dreamily, but no one noticed, so he sped out of the hospital's parking lot, squinting the spring sunshine from his puffy eyes.

*   *   *

Roy Vachon pointed to a door and Junior went through it to stand in front of Randy Ivy's cell.

"Thank God," Randy said, and reached for his jacket on the narrow cot. "I thought I was going to rot in Mayberry."

Junior eyed his son steadily, a look he remembered well from his own father.

"I told them you were my old man," said Randy. "But they wouldn't let me go."

"Why should they?" asked Junior. "You're a goddamn car thief."

"Oh, come on, man," said Randy. "I've had a real rough night here. Don't start in on me."

"You listen to me," Junior snarled. With a flash of his hand he reached through the bars and grabbed Randy's shirt collar, yanked him forward. Junior looked into his son's pupils, the eyes of Marvin Randall Ivy III, the namesake, the recipient, the inheritor of genetic coding, of human notions, of the Ivy Funeral Home, of the late Marvin Ivy, Senior.

"Don't you ever call me *man* again," Junior said to his startled offspring. "Now I'm gonna tell you something and you'd better listen." He released Randy's shirt and the boy dropped down to his cot and put his oily face in his hands.

"You'd better get your horse manure rounded up into a meaningful pile pretty goddamn soon," Marvin Ivy, Junior, told his son. "You'd better get your dog doo-doo all in the same bag, because I've had it with you. You understand me? *Had it!*"

"This isn't fair," Randy pleaded.

"And don't *yammer!*" Junior shouted.

Roy Vachon ducked in to investigate the disturbances.

"Well?" he asked Junior Ivy.

"I've never seen him before," Junior said evenly. "He must be a Gifford."

"Dad!" Randy shouted, and grabbed the bars of his cell.

"So now it's Dad, is it?" Junior thought, and left the room. Outside he looked at Sheriff Roy Vachon. He wouldn't bother to report the vandalism on the Cadillac. He had visited Mattagash enough to have learned one of the local truisms: Like elves, the Giffords have no fingerprints. But instead of chalking it up as a loss, Junior Ivy would consider it just another expensive lesson. Besides, he had suffered a much greater loss than the creamy, dreamy Caddy. He had lost the Senior in his life, his immediate ancestor, and if he wasn't careful he would remain floating. Even his name, even Junior, was now a name in limbo, with nothing to attach itself to.

"That *is* my son," Junior told the sheriff. "If you don't mind keeping him a little longer, I think it might be a valuable piece of education for him."

"No problem," Roy Vachon said, and winked. "Nice thing about us. We don't charge any tuition."

PROFESSIONAL MOURNERS
PROVIDE A MOON FOR THE MISBEGOTTEN
FUNERAL: LESSONS OF LIFE
IN THE GRAVEYARD

....

"Well, first of all, Frederick went to the hospital and proposed to Natasha, right after she told Maximilian she was up the stump. Then the doctors took a fibroid tumor the size of a basketball out of her, so she ain't knocked up after all and won't have to marry that sleaze-bag little fairy. But Tiffany ain't gonna be able to adopt the baby 'cause now there is none and, if you'll remember, she's so barren she couldn't have a *kitten*. But if you ask me, when Roberto gits back from that business trip to Mexico, down there in Rio de Janeiro, he's gonna put the goddamn boots to the whole miserable bunch of 'em."

—Vinal Gifford, regarding the soap opera episode
that Pike missed due to a court appearance

PEARL MCKINNON IVY INSISTED THAT CUSHMAN'S FUNERAL HOME handle the details of Marvin Ivy, Senior, a business decision Marvin would have agreed with, unbeknownst to Pearl. Junior didn't argue with her. Major decision making was still new to him. He would have to try out a few of his own, in privacy, before he sprang any on his incorrigible mother.

"I'm staying on in Mattagash," Pearl said to her son. "I want him up here. I want him close by. He had no friends in Portland anyway. His business was his best friend. Now it's yours. If you're smart, you'll let it be an acquaintance, not a friend. Look to the living for things like that."

"What about the house?" Junior asked.

"Sell it," said Pearl.

"But your stuff," said Junior.

"I took every single thing out of that house I consider valuable," said Pearl. "You see anything there you want, you go ahead and take it. Then sell the rest."

"But that was *our* house," Junior almost whined, then checked himself.

"Yes," said Pearl. "You're right. It was. First it was mine and Marvin's. Then it was mine and Marvin's and yours. Then you got your own house, and it was just mine and Marvin's again. Now it's just mine. Sell it. *This* is the house I knew before I ever dreamed of Marvin Ivy, or you. This is where I belong."

◆   ◆   ◆

The next afternoon, Junior Ivy had Thelma drop him off at Watertown's bus station in the family business car. Peter Craft was busy at his filling station, rounding up a new battery and four tires for the Cadillac. Junior would have to limp it back to the Cadillac dealer in Portland for the snobby stuff. While he sat waiting for his two daughters to arrive from Portland, Thelma drove over to the police station and managed to get Randy released without getting herself locked up. It was her first day in months without the warm companionship of Valium, a mother's companionship, a loving sister's, an eighth cousin's. Whatever companionship you wanted it to be.

"Lord love a duck, but I'm gonna make it," Thelma thought. "Your grandfather's dead," she said to Randy. "Now get in the car."

"Balls," said Randy. "And I thought *this* was a bummer." Mattagash, it seemed, had different effects on different people.

◆   ◆   ◆

"I thought you were coming to a *wedding*," Cynthia Jane complained, as she and Regina scooted down from the Greyhound.

"You might say even the wedding turned into a funeral," Junior said, hoping to make light of the situation, hoping to console his daughters on the occasion of their grandfather's death.

"I hate funerals," Regina said firmly.

"So do I," said Cynthia Jane, and tugged at the legs of her panty hose, hoisted them down a bit.

"Your grandfather couldn't help it," Junior reminded his girls.

"Well," said Cynthia Jane, "it seems senseless to come all this way to a funeral when we have our own place." *Your grandfather has just died*, Junior almost said to her, but instead he realized something about his eldest child. He wished suddenly that she would marry her thin-faced dental student and get to hell out of his house, take her goddamn psoriasis of the crotch with her.

"They're both barbaric rituals anyway," said Regina, and slipped a book from her carry-on bag. "Weddings and funerals alike. They're emotional chain letters. They prey upon the superstitions of the ill-read. Tell me, have you hired any professional mourners for the occasion?"

Junior looked at his second daughter. Now this one, this one with her pale, homely face and inquisitive eyes, might have a chance. This one might just be a modern chip off the old Pearl McKinnon Ivy block.

"One out of three," thought Junior, as he visualized the futures of his three children. "Thirty-three percent success possibilities. That ain't half bad nowadays." He realized his father had gone to his grave thinking he had batted zero, had struck out completely, one hundred percent, with his only child. Maybe that's why large families had been so prevalent in little towns like Mattagash. The failure ratio didn't appear so drastic. Maybe the Catholics were onto something.

◆　◆　◆

"People don't wear mourning like they used to," Sicily mentioned to Pearl, as she eyed the bright pastel colors that adorned Marvin's granddaughters. The gathering at Cushman's Funeral Home was small. Pearl, Sicily, and Amy Joy representing the old McKinnon clan, sat like mismatched sisters in the front row. Junior Ivy and Thelma, with their three children, representing the Portland clan, or maybe the future clan, sat directly behind Pearl. Junior reached a hand out to touch his mother's shoulder occasionally, and watched as she took it gratefully in her own hand, squeezed it, and then let it go. His mother could only lean on someone for so long, Junior noticed, before she straightened herself again. Yet he did not see this as a weakness but as a strength, as her inheritance from the old pioneers.

Winnie Craft had come, *to pay her respects to Pearl and Sicily*, or so she told Pearl, who inspected her with steely McKinnon eyes. And Claire Fennelson had come along to keep Winnie company, or so she told Sicily. Dorrie Fennelson had come along only to drive the two women, or so she told Amy Joy, who cringed to see her. Pearl cringed to see all three of them. They sat stiffly, dressed in black getups, staring straight ahead, seemingly uninterested in everyone and everything but the pure grief of the beleaguered family. To a passerby, to a tourist, to a canoe or white-water enthusiast, they might appear to be sincerely paying their respects to the deceased. But Pearl McKinnon Ivy knew better. She knew the truth. The living interested these woman far more than the dead. Like irritating houseflies, Pearl knew, these women had eyes all over their heads when it came to gossip.

With Pearl's consent, Marvin Ivy, Junior, stood to say a few words.

"We don't need a preacher," Pearl had reminded her son. "Your father was never a man of the church. There's no need for us to pretend now." Sicily had done that with Ed, Pearl remembered, and everyone knew that Ed Lawler was an atheist.

"Let Mattagash do things their way," Pearl decided. "I'm home, but I'm my own woman."

So Junior Ivy stood, with eyes tearing but without any yammering, and spoke a short eulogy in his father's memory.

"He was a good father," Junior said, and looked at Randy, his own son. "I wish I'd let him know that more often when I had the chance."

Claire Fennelson elbowed Winnie. This was something to feed into the Mattagash Intelligence Network, a little tidbit to make it purr and hum.

"He was a good husband," Junior said, and looked at his mother, who sniffed softly as Sicily reached for her hand. "Being a work-aholic was his only vice, if it can be called that."

Winnie stiffened. Had he said alcoholic? It was some kind of "holic." Maybe Claire had heard. She must inquire on the frost-heaved ride back to Mattagash. Beside her, Claire Fennelson had indeed heard. Marvin Ivy, Pearl McKinnon's husband, had been an alcoholic!

Sicily felt uncomfortable suddenly, her black suit about to squeeze her out of it. Ed had been an alcoholic. Did Junior's use of the word *workaholic,* a city word, a word that would never wing its way north for there was no need of it, did it remind everyone of Sicily's own husband? Were they all feeling sorry for her right now?

Amy Joy sat in a black skirt, a white blouse covered with a black sweater, black pumps, and thought about how Dorrie Fennelson had driven all the way to Watertown, to the funeral of a man she'd never met, so that she could flaunt her married self in Amy Joy's face. Amy Joy was surprised she hadn't brought that noisy baby.

"Workaholic. Alcoholic. Cath-o-holic," Amy Joy thought. "They're one and the same. They all mean too much of what could have been a good thing."

◆   ◆   ◆

The Cushman hearse pulled slowly out of the funeral home drive and pointed its nose toward Mattagash. In the car immediately following, Sicily and Pearl, large McKinnon women, sat in the front seat next to the furnished driver. Junior claimed half of the back seat for himself, while Thelma and Amy Joy shared the meager space which was left them.

Cynthia Jane drove the family car, Regina on the passenger side, Randy scowling in the backseat. When would the nightmare of Mattagash end?

The fourth and last car carried the good wives of Mattagash, happy to find themselves behind all the rest, where they could survey the events at their leisure.

"Pearl hardly looked like she'd been crying," said Claire.

"Well," said Winnie. "I suppose she'll come into a good sum of money with him gone."

"Crying don't mean nothing," Dorrie said, dodging a pothole. "Look at how much Jackie Kennedy didn't cry."

"Yes," said Winnie. "And I suppose she come into some money, too, just like Pearl."

"Even her kids didn't cry," said Claire. "Poor darlings. Saluting their little hearts out."

"Only John-John saluted," said Dorrie.

"Dear, dear children," said Winnie, "to go through something like that. But I suppose they all come into some money afterwards."

"They ought to mark that pothole," said Dorrie, thinking how helpful the sticks driven into the ground along the sides of the road, and displaying a red warning flag, could be when one was miles from home and somewhat unfamiliar with the topography.

"The warm weather'll take care of the frost heaves soon enough," said Claire. "But I don't think the State is ever gonna fix them potholes."

"Did you see how them granddaughters was dressed?" Winnie asked. "You'd swear they was on their way to a prom."

◆　　◆　　◆

"I'm so embarrassed to be driving this car with that writing on the door," Cynthia Jane complained. "We look like a funeral convention."

"I've read they have the rowdiest in the country," said Regina, and pulled her visor down to break the spring sunshine.

"You can't even imagine what this has been like," Randy told his sisters. He sat forward and folded his arms on the back of their seat.

"Oh, I can imagine all right," Cynthia Jane said, then "Jesus!" as she hit a pothole. The car jarred out of it and straightened again.

"Wait 'til you hit what they call a frost heave," warned Randy.

"Did you see how Amy Joy was dressed?" Cynthia Jane snorted. "Did she look like some old spinster, or what?"

"Barbaric," said Regina, and turned her face to watch the thirty miles of bright blue river unfold as the road followed it, not realizing it had been her great-great-great-grandfather's passageway to Mattagash.

•   •   •

Vinal and Pike Gifford had just left Henri Nadeau's, where they purchased hot dogs and beer with some fresh money that had suddenly fallen into their palms, when the funeral procession wound past.

"We oughtta splurge and get the Plymouth an eight-track," Pike said to Vinal, as they fell in behind Dorrie Fennelson's car, and joined the mourners. "I kinda miss Julie Andrews."

"We can always buy that eight-track back," Vinal advised. "Old Sambo'd probably sell it back to us for the same price. We're good customers."

It was true that the Giffords kept Old Sambo's little junk shop, on the Mattagash–St. Leonard line, full to the rafters with sundries. Old Sambo asked no questions, which was good business conduct as far as Vinal and Pike were concerned. They offered no answers, anyway.

"I wasn't talking of *buying* one," Pike said, a bit chagrined. "There must be somebody else in northern Maine with one of them things."

"I wouldn't mind taking that hearse for a spin," Vinal said, leaning over for a quick view past the other autos in front of him.

"You'll be doing that sooner or later anyway," said Pike, and felt one of Henri Nadeau's hot dogs rise dramatically up his esophagus. He burped a long, lusty belch, mixed with beer. "We ought to hold Henri Nadeau down someday and make him eat about three dozen of them damn hot dogs," Pike prophesied. "They cling to a person's food pipe forever."

"When they do go down," Vinal agreed, and belched in testament, "they're real gut bombs."

"This is beginning to wear me out," said Pike. "Can't we pass 'em?"

The funeral procession had finally reached the WELCOME TO MATTAGASH sign. Giffordtown wasn't too far away now, but Vinal's heavy foot had grown restless with the censorship placed on it all the way from Henri Nadeau's Quick Lunch and Gas to the Mattagash line.

"Hey," he said to Pike, "let's moon 'em." He pulled out into the passing lane and pushed the accelerator to the floor. Pike unwound his side window and tossed an empty Bud bottle at the Mattagash sign. It hit wood with a thick thump.

"Five hundred and thirty-eight!" Pike shouted. "It ain't likely you'll break that record, Vine. You can't aim as good as me."

"You're just guessing," said Vinal.

"No, I swear," vowed Pike, and held up his right hand. "I started counting in 1957."

"There's old Winnie-the-Pooh," said Vinal, and slowed the Plymouth. "Show her the moon, Pike!"

The Plymouth lunged forward, riding the crest of the frost heaves as though they were magnificent waves. When it came abreast of Dorrie Fennelson's car, it floated alongside. Dorrie was too frightened to take her eyes from the road, but Claire and Winnie were gaping at the shark and its pilots.

"Hurry up!" shouted Vinal. "I'm bound to meet something head-on soon."

"H . . . e . . . r . . e . . . 's John-neeeeee," said Pike, and maneuvered his bare ass up into the passenger window.

"Kiss that, Winnie!" Vinal yelled. Dorrie quickly closed her side glass, as Winnie turned white as last week's snow and Claire Fennelson screamed heartily and covered her eyes.

"She's pretending not to see," Vinal informed Pike. "But she'll be telling everybody by nightfall how many pimples you got."

"I ain't got no pimples, do I?" Pike Gifford had always been a vain man.

The Plymouth left the wives of Mattagash behind, in genuine shock, and buzzed up next to the car full of the Ivy grandchildren. No one looked. Used to the rudeness of the city, dulled by the unpredictability of what their fellow man might attempt next, Cynthia kept her city eyes ahead, on the lookout for potholes. Randy lay in the backseat and bemoaned the geographical limitations forced upon his recreational habits. Regina kept her eyes down, on the even sentences of her book, where there were no lurking road hazards, just smooth literary sailing.

Disappointed with their audience, the Plymouth lurched up to the car following the hearse.

"That's Pearl and Sicily," Vinal told Pike, whose head was beneath the level of the car window.

"Hurry up," Pike told Vinal. "I'm freezing my ass off!"

"Hey, McKinnons!" Vinal shouted, keeping a quick eye on the road. He wanted no part of a head-on collision. He tooted loudly until Sicily and Pearl and Amy Joy and Junior and Thelma all turned their heads, like well-trained ducks.

"Sweet Jesus," said Sicily. "Who *is* that?" She would recognize Pike's upper body parts, but the part he was now exhibiting, the part that was filling up his entire window and turning pinkish red with cold, could have belonged to any man in Mattagash. And she couldn't see the driver of the car because of the huge hairy buttocks filling the window.

"Giffords,"said Amy Joy. She recognized the shark. "Vinal and Pike."

"Grown men," said Pearl.

"Oh sweet lovely Jesus, deliver us," Sicily whispered, and collapsed against Pearl in a soft, emotional heap. She had never even viewed Ed thusly, let alone a Gifford.

"Okay now," Vinal, the ringmaster, commanded. "You showed 'em the moon, now give 'em some sun. Flash 'em, little brother! Blazon forth!"

"All right," said Pike. "But only for a minute. I'm gonna throw up a hot dog. And if gangrene sets in, I'll lose my balls."

"There's more where them come from," Vinal assured him.

"More *balls?*" Pike inquired. He had heard of skin being grafted, but had no idea that medical science had launched into spherical shapes.

"Hot dogs," said Vinal. He leaned ahead to grin at Sicily and Pearl, as Pike rearranged himself in the window of the Plymouth.

"Hey, Sicily!" Vinal shouted, and tooted loudly. The Cushman driver slowed the car down to fifteen miles an hour. Vinal did the same. Pike's dangling scrotum was now bouncing softly outside the car, the penis growing large with excitement.

"I can't feel a thing, Vine," Pike exclaimed, still reluctant to disobey and therefore disappoint his big brother.

"McKinnons deserve the best, Piker!" Vinal shouted. "And women don't call you Pike the Spike for nuthin'!" Pike's immense organ bobbed in response, a sock on a windy clothesline.

"Lord love a duck," whispered Thelma, and then looked quickly at her feet. Even on Valium, where sometimes things did appear larger, she'd never seen the likes of that. Bob Barker would pale in comparison.

"Hey, you two old McKinnon biddies. You old widows," Vinal screamed. "Try not to fight over it!" Pike smiled proudly over a well-known Gifford genetic trait, well-known at least among Giffords.

"I can't feel anything now," Pike cried with glee, as the anesthetic weather took away all sensitivity. "I'm completely numb."

"Let's pretend not to notice," Sicily sat up suddenly to say. "Let's just look straight ahead and enjoy the nice day."

"This isn't a nice day," Amy Joy reminded her. "It's a funeral."

"Can't someone do something?" asked Pearl. "I wish to God I had a gun."

"A real grandstander," said Sicily smugly.

Junior Ivy had heard Amy Joy's earlier proclamation, had heard her mouth the names. *Vinal and Pike Gifford.* Albert Pinkham had come outside when Junior discovered his defiled Cadillac on Monday morning, and Albert had said it point-blank.

"Vinal and Pike Gifford," Albert had said. "There's no doubt in my mind whatsoever. I'd recognize their work anywhere."

Junior quickly undid the enormously long belt from around his waist. He rolled the window down carefully and hoisted the belt outside, buckle first, as he gripped the other end. Then he let Pike Gifford have it *whack! whack!* across his exaggerated manhood. Pike's accoutrements were suddenly no longer numb. A whipping belt carried more clout than a whipping wind. He screamed sharply and then fell backward, onto Vinal's arms. The steering wheel cut a smooth arc to the left and the shark obeyed the command. The Plymouth plummeted off the road and bounced gingerly down a short embankment, taking down a handful of inch-wide saplings and catching up clusters of dead burdocks around the axle. The oil pan dropped off, like a discarded, messy slop pail, and lay quietly in the brown grass. The motor died away and in its place the songs of the birds rang clear.

◆　◆　◆

"Do you see *now* what I'm telling you?" Randy Ivy asked his sisters, as none of the three grandchildren could possibly ignore the Plymouth once it buzzed past them and hovered like a demented hummingbird alongside the car ahead. "What drug could possibly be worse for me than a week in this town?"

"My God," Regina said softly. "Do you suppose Daddy really did hire professional mourners?"

◆　◆　◆

"Stop crying, Claire," Winnie finally found the voice to say. "You weren't raped, for heaven's sake."

◆　◆　◆

"You can still count on the Giffords for a little excitement," Pearl said, with positive enthusiasm. "I think Marvin is looking down right now and laughing his head off. I think Marvin would enjoy this."

"Junior took care of those scofflaws," Thelma bragged. Her husband was fitting the belt around his massive stomach once again.

"I got to buy myself a belly toner," Junior said, pretending a wish to change the subject. Maybe he would sign up for lessons at Southern Maine School of Karate. One never knew when such things could come in handy. Especially if a man, a Junior, had to protect his family now that the Senior was gone.

"They really are something, aren't they?" Amy Joy said to her aunt Pearl, and they exchanged a knowing giggle. *They're just giving us some mud to wash off, Amy Joy,* Pearl could have said to her niece, but didn't. She could tell Amy Joy already knew. *They're doing their job, so that we can do ours.*

"I, for one, intend to forget the entire incident," Sicily straightened up and boldly declared. "I didn't see a thing. Not a single hair."

• ♦ •

Vinal and Pike sat drinking beer and enjoying the peaceful spring view afforded them by the Plymouth's plunge down the embankment. They had come to a quick stop where the small poplars were leaning inward, shading the brook, and the old pussy willows were still clinging tenaciously, furry kittens, to the willow trees.

"Beautiful day, ain't it?" Pike spoke first.

"Yep," said Vinal.

"Won't be long now and we can go fishing."

"Yep."

"Are you mad?"

"You might say I'm embarrassed."

"But, Vinal," Pike insisted, "he caught me a hell of a wallop. I probably still got marks on my wanger."

"Did you have to *fall* on me?"

"Where *could* I fall?" Pike flailed his arms for emphasis. "Into the goddamn car full of McKinnons? Into the Christly *hearse?*"

"You made us look like two fools," Vinal said, and snapped an empty out into the dead hay. From the trees over the landlocked shark, tiny warblers let their spring songs burst from their throats. Fresh leaves shimmered, casting a mottled shadow down upon the peeling roof of the Plymouth.

"It sure is pretty, though, ain't it?" Pike asked meekly, after a few more minutes and another beer had passed between the brothers. "Look at it this way. We hardly take time out of our schedules to get back to nature, as they say nowadays. Let's just consider this an opportunity to get to know our environment."

Vinal sucked more beer and thought about this.

"Besides," said Pike, "there ain't nothing me or nobuddy else can do to make *you* look like a fool. Not *my* big brother!" Vinal smiled deeply, the tiny brown cave of decay between his front teeth peeping out to say hello to Pike. A good sign, Pike knew, when he saw that brown spot emerge. Pike sang along with the birds of spring, now that social things were settled.

" 'One little girl in a pale pink coat heard. Lay he, yodel lay he, yodel lay he ho.' Can we still get us an eight-track?" he asked Vinal. This had been worrying him deeply, but he'd held the question in his head until the mood lightened.

"I suppose," said Vinal, jovial again. "But we better get us some motor oil first."

◆   ◆   ◆

When the northern raven swirled over Mattagash in his blessed current, he easily saw the Plymouth, a new sight for that wooded area. His brain registered the discrepancy. He knew the territory well, thanks to his swift intelligence and roving eyes. He knew it in different ways than did Winnie Craft, or Girdy Monihan, or Claire Fennelson. But he saw no sign of a road kill. Perhaps had the raven seen Pike Gifford's sprawling pink ass it would have suggested suet to him, but Pike had already tucked his belongings away.

Over the field near Giffordtown, where Vinal and Pike both stood peeing watery beer beside the shiny black car, the raven broke out of its current and flew freely, along the spring-blue river, along the shaggy tops of the jack pines. At the Protestant graveyard, high on its hill, where a meadowy thrust of land jutted out into the river, the raven found another sweet current and rode it up, like a black cinder, into the sky. Below, the fresh grave awaiting Marvin Ivy spilled outward onto the remaining snow like a reddish, anxious maw. The northern raven enjoyed his delicious current a moment longer, watching curiously as the small black figurines inched up the sloping hill, their cars nested quietly below them on the road. The bird swung out of the current, past the graveyard, and its people, and their tiny interests in life. The raven swung away to the St. Leonard dump, where it hoped the gleanings would be more satisfactory.

◆　◆　◆

"This is like déjà vu," said Pearl, remembering how she had stood next to her baby sister Sicily, only a decade before, and watched Ed Lawler slip away into the earth. "Isn't that what the French call it?"

"Don't bring up the *French*, if you don't mind," said Sicily, and smiled. Pearl clutched her hand.

"Oh Lord," she said to Sicily, and her thick ankles and shins and thighs seemed ready to cave in with her weight. "Oh Heavenly Father," Pearl whispered, and Junior took her arm, braced her against him.

"I'm here," he said firmly, and Pearl looked at him with puzzlement, and then pleased curiosity.

"Yes," she said finally, and willed herself to stand alone. "Yes," she said to her son. "I can see that you are."

"We'll make it," Junior said assuredly. Pearl cleared her throat.

"If *he's* not yammering anymore then, by God, I won't start," Pearl decided.

"Here, Mother Ivy," said Thelma. "Lean on me."

"Yes," said Pearl, trying not to watch as Marvin's coffin began its short trip down into the earth, into the old-settler land, far from the Russia of his father, far from the Poland of his mother. But Marvin's own father had told him many times, *Funerals are for the living, son. Remember that and you'll make a killing.* Marvin would have been delighted to go where the living wanted him. And it was important to Pearl.

"I can't drive to Portland every time I get the urge to see his grave," Pearl had told Junior. "His grandkids, let's face it, don't give a damn where he's buried, as long as he's not in their way."

"That's it," Thelma assured Pearl, and held her arm tightly just above the elbow.

"I'm leaning on Thelma," Pearl said, and she looked deeply into her daughter-in-law's dark-rimmed eyes for the first time in, well, maybe for the first time ever. "Poor little raccoon," thought Pearl, as she allotted a bit of her weight to Thelma's shoulders, a bit to Junior's.

"This is what you wanted." Junior looked up to the cloudless spring sky and thought, sure that Marvin Ivy could hear him, or at least cared to hear him. "We're finally doing it for you, Dad. We're getting our buffalo bonbons into one box." He looked beneath Pearl's weighty chin at Thelma, staggering and pale under the burden of her mother-in-law. Junior winked, his eyes red-rimmed with grief, and Thelma winked back.

"We can do it," he had told her the day his father died, when he went to room number 1 at the Albert Pinkham Motel and laid out all his cow chips before Thelma. "Monique Tessier is out to destroy us," he warned his wife, about his mistress. "But she can't hurt us unless we let her. We can keep her out of our lives and we can get our lives back together."

The grandchildren stood in their Easter colors and were silent for a change. Cynthia Jane thought it disrespectful to even tug, and so no audio or video responses came from Junior's children. Pearl looked at them vaguely. They were a part of her, as she was of the old settlers, yet she didn't know them. They were instead, *apart from* her, like soft balloons in pastel colors, bobbing at some park, and not in a graveyard.

Amy Joy looked at the coffin sinking, as if it were her trousseau, her hope chest disappearing.

"Remember when we buried Daddy?" she asked Pearl. Pearl heard the question over her shoulder. The voice that asked it was a young voice and, oh, now that Pearl was back in Mattagash she wanted the input of the young. But this was not a grandchild's voice. This was Amy Joy, boy-crazy, life-hungry, silly Amy Joy.

Pearl half turned until she saw the face, the simple, enchanting, crippled face of youth.

"I still dream about it," Amy Joy said, and Pearl saw, within the eyes of youth, that painful lesson sometimes never learned. She saw a truth one would never find in the eyes of Winnie or Girdy or Claire. She saw the eternal, universal truth for some of the pilgrims who traverse the twisted highways and byways of small towns.

"It takes a real strong person to outgrow their environment," Aunt Pearl Ivy said to Amy Joy. "You'd make ten Dorrie Fennelsons any day. She can't hold a candle to you."

Amy Joy smiled, a small trace of smile, and for the second time in less than a decade the women, those old agriculturists, those *first gardeners,* saw their men folded like seeds into the indifferent earth, and they grew stronger for it.

ALBERT AND BRUCE:
A MAN, HIS DOG, HIS SWIMMING POOL

....

Since most of us are now citified or at least suburban, we've
probably never set foot in a barn.

—Richard Rawson, *Old Barn Plans*

ALBERT PINKHAM SWEPT THE VERY LAST AUTUMN LEAVES OF 1968
away, once again, from his cement walkway. They had blown from
his lawn and from the nearby fields until now they were blown
out. A new autumn would bring others, but 1968 could finally be
scooped up and burned. Spring had no tricks up her sleeve this
day. The temperature had grown steadily higher over the days
since Albert's last hangover, and now birds had arrived from those
distant places most folks in Mattagash could not even find on the
globe. Six herring gulls, their bills like yellow pencils, interrupted

their steady flapping to soar like hawks over the river. Albert watched them diligently. Six was more than he'd ever seen at one time all the way up in Mattagash.

"Probably stormy weather along the coast," Albert explained to Bruce. "Either that or they've found out that our garbage up here in Mattagash is just as good as the garbage down around Portland."

The doors to numbers 3 and 4 in back were gaping open as Albert aired them out. A group of nature enthusiasts would be arriving later in the afternoon, a party of six, with requests to reserve three rooms. Albert had already swept and dusted in number 1, but number 2, his bridal suite, was left untouched. Inside, a thin layer of spring dust, like thin grains of rice, had spread soundlessly over the dresser, the pillowcases, the throw rug, the lamp. Amy Joy's bridal suite in utter disrepair. Albert had already received three advance reservations for the room in June alone. The first, second, and fourth Saturdays of that month, the good old-fashioned wedding month if your head was screwed on straight, had been filled. More of the newest members of the old stock were settling down with the age-old notions of keeping the whole shebang going forward to the future, keeping the family alive, the hearth rosy, the old-settler ghosts appeased.

If hunters needed the bridal suite, they could have it, except for those wedding nights when its services would be greatly required. Albert even decided that once this latest batch of nuisance-enthusiasts was gone, he would move the bridal suite to number 3, the pink room, that lair of mysterious women. All that really dictated that number 2 be the wedding chamber, instead of just an ordinary room, were the small plastic and metal chandelier that Albert had poetically hung over the bed and the plaster-of-Paris statue of one of those naked Greek gods he had found at a yard sale in Caribou. A small candy dish by the bedside was always filled with salted peanuts for the occasion, compliments of the establishment, and Albert tried to remember to toss a few extra bath towels into the deal. *We aim to please* had been, after all, his motto since opening in 1958.

Albert sat on the bed in number 3 to catch his breath. Bruce flopped on the rug near his feet and watched him curiously. A soft breath of perfume still clung to the room, an aroma of hyacinth hovering mothlike in the air. Could it be Miss Tessier's perfume, fresh to the room, or was it perfume from an old memory, an old autumn ghost who had arrived in a swirl of colored leaves and then disappeared in one. It had been almost a month since Monique Tessier had come and gone from Mattagash. Was Violet LaForge still lingering in his memory, in his mind's eye, in the pink room she had painted and then left behind her? That secretary from Portland had stayed just long enough to tear open the wound that Albert had lovingly nursed over the past decade, until he thought it had closed and healed. Now he saw the light, pink as it was, filtering in through the windows of number 3. He was a man alone, and like the old barn builder, he found his very life was disappearing. He needed a change, goddamn it, a *big* one. He looked at Bruce, who yawned a sleepy spring yawn, displaying his crippled fang.

"I'm gonna open my pool this summer, boy!" Albert confided to Bruce, who bounded up in excitement to push his cold nose against Albert's hand. "And then," Albert said, and lay back on the soft bed to gaze up at the pinkish, spring-fevered, lovesick horizon billowing in all around him, "then I'm gonna allow the rich widow Pearl a reasonable amount of time in which to grieve." Bruce was perplexed. He whined, and then wagged an inquisitive tail.

"Why?" Albert asked, and then he answered the dog's question. "Because I plan to whisper some sweet nothings into her big McKinnon ears."

BOTTOM-OF-THE-HILL

GIFFORDS: THE GOOD OLE BOYS

OF NORTHERN MAINE

....

"I guess we're all gonna be what we're gonna be . . .
so what do you do with good ole boys like me?"

—Robert Lee McDill, "Good Ole Boys Like Me"

VINAL GIFFORD HAD JUST RETURNED FROM CONSULTING A LAW-
yer in Watertown. Vinal had intentions of suing the Wilcher Binocular Company for the unfortunate blindness of his youngest son,
nine-year-old Willis.

"He looked straight at the sun with that contraption, and now
he's been stone-blind for three months," Vinal had assured the
lawyer. "It fried his eyes like two eggs."

"So you want to sue the Wilcher Binocular Company?" the lawyer had sighed and asked his client.

"Sure," Vinal had answered. "What else can I do? Sue the *sun?*"

As Vinal drove into his bumpy yard, over the indentations from dried-up mud puddles, past pop bottles and candy bar wrappers, he spied Willis in the middle of a game of hopscotch.

"Willis!" Vinal shouted. "Get your peaked ass into the house." Willis thumped the rock in his hand onto the ground and stomped off.

"He can't stay in the house forever," Vera said, as her husband stretched out on the living room sofa with a beer.

"He can until this law scrape is over," Vinal said.

"How long will that be?" Vera asked.

"Three or four years," said Vinal.

Willis came into the living room and angrily plunked down into a chair to watch television. Behind his thick eyeglasses his pupils loomed large and bulging as a Down East codfish. He had the same problem with his eyes his cousin Irma had learned to live and love with, retinitis pigmentosa, an inheritance from their great-grandmother Caroline McGilvery Gifford. Where the ailment first started is anybody's guess but what is certain is that it crossed the ocean with the McGilverys. Vinal's oldest son, Irving, serving time for robbery in Thompson Penitentiary, was also afflicted with the malady.

"Irving has to hold his face an inch or two above them license plates he's making, or he wouldn't even see 'em," Vera had mentioned several times, with a mother's concern.

"Willis," Vinal sat up on the sofa and said to his son, "I warned you for the last time. I never again want to see you hopscotching in the yard. And don't let me catch you skipping over firewood and mud puddles to catch the milkman either."

"I wanted some chocolate milk," Willis huffed.

"Chocolate milk comes from nigger cows *but Willis wants some,*" sang Molly, Vera's eight-year-old baby. Willis swung his arm loosely in the air to smack her, but missed.

"Four eyes! Four eyes!" Molly taunted, in singsong, and hid behind Vera's thick thighs as if they were sheltering trees. "Willis is blind as a bat! Willis can't see a thing!"

"Yes I can!" Willis's voice cracked poignantly. "I can see as well as you can!"

"No, now, son," Vinal reminded him. "You *can't.* If you want that bicycle we talked about you're gonna have to remember that you're *binocular blind.*" Willis lay back in his chair and buried his head in the cushion of its arm.

"And if someone should come around looking important and asking you big-word questions, I want you to walk into walls. To knock over lamps. You git my drift? I want you to pick up the eggbeater and say hello." Willis hid his head and said nothing.

"Speaking of blind," said Vera. "Can you imagine the little bats Irma and Freddy Broussard'll have if they get married?"

"Priscilla says that Freddy Broussard has been to college," Molly blurted, her mouth full of graham crackers.

"That Priscilla is gonna be just as bad as Goldie," Vera said. She snapped her dish towel at Willis's head. "You poke that pencil into my Naugahyde chair one more time, Willis, and you won't have to *pretend* you're blind," Vera warned.

"And Hodge Gifford told our teacher that he's going to college someday too," Molly added.

"That sounds like something Goldie would put in that poor kid's head," said Vera. Her mouth was still mending from the fight with her sister-in-law, a pale purple line evident on the bottom lip. "A real holier-than-thou show-off."

"I ain't going to no college," Little Vinal said with pride. He picked a scab off his elbow, the last remnant of his most recent bicycle wreck, and snapped it at Molly.

"If you don't go to jail, Little Vinal," his mother said, "we'll all consider you a real big success."

"I'm quittin' school the second I turn sixteen," Little Vinal continued.

"Why bother?" Vera joked. "You oughtta be used to the sixth grade by then."

"Shut up," said Little Vinal, and then leaned back, away from Vera's attempt to slap his face. She must be tired. Little Vinal remembered his mother being much faster than that in the old days.

"If I didn't ache all over, I'd get up and massacre you," Vera threatened.

"Son, there's only two things you need to learn in life," said Vinal, launching into one of his fatherly lectures. "One is don't trust a woman or a nigger. They're all alike. That's one good thing I learned from the army."

"You was only in the army a month before they give you your dishonorable," Vera reminded him.

"What's the second thing?" asked Little Vinal, with growing interest.

"Don't ever admit you're in the wrong, even when all your cards is down," Vinal cautioned. "That only guarantees trouble for you. My way, you still got a chance. There now. Consider that your college education, all paid for by your old man."

"How long is Uncle Pike gonna sleep with me and Little Vinal?" Willis asked. His eyes were large as bluish plums from behind the glacial shields of his glasses. "He snores and kicks in his sleep."

"He farts in his sleep too," said Little Vinal.

"That poor man can stay in this house as long as he wants to," said Vera. "That poor man's been a saint to stay with Goldie Plunkett all these years."

"I wish he was gone," Willis said.

"I have to look out for him because he's my baby brother," Vinal said. "Just like you're Little Vinal's baby brother."

"Don't you want Little Vinal to look out for *you* someday?" Vera asked.

"Not really," said Willis.

"Not really," said Little Vinal.

"Daddy, is it true that chocolate milk comes from nigger cows?" Molly asked, as she inserted a finger into one tiny nostril.

"God Almighty, I hope to hell not," said Vinal, and lay back on the sofa. "It's bad enough it comes from *female* ones."

$\mathscr{G}$OLDIE AND HER CHILDREN:

TOP OF THE HILL WHERE THEY BELONG

....

But in the mud and scum of things
there always always something sings.

—Ralph Waldo Emerson

GOLDIE HAD ALL HER CHILDREN, EVEN A RELUCTANT LITTLE PEE,
out in the yard collecting pop bottles, picking up papers, raking
dead leaves. They collected the strings of Christmas lights, folded
them into boxes, and put them in the attic until the next holiday.
Goldie had made her point, but now it was time to face the summer
ahead, and to go on with life. Vera could leave hers up, unlighted,
until doomsday, for all Goldie cared.

"We're gonna paint this house if it kills us," Goldie told them.
"We're gonna paint this weekend when Irma comes home. She's

using her discount to get us some of the prettiest pale yellow paint you ever saw. We're gonna have the nicest house in Mattagash." Miltie clapped his hands. Little Hodge followed them around with a burlap potato sack, left over from the harvest, and held it open as the family filled it with outdoor debris.

"I asked your father to move them junked cars and pickups and all them tires," Goldie said. She had her hair pinned up in a blue bandanna and the crisp spring air had caused a bloom on her face. The children had never seen her look so young and pretty. "If I have to put flower boxes full of geraniums on all the running boards, I will," said Goldie. "If I have to cover the tires with old quilts and the pickups with couch covers, I will. If he ain't moved that junk by summer, we'll hire someone to tote it all to the dump."

"I found Red Ryder's old soup bone under that pile of leaves," Miltie told his mother, greatly winded. "So I run up the hill and put it on his grave."

"You did?" asked Goldie, and patted his curly head. "How sweet of you, Miltie."

"Is Daddy coming home again?" Missy asked.

"I don't know, honey. I really don't think so. I don't think it's a good idea."

"Me neither," said Missy. "I hate him." Her eyes welled with tears. She looked away from her mother.

"Why?" asked Goldie. "Did he hurt you?"

"Never mind," said Missy.

Goldie squatted down to look into Missy's eyes. "If he hurt you," she said, wiping away the child's tears, "he's *never* coming back. Not over my dead body. Drunk or sober. Does that make you feel better?" Missy smiled and Goldie hugged her.

"You and Miltie get your pop bottles ready," she told the little girl, "and we'll take them to Blanche's Grocery for the refund. You can get them comic books you've been wanting."

Missy ran off to count the rattling sacks and boxes of bottles, some with dead spiders in them, others with bloated cigarette butts, all crowding the back porch.

"Mama, it's Irma on the phone," Priscilla shouted from behind the screen door. "She wants to know, can you start Monday morning?"

"Tell her that's fine," Goldie shouted back.

"Did you get the job?" Little Pee asked.

"Sounds like it!" Goldie said, and clapped her hands with some of Miltie's fervor. She had applied for a job clerking at J. C. Penney's in Watertown. Her sister Lizzie had said she would let Goldie borrow her car every day until Goldie could make a down payment on one of her own.

"If I get this job, I can help get you one, too, Lizzie," Goldie had promised. "That way, you can get away from Frankie." Thank God for Irma, thank God for her oldest daughter, to have paved the way. Goldie might not have been able to do it without a job, and all jobs in Watertown were watched with envy by Watertown girls. But the manager liked Irma. The manager wanted to see Irma get ahead. *Thank God for Irma.*

"Pike?" Goldie said softly, and her son, who had been rolling tires behind the garage, stopped.

"What?" he asked.

"I know Daddy's been getting you to sell stuff to Old Sambo for him," Goldie said. "He pays you a couple dollars to do it, don't he?"

"No he don't," said Little Pee. He kicked his toe at the tire.

"Yes he does," Goldie said angrily. "Priscilla told me."

"So what?" Little Pee looked over at her with narrow eyes. Eyes like Big Pike's. Anger like Big Pike's.

"From now on," Goldie said, "I don't want you to touch a thing he gives you. That's stolen stuff. You can go to jail for doing that."

"I'll do what I wanna," Little Pee snarled, and went off into the garage. This one, this child, Goldie would have to watch closely. But she feared it was already too late.

Priscilla came out onto the front steps.

"My homework's done," she told Goldie. "And I done the dishes, too." Goldie left the others behind to catch Priscilla alone on the porch.

"Did your father ever touch you?" she asked her daughter. "You know, like he shouldn't touch you?"

"Never mind," said Priscilla, and looked instead up at Red Ryder's grave, the grave of her childhood playmate.

"I'll go to the sheriff and report him if he ever steps a foot near any of you kids again," Goldie promised her daughter. "Now come help Missy rake leaves."

"Irma said she's bringing the paint this weekend," Priscilla said, and took the rake from Missy. "Freddy Broussard's bringing it in the back of his pickup."

"Are they gettin' married, Mama?" Missy asked.

"If they want to," Goldie said, and pried one of her IGA marigold plants into the soft earth by her front steps.

"Is Freddy rich, Mama?" Hodge sat on the steps for a breather and asked.

"Richer than most around here, I suppose," Goldie answered.

"I'm gonna marry someone rich someday, too," said Priscilla. "I ain't marrying nobody on welfare." Goldie looked at her second oldest daughter. *Thank God for Irma. Thank God for Irma paving the way.*

"I done something right," Goldie thought. "Even if it took a long time to realize it."

"Our teacher told us about a man who has a mansion in the country," said Missy. "And he has a Rolls-Royce and a swimming pool and a stable of horses."

"And so?" Hodge kicked his feet together, impatiently.

"And so," finished Missy, "he goes to New York City every day and dresses in old clothes and bums money from people."

"He pretends to be poor?" Goldie asked in astonishment.

"Yup," said Missy, pleased that her story was garnering so much attention. "That's how he pays for his mansion and all."

"Imagine," said Goldie. "Pretending to be poor. It takes all kinds, I guess. There's them who pretend to be rich, and right here in Mattagash, so I suppose it's the same thing."

"I wish we were rich," said Missy.

"Know what I'm gonna do with my very first paycheck?" Goldie asked her audience. "I'm gonna buy us some sirloin steaks."

"You ain't gonna mash up relief meat again and tell us it's a real meat loaf?" asked Hodge.

"No," Goldie laughed, remembering the pinkish attempt to fool her children into thinking they had good ground chuck before them. Some things, Goldie realized, you can't imagine away. Some things about poverty were too real. "They'll be real-McCoy sirloin steaks. And this fall we're gonna pool all our potato-picking money and buy us an indoor toilet and a bathtub. This fall we're gonna have hot running water."

"We can take real baths!" Missy hooted. Miltie grabbed her around the waist and they fell upon the grass, expressing their exuberance in the rough-and-tumble language of childhood.

"Oh God!" said Priscilla. "How much will that cost?"

"You just do your share this fall and let me and Irma worry about the rest," said Goldie. "We're the ones with jobs," she added proudly.

"Are we gonna go look at them puppies advertised in St. Leonard?" asked Hodge.

"They're *free to a good home*," said Missy.

"Can we?" asked Miltie. "Can we get another puppy?"

"Why not?" Goldie said, as she planted more good things into the soil which Joshua Gifford first squatted on in 1838. "Why not?" Goldie said again, and the remaining marigold plants went into the Gifford soil, their roots dangling like the arms of small children. "This is as good a home as any," Goldie said.

ℐICILY AND AMY JOY:

THE OAK AND THE ACORN

....

Al-lo, I am apologies for what go on. My brudder is brought
me to Conetticut widout my permiss. But I like N. Britin
bedder den home. May bee it for da bedder. How is you mudder? Bon Chance!

—Letter to Amy Joy from Jean Claude,
New Britain, Connecticut, received May 15, 1969

"GLORIA MULLINS HAD HER BABY LAST NIGHT," SICILY SAID. "HER
water broke at the IGA, so the man in the produce department
rushed her over to the hospital. It was lucky she was already in
Watertown shopping."

"I'm surprised a little water stopped Gloria Mullins from shopping." Amy Joy was uninterested in new additions to the old town.
"Too bad she didn't have some hip waders with her."

"Winnie told me this morning that Kevin Craft's mother said he intends to enlist in the army," Sicily said to Amy Joy. They sat on the front porch of their house and stared out at the road, at cars passing.

"Like two old dogs," Amy Joy thought.

"That'll be the fifth boy from Mattagash to be in the services," said Sicily, "and already three of them is right in the heart of Vietnam."

"Well," said Amy Joy, and crossed her legs, "it's a man's world. Let them fight for it." She finished polishing each of her fingernails a different shade. Sicily winced, but at least the silver streaks had not resurfaced.

"Sometimes you say the blackest things." Sicily's tone was one of worry, a doting lilt. "But I suppose we got enough wars right here at home to keep us busy." She was thinking of divorces, and weddings, and births, and funerals.

"I wish we could see the river from here," Amy Joy said. "The way you can from Aunt Marge's back porch."

"Winnie says it's a form of suicide, is what it is," Sicily continued. "Ever since Bonita left him and moved to Connecticut with them kids, he's been drinking and acting the fool."

"Lucky little kids," said Amy Joy.

"Poor soul. He must be lonely."

"He can't be too lonely," Amy Joy added. "He's dating his first cousin Lola Craft."

"No!" Sicily gasped. "He ain't even divorced yet!"

"Well, it's true."

"Winnie says they're just real close," Sicily protested. "After all, they *are* double first cousins."

"Well," Amy Joy said flatly, "miracle of all miracles, Winnie is wrong."

Lola Craft was no longer Amy Joy's best friend. She had told too many fantastic versions of Amy Joy's reaction to being jilted by Jean Claude Cloutier. The first time she had seen Lola since the wedding fiasco was at Blanche's Grocery the day before, with Kevin Craft. Lola probably needed the company. Amy Joy knew through her aunt Pearl's grapevine that Lola had besieged the Ivy residence in Portland with phone calls and letters, neither of which Randy Ivy answered. It would chagrin Winnie Craft greatly to learn that Junior and Thelma Ivy did not think her daughter, or any other nubile virgin in Mattagash, worthy of their son. At Blanche's Grocery, Lola had appeared sheepish, Kevin dazed with his own denial of life's events. They both seemed to have taken up an unusual new hobby since Amy Joy saw them last. Cynthia Jane Ivy wasn't the only one, or so it seemed to Amy Joy, to be suffering from the heartbreak of psoriasis of the crotch. The city crabs had settled down like pioneers, like homesteaders, in a pastoral setting.

"Why ain't you called me?" Lola had stepped away from the side of Kevin's pickup to ask her.

"Oh," said Amy Joy, "I guess your story that I cut my wrists, then tied them up with your pantyhose, was the straw that broke the camel's back."

"Well," said Lola. "Then I'm not your friend anymore!"

"Ditto," Amy Joy had said, and watched the weary taillights of Kevin Craft's pickup as it disappeared in the dip past Blanche's Grocery.

"Did you know there used to be camels in Alaska?" Amy Joy asked her mother.

"Go on," said Sicily, and smiled.

"Who knows?" said Amy Joy. "There was probably even camels in Mattagash, Maine, once upon a time."

"Oh, I don't think so," said Sicily. "There's too much snow in the winter."

"Good Lord, what will she think of next," thought Amy Joy, as she tried to imagine camels up to their asses and humps in snow. What were the thoughts, the doubts, she'd had since her eighteenth birthday? What were Amy Joy's greatest fears about this moment, this event of two women sitting idly on their front porch? To make Sicily happy in her old age, Amy Joy knew what she was expected to do. She would need to stay in the Lawler house and share Sicily's old age. She'd seen daughters growing old within the shadows of their mothers. They were gnarled *young*, bent and twisted without sunlight, too close to the mother oak. They became children again, together. They grew into sisters. They shared old age like a crust of bread. They shared the aging disease until the day came when no one could tell them apart anymore.

"But if there were camels here," Sicily said with pride, "you can be sure the very first McKinnons brought them."

Amy Joy closed her eyes and felt her thoughts reel. Like the raven, they rode up on a warm current, up, up, far away from Sicily.

"I meant hundreds and hundreds of thousands of years ago," Amy Joy said. "The McKinnons got here in 1835."

"Be careful now," Sicily warned. "You know Reverend Glass says that the earth was created only ten thousand years ago. It says so somewhere in the Bible." Amy Joy thought heavily about this. My God, but she knew from school that the pyramids were six thousand years old, or older.

"Somewhere in the Bible," said Amy Joy, "it probably says that pigs can fly." But she was at least relieved to learn that her mother didn't believe the world had been created in 1835 by the McKinnons.

"You're starting to talk just like one of them freethinkers," Sicily said. "I swear, Amy Joy, but you sound more like your father every day."

Amy Joy closed her eyes again. Suddenly she was far over Mattagash, looking down on everyone, at the black, insignificant speck of Dorrie Fennelson and her baby carriage, at the foolish glint of her wedding ring. She saw Kevin Craft's inch-long pickup turn off the main road and onto a leaf-riddled dirt road where he could touch Lola's warm breasts and try not to imagine they were Bonita's. Amy Joy went far up, on thoughts warm and tender as thermals, to look down on the pirogues bringing the first settlers up the clean blue river with their papery grants from the king of England. She no longer heard her mother, sitting in the warm sun, so near to her.

"Come to think of it," Sicily was saying, a stern, theosophical look on her face. "If there was camels in Alaska, why *can't* pigs fly?"

Amy Joy heard nothing, as she imagined her arms to be wings, imagined the old river falling away beneath her like a blue dream.

"I am my father's daughter," she thought. *"Finally."*

$\mathcal{T}$HE WIDOW PEARL

SETTLES IN: LESSONS IN GENEALOGY

....

"It's no big deal, man, but I seem to have misplaced a houseguest."

—Randy Ivy, back at work in the family business

PEARL HUNG UP THE PHONE FROM TALKING TO JUNIOR. THINGS were back to normal in Maine's southernmost city. People were still dying, on schedule these days, and other people were paying someone to bury them. The dry spell was over, her son was happy to report. And people were still getting married. Thelma came on the phone to inform Pearl excitedly that her granddaughter Cynthia Jane had announced plans to marry in August.

"Timothy will be a full-fledged dentist then," Thelma had said, a calmness, a steadiness in her voice Pearl had never noticed before. "We'll all get discounts," Thelma had added. "The whole family, and that means you, too."

"Good," said Pearl. She could almost imagine Thelma simple-minded enough to expect Pearl to drive to Portland for cleanings, and fillings, and root canals, and discounts. But the truth was, Pearl recognized, that Thelma was just trying to be nice.

"Tell Timothy thanks," said Pearl. "You can be sure I'll be there for the wedding."

"He's doing just fine," Junior had lied, when Pearl asked about Randy. "I think he's finally gonna get his rabbit raisins together." Pearl smiled warmly to hear this analogy still in use.

"We'll come visit you this autumn," Junior promised. "After the leaves change."

"That'll be nice," said Pearl, and realized she meant it.

"I won't be bringing my new Caddy," said Junior. "I'm taking the Greyhound. A fancy car hasn't got a prayer in Mattagash."

"How's the old house?" asked Pearl.

"It's still up for sale," said Junior. "Like you wanted."

"Good for you," said Pearl.

"I kinda hate driving by there, though, and seeing the sign. I been taking a longer route home."

"Soon," said Pearl, "when another family moves in, and you see someone's kids in the yard, someone's curtains in the window, someone's car in the driveway, you'll get used to it. Soon, it'll seem like you never lived there."

"If that's true," said Junior, "then why are you back at your old homestead?"

"This is different," said Pearl. "This old house ain't been doing nothing but *waiting*."

◆   ◆   ◆

In the afternoon, when the sun broke out of the clouds and cascaded down on the roof of the old summer kitchen, Pearl put her coffee cup in the sink and decided the time was now. She took her sweater from the back of a kitchen chair and draped it over her shoulders.

Then she went out into the river-sweet air of the old McKinnon backyard.

The latch to the summer kitchen creaked, as did the door. But it was time to lay the dusty ghosts to rest. They had been coming and going sporadically, boisterous some nights, silent others. Like tourists, they did what they pleased. Pearl was ready now to face them, be they Marge, Marcus Doyle, or any other spectral baggage they might have picked up along the way.

Pike Gifford lay on his stomach beneath the newly leaved hazelnut bushes and focused the same Wilcher Company binoculars that had reportedly blinded his nephew Willis. He watched the sturdy Pearl leave the house and make her way along the gray shingles of the summer kitchen. He watched her lift the rusty latch and push open the wooden door.

"Uh-oh," said Pike, to the Canada warbler overhead. "I think the jig is up."

Pearl adjusted her eyes to the tiny building's interior. It seemed veritably stuffed with things. Sundries. Items. These couldn't be Marge's things. She and Sicily had gone through most of Marge's belongings and then tossed them out like leftovers. There were only chairs, a table, a trunk, and rows of mason jars left. Pearl pulled the curtains down from the upper window and sunlight spilled in on all the goodies: batteries, hubcaps, rearview mirrors, sideview mirrors, aerials, skidder chains, chain saws, axes, pulp hooks, gas cans, wrenches, screwdrivers, and hammers. Pearl saw that the mason jars had been filled with nails, bolts, nuts, and shiny car keys.

"What kind of ghosts are they?" Pearl wondered. "*Mechanics?*" She looked further. There were car mats, women's purses, radios. Then some of the spring light bounced off something shiny. Pearl picked it up and turned it over in her hands. It was a tiny crown emblem with wheat growing up around it. A Cadillac emblem.

"I'll be damned," said Pearl. "The Gifford storehouse."

"Goddamn!" said Pike Gifford. "She's found our surplus."

When word bustled around town that Pearl McKinnon Ivy was home to stay, Pike and Vinal had begun looking for a new lair. It was just that morning that Vinal remembered the old barn builder in a way he perhaps didn't care to be remembered.

"Ain't that barn still standing out in the field behind Albert Pinkham's?" he asked Pike.

"I think so," said Pike.

"I ain't surprised," said Vinal. "That old son of a hoot could build himself a barn."

"Nobody'd ever look out there," said Pike. "But it's a shame Pearl relocated, as they say. That old kitchen was sure handy."

"You keep your eye on Pearl," Vinal instructed. "The very next time she hoofs it to Watertown we'll drop by and do some relocatin' ourselves."

Pike watched Pearl scurry out of the summer kitchen, in what looked like a lawful rush, a legal hurry. He lowered his binoculars and looked down at them.

"I might as well look at the sun with these," Pike lamented. " 'Cause what I just saw has burned my pupils forever."

* * *

After the sheriff assured Pearl that he would be back with a truck to empty the summer kitchen, he nailed the door shut.

"I'll need to go over a lot of old paperwork," he told her, "to try and contact folks who've filed reports. That way, they can come down to the station and claim their possessions."

"Can't you arrest them?" asked Pearl. "Can't you arrest Vinal and Pike?" Roy Vachon shook his head.

"Why?" she asked.

"Haven't you heard?" the sheriff said wearily, and then smiled. "Giffords don't have fingerprints."

* * *

It was suppertime, Pearl's loneliest time of day, the time she had learned to expect Marvin home for the night. She had just finished stirring a can of tomatoes into a pot of rice soup when the phone rang. It was Amy Joy.

"Can I come over?" she asked. "I wanted to ask you about the old settlers. Mama says you know a lot more than she does about how that all happened."

"I probably do," Pearl agreed happily. "There's always one in each family, in each generation, who carries the torch. I guess I'm the one in mine."

"I got a lot of questions," Amy Joy warned.

"I got a lot of answers," said Pearl. "Did you know that your grandpa Ralph suffered from soldier's heart? That he imagined almost every day of his life that he was having a heart attack?"

"I didn't know that," said Amy Joy.

"Did you know that I even got the original grant which your great-great-great-grandfather William McKinnon was given by the king of England?"

"God," said Amy Joy. "I've heard about that. But if you listen to Mama, you'd have to believe William knew the king personally." Pearl laughed.

"Come early enough for a bowl of rice soup," she told her niece.

When she opened the door to find Amy Joy standing there with a suitcase and two cardboard boxes full of her belongings, Pearl was surprised.

"I guess you do have a lot of questions, Amy Joy," she remarked.

"I used to have a room here, too," Amy Joy told Pearl. "When Aunt Marge was alive."

"I remember," Pearl said. "Come on in."

"The truth is," said Amy Joy, "that as much as I love her, Mama's driving me crazy."

"I remember that, too." Pearl laughed. "Pull up a chair and put up your feet, as they say."

After bowls of hot rice soup, Amy Joy and her aunt Pearl sat out on the back porch, next to the summer kitchen, and listened to the old river.

"Well," said Pearl, and began the speech that had been stuck to her tongue for years. "Jasper, Ransford, and William McKinnon were the first of your ancestors to come up that very river you see before us, and stake their claims in the piney undergrowth."

"In 1835," Amy Joy nodded.

"They were really something," Pearl said to her niece, "to come all the way from Campbellton, New Brunswick, in pirogues."

"I know," said Amy Joy.

"They had their faults, I'm sure," said Pearl. "Like we all do."

"I imagine," said Amy Joy.

"But, by God, they were tough, and so are we!" Aunt Pearl raised her cup of tea to Amy Joy's and they toasted each other, the old settlers, the wash of the Mattagash River.

"Affirmative," said Amy Joy, just as the frogs and crickets began their evening serenades. Far over their heads, the northern raven was anxious to make its way to a night roost. Beneath it, the soft lights of town flicked on, little fireflies dotting the black river. Electricity lived along the sleek wires between the toothpick telephone poles, as it lived still in the people, in the old stories, in the stories fresh off the press, in the stories still to come. The firefly lights winked softly up at the raven as it found a heavenly current and, like the dreams of young children, like the wishes of trapped spinsters, like the prayers of aging widows, it was carried high up, over the crest of town, untouched, unharmed, unnoticed by Mattagash, and was finally gone.